CAFFEINE NIG

ROGER ALLAN
NEWBURY

THE TIP OF
THE ICEBERG

Fiction to die for...

Published by Caffeine Nights Publishing 2022

Published in Great Britain by
Caffeine Nights Publishing
Amity House
71 Buckthorne Road
Minster on Sea
Isle of Sheppey
ME12 3RD

caffeinenightsbooks.com

British Library Cataloguing in Publication Data.
A CIP catalogue record for this book is available from the British
Library
ISBN: 978-1-913200-24-4

Everything else by
Default, Luck and Accident

To Anthony, (verisure!)

The Tip of the Iceberg

By

Roger Allan Newbury

Enjoy the Book,

Roger A Newbury

I would like to dedicate this first edition to my late parents, Reginald and Grace. Unfortunately, they never got to see it come to fruition. To my older siblings Steve and Bob who will get a copy. And especially my four children who are grown up with their own families. To Mick and Chelby Kenten and their family for keeping me thinking straight and not giving up!

Acknowledgements

To Darren E Laws, who took me under his wing of experience, giving me the opportunity to work with the novel and improve it exponentially (I hope!) For my friends far and wide around the globe from the BTZ especially the author Mark Billingham, a source of encouragement and inspiration.

About the author

Roger Newbury lives in North Kent, on the sunny Isle of Sheppey. In his past he has worked as an office clerk, hospital porter, forklift driver and house removals. He even spent 10 years with a local theatre am drama group, treading the boards (he's no Laurence Olivier) or operating the lights.

The Tip of the Iceberg

Roger Allan Newbury

Prologue

Saturday, December 29th.01:05 AM.
London's Docklands Area: Canary Wharf.

The section where the first captives were, was mostly dark. They were on the fifth sub-basement floor of the building, in a purpose-utilised area which in truth were nothing more than concrete cells, each one almost empty of furnishings along with being dark, damp and cold.

In each, there was a low bunk bed with a thin mattress and one woollen blanket, a chair and a small metal table, all securely bolted to the floor. What was the only door into the cell was a two-inch-thick steel plate barrier, with a narrow but wide opening at waist height; a small shelf where the food and water, what there was of it, was passed through, by an unknown individual.

The cells ran beneath and around the building's storage levels; these were below the upper basement underground parking garage level and inbound delivery ramps that connected to the street.

These cells had the grilles retro-installed to aid ventilation and were five feet from the floor, one foot high by three wide. The grilles consisted of metal mesh-style cover, screwed into the wall.

In one corner was a crude toilet; simply put, it was nothing other than a hole in the floor, with a flip-down stainless-steel seat attached to the wall, which forced the unfortunate occupant to squat. The hole fed waste down a hard plastic tube to somewhere else. The constant smell emanating from it was nauseating, even though there was a rudimentary flush mechanism close by, attached to the wall, along with the worst kind of toilet paper, a rather meagre sink and one tap with just cold water.

There were light fittings in the ceilings, but the light from these were minimal and sporadic, with buzzing sounds coupled with intermittent flickers.

As the female slowly regained a modicum of her senses, she heard a male voice asking in a croaky voice to no-one in particular, where he was.

'I need to speak to you,' she said, her somewhat sleep-induced voice quivering nervously, becoming stronger. The lighting unexpectedly increased, illuminating the stark reality of their predicament. Their eyes compensated to the sudden brightness, and they had a layout of their cells. She wasn't sure if the person in the next cell was looking around as well, but the female was looking for anything that might explain why they were here.

'Who are you? Have you kidnapped me?'

'What for, I'm of no...' he began saying, before the female abruptly interrupted him.

'Of course I didn't kidnap you. I'm a prisoner as well. Have you any idea how long you've been here for? Have you seen the people responsible?' she asked, her voice returning to a more relaxed level.

'No, not that I'm aware. Do you know where we are?' he replied, then he started coughing.

'Do you want to get out of here?' the female said, her tone showing annoyance.

'Yes, yes of course I do, it's just, I don't remember how I got here, or how long ago it was. My mind is still a bit fuzzy. The last thing I remember was being chatted up by this really gorgeous bird in a night club in Soho,' the male said.

'That... that's strange. An attractive man, also in Soho, chatted me up. The Clandestine Club in Wardour Street?

Last thing I remember was being offered a drink by him, and then I woke up in here, naked,' she said.

'You're naked too? Jesus. Do you think we are alone? I mean, do you think there are more like us?' he asked, then added as the recollection came to him, 'The Clandestine Club... yes. I was there too. Friday night.'

'I'm not sure if there are any other people or not, however you're the first person I've spoken to,' she said, then remembering, 'Friday night, the eighth, that's when I was there as well.'

'I'm sorry. I just can't figure out why we've been abducted, or what's going to happen to us. If I could get my hands on the woman who drugged me,' Dean said.

'Don't be sorry,' she said quietly. 'I'm as angry as you are, and scared. Do you have any idea where we are or what time it is, or what day?'

'Nope. Not an inkling whatsoever. By the way, I'm Dean, Dean Morgan, what's your name?' he asked.

'Verity, Verity Bracknell. I'm from Cambridge, where are you from?'

'Canterbury in Kent,' Dean replied. 'I was meeting friends in the city. But I ended up by myself in that club. Then here, wherever this is.'

While she'd been talking to Dean, Verity had been working on trying to manipulate the recessed cross-drive screws that held the ventilation grille separating the two of them in their cells. For some reason, in the cell's construction, the grille had been fixed only on one side, which was the side occupied by the woman.

Using a metal hair clip Verity fashioned it so that she could get the head of the first screw in the gap. She then twisted the clip so it gripped the screw and after several failed attempts, and much swearing under her breath, she succeeded in removing several of the twelve screws.

Dean had heard the scraping sounds coming from the other cell. 'What are you doing...?' he'd been about to ask, when a louder scrape heralded the removal of the grille's frame from the hole, and a head framed by dirty blond hair cut to shoulder length popped through.

'Hi there,' she said, still keeping her voice low. 'Get ready, I'm coming through...'

Suddenly footfalls outside in the corridor, heavy clumping footfalls. Someone wearing military combat boots or something similar coming their way.

'Quick, get back in your cell,' Dean said, his whispered tone showing concern.

Verity, who had manipulated the top half of her slim body through the hole retreated back, and swiftly replaced the grille as quickly and quietly as she could, before she heard the lock mechanism of the door turning. Where to put the screws though? She decided where, throwing them into the maw of the makeshift toilet, just as the cell door pulled outwards into the corridor. She had managed to get back to her bunk moments before, pulling the single wool blanket over her naked body, hoping to give the impression that she was still unconscious.

Silhouetted within the bright light of the corridor, were three figures. Two of the figures advanced and swiftly grabbed the twenty-seven-year-old woman. She thrashed trying to escape the iron grip of the two men, who wore dark blue uniforms with red roll-necked sweaters underneath the tunic-jackets. One of the men laughed, 'I think she presumed she could pull the wool over our eyes.'

The third figure came in, a tall slim female with dark hair pulled back into a tight bun at the back of her head, giving her a severe appearance, wearing a beige trouser suit with a protective white overcoat. She appeared to be holding something that glinted in the light. Verity realised it was a hypodermic syringe. She thrashed again, the fear that it was heroin or something worse stimulating her to fight with all that was left of her strength.

The two men forced her backward onto the bunk, one held her wrists together behind her head, after ramming a wadded ball of cloth into her mouth. The other male whipped the blanket clear exposing her lithe figure. Her breasts were of moderate size yet firm, above a flat stomach, she wore a belly button silver stud, and the man holding her ankles leered menacingly at her nakedness.

She looked down, following his gaze as he stared intently at her *'runway'* of pubic hair. On the left side of the thatch of pubic hair, she sported a small tattoo of a dog with a Chinese symbol. The man looked up towards the female, brandishing the syringe. She nodded to him, the paper mask covering her nose and mouth, obscuring her identifiable features; she mumbled something Verity could not understand.

The man holding her wrists transferred his grip to one hand and allowed his left hand to move down and cup Verity's right breast, squeezing it, rubbing the bud in the centre making it react, against Verity's will. The man kneaded the mound roughly, enjoying the firmness in his palm. Verity squirmed, the resistance she'd been trying to expel to her legs, keeping them from being forced apart for fear of being raped, was weakened and the man holding her ankles easily separated them widely.

'That looks nice and inviting,' said the man gripping her ankles.

'Cut that out,' ordered the woman, 'you know the rules. If you try anything, our employer would be very displeased with all of us. I shall administer this and then you two take her to him.'

'Yeah... right,' the man ogling Verity's naked form answered, as he tried to contain his aroused state.

Verity saw a scar on the right hand of the man holding her feet, shaped like a thick crescent with a starred blotch within the curved design. The skin was far paler than that of the rest of his exposed flesh.

Verity relaxed herself. 'Good girl, that's better,' said the woman as she closed in and prepared to inject the syringe into a spot on the inside of the young woman's right calf.

Verity's eyes widened in stark terror, as she felt the cold point of the syringe touch her flesh and she suddenly jerked, the adrenaline pumping wildly through her veins at that exact moment and giving her the energy to enable her to free her foot from the man's grip. She managed to force the ball of cloth from her mouth, and screeched loudly, an ear-piercing scream that echoed within the cell. She lashed out with her foot striking the hand of the woman holding the syringe; the force was sufficient to cause the woman to unintentionally release the surgical implement from her hand, it struck the ceiling on the needle-tip, before coming back down. Then as the two men released Verity, all three instinctively attempted to grab the syringe before it was broken.

Verity darted off the bunk and ran to the open doorway. She grabbed the edge of the doorframe as she exited the cell, while the three strangers ended up in a crumpled heap on the floor realising they'd each missed the syringe. Then as it struck the concrete wall the glass smashed and the fluid reacted with the unpleasant atmosphere, created by the contents of the makeshift toilet.

Verity wrenched the door towards her, closing it. She looked down as it clanged shut; she could not believe her eyes.

A bunch of fucking keys.

Hanging on the outside of the door next to the feeding slot. One key still protruding from the keyhole. Grabbing the larger end of the key, she twisted it and it engaged the locking mechanism.

She only opened the feeding slot a couple of millimetres but a sickening smell forced her to close it quickly. She could hear grotesque sounds emanating from the other side, shouting, pleading, choking, gurgling, and even thumping noises against the other side of the door... then nothing.

Inside the cell, the chemicals leaking from the now broken syringe were reacting with the ammonia and other noxious gases.

The hallucinatory effect of the drug's constituent parts reacted badly for some as yet unknown reason, and when one of the men stood up after the initial realisation of his predicament, to rush the door, a couple of the hobnails in the sole of his boot created a few sparks. All three heard the crackle and realised instantly the implications. Their faces barely had time to register the shock or to cry out, when the sparks ignited the vapours and an almighty explosion ripped into the three people in the small, enclosed space of the cell with so much contained force, reducing them into a liquefied mush, painting the walls in a myriad of gross slimy viscera.

Verity, who had been leaning against the outside of the door, was thrown hard against the cold wall opposite by the shock wave of the explosion. The door of her cell, although two inches thick, had been deformed by the blast, as a large oval bulge had been formed, virtually dead-centre, deforming the steel plate out by almost five inches from the sides; parts of the brickwork surround of the door and the lintel above it shattered and fell away. The gaps allowed a foul dark smog to filter out into the corridor.

Verity gagged, and then went to the door to her right. She found the right key after five attempts and opened it. The cell was in darkness. On the recessed section of the wall next to the door there was a switch. She pressed the switch and the cell light revealed it was empty. She moved on and tried the last two cells in this block of five, but they too were vacant. There was no sign of them having occupants at all.

Verity, realising she had become disorientated due to the confusion of the explosion, went back to the side of which she was certain Dean occupied. She eventually found the correct key and inserted it into the lock, turning it. The mechanism clicked and the main latch clanked, allowing the door to open. Dean charged out, his fists flailing wildly.

'Whoa there… boyo,' Verity said, as she sidestepped out of his way, almost clobbered by one of the young man's fists.

'Verity? What happened? That noise?' Dean asked. 'What was going on?'

'Nothing to worry about. Not now anyway. I'll tell you later.' The shock and realisation suddenly, unexpectedly hit home to Verity and she slumped into Dean's arms, her naked body against his blanket-covered one. She shivered and Dean opened the blanket then wrapped it around them both. Her arms snaked around his medium build body, and in other times it would be as much as he could do to restrain himself, having this naked woman pressing against him.

'Where should we go? What can we do now?' He asked plaintively.

After Verity had told Dean of what had nearly happened in her cell, of how she had managed to escape, he found himself exceedingly impressed by this woman's tenacity, and her resourcefulness. They moved along the corridor, then they came to a door that was ajar. Inside the room was some furniture, a large, soft, covered futon, a filing cabinet, a desk with a telephone, and a flat-screen PC monitor, which was dormant.

Moving further in, Verity spied a single bed in a separate room. She went into the room first, slowly pulling Dean along with her. She turned and closed the door and locked it, then pulling the blanket away from around Dean's body, much to his embarrassment, and wrapping it around her own, she explored the other rooms that led from this room. Verity saw a phone and picked up the receiver, but the line was dead.

Both areas were devoid of people.

They both wondered why, after the explosion, no one else had appeared to investigate the noise.

'Let's see if there are any spare clothes around here,' Verity said. They began looking in the cupboards in the smaller room and found something to wear.

They also found a small shower cubicle and showered separately, using the products the guards had left in the lockers. Drying themselves using the towels to hand, and dressing in the clothes, they found some trainers that fitted. Verity then used a hairbrush to make her hair tidier. She was not bothered whose brush it was – she needed to keep her hair under control – then she found a couple of hair clips, and she put them in.

'Let's find a way out of here,' she said, her eyes blazing with determination.

'Any idea what the time is?' Dean asked.

They looked around the rooms and found a small travel alarm clock on a table next to the futon. It read 05:24.

'We'd better move. If there is a shift change, they may be here very soon,' Dean said.

Verity nodded, a small grin forming on her face as she agreed. 'Or someone might be wondering why that woman hasn't reported in yet.'

They exited the outer room, closing the door and locking it behind them with the set of keys Verity had with her. They followed the corridor along to where a locked steel door barred their way. Above it stencilled in white paint was the legend: GARAGE LEVEL STAIRWAY

Fishing the keys out of the overall pocket, Verity eventually found the right one and unlocked the door. She pushed the bar running horizontally downwards and it creaked open. They passed through and closed the door. Verity tried to lock the door, but for some reason the key got jammed and she was unable to remove it. Dean tried but he too failed. Verity wrangled the key ring off, leaving the seized key in the lock. Ahead of them were stone steps leading upwards within a dimmed stairwell. Tentatively they began climbing the steps cautiously, pausing every few steps to listen.

They reached a turn-back and had to climb another level, then another, and finally one more before they reached an opening that brought them to a garage area, lit by a few strip-lights, a few of which were flickering and buzzing erratically. Parked in a few of the spaces were various vehicles. Verity stopped beneath one of the strip-lights and looked at the keys again. Most were the same type, but three were different and looked like they belonged to a car.

Though which one? There were no distinguishing logos embossed on the keys themselves and no fob to activate or deactivate an electronic alarm. With Dean following close behind her, Verity began scouring the vehicles, trying to assess which vehicle might be the right one.

Dean thought he heard something, an unexpected motorised whirring from somewhere else in the garage level. Then an engine revving and tyres were making contact sounds with the rough garage floor, squealing as the vehicle approached him and Verity. He grabbed her upper arm pulling her to his side against a wall, as a set of car lights almost illuminated them from an upper level of the three-tier underground garage, as they stood looking at a similar vehicle.

The approaching vehicle rounded a corner, its engine noise became louder as it drew closer. Grabbing Dean's arm this time, Verity pulled him further out of view as the large black 4x4 Mitsubishi Warrior pickup came into view. As it passed them by, Verity saw that all the side windows were tinted. She guided Dean between two vehicles and they stayed down, crouch walking towards the rear of the vehicle they had been hiding behind, and out of sight. It drove past and down further into the barely illuminated parking garage, following the arrows painted on the concrete. Dean and Verity, still holding the keys tightly in her hand, ducked down at the squealing screeches of the tyres becoming louder. The engine noise echoed loudly in the subterranean garage parking area, and finally the 4x4 finally reached the lowest level.

The 4x4 having rumbled by disappeared, the sound of its engine eventually fading into the distance. Coughing due to the exhaust fumes in the subterranean area, which had no proper ventilation or exhaust removal system in place, Dean and Verity moved out and edged to the ramp the truck had just come down.

Checking first cautiously to see if there were any more vehicles approaching, or anyone walking their way who potentially might be looking for them, the two escapees moved as swiftly as they could up the ramp to the next level and saw that this one had only one vehicle parked up. This was another Mitsubishi Warrior painted in dark red but with a closed-in back end, over the cargo-bed section.

Verity hoped that the car key she held might be for this vehicle. Cautiously she approached the truck and slipped the key into the lock on the left-hand side door. It turned easily and she noted the click as the electronic locking mechanism disengaged.

She opened the door and found that this vehicle was a left-hand drive, which she thought strange for the UK, but she knew some people liked them. Motioning for Dean to go round to the other side door, Verity climbed in behind the wheel and inserted the key into the ignition. Dean closed the passenger door as Verity turned the truck's ignition-key three notches for the glow plugs to warm up, since it was a diesel engine. When the orange light on the display went out, she turned the key right over and the engine fired into life.

'Do you know how to drive one of these? 'Dean asked nervously.

Verity glanced over at Dean, rolling her eyes in mock despair. 'My brother Jim has one up in Yorkshire on the farm he runs. I get to drive it. It's easy really,' she said, as she put it into gear after checking it was not set for four-wheel drive. The smaller gear lever to the right of the main gear stick, used to initiate the off-road utility, was pulled back towards the rear seats.

Selecting first, she slowly pulled the truck out of the parking space, flitting her head, looking for any sign of someone ready to dart out of a hiding place to recapture them. Then she remembered that you could lock the doors by flicking the switch on the driver's door panel. She did this and immediately felt to some degree safer, more comfortable.

She drove the vehicle, following the painted arrows leading her to the main exit, picking up speed as her confidence grew. As the main gateway came into view, her heart sank back down when she saw that there was a steel mesh barrier blocking her escape. Taking her foot off the accelerator and slowing down the truck, she wondered how she was going to get them both free from this God-awful nightmarish place, but unexpectedly the barrier began to slide open upwards. A beeping noise began to sound in the truck's cab just below the CD player where a box showed a flashing series of coloured lights.

Verity realised this must be an auto-sensory unit for the person that owned this vehicle. Either way she was grateful it had not been disabled. She began to edge forwards once more as the barrier continued to reveal the outside world.

It was still dark and now teaming down with rain outside, as the opening was now wide enough for her to pass through; she drove out into the wild dark yonder, then the barrier stopped and began to close again.

***

The other 4x4's occupants were the relief security officers. They had exited their vehicle and taken the lift down to their sector in the building's basement. When the three arrived, they each knew that something was terribly wrong. Usually met by at least one of their colleagues, but no-one did. Arriving at the lower containment level, they found the buckled cell door, and managed to force it open, retching at the disgusting smell and scene that befell their eyes. One of them set off the internal silent security alarm which would alert the CEO, then they ran back towards the garage area as quickly as they could, grabbing their weapons from their lockers, en route to returning to their vehicle.

Jumping back into the black Warrior, the driver floored the pedal and the vehicle's wheels spun madly creating not only a high-pitched squeal as the tyres burned rubber on the rough concrete, but an almighty roar as the engine protested from being ill-treated.

The guard in the driver's seat accelerated, wrenching the steering wheel of the normal right-hand drive from one side to the other as she negotiated the tight turns at high speed, bouncing up the ramp to the next level, racing towards the main exit. She knew that the person driving the other vehicle would only be able to follow the roads leading back into the city from here, so she was confident it would not take very long to catch up with the escapees.

The female security guard and her two colleagues were also very aware that if they failed to re-capture the escapees they would definitely suffer the consequences from their employer's personal bodyguard.

She drove fast through the early morning traffic, snaking around buses and overtaking taxis, receiving blasts on horns and loud obscene comments. She eventually caught sight of the rear of the red Warrior as it turned right onto South Colonnade, and again when Verity sped along the road towards West India Ave, and on towards West Ferry Circle Roundabout.

Verity glanced into the rear-view mirror and gasped when she saw the other Warrior weaving its way through the traffic and gaining ground behind them. Horns blared and headlights flashed as angry drivers remonstrated towards the aggressive driver succeeding in moving closer. Verity slammed her foot down, changing gear frantically but with almost the precise finesse of a Formula One racing driver, she picked up speed and changed lanes, often driving on the wrong side of the road, in her effort to slip around the other cars, buses, coaches and commercial vehicles on the road. She too gained remonstrations from the other road users, but she did not really care.

She barely slowed down as she entered the roundabout, narrowly missing clipping the nearside front of a taxicab entering from the A1206 northbound. The driver of the taxi slammed his brakes on so hard forcing his car to slew into a sideways slide on the slippery wet roadway.

Dean, with both hands pressing against the soft leather-covered dash, had sensibly put on his seatbelt, his face showing his fearful concern towards his companion's driving abilities. Verity drove with determination to escape, as she headed right onto the A13; now she was on East India Dock Road heading westwards.

Still looking in the rear-view and the side mirrors, she stayed on the same road as it became Commercial Road, heading through Stepney.

Another Mitsubishi Warrior vehicle, crewed by four members of the company's in-house security employees had managed to close the distance on the fleeing captives, and were now a few vehicles behind them.

The trailing Warrior had closed the gap. Two of the guards armed with semi-automatic Glock.45 machine pistols loaded with .45mm rounds fired at the red Warrior indiscriminately.

Without warning and from behind them, gunfire fired by the pursuing security team. Bullets struck the rear of the vehicle; the rear window disintegrated. With the glass gone, she could hear the screeching of tyres and horns from behind, forcing other road users to get out of the way. Verity knew she had to find a new route and veered aggressively, forcing the oncoming traffic to react, and hopefully create space for her to get away, as another salvo of rounds impacted with the vehicle.

Verity remembered the gun she had grabbed before leaving the cellblock. 'Dean, use the gun, shoot back at those motherfuckers.'

'I don't know how to, I've never fired a gun before,' Dean replied feebly.

'Jesus fucking Christ. All you have to do is pull the fucking trigger. Fire back at those tossers or we're dead. And don't forget to release the safety.' Verity immediately felt guilty for swearing at Dean in this manner, but she justified it by convincing herself that they would both most certainly die if she had not.

Dean grabbed the gun and flicked the safety off just as another salvo of rounds clanged and struck the lead Warrior, forcing Dean and Verity to flinch. Incensed by this aggressive attack, Dean unclipped his seat belt and turned to face out of the busted rear window. He aimed the weapon and fired, several rounds spitting out, and the vicious recoil made his unaccustomed wrist ache.

Two rounds struck the advancing black Warrior's windscreen creating holes close to the female driver, who jerked and swerved striking a civilian's car on its driver's side, badly scraping the paintwork and tearing off the bump-strip of the Peugeot 207.

Verity took corners wildly, her adrenaline rushing through her bloodstream diluting the fear and increasing the determination to flee the pursuers. She weaved her way through the already increasing pre-dawn morning traffic towards Westminster, taking roads along the centre white lines, forcing traffic out of her way. Verity ploughed the red Mitsubishi through the traffic on the A1203, as she led the other vehicle and its occupants, still firing their weapons without concern, along East Smithfield towards Tower Bridge, the first main bridge that spanned the river Thames. Verity twisted the steering wheel, the tyres screeching and protesting around the left-hand turn onto the A100.

Often managing to increase the distance between herself and the other truck, sometimes backtracking from one bridge over the river and back over another bridge, slipping down side-roads, once she was certain she couldn't see the other 4x4 behind them and stopping briefly to catch her breath. After a brief stop, she glanced at the fuel gauge and sighed hesitantly; the needle was just under the quarter mark. Unfortunately, Westminster Bridge was still closed to traffic due to major road works and enhancements to the pavement and the lighting.

Driving around aimlessly on roads south of the river, Verity began searching for a petrol station. She had no money on her, and she suspected neither did Dean, so she would have to do a runner. It was not even her vehicle; even so, she had already begun to feel guilty for even thinking it.

Cruising along trying to conserve what fuel remained and keeping her eyes alert for the pursuing truck and a petrol station, her spirits lifted when she saw a BP garage looming up on her right. She gauged the moment and slipped through a small gap in the oncoming traffic. Her heart pounded in her chest as she pulled up next to the diesel pump. Verity asked Dean to get out and fill the tank while she prepared herself by not turning off the engine, keeping her foot away from the accelerator. She pulled the small lever to release the filler cap flap. Thankfully, even at this hour, the forecourt was devoid of other customers, so no one was close enough to notice the bullet-holes that peppered the bodywork and had taken out the rear window.

Verity jumped when a loud female voice boomed out via an external speaker. 'Would the female driver of the red Mitsubishi Warrior at pump five, please turn off your engine... this is a garage you know.' Greatly embarrassed and reluctantly, she complied.

Dean took the fuel spout and slipped it into the filler opening. He looked over at the shop, directly at the person behind the counter, and smiled, hoping that she would press the button to allow the fuel to commence flowing. Almost immediately, the pump fired into life and Dean was able to begin filling the tank.

As he stood beside the truck, he began checking the pockets of the clothes he had taken from the guard's room and found a wallet. Looking slightly perplexed, he opened the wallet and found it contained at least two hundred pounds in notes. He almost jumped for joy, and after filling the tank with almost ninety pounds worth of diesel, he replaced the fuel cap and closed the flap, then he sauntered painfully over to the door of the shop and went inside.

Verity looked on with dread, wondering what Dean was doing at a time like this. Turning her head this way and that, Verity waiting for the other 4x4 to make an appearance, she could not believe her eyes when Dean returned carrying a bag of shopping. He climbed back into the truck and grinned knowingly.

'What the hell do you think you're doing?' Verity spat angrily.

Dean showed her the wallet with the remains of what money was inside. Verity sighed with relief and smiled.

'I'm sorry,' she said, resting her right hand on his left, across the centre console. Dean grinned once more, opened a bottle of orange flavoured Lucozade, and passed it to her, along with a Mars bar which he had partially unwrapped. Verity took a quick gulp of the drink and a bite of the confectionary, then started the engine and eased back into the main road in the same direction that she had been going.

Driving past Waterloo Station, on York Road, both she and Dean kept their eyes on the roads, either side, in front and behind them. She followed the road around to cross over the Westminster Bridge a little way ahead, and then she saw the warning signs telling drivers: Closed to Traffic. Chastising herself for forgetting, Verity continued along the road parallel to the Thames, realising that they would have to go towards either Lambeth or Vauxhall Bridge, then she looked in the rearview.

'Shit.'

'What?'

'They've found us again. However, the good news is the traffic is much heavier. They're not going to risk forcing their way through it to get to us. It'll draw more attention... besides...' Verity paused, waiting for Dean to ask.

'Besides?'

'There's a police car two cars behind us,' Verity answered.

'Why don't you stop, get their help?' Dean said.

'Too risky, both for the police and us. If we stopped, those bastards *could* just drive past and shoot all of us, the police... anyone who witnessed anything. Get ready, I'm going to floor it,' Verity said, as an idea formed in her mind.

When a suitable gap appeared ahead of her, she swung out slightly to see what the oncoming traffic was like. Great, there was a gap looming within the approaching vehicles right now. Just as she prepared herself to make her move, the blues and twos of the police car made her jump, and the police vehicle burst out from behind the two cars following Verity and Dean and sped past them. As it went by, the passenger officer glanced at the rear end of the Mitsubishi, and noticed the smashed rear window and the holes, but said nothing.

'Great, well done,' said the female guard leader of the three people in the black Warrior, as she commended the male guard who had phoned nine-nine-nine and called an emergency in a nearby location, believing the control centre would call the closest police crew patrolling to attend the emergency.

'This'll soon be over. If only this fucking traffic was lighter. Damned congestion,' said the second male guard.

With the police car speeding out of sight, Verity's confidence took a dive yet again. She looked ahead and saw that the gap in the traffic in both directions was about to close up after the police vehicle had passed by, she swung out clipping the rear of the car in front, denting and scratching the bodywork. She floored the red Warrior's accelerator, tyres screaming and burning rubber onto the tarmac creating a plume of blue smoke. Deciding it was her *only* option, having now reached the junction to cross Westminster Bridge Verity turned right and blasted her way through the barriers that barred the traffic from using the bridge's roadway, feeling and hearing the metal scraping against the bodywork. She weaved the large vehicle around the main obstacles that might have hindered another person, as well as a few construction workers, shocked and angry at a driver choosing not to abide by the restrictions. There was a large tarmac layer machine, slightly askew across the roadway, a road-rolling machine and a couple of bulldozers and tippers, as well as mounds of broken older tarmac and grade 2 shingle.

Once over Westminster Bridge, passing the Parliament buildings and Big Ben tower, Verity turned left onto the A3211, weaving the Warrior in and out of the traffic, not caring anymore what cars she hit, she just hoped she did not hit any with children. She glanced into the off-side door mirror and saw the black Warrior, the only other vehicle to dare cross the bridge, and in doing so, making ground swiftly forcing its way through the traffic, sending unfortunate drivers swerving out of the large pick-up's way, and crashing into other vehicles, or forcing them onto the pavements, scattering pedestrians and cyclists. The female driver of the black 4x4 did not seem to care who was injured.

One poor driver was almost on an unavoidable head-on collision, and as the middle-aged driver reacted, he overcompensated the steering and pulled the car, a 1980's yellow Datsun Sunny over to his left so sharply, kerbing the wheel so that his brakes unexpectedly failed. Then he realised he was heading straight towards a bus stop shelter, with several people waiting for a bus.

He wrestled with the wheel; his left front tyre blew out forcing the car to slew then it mounted the pavement and ploughed into the shelter at more than twenty miles per hour, striking the innocent people, some of whom had begun to scatter and escape being hit, but failed. The driver of the car struck his head on the wheel extremely hard, as the front end collided with an upright post and three people tumbled over the bonnet, windscreen and roof, leaving a torso-sized dent in each.

The car immediately caught fire, the bonnet flying upwards, taking a person unfortunately laying atop it, as an explosion in the engine bay caused by the fuel pipe rupturing and the fuel striking the hot exhaust manifold igniting, tore it free from its hinges.

Screams began to permeate through the roar of the fire, as other people immediately went to help those involved in the crash.

Verity never saw the aftermath; she was staring ahead, only occasionally glancing in the mirrors to check where the other Warrior was. She turned her head again and looked to her right then had a start when she saw the face of the passenger in the black Warrior pointing a weapon directly at Dean's head, through the open window of the other door.

Dean, who hadn't realised he was in the firing line, turned and looked at Verity as she immediately slammed her foot on the accelerator. The red 4x4 shot forward as a salvo of rounds blasted through the rear side window narrowly missing both Dean and Verity's heads, blowing out the glass on Verity's side, small pieces of glass littering the roadway. The guard in the passenger side of the black Mitsubishi 4x4 grimaced in annoyance. Then Verity was forced to slow abruptly once more when she saw that she was about to rear-end a stationary bus. The black 4x4 overtook them as the bus pulled away, the bus driver thinking that the red truck driver was letting him pull out from the bus stop. The female security Mitsubishi driver pulled directly in front of Verity and Dean and continued moving forward.

Now that they were ahead of the escapees, the female guard believed that she could control the situation, but Verity had other ideas. She slowed down to increase the gap between the two similar vehicles, just as they reached the turning on the North London side of Waterloo Bridge. Verity slammed her right foot down and rammed the nearside rear corner of the other Warrior, forcing it to slew off to its right, and then Verity backed off and slipped up the other vehicle's nearside, taking the corner of Lancaster Place sharply. So sharply, that as she took the corner, both of the offside wheels lifted clear of the road, and she had to throw her weight and shove Dean far over to the right to get the truck back down, without taking her foot off the gas.

She then gunned the vehicle until the engine was straining at the bit, along the road, weaving in and out of honking vehicles, in a 'Devil Don't Give a Fuck' attitude.

After being struck by the red 4x4 on the offside rear quarter, forcing the vehicle over into the oncoming traffic, the female guard opened her eyes in horror as a motorcyclist was heading straight for the front of the vehicle. The unfortunate motorcyclist had no time to avoid the impact, and the front wheel of his Suzuki 1300 cc touring bike struck the front of the 4x4 at thirty miles an hour. The front wheel buckled and the rider flipped upwards and over the roof of the truck, somersaulting in mid-air and coming back down onto the road surface behind the truck on his back. The force of the rider's body slamming into the tarmac ruptured his kidneys, tore his spleen and seriously bruised his liver. Several bones were broken in his arms and legs, and his pelvis shattered in several places. He also broke his neck when the lower back edge of his crash helmet dug into his flesh.

The female security driver had overcompensated due to the wet surface, the 4x4 slewed to face in the opposite direction.

Nevertheless, the biker was alive. Nearby spectators rushed to his aid, two of them medically trained, and aware of potential injuries to motorcyclists, they acted accordingly.

By now, several calls to the emergency number had resulted in a major call-out of police cars, ambulances and fire engines. Blues and twos sounded in a cacophony of wailing sirens that echoed close by, bouncing off the buildings, beginning to sound like banshees. Verity knew that time was running out. She had one last idea to put to the test. She slowed down.

'What's happening?' Dean asked, craning to look at the fuel gauge. 'We've still got diesel.'

'Keep a lookout behind us; let me know when those ass-wipes catch up.'

'Are you crazy? I thought you wanted to lose them,' Dean moaned.

'We will, if this works,' Verity said, her voice edgy with determination.

'What plan?' Dean turned and looked out of the rear window.

The female guard having shunted the motorcycle out of her way, brought the truck back under control and turned it round, her hands a blur on the steering wheel, clipping three stationary cars in the process. One of them was a police car; the two uniformed officers swiftly got out and began to approach the truck but were both shot in their lower legs by the passenger with the Glock.45 automatic pistol, reloaded with a new magazine.

Crippled by the bullets the two officers fell, but one managed to radio for assistance and give a description of the two Japanese trucks heading towards Covent Garden.

and saw the black Warrior come into view. 'It's moving up.'

'They're closing the gap!' Dean shouted.

Verity pressed down on the accelerator a few times quickly and revved the engine, she depressed the clutch, rammed the stick into first gear and slipping the clutch again wheel spun the truck. It shot forward suddenly, causing Dean to lose his hold of the weapon and drop the gun onto the floor. Verity shot onto Bow Street just as the black Mitsubishi weaved from side to side, trying to get past. The passenger fired shots at the red Warrior, having come up on the driver's side, three shots striking the driver's door.

One bullet went through and struck Verity in her left thigh, ripping into muscle, and taking a chunk out of her femur, but thankfully missing the femoral artery. The searing pain made her grit her teeth; another bullet hit her left wrist shattering both forearm bones close to the joint. The third bullet went into the back of the seat, deflected and came out the other side tearing the leather sheathing of the gear stick's head.

Verity wrenched the red Warrior aggressively over to her left, striking the driver's side of the black truck. 'Dean. Shoot that fucking bitch in the head, now,' she ordered.

'I've lost the gun; I dropped it,' Dean said sounding pathetic.

'Then fucking get it, you dickhead… quickly,' Verity answered angrily.

Dean took a deep breath, shocked at Verity's sudden aggressive outburst. Swiftly he searched between the front seats, scrabbling on the floor. His hand touched the grip and closed around it. He turned in one fluid movement aiming the barrel directly at Verity's right side of her head. She was level with the other vehicle. 'Duck,' Dean said sharply into her right ear.

She did so, throwing her head forward and down but still looking where she was driving through the steering wheel over the dashboard. Dean fired and five successive rounds escaped the barrel, then the gun clicked.

The first bullet struck the driver in the right shoulder ripping through the scapular bone. The second ripped a huge rent in the side of her neck, creating a maw the size of a boxer's fist out of her throat. Blood shot out striking the windscreen and obscuring the view.

Two completely missed the driver but hit the front passenger, one dead centre in the forehead, as he had been staring wide-eyed at Dean, the second ripping through the left eyeball with a slight upward trajectory. The round macerated the brain into pulp before taking a massive piece of skull bone out the back of the head and covering the interior roof lining with brain matter, bone and claret.

The female driver lurched to the right, as Verity swung out then back to her left, striking the driver's side engine compartment of the black Warrior with so much force the driver completely lost her one-handed grip on the wheel. Her right arm hung limply at the side. Then Verity side-swiped the other vehicle again just as they reached the leading corner of Covent Garden's Royal Opera House, on Bow Street.

Verity, pushing the pain from her wounds out of her mind, rammed the other truck again mostly using her right hand to steer, with a pain-jarring crunch as the other driver finally slumped forwards, her right foot pressing down on the accelerator, her life now extinguished. The third guard tried to reach forwards from the rear to grab the wheel and steer it, he did not think to knock the gear lever into neutral. The impact sent him flailing sideways losing his meagre grip of the wheel.

Verity forced the truck to the left into Floral Street. The yellow stone Opera House building set back from the kerb by about ten to fifteen feet or so. With one final grinding shove, Verity rammed the truck to the left; the nearside wheels striking the kerb in such a way the still speeding truck flipped sideways up into the air and rolled on its longitudinal axis. It became airborne to a height of about fifteen feet before it slammed into the upper flat yellow stonework façade below the columns that formed the architectural frontage of the building.

The truck hovered briefly, while people nearby and below scattered madly out of the way. Then it fell, landing on its roof, which immediately caved in. The front passenger guard's head, *or what was left of it,* was severed at shoulder level as the sharp metal of the window edge of the door sliced it clean off on impact with the ground. The head rolled a few feet, stopping at the feet of an elderly man, who looked down at a one-eyed face. He keeled over from a massive heart attack and was dead before his body struck the pavement.

Verity pulled up a few feet away. The engine stalled. She was bleeding badly and had already lost a lot of blood. She turned to look at Dean, smiled, and passed out.

Moments later the area was awash with police cars and vans, the first police officers on scene called ambulances and fire engines. Blues and twos filling the enclosed area with ear-shattering noise. One-by-one the sirens switched off, leaving the flickering blue lights. Fire trucks and ambulances arrived to deal with the injured and the dead, cut free anyone feared trapped, and to make the vehicles safe.

Deputy Chief Commissioner of the Metropolitan Police, Felicity Conway, arrived in her chauffeur-driven Jaguar S Type to oversee the situation. Accompanying her was Chief Superintendent Charles Warwick, who looked far from pleased at seeing the carnage, not just here at Covent Garden, but witnessing the aftermath of the numerous traffic violations caused by the drivers of both of these large vehicles, as they wreaked havoc all the way from London's Docklands. He was also less than happy at hearing earlier reports that someone in the black 4x4 fired shots at police, and seriously wounded two officers.

Someone was going to pay dearly for this, and he desperately hoped it was not going to be him, but he felt butterflies in his stomach, and his fingers tingled.

The news spread fast. People with video cameras and mobile phones had been taking pictures and videos, and sending them direct to the news channels, happy to make some money out of other people's misery.

Vultures.

Chief Superintendent Charles Warwick looked at his watch. It read:

10:14 AM.

The paramedics worked alongside their fellow professionals, the police and fire crews, to deal with the injured parties.

The dark red Mitsubishi Warrior was in a far better condition than that of its sister vehicle, albeit less a few windows, and damaged bodywork, plus several bullet holes. The fire crew still had to cut the roof free, as all of the doors were badly wedged into the bodywork.

Verity, unconscious and slumped to her right was being tended by three paramedics who had climbed into the cab while the fire crew cut the roof free, and after pulling the doors away they carefully placed her on a spinal board. The paramedics treated Dean similarly and both were immediately taken to the nearest A & E department.

***

Early Morning. Sunday 30th December 2007: 01.44 AM.

The office block was quiet, but then it was the weekend after Christmas. The only people working were the hard-pressed, underpaid and undervalued security officers and essential cleaning operatives.

The rookie security officer, Jake Bunton, who like his colleagues worked for a London-based cover security company, sat half-looking at the screens in the control room. He was not supposed to be, but he was watching a DVD on a portable TV he had brought in whilst working over the festive season, or what was left of it.

Supervisory Security Officer, Dee Fielding, sat facing a wall of security TV monitors. She constantly viewed up to one hundred and twenty visuals of the building, all of them digitally recording 24/7. Centred within these smaller screens was one much larger screen, so suspicious activities caught on the smaller screens might be enlarged and viewed in detail and clarity.

Unexpectedly, all of the screens covering the fiftieth floor went completely blank. 'Damn,' Dee said, as her perfectly manicured fingers began tapping the keyboard, attempting to reboot the cameras for that particular floor. 'Every week the cameras on the fiftieth glitch out. How come the maintenance guys never seem to find the fault?' she asked.

Jake grunted. He was too busy watching the film.

Dee turned in her chair to face the younger man, a look of utter disdain upon her face. 'You are taking one hell of a liberty sitting there watching that bloody DVD, instead of doing your job,' she told him sternly.

Dee looked at the clock. It was just after one-forty in the morning, so she grabbed the internal radio microphone. 'George? Wesley? What floor are you guys currently on?'

Loud static came back which caused Dee to wince, then a voice, which sounded almost alien. 'George here, Dee, I'm on the forty-third. Wes is on the next one up, what's the problem?' George Murray said. His gruff voice unmistakable, even through the close-knit radio electronics system.

'I think the cameras on the fiftieth are on the blink again. Could one of you two go check it out, please?' Dee asked.

George muttered something unintelligible under his breath, then he pressed the call button on the side of his hand-held radio, 'Okay, will do Dee... Wes, wait at the North Side elevators. We'll go up together and check, besides it's nearly our break period.'

After meeting by the elevator and exiting on the fiftieth floor, the two security staff walked along the wide corridor when there was a loud bang that made the two men jump.It sounded like something striking the exterior of the building, against the plate glass windows that covered the majority of the upper office floors. George Murray and Wesley Jenner stood dumbfounded, their mouths agape in utter disbelief, when they saw the silhouette of a person suspended briefly for a few seconds.

Light from a roving source from somewhere outside illuminated the side of the building in random arcs, across the exterior windows of the intersecting corridor ahead of them.

As the two security men cautiously moved forward and reached the plate glass barrier between them and the person outside the building, a blustering gust of wind caught her body in its grip, twisting her around, moving her away from the side of the building then slamming her violently face first against the thick, toughened glass.

A smear of blood leaking from a viciously long slash on her right cheek left a sickeningly wide meandering trail against the glass. Because of the powerful lighting that occasionally swept the building, the two security men could see her bruised wrists and ankles.

Then without warning, she fell out of sight.

One

Sunday 30th December. 09:33 AM.

'Detective Chief Inspector Philip Lomax?' asked the voice on the other end.

'Yes, who is this?' he said, his tone showing his annoyance.

'Chief Superintendent Charles Warwick, I apologise for calling during your vacation. I understand you once knew a woman by the name of Amanda Waterman?'

Lomax was stunned. He had not heard from or seen Amanda for a long, long time. The last he knew of her, she had moved to the US to work for a pharmaceutical company in Virginia.

That was many years ago.

'Yes sir… if it's the same Amanda Waterman, don't forget, she won't be the only woman by that name. Especially in London,' Lomax said.

He had heard during his holiday that his superior Chief Superintendent Nick Huntley now fully transferred to Fulham, and that a new Chief Superintendent was to take control of his Section. He scoured the vista before him. He was laying on a sun-lounger on the balcony of his hotel in Brixham, Devon, where he had taken the briefest of breaks, where down in this part of the country the weather was unseasonably warm and sunny, compared with London and the North. 'Excuse me for asking sir, but I feel that I have to ask, how is it that you believe this Miss Waterman and I could be acquainted in the first place?'

'One of the uniformed police officers on the scene, found a piece of paper near the corpse with your name and your office landline number written on it, CS

Warwick answered. The line went silent for a few moments before CS Warwick spoke again.

'Lomax, are you there?'

Lomax rebuked himself for allowing his thoughts to slide away from the call.

'Yes sir, I'm sorry,' Lomax lied. 'What would you like me to do?' He asked, hoping he would not hear the answer.

'I need you to get back to your office,' CS Warwick began. Lomax's heart sank straight away, he was just getting relaxed, and his recharged batteries were definitely feeling as though they were helping his mood. 'As soon as your holiday's over, of course. All data relating to the incident will be on your desk. Your subordinate officers will of course have taken statements, and reviewed the forensic evidence recorded. How many days left have you, by the way?'

'Six, sir,' Lomax said.

'See you when you get back then,' CS Warwick said, and then the phone line went dead.

No matter how he tried, he had not been able to relax properly for the first few days of his break. Lomax's older sister, Hillary, telephoned minutes before CS Warwick had called, to say she had to go away on an emergency concerning her husband's family and that Gerald would take over her duties.

Lomax knew that this was a bad mistake, and so realising that it would be a pointless exercise to remain there, he drove back early from Devon. Besides which, he needed to be assured whether or not the victim was indeed the Amanda Waterman he knew. Lomax drove back through Devon towards the A303, aiming to reach the M4 before the traffic built up, and get back to the city as soon as possible.

Two

Sunday December 30th.11:40 AM.

Detective Sergeant Roma Clarkson was seated in CS Warwick's office on the 4th floor of Dunne House, with DC Christopher Crosse in the other chair facing the moderate-sized desk. Behind Chief Superintendent Warwick, the window blinds were open allowing a bit of light in through the grimy glass that seriously needed a damned good clean.

'How have you found taking overall charge of the team during DCI Lomax's absence, Roma?' CS Warwick asked.

'It's been fairly straightforward sir, apart from this recent situation with this Amanda Waterman at the Canary Wharf site.'

'What do you mean?' CS Warwick asked.

DS Clarkson immediately felt uneasy by Warwick's unexpected question.

DC Crosse also shifted in his seat, then spoke. 'I think DS Clarkson means that if Lomax is… or *was* acquainted with the victim, perhaps it might conflict with the investigation, due to personal associations?'

'Is that so, Clarkson?' CS Warwick asked. 'Might that be your concern?'

Coughing to clear her throat, DS Clarkson smiled and nodded. 'Yes sir. I'm not trying to cause undue issues with the case before Phil– I mean, Lomax gets back from his break, but if he was indeed acquainted with Ms Waterman, surely we should offer this investigation to another division?'

'I understand your concerns Clarkson, and I admire your dedication not only to your immediate superior, but to the Serious Murder Enquiry Team based here at Dunne House. I'm certain that when DCI Lomax returns, he'll have little to do with the investigation, apart from overseeing the final tidying up, because your leadership and the team will have it all sown up by the time he gets back in a few days.'

On their way back to the S.M.E.T. enquiry suite, Roma and DC Crosse went into the office that she and DCI Lomax shared, she took the chair behind Lomax's desk, while Crosse sat in one of the spare chairs after setting it closer to the desk.

'I'm really not sure it was wise of Warwick to call Philip and tell him of the situation, considering that he was on a well-deserved break, or while we were in his office.' Roma said.

Crosse simply nodded his agreement, giving him time to formulate a response. 'Perhaps he was fishing for a response from you.'

Roma's eyes widened in surprise. 'What are you implying, Chris?'

'All I'm saying is that it's obvious that Warwick senses that there's more going on between you and Lomax than meets the eye. In addition, the rest of the team can sense it too. I have had my suspicions for a while... so, am I right? Just let me know, and I'll try to persuade everyone else that they're barking up the wrong tree.'

'I'd rather not imply anything. All I will say is that Lomax and I have a strictly professional relationship, nothing more, now let's leave it at that.' Roma started shuffling through some papers on Lomax's desk relating to the Waterman case when the phone rang. Roma snatched the receiver from the cradle. 'Yes? DS Clarkson here.'

'Morning Roma, Sally Hickton here. Just calling to let you know that I am on site. About to begin my preliminary examinations. Have you heard from Philip?'

'Morning Sally, no he's still in Devon. He still has a few days' leave. DC Crosse and I will pop along in a short while. Any ideas as to how long it'll take before you'll be moving the deceased?'

'It's going to be some time I should think. There's a lot of ground to cover and it's very messy. Tell Philip that he'll have my report ASAP. Bye.'

'So, what happens now?' Crosse asked.

'Follow me; we have to let the team know what's currently happening.' Clarkson and Crosse then briefed the assembled officers and civilian staff working on the case, and that Dr Hickton was on site. After assigning members of the team to specific duties, and checking on the other officers and civilian staff with other ongoing cases, she told Crosse, 'I'm going to get us a coffee before we head off to Canary Wharf,'

When Lomax arrived at Dunne House, and was walking through the investigation suite, he saw Roma walking towards their office, two polystyrene cups of strong coffee in her hands.

The shock at seeing her immediate superior back so soon dissipated and she smiled briefly. 'How was the bre...' she began to say, but when she saw the glum expression cloud across his face, she stopped herself.

'Where are the notes on the suicide in Docklands?' He asked. His tone curt and to the point, before he swiped one of the cups.

'Suicide? What are you doing here? Shouldn't you be in Devon?' asked Crosse, as he came to the doorway of the inner office. He wiped his forehead, beaded with perspiration from the clammy heat of the office heating system. Although his family originated from Trinidad,

Christopher Crosse was born in Brixton, London, and he had the typical south London accent; but slightly posher than *one* would have expected.

Lomax sighed audibly. 'For the moment, we have to give the impression that she committed suicide. Regardless of what you've been led to believe may be the actual cause of death.' He sat down at his desk, as Roma handed him the case folder. He sat back, opened it and began to read, digesting the information. He took a sip of the coffee and winced, looking at Clarkson ruefully. 'Machine coffee?' he asked.

Roma nodded guiltily. Lomax returned his attention to the written report, gingerly placing the Styrofoam cup on the corner of his desk. There was not a great amount of information inside. Even without the forensic data, the report was, for all intents and purposes, useless.

'So? How *was* your break?' Roma finally dared to ask. A sheepish look of interest on her face.

'Disappointing, considering I cut it short,' Lomax replied, nonchalantly. 'Roma, get the pool car ready, I need to see the scene and the body…' he paused, as he tried to recall whether he had read that Amanda's corpse had already been removed from the scene, and taken to a mortuary for autopsy.

Roma read his puzzled expression. 'The answer is no, her body is still under a forensic tent, and is being examined as we speak by Dr Hickton.'

Lomax smiled. Even though he had not really been in charge of this particular team for very long, he believed that they were working exceedingly well together, and forming a strong bond. Whether that would last would be anybody's guess.

During the ride in the unmarked silver Vauxhall Vectra 2.0, Lomax felt distracted. On one hand, he was thinking about how and why Amanda was dead. On the other, he knew he had to sort some personal things out. Mostly concerning his own father's well-being and having a serious discussion with his older siblings about their utter lack of respect for their father's health.

The moment he arrived back in the capital, before he went to the 'office' he nipped round to his father's home, in Arlington Gardens, Acton, and was surprised to find his older brother Gerald, vacuuming and tidying the place up. There was no mess anywhere, not even in the kitchen. After the briefest of greetings, Lomax went upstairs to his father's room. There was no musty odour. Propped up in bed, his father was reading the newspaper and listening to Radio 4.

'Hi pop,' Lomax said.

'Hello son,' James replied rather cheerily, 'how was your holiday?' His mood seemed buoyant and he sounded healthy, even though he was far from it. This however appeared to be one of his better and more lucid days.

Lomax sat and talked for about forty minutes before he had to leave and go to work. He told his father he would pop round again the next day. After another brief chat with Gerald, Lomax left for work, but on the way, he called Social Services, making certain a nurse or care worker was regularly checking on his father, ensuring that he took his medication, and had something decent to eat.

***

Amanda Waterman however was an entirely different matter. Lomax was attempting to piece together the smidgen of information gathered in the case file, plus what he knew about Amanda's past, which in fact was not a great deal.

16:29 PM.

As the questions continued piling up in his mind, Roma pulled into the underground car park of Vortexa Pharmaceuticals and stopped the car in an available bay. Well away from where Amanda's bright blue Lexus convertible was cordoned off by blue and white police tape.

The SOCO team had fingerprinted the car and had thoroughly searched the exterior and interior, once they retrieved her personal possessions from her handbag in her office, particularly the car keys. Now they were waiting for the tow-truck to take it to the lab for further tests.

'What do you want to see first, sir?' Asked one of the uniformed police officers securing the area from casual onlookers, 'The victim or the security staff who witnessed the body falling?'

'We'll go speak to the security staff, before they get their facts screwed up,' Lomax told the officer.

'In that case then sir, take those elevators over there, when you get to the upper level another officer will direct you on from there.'

Lomax hated elevators. He was not claustrophobic, he just detested them, usually smelling of staleness, body odours and the residue of sickly perfumes, and more often than not vomit and urine – even in flash offices like these, and more usually after the obligatory company Christmas do.

They had to get out and change to another set of elevators on the north-west side of the building to get to the executive offices, and as the uniformed officer said, another was waiting to show the two S.M.E.T. officers which direction to take. After reaching the designated floor from the elevator, the views ahead of Lomax out of the huge picture windows showing off the city were incredible, yet Lomax realised he preferred the gritty, run-down aspect of his own world at Dunne House. Not this tasteless and tacky lifestyle of corporate bullshit.

The floor was covered in thick beige carpeting, which felt like you were moving barefoot through soggy marshland. Plaques beneath photographs festooned on the walls declared the dog-eat-dog attitude of big business. Everyone fighting to be better than the next employee.

Dog eat dog.

Intermittently spaced were small octagonal ceramic pots on wood tables, with different plants in them. Lomax detested this also; to him it represented everything that was corrupt in global companies such as Vortexa Pharmaceuticals. So-called companies that developed vaccines and medicines to combat diseases such as all known cancers, and other debilitating ailments like Alzheimer's, (one of the conditions his own father suffered from), senile dementia, CJD (Creutzfeldt-Jakob disease), and diabetes to name a few.

Lomax was also pissed off at NICE, the organisation that made the executive decisions as to which patients got certain drugs or medicines, according to the cost factor implemented by their postcode, and which NHS district their hospital resided in. It did not stop there either; the pharmaceutical companies themselves were on Lomax's Hyde Park Corner soapbox hit list, for charging far excessive prices for the products in the first place. He disagreed with their excuses that it costs a lot of money in research, and time.

Was it any wonder people were dying needlessly or suffering long-term, when they did not need to?

Lomax mentally chastised himself for allowing his thoughts to cloud his purpose.

Roma noticed he was sweating and offered him a paper tissue from her handbag, which he accepted wiping his brow and face, before tossing the item in a nearby trashcan.

They reached Amanda's expansive office; looking through the wide-open door Lomax found a sparsely furnished room with a long leather sofa adorning part of a sidewall, and an ornate desk, in the centre behind which sat an equally lavish leather chair. The partially carpeted floor of the office from the doors leading from the corridor mixed with highly polished hard wood flooring. Lomax heard the soles of his leather shoes squeaking irritatingly on the hard floor surface. After a cursory look around her office, stopping to glance briefly at a family photograph on her desk, he retreated back to the corridor, constantly looking around.

Walking up to the large window at the end of the corridor outside of Amanda's office area, Lomax saw the large external crack that had eventually appeared, even though it was toughened glass. He saw the smear of blood, frozen into the crack by the arctic temperature outside.

Stepping even closer, Lomax saw that the crack had not moved all the way through the glass to the interior surface. Carefully examined by SOCO, photographed and swabbed for fingerprints. He refocused his vision and peered down. Under the illumination of the portable lights of the SOCO team members, of which there were at least seven, he saw the large white tent, erected over the spot where the body of Amanda Waterman had fallen.

The corpse was still in situ and had been forensically examined thoroughly; unusual given how long the body remained where it fell. Due to the location and circumstances, Home Office Forensic Pathologist Dr Sally Hickton demanded that the corpse remain until the entire area was checked. Lomax saw the intermittent bright flashes as one of the SOCO team took photographs. The sudden and brief flashes of light looked eerie, as though lightning was restricted to within the confines of the SOCO tent. Added to which, with the city shrouded in winter darkness, and the immediate area bathed in the orange street lighting, the whole scenario looked ill-omened. Although Lomax could not see what was happening inside the tent, he knew the forensic personnel were doing their job professionally.

Down within the tent, Dr Sally Hickton confirmed that the victim was female, aged about forty-one years, and had suffered from serious injuries around the neck, notwithstanding the added trauma of falling from extreme height.

Sally Hickton made requests to retrieve whatever evidence was visible from the immediate area and to look for anything that was not natural. The body was then turned over and photographed again. Hands covered with bags to protect any trace under the fingernails, and any other parts of her body recovered.

Reading the brief report, Lomax read that her brain had 'popped' clean out of her skull from the ground floor level impact as her head had struck the walkway below first, the back of her skull had been wrenched apart. Her brain ended up nearly forty feet away, in a flowerbed. The force was so great upon the base of the skull where the cervical part of the spine connected that the brain stem was instantly severed, allowing the spongy organ to be fired out with relative ease – a direct result of the terminal velocity impact.

After examining the executive offices on that floor apart from those of the – at present unknown – CEO of Vortexa, which were of course securely locked and alarmed, he went down to the exterior scene. Having donned a one-piece – *one size fits all* – waxed paper suit, latex gloves and a surgical mask, Lomax poked his head in through the flap of the tent and immediately felt queasy when he looked at the bagged corpse, as it was moved on a trolley out from the tent and loaded into a coroner's van.

He noted that Dr Hickton was no longer in the tent, discovering that in the time it took for him to make his way back to ground level she had avoided bumping into him and headed back to her office. Lomax removed the suit, gloves and mask, depositing them into a waiting bio-hazard bag, held open by one of the SOCO team members. He asked Roma to drive him to the mortuary. The journey was silent.

Driving through London at peak time was murder, but DS Roma drove like a woman possessed, she guided the vehicle through the congested traffic with ease, often causing near misses with other drivers, and generating the obligatory middle finger response, often coupled with some profanities.

Mortuary: 18.50 PM.

Once there, Lomax asked Roma to stay with the car. In his current mind, he wanted no distractions. He walked down the clinical corridor, the green linoleum making annoyingly loud *schlapping* sounds as his leather-soled shoes made contact. There was also that cloying antiseptic smell, which coupled with the bleach and disinfectant, always made his teeth itch and his eyes water. He reached the mortuary department shortly after the corpse of Amanda Waterman had been delivered; laid out stark naked on a dissecting table.

As Lomax pushed open the double doors to his left, he was immediately assaulted by the unmistakable cloying stench of death. In the autopsy room, there were six stainless steel tables. Each with a slight downward angled centre channel in each one, which led to a drain at the foot end where released fluids would travel.

Above the tables were powerfully bright moveable lights, so that the pathologist could examine from virtually any angle, before they cut flesh or removed organs. Attached to these lights were video cameras and microphones on gimbals to adjust separately for the benefit of the pathologist, which recorded the entire post-mortem examination. There was also a showerhead with a retractable hose; the showerhead handle had a trigger mechanism, which made it easier for the mortuary attendant to control the flow of water when they washed the corpses down; usually immediately after a meticulous examination.

Only three of the tables had 'occupants', each one naked and having been preliminarily examined and washed down. Two were male, one a white victim of a traffic accident on Oxford Street, the other the apparent unnecessary and random stabbing of a smartly dressed young Asian man in Ealing Broadway tube station.

It was the third body that Lomax had come here to see, out of necessity, personal curiosity, and respect. He moved closer to the table and balked at the recognition of the person he once knew.

He could not actually see what was left of the once-beautiful face; with blood-smeared hair matted against the flesh, the head turned away from him at an obtuse angle due to the acute trauma of the upper cervical vertebrae. He saw the gaping maw and the splintered edges of the cranial and parietal bone, as well as the cranial blood vessels that were torn when the brain mass was wrenched from its housing.

Sitting in a large kidney dish was the brain itself, a sagging lump of pallid grey/white organic tissue now barely resembling the human mainframe, which normally governed practically every physical and intellectual activity. There were clear visible signs of injury to the

55

brain, and small fragments of bone embedded into the fleshy sponge-like organ.

Lomax had been present at many post-mortems during the course of his work; this however was in fact the first of someone he knew. It was unsettling to say the least, and now he remembered just what it felt like to lose a friend, or perhaps... a member of one's family.

Having already mourned the loss of his mother when he was eleven years old, Lomax felt a sudden discomfort. He shook his head to try to dispel the thoughts filling his mind. 'Did you get any trace evidence from the bindings around her wrists and ankles?' he asked.

The pathologist looked up from what she was doing and rolled her eyes in mock exasperation. 'I do wish you wouldn't use those American phrases, Phil. Trace evidence indeed,' Sally Hickton said. Her slightly husky voice warmed Lomax's heart. Sally was a Civil Servant, who had also been at school with Lomax, and was in fact one of the few true and loyal friends he would make during school and since leaving. Lomax's friendship with Hickton had travelled through school to one of the new colleges but whereas Lomax only stayed on to get his academic qualifications in English, Social Studies, History and Mathematics, Sally went on to university to gain her NHR biology/chemistry and physics degrees.

Sally Hickton was a tall and well-built woman, standing at six feet-three, which often made things awkward examining corpses in strange locations. A wider nose with a slight bump midway from a sports injury at school, where her nose had been broken during an aggressive netball match with another college, but never properly mended. Brown eyes shone with energetic fervour for her work. Her lips were nearly always pouting.

'Oh come on Sal,' Lomax said, adding 'you know I like American cop shows.'

'To be honest Phil, there was not any foreign DNA or epithelial evidence present on the rope or the tape apart...' She paused purely for effect. 'Apart from *her* own.'

'Are you certain?' Lomax asked incredulously, his eyes opening wide in surprise. 'You found no foreign material?'

'Not really, apart from some common grit found on the roof where the rope was tied off. I'd be inclined to hypothesise that unless the *'murderer'* wore protective clothing, gloves or whatever to lessen the chances of leaving anything specific, this was indeed a suicide, possibly made to look like murder, or... or a murder made to appear as suicide. I cannot be certain at the moment.'

Lomax was about to ask something, then paused as he changed the way he wanted to phrase it. 'Why would a healthy woman, with everything to live for, commit suicide? It doesn't make sense.'

Hickton merely shrugged her broad shoulders.

'Do you have an approximate time of death?' Lomax asked.

Sally turned to look at Lomax with an expression of utter disdain, then spoke curtly. 'It's not definite, but due to the fact that her body had been suspended outside in the freezing cold, and the time factor between the security guys seeing her fall to the ground, and then calling the paramedics, who then called your lot, I'm of the assumption she died some time the previous evening, or perhaps during the day. As I said I cannot be more definitive.'

'You'll let me know what you discover. Right?' Lomax asked, not waiting for a reply as he swiftly left the autopsy room and re-joined Roma at the car.

While Lomax was talking to Sally Hickton, Roma had nipped to a nearby petrol station, bought two coffees, and heated Cornish pasties. As Lomax climbed back in, Roma handed him one of the coffees and the remaining pasty. He took a sip and winced.

'This hasn't any sugar in it,' he said, as Roma swiftly swapped cups, grinning sheepishly. 'You did that on purpose,' Lomax said, pretending to look annoyed.

'No… not really,' she replied, failing to prevent herself from grinning. 'So, where to?'

'Back to the office, drop me off there to get my own car, then I'm going back home, I have a few things to tidy up there. Pick me up from my place in the morning. At seven-thirty.' He did not say anything further during the ride back. After she pulled into one of the vacant car spaces back at the station and she had alighted from the vehicle, Lomax waved to acknowledge his colleague, then she went up to the office to make some brief enquiries with the Investigation Team, and to change some of the assignments for particular staff.

Lomax went to his car and began the drive home, then he diverted. The drive towards Acton was annoyingly slow in the traffic, and Lomax detested driving at the best of times. Eventually finding a parking space nearby on Arlington Road, Lomax walked up the path of his father's home, he put the key into the lock and let himself in. Having been a police officer for many years now, Lomax was well versed in detecting odours left behind by the smoking of marijuana or cannabis. His heightened sense of smell immediately detected the odorous remnants of marijuana floating in the air.

Gerald was asleep on the sofa in the front room; several empty beer cans littered the floor, along with the wrappings and uneaten remnants from a kebab and chips supper, there were the remains of a joint in between

Gerald's right index finger and middle finger. After the concerted effort Gerald had put in earlier, vacuuming the house, Lomax had an uncomfortable sensation begin to develop in his gut.

The telephone answering machine beeped, so Lomax went over to check it. There were several messages, so he quickly went through them. Most were illegible cold-callers, from days earlier promoting questionable goods that Mr James Lomax could have wanted? Two calls were from associates of Gerald's asking for some class B and C drugs that he occasionally peddled.

One specific message came from Amanda Waterman timed and dated by the electronic device at eleven-twenty-one on Thursday twenty-seventh. Four nights before she had died, while he was in Devon. Before Lomax pressed the play button to listen again, he hesitated; with his finger poised, he noticed that he was trembling.

His breathing laboured in his chest as he felt his heart beating against his ribs like a xylophone. He felt his shirt begin to stick to his back, and the hairs on the nape of his neck began to rise, tingling, making him more nervous.

He knew he ought to go up and check on his father first, but this one message may be so damned important, and more likely pertinent to Amanda's death. He played the message right through. However, he had not really taken a great deal of what Amanda had been saying. He had recognised her voice, and it triggered many deep-rooted memories from years before.

'Dad?' He called up the stairs.

'Yes son… I'm here,' James Lomax croaked back, adding, 'I don't think I could run anywhere even if I wanted to.' Followed by a bout of muffled coughing.

'I'll be up to see you in a moment.'

'Very well then, don't take too long. I need to pee,' James Lomax cackled.

Lomax chuckled. His father had been fitted with a catheter and an over-sized bag to collect the urine. Unfortunately, his father had also had to have a colostomy operation a few months earlier due to damage to the colon through ill health and disease. Lomax had arranged to have a home nurse visit, to attend three times a day since the operation to deal with the *awkward* and unsettling nature of his father's health. He knew his sister and brother would never be willing to deal with their father's sanitary needs.

After deleting the unnecessary calls, Lomax pressed the play button again and listened carefully once again to the one left by Amanda.

'Phil… its Amanda… Amanda Waterman, you know me from school, remember? Listen, I'm sorry you're not there right now to take this call personally, but I need to see you. I need to see you, urgently. Please call me on…' She gave a mobile number. *'I think there's something you ought to look into.'*

Lomax replayed the message several times, so that he could write down the number. He could not understand why he was not made aware of the call earlier when he had called round. Another item about which he would have to speak to Gerald.

After making something to eat for the both of them and chatting to his father for at least an hour, Lomax checked the contents of the catheter bag and the colostomy bag, which were barely a quarter filled; he went back downstairs to the living room. The TV was still on and Gerald was still asleep, *a drug-induced sleep.* Lomax lightly punched his older brother on the shoulder several times before he stirred.

'What? Why are you here again?' Gerald asked, his tone becoming angry at being disturbed, as he twisted his head around and rolled onto his back to look at his younger sibling.

'Pissed and drugged out of your fuckwit brain again I see,' Lomax said, adding for good measure, 'smoking pot in the house, how many times have I told you not to do that? I had smoke alarms fitted for Dad's…'

He nipped into the hallway and looked up. One edge of the plastic casing had not closed properly. He instantly knew what his brother had done. Lomax's anger immediately intensified: he charged back into the living room and stood in front of the sofa facing Gerald, who had now moved into a sitting position.

'You stupid, ignorant, selfish fuck.' Lomax grabbed his brother by his shirt collar, yanking him from the sofa, and pulling him close so that their noses were almost touching. Lomax glared into Gerald's face. 'You're going to burn this fucking place down one day. I've told you never remove the fucking batteries from the smoke detectors, they're there for a damned reason.'

'Get down off your soap-box. No harm done,' Gerald said grinning, his breath thick with the stale and cloying stench of marijuana and beer. Lomax let go of his brother who slapped his younger sibling's hands away in an act of further defiance as Lomax stepped back.

'I want you out of here. Dad doesn't need your help, not that you actually bother doing anything anyway…' Lomax said forcefully.

Gerald interjected angrily, 'You saw me hoovering this afternoon, didn't you? The place *was* tidy and clean, wasn't it?' Gerald said through pursed lips.

Lomax hit back, 'That's not the fucking point, Gerald. You and Hillary might be older than me, but I'm the one organising father's care, and I'm sick and goddamned tired of you using this place as a dope den. You do realise if you are raided, not only could the shock of armed police breaking into this house frighten our father to death, I could lose my job. I might even decide to turn you in myself,' Lomax said, his expression deadly serious.

'You wouldn't fuckin' dare,' Gerald said. 'I'm your brother, we're family, and family don't grass on family.'

'Wanna bet?' Lomax said, vehemently. 'If you think I'm losing my job because you prefer to sit around all day, peddling your weed to other lowlifes, risking our father's health, you should think otherwise. Have you any idea what the effects of the smoke coming off your joint might have on Dad?'

'I regularly give him a couple of drags of a joint,' Gerald said, a sardonic smirk appearing across his gaunt, ragged features. 'He seems to like it.'

That was the final straw, Lomax's blood boiled in his veins and arteries. His mind began to overload as his anger raged.

Lomax kneed his brother very hard in the lower gut, causing Gerald to double-over, forcing breath from his lungs. Lomax then pulled Gerald wheezing to one side, and launched his older brother into the sofa, which tipped over from the force; as Gerald landed heavily on the floor, he almost collided head first with the drinks cabinet.

'Get out... get out now before I fucking kill you myself, you useless bastard,' Lomax said, the ridges in his brow above the nose deepening.

'Where can I go for fuck's sake? This... is where... I live.' Gerald groaned as he spoke, getting onto his knees and looking up into Philip's anger-filled face. 'Besides, look at the time, it's late, where can I find a hostel?'

'I don't give a toss. I'm sure you'll find a cardboard box somewhere. Go to Hillary's, you two seem to have the same ignorant attitude towards me and Dad anyway. It's not as if you have many possessions, and neither does Dad, now that you've sold most of their jewellery. Just get out before you make me do something to you, that I likely *won't* regret,' Lomax half shouted, as he advanced once again on his older brother, his face set in a rictus of pure malice.

Lomax realised that all of the crashing and shouting must have caused some alarm for the neighbours, and likely as much for his father, if he was still awake.

Once Gerald had reluctantly left gathering what few items of clothing he could, and after Lomax had taken any spare keys away from his brother, he called for a 24 hr locksmith to come in as soon as possible and change all the locks. He then went back upstairs to check on his father who *was* surprisingly still fast asleep. Lomax pulled the covers over his father, making the old chap as comfortable as he could and lowered the adjustable bed slightly, after checking both of the waste collection bags once more.

He could not return to his own place – not now – not after this. He was thankful Gerald did not know where he lived. Gerald also only had a special mobile number to call in the event of an emergency concerning their father, but deep down, Lomax knew full well that Gerald would rather allow his own father to die than call his younger brother, or the emergency services. Besides which, he'd have to wait for the locksmith.

Especially now.

The favourite son.

Lomax sat in one of the armchairs and replayed Amanda's message several more times, having trailed the telephone and the answer-machine power cords into the living room from the hallway. For now, he would be keeping this to himself. He removed the tape and replaced it with a spare, putting the one with the message from Amanda Waterman into his inside jacket pocket for the time being.

It was fair to say that as families go, his relationship with his older brother and sister had never been amicable, right from the moment he had been born. There seemed to be a large degree of resentment from both Hillary and Gerald when Philip arrived on the scene in 1966. Then after Philip, when Ruth and Byron the twins were born late in 1976, things only got worse.

Their mother Brenda died a few months after the twins' birth, from severe kidney failure and internal haemorrhaging. James struggled to bring up the family on his own. Brenda's sister Margaret helped out, looking after the children while James Lomax continued to work. A few weeks later Gerald was accountable for giving Philip bleach to drink in 1972, which nearly killed the young Philip as he was only six years old at the time. The younger Philip was sick immediately and vomited the small amount, much to Gerald's amusement. Philip was taken to hospital to be observed overnight by his father, who had some choice words to say to Gerald when he returned.

Margaret took Ruth and Byron to live with her as she was unable to have children, but due to a rare hereditary defect, Ruth and Byron did not survive for very long afterwards.

At the time Philip was almost poisoned, Gerald was twenty years old, he got away at the time, due to his being addicted to LSD, the hallucinatory drug, which he said at the time of the investigation, made him hear voices telling him to do it. Social services were assigned to look into the welfare of the younger surviving child.

Gerald had been exceedingly lucky to receive psychiatric care and placed on a drug rehabilitation program; however, it never really worked for him.

As if on cue, Lomax was interrupted from his irregular mind wanderings by the telephone ringing. He glanced at the trim phone sitting on the side table next to him, as the shrill declaration of someone calling interfered with his train of thought. Snatching up the receiver, he spoke. 'Yes? Who's calling?'

'Philip, it's Amanda again. I'm sorry if I worried you earlier. Could we meet up soon? Give me a call on the same number I gave you earlier. Thanks.' Lomax nearly dropped the receiver.

How the hell was she calling… she's dead, she has been since sometime in the past twenty-four hours. Cautiously Lomax replaced the receiver, and began rubbing his temples, sucking in deep breaths trying to stem the tears that were threatening to cascade down his cheeks.

Three

Again, he checked the telephone message tape; it *had* recorded the incoming call, as the answer-machine was set on *auto record all calls*.Probably by Gerald, so that he did not miss a sale.

Lomax took this tape out also, putting it with the other one in his pocket. Taking out his mobile, he dialled Amanda's number. The ringing continued unanswered until it cut-off automatically and the phone's pre-programmed voice told Lomax the recipient was unavailable.

This of course was an understatement, and then he wondered why he had even bothered thinking where Amanda Waterman was – he knew precisely where she was: in the mortuary. Nevertheless, why was she calling him now, how was that even possible? Then Lomax dialled DS Clarkson's private number. He had not noticed the time.

***

02:16 AM.

The hand snaked around her midriff, moving casually up over the soft flesh, gently caressing the fine downy hairs, causing her to shiver, his hand moved up her body until her pert left breast filled it, then he squeezed, his thumb gently increasing pressure on the already aroused bud in the centre. She gasped, rolling onto her back as a male set of lips found hers. She could feel her heart thudding in her chest, ripples of undulating pleasure cascaded across her body, fuelling her senses… building up to the point when…

The phone rang seven times before being answered, 'Hi Roma, yes, I know it's late, I'm sorry for waking you. Look don't pick me up tomorrow as planned, I'll drive in myself, and meet you there. Cheers.' He switched off before Roma could respond.

She hoped she could get back into that specific dream, almost right at that point, just when things were becoming interesting.

***

Monday December 31st. 06:48 AM.

The items of personal effects and clothing no longer required for forensic examination were in Lomax's office when he got in. The large yellow paper evidence bag sat on the blotter and seemed out of place in the surroundings. Opening the bag, Lomax tipped the contents out; there was no mobile phone.

Crosse peered into his boss's office, 'You okay, Guv?'

'Where's Miss Waterman's mobile phone?' Lomax asked, as he sat down heavily in his chair. A supposedly ergonomic design developed to alleviate back pain but which did nothing of the sort for Lomax.

'What mobile?' Crosse replied. 'There was nothing else with her personal effects from her car or handbag, and nothing in her office, we searched it thoroughly, boss,' Crosse said.

'You're certain?' Lomax asked, his tone seemingly curt.

'Positive,' Crosse replied. 'Oh, and the SOCO peeps didn't find one in the grounds at the base of the building either, by the way.'

'What about her home, has that been visited yet?' Lomax asked as he rechecked the few details from the report he had from the day before. He did not know where Amanda Waterman lived until he had read the file.

He had been surprised to find out that her apartment was less than a quarter mile from this very building. He wondered why he had not bumped into her long before now. He instantly realised that she more than likely spent a great deal of the time travelling abroad for the company.

'No sir. We weren't sure we could get a warrant,' Crosse said.

'Well… we don't need one now. She's dead, and she has no family.' Lomax grunted. The annoyance was clear by the timbre in his voice.

'How would you know that sir?' Asked Crosse, his furrowed brow emphasising his concern. 'I mean… that she has no immediate family?'

Crosse seemed a bit put out from not being given an answer to what was in truth a reasonable question, when Lomax got up from his chair and began moving towards the door tugging the chair in a half-hearted attempt to swap it for one of the others in the main room, then thought better of it. He collected the items from his desktop and poured them back inside the bag, tucking it beneath his arm as he exited his office and closed the door, leaving a bemused Crosse still standing inside and feeling very uncomfortable. Crosse opened the door again and stepped into the briefing area, feeling unnerved.

***

07:33 AM.

Sketchy pieces of information were written on the whiteboard in the briefing room with a red marker pen, coupled with photographs taken at the scene. Some were of Amanda Waterman's corpse and of the cracked window with the blood smears, a small section of a street map of the area, a blueprint of the building itself and some questions posed by Lomax, Clarkson and Crosse.

TIME OF DEATH?
SUICIDE OR MURDER?
MOTIVE?
AMANDA'S REASON FOR RETURNING TO THE UK?

Once the full team had arrived and taken their seats in the area reserved for the briefings, Lomax called for order and the muted chitchat died down.

'Okay, this case takes precedence over the others for the time being. Even though what viable information we do have is limited. I need you to focus on gathering anything you can on Amanda Waterman's full employment with Vortexa Pharmaceuticals: how long had she worked for them? What was her status within the company? What was her relationship with her colleagues like? That sort of thing, you know the drill. I want you to dig into every nook and cranny on this case.'

A hand shot up and Lomax's eyes darted towards the owner, an inverted sigh wallowed through him. 'Yes, Greggs?'

'Might I ask just *why* this case is so important, and why it's deemed urgent to overshadow the others we're working on?' Greggs had the annoying habit of asking inane questions recently.

Lomax felt as though his command of this team was called into question. It was fair to say that his working relationship with the young DC Neil Greggs had never been an amicable one. The man was eager and usually very productive, if a little over-zealous with police protocols and procedure. There had been several occasions when the two men had clashed.

'Due to the high-profile status of the company, although we have very little background on what they actually produce and how they market it, I want to uncover every little detail. I need to find out what Miss Waterman did for the company and what her associations with anyone at work or outside work were. In other words Greggs, no different to any other case, just better and quicker.'

A few heads turned to look in Greggs' direction and whispered derogatory quips made towards Greggs, whose face reddened in embarrassment. After taking questions from other members of the team; giving out his requirements for the civilian staff members, who he wanted to chase up the enquiries regarding the actual manufacturing, processing and delivery practices of Vortexa Pharmaceuticals. Including if possible, finding out who their main customers were, as well as making general enquiries of the staff there. After fifty minutes for the morning's briefing, where other questions were raised and answered, Lomax went to his office to sit quietly while he gathered his thoughts and waited for developments.

He jumped when the phone on his desk in the cramped office began ringing. He grabbed the handset and cleared his throat before he spoke. 'Hello, DCI Lomax.'

'Morning Philip, Chief Superintendent Warwick here.'

'Sorry sir, I meant to call you back, but I've been busy since I returned.'

'That's okay, I just thought that seeing as we haven't officially been introduced since you went away, and I took over from CS Huntley, I'd like to make your acquaintance officially. Would it be convenient for you to pop up to my office and see me now?' CS Charles Warwick asked, keeping his tone as friendly as he could.

Lomax realised that there was no way he could get out of having to have an official meeting with his new superior; he had deliberately taken his leave prior to having this meeting, but he knew it was inevitable that he couldn't get out of it indefinitely.

'I'll try and get along this morning, sir. I have some things to do first, unless you'd like to put something in your diary for a later date?'

'I have your work mobile number; I'll get my PA to give you a call later today?'

Lomax acknowledged the request and replaced the handset carefully yet with a degree of annoyance. For another twenty minutes, Lomax sat in his office pondering why this case was already giving him such a headache. He could feel the beginnings of one pulsing across his forehead.

***

08:46 AM.

Roma joined Lomax as he was leaving the station after explaining where he was going, and why, heading towards Amanda's apartment. Crosse and Greggs along with two uniformed officers also attended.

The pavement was still frosty as the sun slowly made its way above the buildings to lighten the sky, its meagre energy struggling to melt the ice underfoot. Moving northwards, Lomax and his team turned into Kensington Church Street, and eventually came to number sixty-four, part of an Edwardian row of four storey buildings that had once been elegant single houses and were now converted into quite spacious apartments. Amanda Waterman occupied the entire top floor apartment, and to gain entrance Lomax pressed an intercom button on the panel next to the main door, with 'Apartment Manager' written on the brass plate.

'Yes? Who is it?' the disembodied voice said.

'Detective Chief Inspector Lomax,' came the response. 'Please open the main door so that I might enter. Police business.'

The click and buzzing sound alerted Lomax and his colleagues that they were now able to advance. Pushing the right-hand glass panelled door, Lomax, accompanied by Roma Clarkson, Crosse and Greggs, entered the building, requesting the two uniformed officers to remain outside.

Lomax was met in the well-maintained communal foyer by the manager – who also doubled as a sort of concierge – a broad-built man, just less than six feet tall, and even with the smart but casual clothes he wore, Lomax could tell he had some muscle. The thick dark hair neatly combed with a right-hand side parting, yet it was the dark grey eyes, which burned with a determined edge that caught Lomax's attention. The nose, wide and almost flattened parallel to the face, with barely enough of a nasal opening to breathe through. Lomax eyed the apartments' manager steadily, taking in the man's appearance and tracking it to memory.

'So, what is all this about then?' The man asked.

'Before we go up to Miss Waterman's apartment, would you mind telling me your name?' Lomax asked, his request made to sound overly officious.

'Oh, yes, sorry. Eddie Whelan. I've been the manager here for the past eight years.'

Lomax smiled. 'Eddie Whelan... I thought I recognised you. Ex-boxer almost won the British middleweight title five years ago, and only just lost out during the Commonwealth Games finals.'

A visible deep scar ran down and across Whelan's left cheek diagonally from his ear to the edge of his nostril. The result of a metal blade in an opponent's glove. He had a wide mouth with quite puffy lips. His skin tanned as though he regularly travelled abroad, or – more than likely – frequented tanning salons. His right ear had been badly cauliflowered, caused by far too many hefty blows on that side in official and 'unofficial' boxing matches.

'That's right. Do you follow boxing then?' Whelan asked, a broad yet warm smile of contented recognition spreading over his features.

'No,' Lomax said sarcastically, then he asked, 'now then, could you tell me the last time you saw Miss Waterman?' Lomax's negative response that he didn't in fact follow boxing as a sport; although that he recognised Whelan's name and status was a deliberate ploy to put the man on the back step.

Whelan was indeed unexpectedly taken aback for a few moments, the welcoming smile swiftly evaporating, then he considered the question. 'If I'm right, she left for work on Friday. That was Boxing Day at about half-three in the afternoon. I thought it strange she'd be going in at all.'

'Did she say anything to you?' Clarkson asked.

'Only to wish me a Happy New Year,' Whelan replied while absentmindedly scratching the scar on his cheek… the very cheek on which Amanda had planted a friendly kiss. A kiss that Eddie Whelan thought or believed meant much, much more. 'I hadn't really seen her much over the Christmas period, due to her having been working in Holland, Germany and in America, as I recall. She returned on Boxing Day morning, at about eleven-fifteen.'

Crosse was taking notes in his notebook as a matter of necessity.

'I'd be grateful if it would be at all possible in that case, to have a look around her apartment,' Lomax asked.

Whelan's expression showed obvious concern, he hesitated as he was about to turn on his heels to lead them up, he stopped and looking directly into Lomax's face he asked, 'Shouldn't you have a warrant or something, I mean, what if Aman… I mean, what if Miss Waterman comes home and finds out I've allowed you into her apartment?' Whelan's voice sounded feeble in comparison to his physique.

'I doubt that. She's dead,' Greggs unexpectedly announced, with a total lack of empathy and as though he had actually said nothing at all. Lomax glared at Greggs briefly.

Whelan's face immediately drained of colour, and then he led the group to an elevator.

The journey upwards was devoid of further discussion. On the floor to Amanda Waterman's apartment, the elevator stopped, and the passengers stepped into an entrance hallway of bare wood flooring with patterned scatter rugs carefully placed at angles to the walls. The walls themselves were light oak-stained tongue and groove panels, with different sized framed reproduction prints by Monet and Matisse spaced evenly. Along the walls between the apartments' rooms were different sized, coloured and shaped planters, each with an array of expensive looking flowers or small trees.

Lomax felt the pangs of uncertainty and concern: had he ever known Amanda at all? Butterflies began dancing around in the pit of his stomach and his fingers tingled with pins and needles, as Eddie Whelan approached the main apartment door and took out his master electronic key. Whelan unlocked the door by inserting it into a reader, entering a six-digit code and pushed down on the handle, easing the door open. Lomax brushed past him and opened the door the rest of the way himself. 'Stay here Mr Whelan, please. Thank you for your assistance.'

As the police officers disappeared inside Amanda Waterman's home, Eddie Whelan couldn't help but notice Clarkson's allure, his eyes lingered a bit too long on her figure before she entered the apartment, her eyes stared back at him, and she closed the door. He whirled on his heels and retreated to a chair nearby.

Four

Berlin: Vortexa Pharmaceuticals Corporate Offices, 244 Heinkelstrasse Nort.

Monday 31st December.10:45 AM German time.

The extensively long conference room table was surrounded by chairs. In these chairs were highly paid executive members of staff of the Vortexa conglomerate, including the CEO and ultimate owner of the company as a whole. Each member had been urgently ordered to attend this meeting, regardless of the time of year, with it being New Year's Eve.

Gerrard Banksworth-Tilburne was an Anglo-American, currently hailing from Denver, Colorado; he was brash, arrogant and above all totally selfish. Blond-white hair cut short and neat, a broad head resting on an equally broad neck above a barrel-chested torso, with bulging muscles which regularly threatened to rip his tight-fit expensive clothing. His single steely blue eye could almost cut granite if he was angered.

He *was* angry now, and he surveyed the four men and three women. The black leather mask shrouded most of his facial features, covering the other eye-socket without the organ, leaving a grotesque maw which he rarely allowed anyone to see, and with a small, disfigured area visible beneath the mask; the flesh was scarred with striations of bubbled skin, burned by acid.

'I was informed not fifteen minutes ago, that one of our executive colleagues from the London Docklands Laboratory Complex was found dead at the weekend,' he said, his voice firm yet tinged with sadness.

'Who was it?' Asked Patricia Kohl, the red-haired woman seated immediately to Banksworth-Tilburne's left. Her tone didn't seem to carry an air of sincere concern.

He looked at her blankly at first. 'Amanda. Amanda Waterman,' he said.

Whispers filtered around the table as the others leaned in and began asking questions.

A hand immediately went up. Tilburne nodded and the quiet talking ceased.

'Excuse me sir,' the voice of the Dutch exec, Kurt Anderlich, boomed loudly, his thick Netherlands accent cutting through the tension, 'would I be correct in assuming that Vortexa might be implicated in a scandal, involving either a murder or suicide?'

Tilburne pondered this question briefly. 'No. No, we shall never be implicated in anything of the kind. The death of our colleague is... unfortunate. Especially at such a crucial moment in our development of the latest series of multi-cancer fighting drugs from the Vortexa CHX-485 range we're about to launch onto the world-wide market. Seeing as you brought up the subject, as to whether or not her death will be investigated as a homicide, from the information I received, it is likely that it will be classed as a sad suicide, due to the festive season.'

'They say Christmas usually brings an increase of suicide, so I doubt this would be implausible for the police to accept this,' Maxwell Burroughs, the Texan member of the panel said, brushing his stodgy tanned fingers through the thick white hair on his head. He replaced his Texan hat and sat back, a slight sneer appearing across his face.

For a further forty minutes, Tilburne discussed other issues and business matters that for him were of far greater importance than the death of someone he had quite recently enjoyed an intimate time with.

Tilburne needed to conclude any further matters quickly, as he wished to return to London and address his personal agenda. His Gulfstream jet was waiting at Berlin's International Private Airport for his arrival.

Liam Garratt greeted Tilburne as the tall man exited the Corporate Offices of Vortexa and opened the rear door of the Audi Executive limousine. The journey to the airport lasted twenty-five minutes, and the journey for the flight plan to London City Airport would take approximately one hour and forty-five minutes, depending on the weather.

Once back in the UK, Garratt drove Tilburne to his expansive mansion in Virginia Water, Surrey, before he would eventually return his employer to his private suite at Vortexa Tower, once the police presence had waned and business could continue.

Five

The mobile phone rang incessantly in Lomax's pocket.

He was annoyed, as he was carefully threading his way through the mess of Amanda Waterman's apartment. Furniture had been ripped or torn with a sharp implement and turned over. The expensively huge fifty-inch flat Samsung plasma screen television was smashed, as was the hugely expensive integrated Bang & Olufsen system built into the wall. Cushions and vases littered the floor, as did paintings and ripped reproduction prints in broken frames. In the bedroom the carnage was the same; the bathroom looked like a bomb had exploded, all of Amanda Waterman's cosmetics, medicines, toiletries, and bathing oils smeared over the white porcelain bath and toilet, walls and floor.

Lomax asked Crosse to bring Mr Whelan into the apartment. 'How do you explain all of this?' Lomax asked.

Whelan couldn't fathom how this could have happened, he explained that the tenants had special entry card-keys, and personal security codes which logged them in or out and was in fact the only method of gaining entry. 'I'm completely at a loss to explain any of this.'

'You're saying neither yourself nor the other tenants heard anything?' Greggs asked incredulously. His tone conveyed his suspicions directly at Whelan.

'Whoever did this, had to have discovered the special digit code known only by each tenant,' Whelan told them. 'Although I suppose they must have bypassed the system somehow.'

'Or they paid someone to help them,' Greggs added.

Whelan was incensed. 'Are you suggesting that I allowed someone to gain entry to one of my tenant's apartments?'

'No… none of us are suggesting that at all, Mr Whelan,' Crosse said as calmly as he could.

'That still doesn't answer why?' Roma said, adding for good measure, and mostly Greggs' benefit, 'I don't believe for one moment Mr Whelan would be inclined to trash one of his tenant's places, nor allow anyone in who wasn't invited. This has to have something to do with Miss Waterman's death. Someone managed to get in here; they were looking for something specific, but what?'

Shaking his head the manager frowned, an angry and concerned look across his face.

Lomax felt the vibration from his phone in his pocket; retrieving his phone, he pressed the receive button, 'Hello?'

The voice on the other end was that of his sister Hillary, they spoke briefly. *Jesus.* It had been less than twenty-four hours since he'd kicked his brother Gerald out of his father's home. Lomax sighed loudly. This was precisely what he didn't need, not now… not *right* now. He listened quietly to what Hillary had to tell him, and which *did* not go down at all well.

Lomax spoke briefly and curtly in response to his sister, then he pressed the end call button and was about to slip the phone back into his pocket when it rang once more.

Now he had a phone call from Warwick's PA Brigitte Ellis, demanding that he return to see his superior immediately.

'Roma, I have to go. Chief Superintendent Warwick wants to see me. Take charge of this for now, would you? See if you can find Miss Waterman's mobile, or anything else, no matter how insignificant, which may have been overlooked by whoever broke in here,' Lomax asked.

Roma continued searching, her hands enclosed in the statutory blue forensic latex gloves, as were all the officers attending. Lomax glanced at Whelan as he passed him in Amanda's apartment, then he followed Whelan back down to be allowed outside. And wondered.

Lomax took the shortest route back to Dunne House. He wanted to get this bollocking over and done with as soon as possible, although he couldn't be certain as to what he'd done to warrant this intrusion into this case by his superior.

He walked through the main door, then took the stairs up to the fourth floor where his own office was and the large open plan area where several civilian members of staff were busy making phone calls; others, the plain clothed team members were accessing the NPC system, trying to access any background information on Vortexa Pharmaceuticals. Walking past his team moving through his floor, he immediately noticed the expressions on the faces of the officers. They seemed accusatory: suspicious and uneasy.

As Lomax passed by, his acute hearing picked up the muted whispers. It would appear they knew something he didn't. He wanted to stop and turn. Say something, yet he knew it would be pointless.

He walked through the open-plan area to another set of doors and up a series of stairs to the sixth floor, then went into the ante-office, presided by Warwick's P.A., Brigitte Ellis, at her desk. Although she was only in her mid-fifties, she looked much younger. She didn't smoke, didn't drink excessively as far as he knew, and for all Lomax knew, she was unattached.

Her dark brown hair, fell well past her shoulder blades, and was cut in a fashionable style, framing a slim face with oval grey/blue eyes. Rouge and foundation covered high cheekbones and this accentuated her very thin nose, almost as sharp as a pencil-point at its slightly upturned tip. Her mouth was average in shape and form.

Her overall figure was of a medium-yet-alluring build. She looked up as Lomax entered without knocking, giving him a distasteful glare. Ellis rose from her desk and went to her boss's door, knocking and then entering without being addressed. She said something in a muted voice, then came back and opened the door wider, she motioned for Lomax to move past.

He caught a whiff of the perfume she wore. It was potent and made him cough and wince. He entered his superior's office noting immediately that there were two other people in the room, seated in chairs just off to the right of Warwick's desk.

'Aahhh, Detective Chief Inspector Lomax, I appreciate you returning here so quickly,' Warwick said, his tone distinctly cynical, albeit not directly accusatory nor was it demeaning.

'Sir? You called me at a very urgent time in the investigation. You have no idea how awkward this is,' Lomax said, he felt his voice falter, sounding weak and unprofessional. He added quickly as an afterthought, 'You know how important an investigation is during the crucial first few hours.'

Warwick looked sternly at his subordinate. Lomax instantly knew this was far more serious than *he* needed it to be. *'What now?'* he wondered to himself.

'I'd be surprised if you *were not* already aware Detective Chief Inspector Lomax, but the body of your older brother Gerald was found very early this morning,' Warwick said, his tone almost devoid of sympathy.

Lomax felt sick. Nausea rushed up from the pit of his stomach like an express train, and he immediately felt dizzy. He lurched forward, gripping the back of one of the chairs occupied by one of the visitors. He took a deep breath, and as soon as the wave of shock eased off, he stood upright.

'Yes, I did know, sir. My sister Hillary told me by phone less than twenty minutes ago about his death, but not where he'd been found. Where exactly?' Lomax asked, fearing he had a clear idea.

It was one of the strangers that answered. 'He was discovered lying in an overturned industrial wheelie-bin, beneath one of the arches of Constance Row Railway Viaduct in Walthamstow. He'd taken heroin, a lethal overdose we believe,' said the larger-than-life man. Detective Sergeant George Wheeler's voice was deep and almost raspy. He was a short but thick-set black man. Warwick introduced both officers, who refrained from extending their hands; their overall lack of pleasantries was discomforting.

A chubby face with equally thick neck struggled to fight its way out and over the fastened collar of Wheeler's pale blue shirt. The bright red with yellow spots tie with its wide Windsor knot looked out of place on this man. His pockmarked face gave, however, a kindly outlook, with his deep-set brown eyes, along with the high and prominent brow of his Anglo-African descent.

'Thank Christ,' Lomax said.

'I beg your pardon?' said the second visitor, his voice obviously filled with suspicion.

'Detective Superintendent Miles Hancroft, from the Internal Investigations Division,' Warwick said, introducing the second man. Lomax sighed audibly. This *was* worse than he'd imagined. It was obvious to him that he was suspected of being involved with his own brother's death.

'Sir, I apologise if my response sounded… uncaring. I haven't told anyone about my personal situation at home, for fear that it might infringe on my continuing with this case; a case that you requested me to undertake, I might add. My father has been ill for some time. Gerald and my elder sister Hillary, apart from myself, are the only members of our family that continue to live in the UK. Most of my uncles, aunts and cousins are far flung around the world. We don't have much contact as we're not strictly a close-knit family.'

On his way over, Lomax had checked in with the all-day carer service by mobile, while he was running through the streets. So far everything was fine. No problems. His father was comfortable.

For the next two hours, Lomax explained as best he could about his father's deteriorating health, his brother Gerald's criminal past, (particularly the incident with him when he was six years old) and Gerald's activities involving drugs, as well as his sister's selfish attitude.

'To be honest, if I had told you everything, would I have been allowed to remain a police officer?' Lomax asked.

The room remained silent for several moments. The three officers looked pensive as they pondered Lomax's question.

It was Warwick who finally spoke up. 'I cannot be certain, Lomax. However, in my own opinion it would have been prudent of you to have made us aware of your situation. You do realise that through the Police Federation, you may have been entitled to both social care funding regarding your father, as well as legal support if any member of your family were to engage in unlawful activities?'

'Yes sir, I was aware, but felt it would be an infringement of my career if I allowed my personal life to make such matters public knowledge within the force,'

Lomax answered, adding, 'I'm sorry, sir. Gentlemen, for involving you in this matter.'

Detective Superintendent Hancroft stood up and extended his hand. Lomax took it and they shook. 'You realise you were very lucky? If you hadn't explained things, you could have been in very serious trouble. I doubt even the Police Federation lawyers would have been able to help you out.'

'Yes, I know. Thanks,' Lomax said. He also shook hands with George Wheeler, after both men had left, he was alone with his immediate superior. Warwick glanced at Lomax then leaned back in his chair, forcing it to tip backwards slightly, so that he could stretch his legs out, relieving the tense cramping in the backs of his knees and thighs that threatened to give him gyp. For a further forty minutes, Lomax appraised his superior of the current status of the case; what his team had discovered to date.

'You'll be a damned lucky son-of-a-bitch, if those two officers keep this matter to themselves as they promised,' Warwick said, just before Lomax opened the office door, and stepped out. He turned to look at his superior, gave the man a knowing smile, and then he was gone.

***

'Damned lucky son-of-a-bitch,' Roma said when Lomax finally returned to Amanda Waterman's apartment building. Lomax briefly explained why he'd been called away urgently, pulling Roma aside away from any of the others being able to catch what he was telling her, as he kept his voice low.

Crosse, wiping his face of perspiration, slowly got up from kneeling down, meticulously searching for anything important in a set of drawers, already fingerprinted and checked by the accompanying SOCO personnel, called in by Clarkson. His knee joints clicked quite audibly as he did so.

For some unknown reason, seeing Crosse rise and hearing his joints making those sounds gave Lomax an idea. He knew it was a long shot, and he also chastised himself for not thinking of it sooner. He took out one of the tapes from his father's answering machine and put it into his personal dictation unit he always carried with him. Luckily, they took the same C-80 type of cassette.

He connected the dictation unit to his own mobile via a special adapter lead into a socket on the side of the LG phone. He then pressed the play button on the diction unit from the very start. The series of electronic beeps showed up on his mobile's screen, as the number from Amanda Waterman's other mobile. He wondered why he hadn't thought to check with the phone company and ask them to relate back to him the calls made to his father's home number at a specific time; but then he knew he would have had to do that himself, without the others becoming aware.

Disconnecting the lead, Lomax immediately saved the new number into his mobile, and then dialled it. Everyone had been told to keep quiet, not to move.

It was indistinct, hardly perceptible. A feeble warbling sound coming from somewhere within the apartment. Lomax moved to his right through a set of doors into another large room, being careful where he stood amongst the debris.

Nothing.

The sound faded.

Roma tapped him on his left arm and pointed. Lomax nodded and moved in that direction. The sound became slightly louder, increasing as he returned to the kitchen area. Pots and pans littered the floor. He accidentally kicked a metal saucepan that skittered across the tiled floor noisily, obscuring the sound. When the utensil had stopped spinning, Lomax could no longer hear the warbling noise.

Damn.

He glanced at his own mobile and saw that the call time-out had finished. Lomax grinned inwardly and redialled. However, this time he only heard an even fainter warble and knew that Amanda's mobile battery was more than likely losing power. He sped up his movement and got to a spot in the large kitchen dominated by a huge cabinet situated between the Rayburn cooker and a large American-style refrigerator-freezer set into a recess on the west wall.

The ornaments and hanging kitchen utensils, books and drawers which had been in place were now as almost everything else, scattered around, broken if breakable. Several porcelain figurines were smashed on the tiled floor. The two waist-height drawers were pulled out to their furthest extent and emptied. Lomax pressed his ear to the pine wood back of the unit and could barely still hear the fading sound.

'Come here,' he yelled to no-one in particular. Crosse and Greggs came to Lomax's assistance as they saw him struggle to pull the unit away from the wall. Even with all three men pulling as hard as they might, the kitchen unit held fast.

Roma stepped up.

'Oh, so now you're going to have a go, and show us big strong men up, are you?' Greggs asked, his sardonic tone was not lost on Roma, as she gave him a look that instantly made him back away.

She examined the sides of the unit that seemed unusually flush to the back wall, and then she stood on a chair to examine the top of the unit, careful not to run her fingers along the edge, she then climbed back down off the chair, crouched, and peered into the opened drawers. She called in the SOCO team and asked them to swiftly dust the surfaces of the pine dresser. After they had finished their task, Roma climbed back onto the chair and looked over the top, running her fingers along the sides to the back. Her fingertips finding purchase in a small ridge, she lifted a false panel and peered beneath it. Satisfied she was correct, she climbed down off the chair once more and placed each of her hands in a drawer and felt around.

'What's she looking for?' asked Greggs.

'Fucked if I know,' Crosse answered curtly.

'I'm looking...' said Roma, pausing as her long slender fingers explored the openings, '...ah-ha. Got it.' Her left hand found a recessed button, which she pressed and swiftly removed her hands from the drawers.

A low hum emanated from somewhere behind the wall, then the dresser lifted about three inches, moving away from them, and opened up into another large area.

'Clever, very clever. Look, there are no markings whatsoever and no scratches on the floor to signify anything such as this,' said Greggs.

'That's because it runs on an oiled ball-bearing and hydraulic retraction system hidden on the upper surface of the top edges, concealed by the false panel at the top of the dresser, likely as much controlling the hidden rubber runners underneath,' Roma said, trying not to smile, as the dresser then began to swivel to one side.

Everyone stood open-mouthed as bright lighting automatically came on inside the unseen room. Lomax mentally assessed the layout, trying to figure his bearings. It dawned on him almost instantly.

'We're in the building next door. The one not officially leased to these apartments,' Lomax said.

'Wow,' exclaimed Roma as she stepped through the opening. 'Look at all this stuff. What on earth was she up to?' She asked.

Inside the room was a multitude of high-tech electronic equipment. Benches cluttered with specialised testing units. Free-standing bottles of various gasses and pressurised liquids were intermittently spaced out, connected via glass tubing to specific machines.

'That's a gas-spectrographic-thingy machine,' said Crosse pointing, 'I've seen them on TV and in films… oh, and our SOCO chaps use them too.'

'What on earth was Amanda doing with all this stuff though?' asked Lomax. His puzzled frown adding to his already extremely frustrated feelings of anxiety.

He remembered what he was looking for. He re-dialled the number, and a short *bleep-bleep* came from somewhere over to his left. There were no windows; they had been bricked up, although from the exterior of the building it would be practically impossible to tell. He followed the steadily weakening sound being emitted from Amanda's mobile; it had almost stopped when he saw a cupboard door slightly ajar on the wall. He opened it using the biro from his pocketbook and found an LG mobile model similar to his own, whose light blinked out as he looked at it.

'Found it,' he said, as a brief smile appeared on his face. He carefully took the mobile in his blue latex-gloved fingers and passed it to one of the accompanying SOCO experts who checked it over, shining an ultra-violet light over it to see if there were any latent prints on it. Seeing that there were several, and that they were all badly smudged, she handed it back to Lomax.

'No good, sir,' she said, her voice muffled by the mask covering her face. 'I won't be able to get anything off this that isn't likely to be anyone else's except the owner.'

As the female SOCO went back about her business with her colleagues, all dusting for prints, and DNA samples, Greggs looked at Lomax, who began looking for a power-connecting lead in the cupboard. He moved a few items about and found what he was looking for. 'Ah-ha, here it is.' He then found a socket and plugged in the charger, then the other end of the lead into the bottom of the mobile. He flipped the switch on the electrical socket and turned on the LG, to make sure it would charge, but also to be able to go through the menu.

He meandered through the memory but found nothing much, except for a strange message in the memo.

Teak.Bedroom Furn. IKEA Sale. Wednesday 2nd Jan 2008. Oxford St. Store. 14:44. Deposit left 24th December, via online bank transaction; items held in advance for January delivery.

Roma and the other two detectives who had been searching the room, having checked through some other cupboards, suddenly stopped when Crosse called out 'Hey, see what I've found.'

Lomax crossed the room and joined his colleague, as the man placed a laptop on the counter. Crosse flipped the cover open and switched it on, he stepped back as it powered up and a screensaver showed a sickening video of experimentation on lab animals.

'Jesus H. Christ,' exclaimed Crosse as he winced and pulled an expression that bordered on gurning.

The others moved closer, crowding the laptop as a pre-programmed video sequence continued. The scenes played out like an amateur videographer making their first film, single-handedly using a digital camcorder. The camera panned around the large room. An extensive laboratory, on a far greater scale than the one Lomax and his colleagues stood in at the present.

Even with the slight camera wobble, the camera showed a dimmed room. Along each wall were benches in an organised fashion with multiple machines and chemistry set-ups. Glass tubes and beakers lined the tops, while arranged in sequences were flow units, larger glass containers with coloured liquids, which were transported via a vacuum process through tubes and via special one-way valve-taps. These were electronically controlled, as they mixed with the compounds in funnelled glass hoppers, filled with powdered chemicals and strangely code-named substances.

The named labels didn't look familiar, as the compounds had been ciphered into a code, specific to Vortexa Pharmaceuticals. The security taken in case of infiltration, which the CEOs believed was impregnable.

*The person wielding the camera moved along, switching on enclosed sampling electron-microscopes and the flat-screen monitors beside them so that the camcorder could see and record the images. The film lasted approximately forty minutes. Different rooms included smaller dissection labs where the dead animals, mostly chimpanzees and larger simian species, as well as oversized scorpions, beetles, snakes and frogs, as well as other lizards, which were being dissected for further analysis. There was one section of one area that was particularly impossible to gain access to. The specialised security panel next to the stainless-steel door with its decontamination booth, was strictly for the higher echelon level of scientists, and therefore only **they** were able to access the labs and pursue their work through there.*

Once the film had finished playing, everyone found it difficult to voice their thoughts.

'Do you think this is what she was killed for?' asked Crosse, to no-one in particular.

'So, you reckon she was definitely murdered?' Greggs said, turning to face his colleague.

'Well, I wouldn't have thought she'd have committed suicide without telling anyone about this. Come on Neil, Detective Chief Inspector Lomax told us he received a pre-programmed mobile message from the deceased, on which he heard her being attacked by someone, obviously the same night she was found, snuffed out, in what I personally would call extremely suspicious circumstances,' Crosse said bluntly.

Lomax had copied the third message he'd received from Amanda Waterman onto another normal cassette tape and played it first to his superior after the meeting with the two officers from the Internal Investigations Division, and then to his colleagues immediately after he'd returned to Amanda's apartment. He felt certain he had finally gained the support and confidence of Crosse.

Greggs however, seemed reluctant to agree.

Roma used the tracking ball to replay the second to last scene, where the hand that became visible in front of the lens, with a key-coded entry swipe card had tried to gain access to that particular area. The elasticated left-hand sleeve of the leather bomber jacket moved up and showed a watch. A square shaped body and blue face with white Roman numerals, luminous hands, with three rectangular chronograph dials and a very unusually designed strap. There was also a faded tattoo just below the watch face near the wrist joint.

She rewound again, played and paused the video. She then moved in closer to the screen and studied the image closely. Blowing air between her teeth she nodded. 'We need to get this to the video forensic boys,' Roma said, 'I'm not sure, but I think I recognise that watch and tattoo.'

'You recognise the watch *and* tattoo?' Asked Greggs incredulously.

'I wasn't always a CID officer, you plank. I was a WPC, I arrested an environmental and animal rights activist, about eight years ago for committing illegal entry into cosmetic production facilities all over the UK, and causing damage,' Roma said, a slight tinge of affection crept into her voice, and it definitely wasn't lost on Lomax or Greggs.

'Let me guess,' said Greggs, his voice showing contempt, 'you fell for him, and began a relationship, but when you realised you couldn't persuade him to stop his involvement, you chucked him?'

'No,' she replied, 'but he was… is a cousin of mine. I didn't actually realise we were related until later on when his father came to bail him out. I was the officer dealing with the paperwork, and I recognised my uncle. They'd emigrated to Australia in the late 1970s, when Raymond was two years old, but they returned to England in the mid-nineties, many years before I caught his son, my cousin, trying to escape from the cosmetics production facility, in Woking, Surrey.'

'And so? What does that have to do with this? How come you recognised the watch and tattoo?' asked Greggs.

'Simply because my mother had bought the watch for him as a gift, on his returning to the UK. Also, I know that he had a tattoo done on that wrist, but I can't be certain that's it, as we haven't had a lot of contact since I'd seized him. I also think he took umbrage to the fact I was a rozzer, as much as that I'd arrested him personally, but in my defence, he was wearing a Balaclava and face-paint to obscure his features at the time of the arrest at the laboratory,' Roma said, a hint of sadness in her voice.

'How old is he now then?' asked Crosse.

'At the time I arrested him, four years ago in 2004, he was twenty-seven years old, so that makes him… thirty-one, roughly,' Roma said, adding, 'I can't pinpoint at this time when his birthday is.'

Lomax gently laid a reassuring hand on her right shoulder. He spoke softly, 'You did the right thing, Detective Sergeant. I'd have done the sam–'

Greggs interrupted again. 'What? Arrest a member of your own family? Grass on them?'

'You're damn fucking right, I would,' Lomax exploded, adding, 'Just as much as I'd turn in any fellow officer I found to be breaking the law. Now shut the fuck up. And if you don't toe the line Greggs, I'll have you removed from this investigation, and from my team. Believe me, I will.'

Everyone stopped what they were doing and turned to look at Lomax, as he'd reprimanded the officer in front of their colleagues, and also looked at Greggs. As Lomax glanced around at them showing his displeasure at their encroaching on the heated debate, they quickly went back to work.

After giving the SOCO team instructions to go over the hidden laboratory area carefully, and to report immediately anything they deemed important, Lomax and Clarkson left the apartment, the laptop carried by Roma. Crosse and Greggs left shortly afterwards and walked back to Earl's Court Road station in silence.

'So, what do you make of it so far?' asked Lomax, as he sat back in his chair at Dunne House, sipping strong black coffee.

Roma considered the question, and although it seemed an ambiguous one, she still hesitated a bit longer than perhaps she ought to have. 'Maybe I should have kept my mouth shut, and my thoughts to myself?'

Lomax laughed. So did Roma.

Crosse and Greggs passed his office and heard the laughter.

'What do you suppose they have to be cheery about?' asked Greggs.

Crosse said nothing, but he was certain he knew.

Six

No-one was even acutely aware at Dunne House that the CID office suite was covertly under surveillance, by person or persons unknown.

If any member of the general public, walking in both directions down Earl's Court Road, this main artery of London, had paid any attention at all to the large lorry parked nearby in a side street, Abingdon Villas, they'd be none the wiser. The livery on the side stated:

'Interior Renovations Ltd'
A Superior Elegance to Modern Living.

Anyone walking by, seeing men and women wearing bright green coveralls, moving in and out of the side or rear doors would assume they were indeed interior decorator employees, acting on behalf of a client in a property nearby.

Nothing could be further from the truth.

A different vehicle had been shadowing Amanda Waterman for a significantly long time, several months to be exact, prior to her death. Her apartment as well as her workplace was also under routine surveillance by the same people, using sophisticated equipment. However, even they hadn't been able to discover the *'secret'* room that Miss Waterman had been covertly using. It had been very cleverly shielded from infra-red and thermal cameras.

'Why hadn't we found that hidden room?' asked the man with mid-American state accent, seated at a bank of small TV monitors.

'How should I fucking know?' answered the other man, his tone becoming increasingly agitated. 'We've been watching that bitch for some considerable time, day in, day out, and some British PC Plod comes along and finds it as easy as scoffing blueberry pie. Fucking typical.' The twang of his southern Mississippi accent grating as it usually did on the other listener.

'Our superiors aren't going to be pleased,' said the first man.

'Oh, don't you worry… I'll tell them it was all your fault,' said the second man, trying to infuse his comment with a dash of humour.

'Yeah… you would, wouldn't you? Bastard.'

***

Whoever was keeping tabs on Amanda Waterman's apartment, her workplace and the Earl's Court CID investigation, weren't the only ones scrutinising with a fine-toothed comb.

Another subversive group were also watching… and listening to everything going on.

Watching, listening and waiting.

Seven

Since gaining access to the video on the laptop, the video forensic technicians had managed to enhance the watch and tattoo image, confirming for DS Roma Clarkson that it was definitely her cousin, Raymond Deakins.

Just above the tattoo of a Celtic cross with barbed thorns wrapped around it was a scar line, the result of a childhood accident Raymond had had, aged six, when out on the farm in Western Australia.

'I knew it,' she said. Her voice quiet, thoughtful, as she surveyed the photographs on her PC, in the office she occasionally shared with Lomax. He stood behind her, looking at the screen then he rested a hand gently on her left shoulder, and barely squeezed it. He could smell her perfume, a scent that always made him feel warm.

He was still resting his hand on Roma's shoulder when DCs Crosse and Greggs barged in.

He swiftly removed his hand. He gave the two officers a cursory glare of annoyance then moved over to his own desk, sitting down heavily in the chair which nearly tipped him out onto the floor, had he not grasped the side of his desk. 'Well, what is it that you want?' he growled as he regained his composure.

DC Crosse spoke after clearing his throat, 'Sir. We have the warrants to search the property and arrest Raymond Deakins. Are you coming along?'

Lomax stood up and grabbed his long black overcoat. 'Roma,' he said casually, 'maybe you'd better stay here, your cousin might not b…'

'No sir. I need to be there. I've already called his father and explained things, he's meeting us there.'

'You called his father?' DC Greggs said, his tone clearly expressed his disagreement. 'Jesus... I'm beginning to think...'

'And I'm beginning to think that you should keep your opinions to yourself,' Lomax said. Perhaps he should seriously discuss with CS Warwick about having Greggs replaced.

***

Wednesday 2nd January 2008.
34 Bayliss Road, Lambeth, SE11.

It was a typical basement floor bedsit. Stone steps leading down from the pavement to a grimy door, in peeling burgundy red paint which had definitely seen better days.

Better days – many years ago.

It was an asylum for those who simply couldn't afford a better class of cheap accommodation, and chose to allow themselves to be manipulated, along with the local council housing benefit department, to pay well over-the-odds rent, for such disgusting premises by unscrupulous landlords.

At one time, long ago, the bedsits were clean and tidy, but sometimes a clever landlord would fool the housing benefit assessors by claiming that their tenant was residing in a better, cleaner part of the house. When in reality, the room shown to the visiting officer belonged to themselves, and the 'tenant' would be brought up to give the impression that it was his or her room.

Once the council officer was satisfied and approved the rent, the tenant was thrown back into their grotty den. Barely adequately furnished, damp and very smelly. These particular landlords systematically preyed on alcoholics and drug addicts.

Someone was about to get a wake-up call, a very early one indeed.

It was light outside, at just after eight-thirty when the knock on the door stirred Raymond Deakins from his heavy alcohol- and drug-induced slumber. It was inevitable that since his initial arrest by his cousin Roma Clarkson, when he was twenty-seven, almost four years previously, that he was destined to fall prey to the darker side of life; the criminal element.

He rose from the tatty and stained mattress on the bare wood floor of the room, and padded aimlessly to the main door, avoiding the detritus of previous days *'jacking-up'* and empty bottles of spirits and cans of cheap beer. Dirty clothes littered the floor, mixed in with remnants of discarded takeaways. He peered through the spyhole but all he could see was a shadowy figure illuminated from the back by the brightness outside. He opened the door slightly, leaving the security chain attached, and was afforded a better view of the visitor.

The waft of stale sweat and body odours emanating from the short hallway caused the visitor to recoil in disgust, turning his head aside before speaking. 'Your benefactor asked me to deliver this to you, in gratitude for your recent assistance,' the deep voice said, as a hand moved into view from a pocket in the overcoat the stranger wore. Passing the package through the gap, Deakins snatched the small parcel and slammed the door shut, locking the catch down.

The stranger turned and retraced his way up the uneven steps, smiling to himself as he did so, pulling the collar of his coat up close around his neck against the bitter cold, and the scarf and hat tighter, as he walked back south along Bayliss Road towards the underground station, Lambeth North.

'For fuck's sake, sir,' DC Greggs said, his tone expressing his impatience and chagrin towards his superior. 'Deakins' father has probably warned him already that we're onto him.'

Lomax threw his coat onto Roma's desk, covering her laptop and launched himself at DC Greggs, grabbing the man by his jacket lapels and forcing him up against the three-drawer filing cabinet so viciously that one of the upper corners dug into the subordinate officer's back. Lomax's face mere millimetres away, 'Listen you self-righteous prick, at every moment during this case you've been picking holes in DS Clarkson's involvement. Nothing she does is right as far as you're concerned. And don't think I don't know why you resent her.'

'I-I-I don't know what you mean, sir,' DC Greggs said, his faltering voice tinged by the pain down his back as Lomax forced the man harder against the cabinet.

'Sir,' Roma said, 'please let him go, maybe he's right. My cousin might be still pissed off at me. If he sees me there, well, who knows how he might react.'

Lomax released his subordinate and backed off. Then he turned to Roma, 'You're accompanying us and that's final. You two take another pool car, we'll follow on shortly,' Lomax said, his gaze never leaving DC Greggs' pained face.

'You notice how he always takes her side. She's hardly ever wrong?' DC Greggs said as DC Crosse drove the metallic light green Vauxhall Omega 2.0 through the light traffic of six-forty in the morning, while DC Greggs tried to rub the pain away from the spot in his back.

'Perhaps, she isn't wrong,' DC Crosse answered in his usual curt tone, 'and perhaps, she is in reality a far superior CID officer than you. Besides, you really don't know when to keep your thoughts to yourself do you?'

They drove from Dunne House through light traffic, caused by being midweek, and still early into the new year. The streets *were* relatively quiet even at that time, due to many workers still being off work for the holidays, plus added to the fact that there had been a heavy snowfall the previous night across the south of England. They'd had to rush out with snow ploughs and gritting trucks to try to clear the roads before the heavy traffic tried to course its way through the city.

'All I'm saying is that he always takes her side. I think there's something going on between them two,' Greggs commented.

'Cut it out Neil, for fuck's sake. Lomax is right, you're obviously well pissed off that she was promoted instead of you. I never suspected you as being someone that bore a grudge,' DC Crosse said. Then he added, 'Especially being overshadowed by a younger and better looking female to boot.'

'That's not true. I don't bear her any ill-will. Perhaps she was better suited for the job, but I know for a fact, she scored much lower marks than I did in the exam,' DC Greggs said.

Crosse ignored him as he unexpectedly negotiated moving around a completely snow-engulfed car

'How the hell do you know she scored lower than you anyway?' DC Crosse asked, eventually.

'I have my ways and means,' DC Greggs simply said.

DC Crosse pondered the answer for a few moments. 'Oh yeah, that's right you were shagging that bird from the examinations department, I remember now. You do realise of course, that if they found out that you'd obtained confidential exam results, you could be demoted to a common garden beat cop, back in uniform. And your bit of shag could lose her job as well.'

'Yeah, that's as maybe. But they won't. Especially as I don't think you're going to tell them,' DC Greggs said, ensuring that his menacing tone was understood.

***

'Thank you, Phil,' Roma said as they climbed into the police pool Vectra. She turned the key and the engine fired up, Roma revved the engine a few times before putting it into first gear.

Lomax rested his right hand on her left which was gripping the gear selector of the automatic car. He looked at her. 'I just... I just hate it when that stupid fucker Greggs keeps slagging you off. He's not even detective constable material. How he even got into CID only hell knows, let alone into our division.' He removed his hand, as Roma turned to look at her boss's face; she smiled and gave a brief laugh. Then she put the car into drive and pulled away.

Heading south-east into Cromwell Road towards the Natural History Museum, Lomax looked absent-mindedly out of the passenger window at the sandstone brickwork, and the intricate masonry in-filled with decorative stone reliefs of varied creatures of prehistoric life.

Along Brompton Road through Knightsbridge, past Harrods, along to Hyde Park Corner and then round onto Grosvenor Place, past Victoria Station and onto Vauxhall Bridge Road and over the bridge and river Thames.

Turning immediately left onto the Albert Embankment road which ran parallel to the river, until they bore right on Lambeth Road, the A3203, left again on Kennington Road, the A23 and straight on across the junction into Bayliss Road, where they pulled up behind a non-snow covered vehicle.

They were surprised by the state of the roads well away from Kensington, and like DC Crosse, almost clobbered several cars that had indeed been abandoned by their drivers when the weather became far too dangerous to drive in. One vehicle had clearly been struck heavily enough to force it into the vehicle in front of it, and to dislodge a fair amount of the snow covering said vehicles' roofs, bonnets and rear ends.

The thaw for that day had begun agonisingly slowly by the time they'd reached the target property in Lambeth. Unfortunately, due to the severity of the weather, many roads had been rendered unsafe to drive on due to sheer black ice, so diversions had also been implemented, which caused further delay.

***

Deakins lay on the mattress, the needle of the syringe still embedded in the crook of his left elbow, the tip slowly easing itself from his flesh, the contents having been injected directly into one of the veins, already blue and bruised. It had been barely an hour or so since the stranger had delivered the package. He lay in a stupor, his mind being affected by the illicit substance, his thoughts were clouded by visions of his past, as he remembered how his parents did their best to help him, especially his father, Neville Deakins. But his mother, Katherine, soon lost interest when he'd stolen most of her jewellery for a small fraction of what they were worth, to buy his fixes. She completely disowned him. His life spiralled downwards swiftly when he got severely addicted to heroin and crack cocaine. The hits needed to increase, and Raymond soon became a regular visitor to the various police stations, magistrates' courts and even a couple of Crown Courts for serious offences. His parents' marriage broke down shortly afterwards, then his father became seriously depressed, even to the brink of suicide.

'Raymond Deakins… it's the police,' came the booming voice of DCI Lomax, 'open the door, or we will break it down. We have a warrant for your arrest.'

Deakins suddenly sat bolt upright on his grotty mattress, his eyes opening as wide as the muscles would allow, clarity enveloped his consciousness and his heart pounded in his chest. He whipped the syringe from his arm and flung it across the room to join the other detritus. He pulled the sleeve of the shirt down to cover the site, even though blood seeped from it. The only way out was via the front door which was blocked by the police. The short passageway only led to a small kitchen/bathroom, and the lower windows had bars on the outside. The back door had been bricked up years earlier.

He cursed. He'd been raided before many times, in other parts of the city, even when he was staying with his E.A.R.A 'associates', but he realised with the substance – believed to be high grade heroin – he'd injected slowly working its way through his system, that he was well and truly trapped.

'What the fuck do you want from me now? I'm on methadone; I'm coming off drugs. I'm on a programme,' Deakins said, his voice rising a few octaves higher than it normally would.

'He's going to freak out,' said DC Greggs, flexing his muscular frame in readiness for some bother.

Lomax looked at the main door. He scanned the right-hand side, then without any warning he pounded his right foot at the lower hinge, kicking it with such force the door was wrenched clear of the frame, opening up the entrance, the chain was wrenched free of its mountings on the frame. Something heavy was launched through the window from inside, but it landed out of harm's way.

Lomax stepped aside as Roma stole her way past the others and went inside, closely followed by her colleagues. DC Greggs and DC Crosse looked on with mutual disdain.

Roma entered the bedroom/living-room and found Raymond Deakins cowering in the corner by the window. He cautiously looked around.

The recognition was instantaneous. 'You.' He quickly stood up, flexing his arms by his sides, fists balled up, his face deepening to a deep purple rage, his nostrils flaring. The muscles and thick veins becoming more pronounced in his neck, as he rushed towards his cousin.

Lomax barged in past Roma and belted Deakins on the side of the head with his fist, sending the man sprawling back down onto the filth encrusted mattress. 'Sir,' Roma said, her voice loud in the small room.

Deakins whimpered on the floor, curled up in the foetal position. Roma knelt down beside her cousin and quietly whispering she coaxed him back to his feet. 'Raymond Simon Deakins,' began DC Crosse, who'd advanced into the room wrinkling his nose at the stench of stale urine and faecal matter, handcuffs at the ready to be slapped onto the man's wrists, 'I'm arresting you in connection with the break in at a Vortexa Pharmaceuticals Ltd, at a time between August 16th and the 17[th,] two thousand and seven.' DC Crosse then spoke the procedural arresting statement and having locked the cuffs into place, forcibly removed Deakins out onto the street; he offered little in the way of resistance.

DC Greggs remained inside the flat while Lomax, Roma and Crosse exited with Deakins. Greggs removed something from his pocket, and peered up to the street through the window, seeing that Lomax and the others were outside. A few minutes later he stepped up into the street. He looked into DS Clarkson's face.

Roma looked pensive, emotional. DC Greggs noticed it immediately; it didn't sit well with him.

As for Deakins' father, who'd arrived just as his son was being forcibly removed from the bed-sit, his face became even paler when he saw the look of utter disdain on his son's face.

Deakins' father was quite tall though overly very thin, grey hair flowing long at the back past his collar, tied in a ponytail. The face very gaunt and ashen, deep eye sockets and dark half-moon shadows under the once bright, intelligent and caring eyes that seemed far too pale to constitute having any colour in them.

His skin was taut against very bony protrusions, which belied the man's earlier demeanour, once as an extremely well-to-do and highly successful businessman, whose expensive suits would have fitted him like a glove.

He looked on impassively as his son was placed into the back of a police van that had pulled up only moments before.

With Raymond Deakins safely secured in the back, Lomax spoke to the two police officers in the van, ordering them to take the suspect directly to Earl's Court CID, and make certain he was placed in a holding cell until Lomax returned. The van pulled away and turned left onto Waterloo Road heading for the Waterloo Bridge to take them through the city back to Kensington.

The explosion was, in all honesty, totally unexpected. It was intense, a huge ball of orange/yellow flame rose high into the air, rising quickly above the buildings along the street and followed by thick black oily acrid smoke which virtually obscured the skyline above the building roofs. It occurred as the van was passing by the National Theatre at Upper Ground less than five minutes after leaving the flat.

The vehicle was ripped apart. Five innocent members of the public out that early in the day, and passing by the vehicle as it exploded, were killed and others were seriously injured by the blast and by shrapnel. Nearby vehicles caught by the explosive device going off caught fire and the occupants scurried to get out. Several buildings' windows were staved in by the blast, and parts of the brickwork/concrete were scoured by flying debris.

The black smoke poured upwards into the sky, as flames continued to lick over and within the van and other cars, buses and lorries. Those members of the public who were unfortunate enough to get caught directly by the explosion, lay immobile where they fell, their bodies wracked by the violent act. Men, women and children alike.

It was an utter travesty. A deliberate act of violence.

A publicity nightmare.

Lomax, Roma and the other officers ran at full speed towards the sound of the explosion, moments after it went off. Although initially unaware that the explosion had anything to do with them, they each acted instinctively, fearing another terrorist attack on London.

It took them almost ten minutes to reach the scene of carnage by foot on the still slippery paths and roadways. Ambulances and fire engines arrived swiftly after being called by those uninjured and quick-witted enough to do so. The police were also there, uniformed men and women rushing from their daily patrol beats nearby doing their utmost to control the mayhem and help tend to the injured where possible.

It didn't take that long for the press to arrive on the scene either. Several photographers were there, snapping away, whenever they got the opportunity to snatch a shot, as the growing police line did their utmost to keep the press and general public spectators as far away as possible.

Lomax slowed down as he neared the scene.

'Jesus,' exclaimed DC Crosse, covering his eyes with a hand that began to shake.

'Now the shit's really gonna hit the fucking fan,' DC Greggs exclaimed. A note of unbridled sarcasm in his voice. He wasn't going to be proven wrong.

The police van was well ablaze, thick acrid black smoke poured from the windows and the back doors had been blasted apart by the explosion; the heat could be felt from one hundred feet away. The fire service began dousing the flames, and almost thirty minutes later the fire was out, leaving a charred mass of twisted metal, melted plastic and rubber, and something that resembled human remains.

Neville Deakins shivered once he'd stopped. His brow was bathed in perspiration, and he felt the discomfort of his underarms perspiring and making his cotton shirt stick to his skin.

He watched silently as the police officers stood bewildered at the state of the police van's remains.

Cautiously, Lomax, Roma, and DCs Crosse and Greggs approached the vehicle to have a quick look, but it was difficult to make out anything specific. Roma's eyes began to sting due to the acrid smoke and she dabbed a tissue to stem the tears. Inwardly, she blamed herself.

No-one noticed the similarly registered police van driving back across the river via Lambeth Bridge, after it had done a full circle, coming back around and parking near St. George's Circus before continuing with its journey. Its destination known only by the driver and his colleague, with their passenger locked away safely in the rear.

Eight

Thursday 3rd January.11:45 AM.

Lomax felt very nervous.

He was also incredibly angry, not just with himself, but he was absolutely fucked off with whoever had orchestrated such a devious and diabolical attack.

Two brave police officers killed, along with nineteen innocent civilians. Many more seriously wounded.

The media had gone into overdrive. At the press office at Scotland Yard, and even in Downing Street, serious implications were being considered. The Prime Minister Dudley Conran had been called to Buckingham Palace to discuss matters with Her Majesty, her concern of the utmost importance, and needing to be convinced that these incidents were being dealt with urgently.

Lomax was seated outside the Deputy Chief Commissioner's office at New Scotland Yard. He could almost hear the tones of his Chief Superintendent's voice, doing his utmost to quell the embarrassment that the police were facing; assuring *his* superior that this situation would take precedence and be resolved as soon as was humanly possible.

Lomax had already had his own arse severely chewed off by Deputy Chief Commissioner Conway, in front of CS Warwick, as had his entire team, dealing with the Deakins' element to the case. Lomax had had the book 'verbally' thrown at him by Chief Superintendent Warwick, when he'd been in the office as well, the bollocking still ringing in his ears.

'For God's sake, Charles,' said Chief Commissioner Sir William Stonehouse, seated in his high-backed expensive white leather chair, leaning back so it tilted slightly as he began rubbing his puffed face. William Stonehouse, a fifty-four-year-old copper, with well over thirty years in the force, was not in uniform, he was dressed in casual brown trousers, brown Skecher trainers, brown socks, and a beige shirt under a cream V-neck jumper.

At six feet two tall, his muscular and physically appealing frame always generated admiring looks from the women he knew, and of those he met for the first time. His chiselled features were highlighted by his starkly bright green eyes, slightly bulbous nose, well-trimmed beard which like the hair on his head was still richly black, with no signs of greying, even with the intense stress of 'the job'.

He'd seen many things.

Dealt with extremely serious incidents.

Most recently the July 2005 terrorist attacks. The explosions at King's Cross tube station, and the Tavistock Square bus explosion. The Libyan Embassy in London, multiple hostage incident in 1987, when WPC Louise Fletcher was *allegedly* shot by one of the terrorists from an upstairs window; murdered in cold blood as she stood in the street (seen by millions of viewers live on TV).

Each of those situations called for utter diplomacy. The media didn't really care who was to blame, it all made for great news coverage. Accusations were made. The police and political giants were held accountable.

And now this.

'You know how I hate having to come in to work at short notice, and while I'm supposed to be on leave,' Stonehouse muttered, continuing with his admonishment of how this case was developing into an utter shit-cart.

'Sir,' Chief Superintendent Charles Warwick began, 'I'm sure I don't need to explain to you that we're not mind-readers. If we were, then there would be no crime at all. I also cannot explain how or why the van exploded. How or why the arrested suspect was due to be brought in for questioning by DCI Lomax and his team. His investigation was still ongoing; this Deakins appears to have been an integral part of it.'

'That's as maybe Charles, but that doesn't excuse the carnage, and loss of innocent lives. I have to tell you, the forensic team found no evidence of another body allegedly belonging to this Raymond Deakins, other than those of the two police officers, what we now know to be pig flesh, organs and pieces of charred bone. The van was destroyed by Semtex, which as you know, is the prime favourite of terrorists. Just who is this Mr Deakins, and how does he fit in with DCI Lomax's case?' Chief Commissioner Stonehouse asked.

'At the moment sir, I know nothing. I shall ask my people for a full report on this matter,' he lied, then continued 'As soon as Lomax and his team have filed their statements and case notes, I shall let you know.'

Stonehouse and Conway looked at each other after Warwick left the office.

'Lomax. Look, Phil... for crying out loud man. This is one sure-fire fuck up,' Chief Superintendent Charles Warwick said as they drove back towards Kensington, in the rear of the chauffeured dark blue Jaguar XJS Type S. following close behind them in the pool Vectra, was DS Roma Clarkson, with DC Crosse and DC Greggs.

'I know, and I'm sorry sir,' Lomax replied, his voice low, deliberately sorrowful.

'Cut the bullshit Phil, you're a damned fine copper. I know you too well already, having read the commendations from my predecessor to even consider that you wouldn't have sought a warrant for Deakins' arrest, unless you knew full well you had a solid viable reason to arrest him without one. So come on, tell me what the fuck went wrong?' Warwick said.

'To be honest sir…' Lomax began, but his old superior cut him short.

'Phil. I asked you to cut the bullshit. You know far more than you're letting on. Don't forget, I've been in *The Service* slightly longer than you, so I know all the tricks, old and new.' He winked knowingly at his subordinate.

Lomax grinned and briefly chuckled. 'Okay, sir. I'll be straight with you.' He then told Chief Superintendent Warwick everything… or almost everything. He described the information regarding Amanda Waterman's secret laboratory in the apartment next to her own. He felt that he'd have to explain everything sooner or later, and it would all have to be in the case report, so now was as good a time as any to be forthcoming.

Keeping pace with the Jaguar, Roma followed as the car threaded its way through the still icy but busy city streets. Her attention was riveted so intently to the rear of the Jag, she barely noticed the vehicle directly behind her. Even when it suddenly peeled off smartly down a side street, shortly before Dunne House came up, causing several shouts of annoyance from pedestrians and horn blasts from angry drivers coming in the opposite direction.

Inside the vehicle, two of the three occupants were busily checking the 'bugging' equipment in the briefcase, making sure it was operating. The driver was speaking on her mobile, 'Yes… that is correct sir. At the moment the police still have no idea why the police van was blown up. Yes sir, only the remains of the two police officers' bodies were found. It would appear that the police are considering that due to the size of the explosion being centred on the rear of the vehicle, Deakins' body was totally obliterated by the blast, although leaving the blood and visceral organs and a few bones to be found was a master touch. I'm not certain whether they have conducted tests of the bones, blood et cetera as our bugging equipment failed briefly, but I'm certain that they're utterly clueless.'

The driver pulled away after one of the two men transferred to another vehicle parked up the road from the police station.

Nine

If things that are truly bad certainly do come in threes, then DCI Lomax's luck had run out yet again.

Only a matter of hours after his bollocking from Scotland Yard three days previously on the Wednesday, he'd been ordered to go home and rest up for a few hours, to get his thoughts in order, by Chief Superintendent Warwick. Lomax was sure that he'd successfully convinced his boss that there was nothing amiss concerning the way he'd expedited the search and the arrest of Raymond Deakins. Or concerning his prior personal knowledge/friendship with Amanda Waterman.

There was also the unfortunate situation concerning Lomax's brother Gerald's death, which in normal circumstances would, or should have implemented Lomax being taken off active duty for a considerable time; however, Lomax stood up to the suggestion and argued that he needed to deal with Gerald's death in his own way and remain involved in this investigation out of respect for Amanda Waterman. Besides which, Gerald's death was more suited to the Drug Squad investigation team.

He also believed that he'd convinced Chief Superintendent Warwick that none of his officers were implicated in any unlawful behaviour concerning this case. Yet nothing could have prepared him for what happened next. Having been ordered to take a few days' rest, reluctantly he'd agreed, going back to his own home, and contacting the care staff looking after his father, before he attempted to relax. Although no matter how hard he tried, this case was to plague his every woken second, and even in his sleep.

***

The knock on the door of his father's home seemed innocuous enough. Although at just after six-forty in the morning, it did seem strange. Lomax usually called beforehand, notifying the new live-in carers if he was intending to visit.

The nurses and carers had been hired, as a courtesy through The Police Federation Benevolence Foundation; to stay with Mr James Lomax while Philip was at his own home, or at work, would cook meals, ensuring that James took his medication, bathe him and dress him if required, take him out for a few hours, if practical, and clean the house.

They would also keep in contact with Philip to keep him appraised of progress of his father's health. The day shift nurse came down the stairs, a broad woman in her early fifties. Short dark curly hair, just beginning to go grey in places, framed an equally full face, and flushed cheeks; a button nose and a wide beaming smile, which usually seemed permanently attached to her face. The tight fitting dark blue uniform accentuated her muscular build, and yet anyone that knew Frances Willis knew her as a bubbly, friendly and professional person.

She'd not long finished speaking with Philip on the phone, giving him a progress report by the night-stay nurse, Elizabeth Parrish, of how his father had slept comfortably, and that there had been six fairly random and peculiar, strangely quiet telephone calls. No messages though.

After another louder knock had sounded off: 'Okay, all right, I'm on my way,' she called out. She unlatched the front door and opened it. A scruffy scrote stood there, dirty faced, a strong odour of the unwashed was blown into the hallway, causing Frances to wrinkle her nose.

'Who are you, and what the hell do you want?' she demanded.

'Gerald… is he here, I need some gear,' the gruff voice asked.

'No, he doesn't live here… he's gone away,' Frances said, although she knew that Gerald had died almost a week or so earlier, having been informed by Philip Lomax.

The stranger, possibly in his early twenties, tried to barge his way in. Frances stood her ground, blocking the doorway.

'Let me in, I wanna see for myself,' the undesirable rancid-smelling lowlife demanded.

Reluctantly, Frances leaned her face close, trying to breathe out. 'Look here,' she whispered firmly, 'just fuck off, or I'll give you an enema with the rough end of a large pineapple.' She pushed the druggie away with her left index finger and slammed the door in his face.

While Frances Willis took over the day shift, Elizabeth sat and waited until she'd rechecked that James was all right, and was comfortable, then the two women sat in the kitchen drinking coffee.

'So,' began Frances, her eyebrows arched in suspicion, 'how many times did your new boyfriend Allan call you then?' she asked.

'Really Frances… he didn't, how could he? I haven't given him any information as to where I'm working. Besides its early days,' Liz said, blushing slightly. Liz was twenty-six, blonde, slim and very pretty. She'd been seeing Allan Jefferies for only a few days, having met him in the local supermarket.

Sure, like any bloke that had found himself lucky enough to secure a few dates with a great looking woman, he'd been intensely inquisitive, and had asked Liz many questions. Although the answers hadn't been strictly forthcoming.

The two women had been making small talk, Frances teasing Liz about her new boyfriend, when through the large single glazed front room window a brick broke through the glass, exploding it into the room. The extremely loud noise startled the two women, who both screamed loudly due to the unexpected and frightening situation. Tentatively, they went to investigate.

The glass had splintered into sharp shards, covering most of the carpet and minimal furnishings that occupied the downstairs front living room. Pieces of differing sizes lay on the pine coffee table, the magazines on the top and some had even fallen into the large glass goldfish tank, where Jonas the quite large solitary catfish swam around.

'What was that noise?' came the muted voice of James from upstairs. Liz went up to speak to the elderly man, to explain. 'Fucking bastards,' he said, banging his fist into his open palm, 'If I get my hands on them I'll...'

Philip was there within half an hour of being contacted by Frances, as to what had just happened. When he got there he examined the brick and note tied around it, carefully, donning blue latex gloves, though neither Frances nor Liz had read it, Lomax asked. 'Did you touch it?'

Frances simply smiled and wriggled a pair of latex flesh-coloured gloves at him. He smiled sheepishly.

The note was addressed to him personally: the text written in Courier font and printed on cheap A4 piece of paper. With current cheap off-the-shelf printers, it would be damned near impossible to prove where it came from.

DCI Lomax

Unless you wish harm to come to your father, James, and sister, Hillary, just as it did your brother, Gerald, do whatever it takes to close the case forthwith regarding Amanda Waterman at the London Vortexa Pharmaceuticals building.

We know you knew her. Leave it at that. You and your family, friends and colleagues <u>WILL</u> suffer as a consequence if you persist with the investigation. Speak to your superiors and convince them to close the case. You will receive no further warnings. Deposit any 'evidence' you may have acquired in the locker to which the accompanying key relates. Place the key in the envelope provided and post it in the post box on Crouch End Hill N8, near Coleridge Primary School, at 08:20 am any school day. We will be watching. You have three days to comply.

***

A chill ran down Lomax's spine. His nerves tingled with acute anger and dismay.

Just who the fuck were these people? How did they know he was the investigating officer dealing with Amanda's death? Why? Why was he being threatened as well as his family? Incensed with rage and concern, Lomax was about to use the home phone to call his superiors and alert Roma and the team, when it occurred to him that perhaps the phone-line was compromised. Perhaps whoever these people were, they obviously had people watching his every move, and more than likely had been ever since he first began investigating Amanda's death.

It occurred to him that the fact that whoever these people were, they must be deeply connected with the Vortexa Pharmaceutical Company's hierarchy, the top dogs in charge, if it was not themselves. But why? What do they have to hide? He knew of course *why* they wanted the evidence... because it obviously connected and incriminated them in illegal practices. What concerned Lomax, was just what they were indeed up to? And why were they concentrating on him?

The last question which he'd asked himself, he felt was the one that actually mattered. He called a glazier from his mobile to come and repair the broken window, whilst also calling his father's local police station to make an official report of run-of-the-mill vandalism.

They sent two uniformed officers round to take statements from the two nurses, and take notes of the appearance of the druggie who'd called minutes before the brick was launched through the window. They also waited until the glazier had repaired the window. One of the officers, an eager young WPC called Kirstie Ballard, had an inkling that there was something not quite right about the possibility of this being an act of simple vandalism.

She kept her thoughts to herself... for the time being.

Lomax went up to speak to his father. Frances, the district nurse accompanied him, but stayed outside, sitting on a chair until needed, the bedroom door slightly ajar.

'Hello son. What in God's name was that noise earlier on?' James asked.

'Dad, you know I would never lie to you,' Lomax began, feeling a lump of guilt rising to his throat. 'This isn't easy to tell you, but there's been an attempted break-in, either that or just some louts causing havoc. I've got the window people putting in some new glass...' he tried to look his father in the face as he spoke but found himself glancing away. 'There's another thing I have to tell you. Gerald's dead. He died a little while ago, he... he took an overdose,' Lomax sighed.

James Lomax looked at his son, and the elderly man could tell that his son was having a difficult time having to tell him these awful things. He took Philip's right hand in his left and squeezed. Lomax looked back at his father, seeing the intense frailty in how his father's health had deteriorated so swiftly over the past few months, and more so in recent weeks, if not days.

James Lomax had also lost a lot of weight, he was diagnosed as suffering from Type 2 diabetes, he was constipated, and a recent blood test revealed that he also had both colon and pancreatic cancer.

Cancer… the big 'C'. One of many types, yet they were all killers, sooner or later. Not all of the time of course, some lucky so-and-so's gained remission if treated early enough, but just the same, eventually, the cancers got their victims. Philip Lomax didn't know of any that were *good* cancers.

'Jesus.'

It wasn't fair. He was welling up.

'Gerald was a stupid twat,' James said, breaking the uncomfortable silence that had descended.

'What do you mean, Dad?' Lomax asked.

'Don't treat me like I'm a bloody idiot, Philip Lomax. Gerald was an alcoholic drug-peddling berk. You know, he thought I was so fucking senile that I didn't know he'd been stealing my medication to give to children, to raise money to get the harder stuff he needed?' James Lomax said. A pained expression flitting across his face, causing him to squeeze his son's hand as tightly as he could muster.

Philip Lomax swore under his breath. Not because his father still had some strength in his hand, but because of Gerald.

Bastard.

'Bastard… for stealing his father's much needed medication, and bastard for being such a low-life, as to entice young vulnerable children into serious drug abuse,' he thought to himself. He also decided that this was almost as bad as Gerald being

a paedophile, close, and yet another thought suddenly occurred to Philip. '*What* IF *Gerald* WAS *a paedophile as well?*' This made Philip shudder. But at least in a sense it answered a few dilemmas. Dilemmas that had been plaguing the police recently.

Philip didn't feel any sense of loyalty to Gerald at all. His father was right.

'As for that fucking daughter of mine,' James said, breaking through his son's thoughts. 'All she damned well cares about is that loser husband of hers. Never had a mind to give me any grandchildren either. Which begs me the question, when are you going to?'

Lomax was stunned. Was his father being serious? 'Dad, I'm not even seeing anyone at the moment. I'd love to give you grandchildren, but...'

'But perhaps, I might not stay around long enough to see one?' He answered, finishing his son's sentence. A wry smile appearing on his face.

Lomax smiled back. Then his expression became far more serious. 'Dad, would you do me a huge favour?'

'Sorry son, I cannot afford it,'he said chuckling, 'You know I'm on a small pension, and I'm still waiting for that court settlement.' He laughed heartily again, bringing on a long bout of deep wheezing and coughing. Lomax lifted the glass of water to his father's lips, where he took small sips, and the coughing and wheezing subsided.

'That's not what I meant,' Lomax said, his tone serious. 'I want you to move into a care home, just to get away from here for a while, mainly for safety's sake. I mean, you're stuck up here in your bedroom, and it's not as if you can use any of the other rooms upstairs or downstairs. You'd be well cared for, and if you put this place up for sale, you can use that money to pay for your care,' Lomax said. He knew what his father was about to say, but the vibration of his mobile in his pocket interrupted him. He stood up, letting go of his father's hand and walked to the door, taking his mobile out and seeing the unfamiliar number appear on the screen, he pressed the answer button.

As he stepped out of the room, Frances got up from her chair and went in.

'Lomax here, who is this?' he said.

'Sir, it's me, Roma. I really need to see you, it's... it's urgent.'

'Where are you now?' Lomax asked, a tinge of irritation creeping into his voice.

'I'm in Camden Town. The World's End pub, near the tube station,' Roma replied, noting her boss's changing mood, but she held out.

'Why are you that far out from the office?' Lomax asked, his voice suddenly mellowing.

'I'm not sure, but for the past few days I've been getting the feeling that I'm being followed. I really need to speak to you in person, and I thought that this would be best,' Roma said.

He looked at his watch. It was just after ten-thirty in the morning. He couldn't believe he'd been here that long. 'Okay, stay there for a short while. Check around, to see if you think you are being followed, I suggest you check out the punters there. Go by tube to Golders Green; get to a pub there. See if anyone follows you. If you do recognise anyone from the pub where you are now, get back to the tube, and head back to the office, I'll meet you there.'

'What about the car, it's my own vehicle,' Roma said.

'Damn. We cannot leave it unattended. Shit. Okay, change of plan... drive back to my place, all right? But keep your eyes open for any suspicious vehicles trailing you.'

'Yes sir.'

'I'll drive home. Get into your car, we'll go to back to the pub in Camden first, then back to the office with a takeaway.'

'Very well sir. But... if we're being followed, wouldn't those responsible have potentially bugged our offices or our cars?' Roma asked.

'Damn. Okay, change plan again, I'll meet you where you are, stay there and keep your eyes peeled. Catch you shortly,' Lomax said

***

He'd argued with his father for fifteen minutes about the idea of him going in a care home, before he'd left.

'Dad, please. You'll still be independent. You really don't need to live in this house anymore.'

But James Lomax was being cantankerous and extremely selfish. He would not budge on his decision to stay in his own home, in Arlington Gardens, Acton, where he'd lived for forty years, and wasn't about to let some shitheads drive him away.

***

Roma had not only great eyesight, but a pretty good short-term memory as well. Committing the faces to mind, after she'd cautiously scanned the other customers in the pub. She'd counted nine people, not including the landlord, his wife and the suspiciously underaged barmaid.

Lomax arrived almost forty minutes later. The traffic was diabolical, partially due to the continued freezing weather icing up the roads, and certain idiotic drivers not having experience driving in icy conditions and using their mobile phones. Lomax shouted at several drivers for using their mobiles, but they just gave him 'the finger', or mouthed obscenities and continued on their merry way.

He inwardly hoped that they ended up having accidents, without injuring innocent people. He parked his car in Lyme Street, in the only available space, several yards away from Roma's own car, and alighted after switching off the engine. He locked the car and as cautiously and surreptitiously as he could, he scanned the street for anything or anyone he considered acting suspiciously. But to be honest, he thought everything and everyone did appear conspicuous.

Lomax walked along the street towards the traffic lights at the main junction with Camden High Street. He reached the main door of The World's End public house, the maroon paintwork having been recently refurbished with fresh paint. He opened the door and entered and looking around he caught Roma's eye. She smiled and rose from the seat as he approached the slightly raised seating area where the internal decor complemented the exterior of the pub. The seats had also been re-covered with a burgundy velour material and re-upholstered with a more comfortable cushion for the customers to sit upon for longer periods.

'I'll get you a drink,' Roma said but Lomax held up a hand.

'My round, I think,' he said, a beaming smile on his face. 'You hungry?' he asked.

Roma nodded and pointed to a set meal for two on the menu on the table. Lomax nodded and went to the bar. He ordered the meal and drinks and paid. As he stood waiting for the drinks to be served by the young buxom barmaid, short spiky blond hair, with a top that left little to the imagination and a short mini-skirt, even at this time of the year, although to be fair the pub's heating was on, Lomax held the young girl's gaze as she looked him up and down with hazel eyes. He returned the admiring smile, even though he too thought she was suspiciously underage. He then glanced around the large bar area as casually as he could, not having frequented this pub before, his eyes traversing and taking in everything from the various patrons scattered about, along the bar at the men openly leering at the young barmaid, lifting their backsides off the barstools whenever she had to bend forward or over with her back to the customers to reach the bottled drinks in the chiller cabinets, to the thick recently laid new carpeting, stripped parquet flooring in areas and the various items of interest lined up on the shelves above and around the bar and the lounge walls.

On a wall next to a raised platform (set in a corner as a stage for the entertainment) was a large poster, declaring the forthcoming appearance of a Kent-based singer/musician, called Mick Kenten, who had worked with several well-known acts from the seventies: Brian Connolly's Sweet, Les Gray of Mud, Les McKeown of The Bay City Rollers. All of which were brazenly advertised on the poster.

Taking the drinks back to the table, Lomax sat on the opposite side of the table to Roma, took a sip from his pint of bitter, and setting the glass back on the table he looked intently into Roma's face. Keeping his voice deliberately low he asked, 'So why do you think you're being followed, and do you think they've caught up with you in here? There's a few unsavoury looking characters here, that's for certain.'

Roma chuckled, covering her mouth. 'That's for sure. But no… I don't think they know I'm here. That's why I bought a cheap mobile and called you, just in case my 'official' mobile's been compromised… oh shit.'

'What?' Lomax asked.

'I called *your* mobile,' Roma said.

'Yes you did… my new personal unregistered one, not my police mobile,' Lomax replied, grinning.

'Shit. Oh God. I really don't know,' Roma said, keeping her voice low. 'This case has only been ongoing for a few days, and where are we with it?'

'I think you're either getting too worked up with this case, or…' Lomax began.

'Or?' Roma asked, pushing Lomax to continue.

'Or… you're going round the twist. So anyway…' Lomax began before Roma gave him a gentle kick on his right shin under the table, as the food was brought over by the young barmaid and set down for them. They both began eating. The food smelled delicious. Both Lomax and Roma noticed the male customers ogling the young barmaid as she sauntered back behind the bar, a definite and deliberate wriggle as she moved.

'The thing is Phil, I noted five separate vehicles keeping pace with me for several miles as I drove around London. In some places I moved like I was possessed, see if they would keep up with me. I went along the Embankment towards Kensington & Chelsea from Victoria Coach Station, overtaking and undertaking vehicles even in these road conditions. It was the last vehicle that managed to keep up with me the most.'

'What type of vehicle was it?' He asked.

'A 4x4, black… a Mitsubishi Warrior pick-up, one of the newer models, the more sleek versions, but this one had an enclosed rear section, as though it had extra seating. I think it had personalised plates as well,' Roma said.

'How did you lose them?' Lomax asked.

'I took several roundabouts and side-streets at speed and doubled-back on myself before I changed direction again and headed out here. I thought by coming to Camden Town I could ensure they'd lose sight of me,' Roma said before shovelling a forkful of chips and chicken into her mouth.

Roma explained her reasoning for why she believed their investigation into Amanda Waterman was now linked to the E.A.R.A. break-ins, Raymond Deakins' involvement and his subsequent 'death'. Which as Lomax tells her is now unlikely, as he believes that the van that blew up was simply a decoy, and that whoever abducted Deakins was definitely concerned with their investigation gaining ground. He also alerted her of the threats made against Lomax and his father and sister, and that he now also believes that Gerald's death was implicated within the investigation as well.

'I've been warned off. I think Gerald was abducted and shot up with a lethal overdose, then dumped. The note told me to gather all the evidence, the case file investigation reports, even the autopsy results on Amanda Waterman, and post them to an unknown third party, thereafter closing the case,' Lomax said.

Roma gasped as the realisation sunk in, and she reached her right hand across the table and rested it on Lomax's left as he held his beer glass. 'Have you told Chief Super Warwick yet?'

Lomax shook his head slowly. 'No... and I'm not going to unless I'm forced to. I've had an idea.' Then he saw out of the periphery of his vision the unmistakable shape and colour of a black 4x4, as Roma had described, which had stopped in the road, and although the glass was tinted, he could only guess the occupants were looking directly at him and Roma through the pub's window.

'Come... we're leaving... now,' he began speaking to Roma conspiratorially, giving her instructions. She refrained from nodding as she gathered her handbag.

She finished her drink, used the female toilets before giving the customers another cursory glance once more as she passed by, then went to her car which she'd parked in Lyme Street, and drove away. Lomax had slipped out the back of the pub having flashed his warrant ID to the landlord and made his way along the narrow alleyway to the street until he was behind the 4x4. As he made his way through the pub and the alleyway, he'd taken out his own private mobile and made two very brief calls. Now observing the 4x4 hidden by the edge of the pub's wall, making a mental note of the private number plate, which he realised was obviously a vain company purchase.

It read VORTX 244.

The 4x4's driver pulled away as soon as they saw Roma's car enter into the junction traffic, after the lights changed to allow her to enter the yellow box painted on the road. Shortly before the 4x4 driver ran the red light they were facing, and due to their attention being fixed on their quarry, they never saw, heard or felt any vibrations of the rear tailgate of the pick-up being opened over the steady throb of the diesel engine. The one witness who saw Lomax climbing on board under the raised cover and pulling the tailgate closed, was the driver of the car directly behind the 4x4. Lomax fixed her with a cheeky grin as if to convey he was playing a trick on the driver of the 4x4, and he raised his index finger to his lips as if to emphasise this. Thankfully and luckily for Lomax the locking mechanism was well oiled and it simply 'clicked' securely shut, without alerting the driver and passenger.

Roma drove back from Camden Town, towards DCI Lomax's modest three bedroom semi-detached home in Brackenbury Road, Shepherd's Bush, now driving sedately through the traffic in her own dark green Ford Fiesta Zetec. At that time of day it wasn't too bad; it took her a little over an hour, by using a few back streets that she knew of to decrease the journey time, also to check and see if she was still being followed.

Throughout the drive, she kept looking in her mirrors, but she didn't notice any vehicles she felt might be tailing her, not even the 4x4 which was stuck behind a lorry and a double-decker bus. She arrived at Lomax's house at twelve-forty-two. His car was nowhere to be seen.

Her mobile rang. 'Yes?'

'Roma, sit tight for a few minutes as if you're waiting for me to return, then pick up your mobile once more in a few minutes as if I'm calling you, then drive away,' Lomax's whispering voice commanded. 'Drive to BBC Television Centre. I have a friend at security. He'll let you drive in and park up. Go through main reception with him, he'll direct you to the Green Room for studio six. Do as he says.' The call ended.

Roma huffed, and before she pulled away as instructed after a few minutes, and pretending to take another call, she caught the briefest of glimpses of the black 4x4 in her rear-view mirror. It was parked facing the rear of her car a hundred yards away. Having pulled up she saw Lomax who, keeping as low and out of sight as possible, as made a beeline for an alleyway obscured by several wheelie-bins. She grinned, but then wondered if he'd been spotted. During the journey from Camden back to Shepherd's Bush, and before he snuck out of view from the back of the 4x4, he'd dived underneath the back and pulled a very sharp hunting knife from his right calf boot. He cut the fuel pipe, just enough to allow the diesel fuel to leak sufficiently. He knew it wouldn't be long before the engine began to suffer from lack of fuel. Keeping himself low in profile he slipped back to his own home as discreetly as he could, hoping that the 4x4's driver and passenger's attention had been focussed entirely on Roma as she sat waiting. He waited, watching as Roma pulled away again, and he smiled as the 4x4 pulled off and followed her once more. Then Lomax hailed a cab and told the driver to drive him back to Camden where he retrieved his own car and went back to his place to gather some things, fresh clothes and essential toiletries of his own. He made a point of speaking to his neighbour, telling her that he was working away for a few days. Then he drove his car to The Dorchester's car park. He went directly to a reserved room, giving him a chance to shower, shave and change into some fresh clothes.

Starting her car and pulling off, it took her another twenty minutes to course her way to the BBC. Sure enough, a tall black muscular man approached her. Dark short curly hair, a dark pencil thin brooding moustache drooping down each side of his mouth, deep penetrating brown eyes, and a chiselled chin looked at her with slight suspicion.

'Hi, I'm Freddie,' he said.

Roma flashed her ID, he nodded and smiled an immaculately white-toothed grin. 'How long have you known DCI Lomax?' she asked conspiratorially.

'Who?' Freddie answered, feigning that he didn't know to whom she was referring. 'Please, follow me,' he asked.

'Right,' Roma said, deciding to play along with this charade.

Roma followed Lomax's friend Freddie into the building, past the main reception, turning right, and headed towards The Green Room for Studio 6. Freddie opened the door and showed her in. 'Please wait here, miss.'

Freddie returned to his post at the main security entrance, where one of his colleagues was struggling to convince the driver of the 4x4 that without a permit or a valid invitation/ticket to see a show, they could not enter for any reason. Freddie took over and in no uncertain terms told the driver and his three companions to simply, 'Fuck off, or I'll call the police.'

Twenty minutes later, she was ushered into another room by a member of the BBC staff and found herself seated next to the singer/actor Michael Ball. She couldn't believe it.

'Well, hello there,' he said.

'Excuse me, I think you misunderstand, I'm not what you think...' Roma began.

Michael's infectious laugh boomed within the confines of the room. 'It's all right, Roma. Phil asked me to expect you to accompany me in my cab back to my hotel, where he'll be waiting. Phil hopes that whoever's following you, won't realise that you're actually with me. You'll be ushered into the back of the car out of sight. Then I'll get into the car in plain view, then we'll be off.'

'You know DCI Lomax too?' she asked.

'Phil? Yes... known him for years, ever since he collared a female stalker who began making undue and malicious threats against me. Phil was only a DC at the time, and he was injured as a result.'

Roma looked shocked. 'Injured? How?'

'The woman in question came to Aspects of Love. She stayed late and had disguised herself to look quite different from her police record photo. Luckily for me, Phil was there too that night, and he saw through her disguise, just as she came towards me screaming and brandishing a vicious-looking hunting knife. Phil tackled the crazy bitch, and they ended up on the floor amongst a large crowd of other people.' He motioned for Roma to leave the room and head for the private parking area, where stars usually got picked up by chauffeured vehicles, but Lomax felt that might be too obvious, so a black cab with a regular well-known driver was ordered.

Michael Ball continued the story as they were driven back to the Dorchester Hotel. 'They rolled around for several minutes, Phil trying to get the knife away, but she managed to stick it in his lower back, barely missing his liver. He lumped her one on the side of her face, breaking her jaw and putting her out.'

'Goodness me. And so, you've been friends as a result?' She asked.

'Oh yes. Aahhh here we are. You've made good time, Paul,' Michael said to the driver. 'I'm afraid this is where you get out my dear. I'm heading off to rehearsals for my evening show. I do hope we'll meet again, some sunny day.' He smiled that well-known grin as Roma exited the vehicle. The door was closed and Paul drove Michael away.

Roma looked around. She hadn't actually taken much stock of where she'd been driven. She was in awe of Lomax's association with such a warm and friendly celebrity, open and honest. She looked confused and discovered to her surprise that she'd been dropped off directly outside The Dorchester Hotel, near Hyde Park. As inconspicuously as she could, she quickly glanced around, looking for the 4x4, but in this part of Central London, there were many 4x4's driving around, so she concentrated her attention to the number plates. She didn't see or recognise the personalised plates on any of them.

As she looked above her, she saw a dulled shadowy figure looking out of an upstairs window, in a room at the front of the impressive building. It was waving, beckoning her. She realised it was Lomax and so she walked into the main foyer. Roma was expected by the reception staff, where a porter was directed to show her up to Michael's room.

On the Bayswater Road, just before Lancaster Gate tube station, the Mitsubishi 4x4's engine began to cough and splutter. The driver glanced at the fuel gauge and swore as he was forced to pull the vehicle across the traffic and park just past Westbourne Street, making it before the engine died. All three climbed out and saw the trickling evidence of the diesel creating a rainbow effect on the damp road. The driver peered underneath the back of the truck and found the severed fuel line, swearing once again. 'I'm going to cut that bastard's throat when I see him.'

'Who?' asked one of the other two.

'Lomax. He must have been in the back of the truck. He did this, I know it.'

One of the other men opened the tailgate, revealing the empty space.

'Well, if he is responsible then, where the fuck is he?'

***

He opened the door as she neared it. He'd been there almost an hour.

Roma looked around the room *(she'd never been inside any of the rooms at this particular London hotel.)* Particularly as she'd never been *invited* by any of her many suitors, and neither had she been assigned to any murder cases here. Not that there had been any – that the police knew of.

Two high-stemmed wine glasses sat on the dining table in the through-lounge, along with an expensive bottle of Chardonnay, set at a slight kilter in an ice bucket on the table in the centre of the bay window area of the room.

The table had been set for two.

'If I'd have known… I'd have changed as well. You didn't have to go to all this trouble, sir,' she said.

'Drop the *sir* shit Roma, we're officially off-duty,' Lomax said. 'How was Michael?' he asked, a wry smile appearing across his face.

'He was lovely. Such a gentleman… unlike some men I could mention,' she answered, forcing a mock expression of matronly admonishment on her face.

'Good. I ordered a Chinese-style meal for two. Do you mind?' he asked, adding, 'seeing as our pub lunch was rudely interrupted.'

Roma shook her head as he guided her to the table, taking her short brown leather jacket from her and draping it over the back of the cream sofa. He pulled a chair for her and she sat down.

He brought in the two plates already filled to overflowing with the food and set hers down in front of her. 'Ooh… Peking Duck. Lovely,' she said.

They didn't speak much during the meal. Lomax poured the wine every time her glass was emptied.

After the meal, Lomax sat in one of the armchairs; Roma sat on the settee.

'So… what do you make if it all, Roma?' Lomax began.

'Are you referring to the case,' she asked, 'or… about us?' They both spoke briefly about the case, and then discussed at length just how they felt towards each other.

***

He felt the softness of her fingertips drawing trails across his shoulders. The lightness of her lips as she planted kisses on his neck, shoulders and chest as he lay on his back, on the floor on the Persian Rug in front of a roaring coal fire. Roma lying close to him on her left side, her right thigh resting across his. Her right hand rustling through the thick dark mass of chest hair, caressing his stomach and still moving lower.

They'd not long finished making love for the third time. Both their bodies glistened from the exertions and the exchanges of bodily fluids. It *had* started with Roma breaking off from the current discussion about their feelings towards one another, by asking about the attack by the crazy woman stalking Michael Ball.

She looked into his eyes, at his face while he told her what had happened in his own words. 'Michael likes to dress things up a bit,' Lomax had said to begin with. 'It wasn't really that much of a deal,' he explained, corroborating much of what Michael Ball had said, and adding very little more if the truth be known.

'I've been wondering, I thought Michael lived here in London somewhere, so why has he a room here at The Dorchester?' Roma asked Lomax.

'That's an easy question to answer,' Lomax replied. 'Michael has some builders and redecorators in at present, and he'd rather not be there while the place is in a mess.'

'What if he walks in and catches us?'

'I think he'd find the situation rather amusing,' Lomax said, grinning knowingly, and gaining a false look of disdain from Roma.

Roma had insisted on seeing the five-inch scar for herself. Reluctantly Lomax relented after as much persistence as he could stand. He had to take the shirt off, exposing his torso. As he turned to show the scar, Roma moved over and gently touched the spot, running her fingertips over the pale raised bump, a line that was almost seven inches long.

Lomax giggled. He was ticklish. Roma persisted, and they fell to the floor, where she kissed him fully on the lips, her tongue snaked inside and he responded.

Completely.

It had been too damned long since he'd given himself freely to another woman. He'd *'come'* close on a few occasions, but then he'd held back which always turned out to be the right choice, when the woman in question was eventually found to be implicated with the cases he'd been investigating.

The mobile phone ringtone startled Roma. It was her registered one, and when through bleary eyes she looked at the name, she cursed.

She glanced at the clock: 06:57 am.

She turned to her left in her sister Helena's spare room double bed; they'd decided to go there after their mutually initiated – if rather spontaneous – first session of passionate love-making, and importantly in case Michael did by chance return unexpectedly early to his hotel room and catch them at it again. They tidied up before they left the Dorchester at 10:40 pm to remove any *'evidence'*.

They'd arrived at Roma's sister's place in Plaistow, just after midnight.

Roma pressed receive and spoke in whispers.

'Who was that?' Lomax asked, after she'd eventually finished taking the call, and she'd turned back to find him lying on his left side facing her, his entire body exposed. He wasn't smiling though, his face looked serious. 'A boyfriend I don't know about?'

'No. Phil… I don't have a boyfriend,' Lomax feigned a hurtful expression, as if to suggest *"Who the heck am I then?"*

Roma ignored the look and continued. 'That was DC Crosse. They've found another dead body which seems to be connected to Amanda Waterman. They want me over there straight away.'

'Get showered and dressed, I'll go with you,' Lomax said.

'Sir. Phil… you're on imposed leave don't forget.'

'I *was* on leave, you mean,' he said, smiling again.

He drove Roma back to The BBC TV Centre to pick up her car; then he waited for thirty minutes and drove to the crime scene in London Zoo.

Lomax had been very surprised when Roma told him of the location, and what DC Crosse had told her briefly about the recent situation.

Ten

Sunday 6th January.09:49 AM.

He'd had a hell of a job containing his exhilaration in having finally made love to Roma. Deep down he'd been attracted to her, ever since she'd joined his team only three years ago, after she'd transferred from the Vice Squad at Bethnal Green, in which she'd only been working for about a year before she hung up her official PC Plod uniform.

He'd been attracted to her Latinesque looks, attributed (according to Roma herself) from her mother Mariessa, a fiery passionate Italian from Rome, hence her name. Yet not only are work related assignations frowned upon, but they seldom lead to long-term happiness. That didn't deter Lomax, besides... in all fairness, it *was* Roma that instigated the intimacy.

If it had been his idea to initiate the assignation, it probably would have failed before it had even begun.

As he pulled up behind a line of police vehicles, in Prince Albert Road, NW1, including a dark blue Peugeot Expert van, from the SOCO division, he noted with some dismay and trepidation that Chief Superintendent Warwick was in attendance. Lomax was treading a fine line being on the scene, considering he wasn't supposed to be seen officially supervising the investigation of this case at present.

Warwick marched purposefully towards Lomax as he climbed out of his Maestro. He'd been discussing matters with DS Clarkson, DC Crosse and DC Greggs, when he noticed DCI Lomax's car pull up and park.

'What are you doing here?' Warwick asked, his tone full of semi-serious anger.

'I heard it on the grapevine, sir,' Lomax replied, trying not to sound flippant.

'Very droll,' Warwick said, his voice changing to a more comforting level. 'Okay, so what's the real reason you've turned up here?' he asked.

Lomax glanced very surreptitiously towards DS Clarkson who was looking straight at him, but still in deep conversation with DC Crosse and DC Greggs. 'Sir, I think you ought to have a look at this,' Lomax said, pulling the note that had been launched, attached to the brick through his father's front room window, from his pocket. He handed it to his superior who quickly unfolded the piece of paper and read it. Three times.

'Jesus,' Warwick said, then after a few moments of serious thought, he added, 'you do realise of course that we cannot do this?'

'Sir. Unless we do hand over the material, my sister, my father and more than likely myself, are in direct danger. I'm inclined to believe that whoever's behind this note, and indeed the investigation we're trying to solve, has someone deep inside our police service. Possibly even, someone who's currently working alongside us'

'Are you suggesting someone on your team is giving away pertinent information related to the investigation?' Warwick asked.

'They know far too much already. I think this case was compromised from the moment we started, and this is partially why I'm here, I need to get back on board sir.'

'I cannot believe this. It's barely been two weeks since Miss Waterman was discovered dead outside the Vortexa building in Docklands. We don't have a great deal to go on in any case, and they want everything we have?' Warwick asked. Then almost as an afterthought he added, 'You do realise Lomax, that if we hand over the little material we do have, or at least what's been officially logged, and *if* we cease this investigation, it won't be just your head on the chopping block.'

'Yes sir… but. I have a cunning plan.' Lomax took hold of his superior's left elbow and led him along the street, speaking in a low, almost conspiratorial fashion. 'Sir, I have to believe that there might be someone working on my team who has been less than professional, by being in the pay of whoever killed Miss Waterman, and who instigated this note being delivered in such an unorthodox fashion.' Lomax paused for effect and waited while Chief Superintendent Warwick absorbed what Lomax was telling him. Lomax continued, 'I also have to face the possibility that this very same person had something to do with my brother Gerald's murder. So, my idea is, give them copies of what they *think* is the evidence, not all of my team has seen every shred of information or the reports I've written concerning Amanda's death. I'm inclined to believe that the person acting on behalf of Amanda's employer…' Lomax paused then added, 'former employer is potentially a low-grade and low-ranking officer. They only act on what evidence we higher ranking officers supply them, so I'm planning to use what time I have to create some 'new' evidence. Now give me a severe public bollocking… if you would please, sir,' Lomax said.

Warwick exploded. His voice was loud and ferocious. After bawling Lomax out, and making quite legitimate threats to have him dismissed, Chief Superintendent Warwick stormed back to his car, and was chauffeured away.

DS Clarkson accompanied by DC Crosse and DC Greggs walked up.

'Blimey chief, what on earth did you say to him?' asked DC Greggs, his eyebrows arched painfully high.

'Personal stuff,' Lomax replied, succinctly. 'But also, that he thought I was stupid to disobey his orders to continue with my leave, but I don't really give a flying fuck. Right then, let's see what went on in here. I take it there are no members of the general public here?'

'No sir,' DS Clarkson answered. 'It was one of the keepers that found him.'

Lomax followed Roma as she led him through the main entrance. They were immediately joined by Mr Colin McIntire. A short wiry man aged in his mid-fifties. What hair he had was shaped by his barber to form an enclosing circle around the top of his head, framing the balding dome, which was smooth and shiny pink flesh.

Round metal-rimmed glasses perched precariously on his scarily thin nose, his florid face exuded a kindly nature, more so towards the animals than that of mankind. His steel grey eyes shone with an indifference, yet the beaming smile he greeted the police with appeared to be genuine. 'Mornin',' he said, leaving the 'g' off the end of the word. In fact, most of any word ending with the seventh letter of the alphabet always seemed to be missing when he spoke, and sometimes the first.

'Good morning, sir,' began Lomax as he scrutinised the man, who DS Clarkson had introduced as the head keeper of the reptile section of the zoo.

'This way,' McIntire said, as he began marching off towards the relevant area of the zoo with a determined stride. 'You do realise,' he continued, his tone defiant, 'that Mr Har'reaves is extremely pissed off about this. It may not be visitor high season, but we cannot afford any disruption to the staff or the animals' routine. This is most annoyin' indeed, yes it is.'

Mr Hargreaves?' Lomax asked.

'The General Director of London Zoo, sir,' answered Crosse.

'Yes. He is. And he is extremely upset,' Mr McIntire added. 'As soon as it was discovered what had occurred, we had to remove the snakes from their vivarium, there was glass everywhere. Poor little Gertrude might have seriously injured herself.'

Ermintrude?' questioned Greggs.

McIntire stopped suddenly, turning to glare at the detective constable. 'No. Gertrude, not Ermintrude, you nincompoop copper.'

Both Lomax and Roma Clarkson found it exceptionally difficult to refrain from laughing, as did Crosse.

The older man unlocked the outer door to the Reptiles, Arachnids and Snake House, then led the team inside. 'He'd refused to even allow the SOCO members access,' said Crosse.

'Just as well,' Lomax said bluntly.

The section was split into three areas. Reptiles such as lizards: iguanas, monitors and the like lived in a deep watered pit within the vivarium itself, which was huge. There was another just outside for the young crocodiles. The third section held the collection of snakes and spiders, and smaller lizards: chameleons, geckos as well as locusts/grasshoppers and small insects for their food.

As they moved along, they saw that a huge pane of roof-glass had been smashed inwards. The naked body of a male lay with his back folded across a large log. His spine had snapped upon impact three quarters of the way from the cervical section and had literally speared its way through the intestines and out through his stomach wall.

His head and neck were at an obscure and obscene angle, trapped between the smaller branches of the log which angled upwards. His eyes wide open, as if startled. His nose had impacted with one of the rocks and was mashed grotesquely into his face before he'd come to rest a few feet away.

The man's right knee was twisted at an obscure angle, the kneecap shattered and almost completely torn clear, this fact made visible due to the flesh covering the patella bone having been ripped aside, the ligaments visibly white in places where the blood had missed coating them. Lomax immediately recognised that the injury wasn't in any way caused by the fall. But by another far more deliberate type of trauma.

Without waiting for permission, Lomax opened the already unlocked door next to the huge avarium and stepped inside, cautiously moving towards the body, but remaining far enough away so as not to contaminate any evidence. He took the digital camcorder from the bag around his shoulder and began filming the scene in situ, zooming in as close as possible.

After several minutes of shooting images, he exited the avarium and motioned for the SOCO team of five forensic personnel to take over. 'I want everything collected, and I mean everything. Take it back to the lab and examine it closely, please,' he said directly to Sergeant Evelyn Porter, the superior scene of crime officer in charge. She simply nodded with the barest hint of an acknowledging smile.

Not that he could see it in any case behind the mask covering most of her face; in fact, Lomax couldn't say for certain whether he'd *ever* seen what Evelyn Porter's face looked like.

The journey was silent, as Roma sat in the front passenger seat of Lomax's Maestro and he drove back to the station. After parking up, Lomax and Roma followed by Crosse and Greggs arrived after driving Roma's assigned pool Vectra back to the station, went up in the lift to the floor where their offices were, and the incident briefing room.

Seated in his chair, Lomax leaned back cupping his hands behind his head and closing his eyes. No sooner had he fallen asleep, his extension rang. He reached out with his eyes still closed and picked up the receiver.

'I do trust you're still not investigating this case, Lomax,' came the distorted voice.

'No, I'm not. I do have other cases I need to work on you know. I showed the letter to my commanding officer and he's organising the gathering of all the data, so you'll have it very so—'

'Don't bullshit me Lomax. I saw you at London Zoo today,' the voice said, the menace evident.

This revelation almost caught Lomax off guard, but only for the briefest of moments; he did however feel his heart skip a beat. 'I wasn't aware that this particular body was connected to this case, since it was in a completely different part of London and wasn't at Vortexa Pharmaceuticals. Besides, don't you think that that would have been just a little more coincidental, having two deaths at the same place? Now you've just told me that the body at London Zoo *is* connected with Amanda Waterman's death... sorry... murder,' Lomax said, forcing himself to exude an air of indifference.

There was silence on the line.

Had Lomax called the caller's bluff?

'Get the files and the evidence together, Lomax, and drop them as and where instructed. You have twenty-four hours. Stay clear away from this case, Lomax. Otherwise, you know full well what the consequences will be.' The line went dead before Lomax had an opportunity to declare his own counter-threat.

Lomax had the phone to his ear when Roma entered the office carrying two steaming cups of coffee, and a small plate with some rolls. As he looked up at her, something caught his attention, up in the corner of the room. Something that he knew shouldn't have been there. It made him wonder, but he also knew that he couldn't be seen checking it out himself. He replaced the receiver, rose from his chair, a worried expression on his face.

'What's the matter?' Roma asked.

'My father's ill. I have to go to him. Would you drive me?' Lomax said.

'Of course,' Roma replied. She placed the two cups of coffee on the desk as she walked by, then followed Lomax back down to the car park.

On the way towards the underground garage parking area, he spoke quietly, almost a bare whisper in case anyone was likely to overhear, and because the nature of the garage having an echoing effect, 'See if you can get one of the older pool cars to use.'

Roma gave him a puzzled expression, but instantly caught the gist when he rubbed his nose, pretending to scratch an itch. As he waited for Roma to acquire another police pool vehicle that he was certain, or rather hoped, wouldn't have been 'jacked' with any covert bugging devices, he used his knife to deliberately puncture the driver's side front tyre of the regular police Vectra Roma used, having casually looked around the underground parking garage in case anyone saw him. Thankfully the installation of CCTV cameras hadn't been started down there, as far as he was aware.

They arrived at the house in short time. Seated in the passenger seat Lomax adjusted the door mirror and kept looking to see if they were being followed. He was certain that they were. He'd clocked the black 4x4 Mitsubishi Warrior pulling out of a side street near to the station, and it stayed with them most of the way; sometimes it would fall back a few cars, and other times Lomax would see it pulling out of a street up ahead of them, but slowing down outside a row of shops, one of the doors opened as though the driver or a passenger was alighting to go into one of the outlets. As they drove through the city streets, Lomax wrote notes which he only showed to Roma when they were stopped at traffic lights.

Being followed.

Office possibly bugged. Phones too…

Maybe our usual pool and private cars as well as homes.

Roma didn't react, she carried on driving. Lomax glanced in the side mirror and of course he saw the black 4x4 a few vehicles behind them. They finally arrived and went into the house. Lomax introduced Roma to Frances Willis, the daytime district nurse. While the two women chatted, he went up to see his father. Before he did though, he went around the house, acting as though he was checking it was being kept clean and tidy, running a finger over surfaces, or ensuring there was enough food in the cupboards. Surreptitiously he was looking to see if he could spot any hidden devices. He couldn't be certain that there weren't any inside the house. If he was going to have a chance to check, he'd have to come up with a reason; at the moment however, he had nothing.

He went outside, and looked at the brickwork, roof line and windows. Harry Gardner, the eighty-three-year-old neighbour from next door was in his back garden, hunched over a fork. He was toiling the earth on his vegetable patch. He looked up as Lomax walked around looking at the house.

'Hello Philip, long time no see, lad,' Harry said.

'Hello Mr Gardner, yes, how are you?' Lomax replied politely.

'Oh fine. What you looking for?' the older man enquired.

'Oh, nothing really. Just checking the place, seeing if there are any repairs needed. Dad's not as agile as he used to be you know, and what with Gerald dying…'

'Gerald's dead? When did that happen?' Harry asked, his shock coming forth loudly in his voice.

Lomax briefly explained. He knew he could trust Harry Gardner, he'd been a friend to his father for a long time and regularly popped round to do odd jobs to help out the nurses.

'Now you come to mention it,' Harry said, 'a couple of men called round a few days ago, when I checked on Jimmy and got talking to Frances. They said they were from the local council, doing random house checks on the elderly and infirm. They wanted to come in to check the condition of the house, or so they said, but I wouldn't let them in. They had no official ID. I did see some younger man faffing about by the front windows, top and bottom, using a strange looking pole, I gave him a piece of my mind, in fact I told them all to fuck off, so when they left in their van, I had a look all around the outside of your father's house. I found these attached to the windows and walls, as well as the telephone line.'

He showed Lomax the round items with thin wires which had been cut by Mr Gardner, after he'd dropped them into water in a saucepan and boiled them, rendering them utterly useless.

Lomax took the items and looked at them, thanking him, and as casually as he could muster, glanced around the back garden, and at the rear of the houses that backed onto his father's.

He returned inside, surreptitiously looking around for anything that might be out of the ordinary; yet due to the slightly run-down appearance of the decor, it wouldn't be difficult to secrete some more devices, but from what Harry had said, Lomax doubted any more devices had been, especially considering neither Frances nor Elizabeth would have allowed unexpected men access to the property, at least without Lomax's approval. Lomax went upstairs to talk to his father.

'Hi Dad.'

'Oh hello there. Twice in one week, eh? I must be privileged,' James said, a wry smile on his face.

Lomax spoke quietly as he sat by the bed.

'Dad. I have a serious problem at work which has put you in serious danger. A case has come up, and you're being threatened. I want you to go into a nursing home, but only for a short while. I promise you'll be able to come back here, once it's all over.'

'Philip… how many times do I have to tell you, no. I'm staying put here, that's the end of it.' James Lomax's expression said it all. He was adamant that he would not be forced from his home by *anyone* for any reason.

Lomax knew it was pointless. His father was a stubborn old cuss at the best of times. He also knew it was pointless trying to convince the old bugger in doing anything that would impair his independence. Lomax was glad in one way that the Alzheimer's his father was suffering from was still at the very early stage, so he could still remember a decent amount.

He decided on one last attack, as an idea suddenly came to him. 'Dad, how would you like to go and visit Janet? You remember her, don't you? She lives on the Isle of Wight now, in Ventnor.'

'Janet?' James asked, a puzzled frown appearing across his already pallid features. Lomax watched helplessly as he watched what little colour his father's face had, suddenly drain away. The old man's eyes closed slowly; his breathing became shallow.

'Frances!' Lomax shouted, and within moments, she appeared. She checked her charge's pulse, pupils' response to light, and his breathing/heartbeat with the nearby stethoscope. Her facial expression told Lomax all he needed to know.

It wasn't looking good. He grabbed his private/unregistered mobile and dialled nine-nine-nine, calling for an ambulance, becoming frustrated when the operator kept asking for the address to be repeated. Eventually he was told an ambulance was on its way.

The Paramedic arrived and immediately attached pads to James Lomax's chest, which were then connected to a heart monitor. Even though he already had the cannula inserted for the dextrose/saline drips he was being given, and the catheter for his bladder, as well as the colostomy removal bag, it still made it slightly awkward for the crew to administer the attention he needed.

The Paramedics worked for almost twenty minutes before they'd stabilised their patient's condition: in the time since they'd arrived at the house, James Lomax had suffered two heart attacks, bled into the catheter bag through his urine, and suffered several short seizures.

It didn't look promising. He was placed swiftly into the ambulance.

Lomax rode in the back with his father. The ambulance was directed by the despatch operator to take the patient to Acton Hospital, on Gunnersbury Lane, the A4000.

Once there Lomax briefly waited outside, dragging slowly on a cigarette and then he called DS Clarkson, appraising her of his situation, asking her to take charge of the case for the time being, and to inform Chief Superintendent Warwick and the team.

The waiting is always the worst. He sat on a blue plastic chair in the designated outside waiting/smoking area near to the emergency A & E Dept., taking very little notice of anyone else, even the chilly fine winter drizzle that fell from the overcast sky did nothing to ease the anxiety. He ignored the wheezing and coughing, and the lowered voices of those trying to have civilised discussions about the state of the NHS in general.

As he walked along the corridor back to the ICU ward he looked back out of the window across at the small car park, and realised that whatever happened concerning his father, he'd have to call for a taxi. *'Damn. I should have followed in my car,'* he thought, admonishing himself.

He heard a voice calling him, and he turned to see a young nurse running towards him, calling him. He rushed back to his father's bedside. Machines bleeped as James Lomax lay on the bed, barely aware of the activity going on around him. Morphine had been administered to quell the acute pain he'd been experiencing during the few moments he was conscious.

Lomax sat by the side of the bed, looking intently at this frail and pained human being. He sat for over an hour just looking at his father, trying to summon up the right things to say, while he gently held his father's right hand. Then after taking a deep breath, he began speaking in a soft voice: he told his father how he felt, how he truly felt about his family, losing his mother to cancer; Byron and Ruth, although he was very young and so were they, and he never fully understood their deaths at the time. Gerald's untimely demise, Hillary's arrogant attitude. He also told his father that he loved him, but now it was time… time for him to meet up with his wife, Brenda… to go and be with Mum.

Lomax noticed his father's breathing began to become shallower, laboured. The eyelids opened slightly, and James Lomax only moved his face briefly towards his son's face. Lomax saw his father's lips moving but no words came forth, only an almost silent rasping breath. The briefest of serene smiles appeared. Tears formed in the inner corners of James Lomax's eyes, and slowly slid down the elderly weathered skin of his cheeks towards his chin. James' chest rose slowly twice, then sank back down, still, unmoving, quiet. The machines monitoring James Lomax began to sound their alarming rapid shrill beeps, alerting the nursing staff and doctors that rushed in to offer their expertise. However, as Philip Lomax had requested the relevant forms requesting that should his father be likely to suffer further seizures or heart attacks which would render him a 'vegetable', a 'No Resuscitation Order' had been signed and duly respected. The doctors and nurses stood quietly in the corner of the room, after they'd made the necessary checks of their patient's condition and confirming the obvious fact, a life extinguished, observing but remaining professional.

Several minutes passed by before Lomax accepted the fact that his father had indeed passed away; he continued looking at his father's face for several moments, still holding the old man's hand, then his own tears came, and he cried. He tried to quell his emotional state, but he couldn't hold them back. After several moments one of the young nurses stepped over and gently placed a comforting hand on Lomax's shoulder, and in a quiet comforting voice suggested he leave his father's bedside so James Lomax could be respectfully prepared.

After a second doctor had been called for and certified that James Lomax had indeed died, nurses began to prepare the body for removal from the ward. Lomax watched impassively from the corner of the room while the nurses went about their business behind the closed curtains around the bed.

The time on the ward clock showed that it was 20:47 PM.

He took a taxi back from the hospital to his father's home to collect his car. He didn't see the point of staying at his father's home. Frances Willis tidied up after Lomax contacted her and told her of James Lomax's death. She contacted Liz before going home.

As he stopped his car and alighted, he looked at his own modest home from the edge of the pavement, illuminated by the streetlights. Before going in, he never noticed or heard the van slow down, stopping beside him. The side door slid open, and three pairs of hands reached out, grabbing Lomax and yanking him into the interior. He struggled, but these three people were decidedly strong. Once the side door slammed shut, the van peeled off and drove away at normal speed.

Carpet tape was swiftly placed across his mouth, as a hand forced his chin upward to close his lips. Another pair brought his wrists together behind him, and using a plastic cable tie bound them together, as were his ankles and legs just above the knees. Another wider cable-tie was placed around his neck, tightened sufficiently enough to cause Lomax to realise the implications if he continued to resist.

It was too dark to make out any features, but the interior smelled new. Lomax's eyes were adjusting to the meagre amount of light coming from the front of the vehicle, as he was knelt and frisked.

'Mobile phone,' said one voice, in a thick deep northern England accent, possibly Yorkshire, but what specific area he wasn't certain.

'Wallet and police ID,' said another, a female as she felt around in Lomax's left front trouser pocket, her fingertips digging into the far-right corner, and scratching through the thin pocket material into his scrotal sac, causing him to twitch and wrench himself to one side. 'Ooohh, he doesn't like that,' she said, a mannish laugh erupting from her.

'Keys,' said the first voice. 'And a second mobile phone.'

Laid onto his back, Lomax couldn't tell where they were going. Facing towards the rear doors which were windowless, he couldn't tell by seeing buildings he may have recognised, besides, he never even noticed what direction the van was facing, so he didn't know if they were travelling north or south, east or west.

The van took turns slowly and carefully. The driver, whoever they were, slowed down at junctions, lights, and pulled away easily as well. The van's interior must have been sound-proofed. *'This lot are well organised,'* Lomax thought, as the van took a wide corner.

The others were remaining silent; there was no discussion, no idle chit-chat other than when his pockets were being rifled. He knew there were at least four of them.

Overkill?

Four against one?

It didn't make any sense. Neither did the threat to Lomax's family. What possible use did threatening to kill his family make to his investigating Amanda Waterman's death? What was prominently dominating his mind at this moment was his father's death.

He felt a bump as the van went over what Lomax presumed was either a pothole, or the ridge of an entrance ramp, as the van seemed to immediately go downhill at a very steep angle before it levelled out, and stopped, then reversed whilst turning. The engine was killed. Doors opened and slammed shut, the sliding door made a completely different sound which meant that he was about to be hauled out... which he was, unceremoniously.

Dumped onto what Lomax realised to be a wheeled stretcher, he was moved over the rough concrete ground, and a *'Ting'* sound which Lomax knew for sure meant an elevator; so they were taking him somewhere that had several floors. He felt the sudden prick as something was jabbed roughly into his neck. Then a strange sensation as whatever was being injected began to force him into unconsciousness. As the drug began to take effect, Lomax's mind wondered why they waited so long before drugging him. Why now, now that they had reached their destination?

Eleven

Monday 7th January. 09.13 AM.

The weather was turning exceedingly nasty. Darkening clouds began to move swiftly across the late morning sky towards Central London. The forecast was for potential heavy snowfall and black ice.

The man stood in the centre of the western pavement looking at either end of Westminster Bridge, watching for anything or anyone that might be inclined to stop him in his quest. He was standing on the side of the bridge closest to the London Eye, slowly rotating in the early evening, the capsules lit up, most of which filled with passengers. The Houses of Parliament were to his left as the premature dusk began to close in. Directly behind him on the other side of the bridge was St. Thomas's Hospital.

Thick heavy clouds, large dark blue/grey/purple folds of accumulated moisture held in suspension by atmospheric conditions, moved silently low in the sky above the city; it appeared as though the bottom of the clouds were resting atop the roofs of the buildings. Streetlights with automatic light sensors clicked on, as London slowly became enshrouded with a cloak of pelting hailstones, which fell without remorse.

People walking across the bridge ran for cover; those with umbrellas or briefcases held them over their head, to stay the stinging pelts. They basically ignored the man standing almost in the centre of the bridge, removing his clothes. The larger than normal hailstones struck his naked torso, leaving swiftly rising red welts which soon melted into one another.

He removed his trousers, socks and underpants, dropping them without care onto the wet pavement.

Up in one of the London Eye capsules, a young woman in her early twenties with her boyfriend scanned the scene with a Canon digital camcorder, which showed the vista in a reddish/purple/orange hue. She'd pressed the record button by accident and was saving everything she saw onto the memory card.

The veil of hailstones receded to a fine rain then to nothing, as she tried to look at the view while the capsule they were in moved round. Panning to her left she saw something on the bridge. Using the powerful zoom facility of the 1000mm lens attached to the camera, she gasped as she saw the naked man standing, his arms raised, legs placed slightly apart. His lips moving and his head shaking crazily.

He was obviously saying something. She moved the camera up and down the bridge, but it was virtually deserted. Then as she refocused on the man's naked form, admiring his physique, she cried out as he suddenly rushed towards the railing, he took a running dive on to the eastern side pavement, towards the water below.

She followed with the camera and winced as the man's head struck the steel cargo hold cover of a barge being pushed by a tug-boat. Due to the barge's upper surface being illuminated by bright industrial lamps, the recording of the man's behaviour on the camera saw it as clear as day.

His neck snapped instantly, then as his upper torso flipped over, a sharp tapered metal spike which protruded from a corner of the cover sliced through the man's left inner thigh, ripping through the femoral artery, and a gush of crimson, coloured black by the bright yellow lights, sprayed out under pressure. Viewing this grisly scene, the young woman shuddered as the fountain of blood arced and covered the brightly lit barge top cover.

He thrashed on the cover for mere seconds, then immediately went limp.

The girl on the London Eye passed out. Her boyfriend managed to catch her before she hit the hard floor of the capsule, but his main concern was his expensive camera. Other travellers in the capsule rushed to offer assistance. One woman, who was a trained first-aider, attended to the young woman, while the boyfriend called the emergency services.

It was a further nine minutes before the capsule reached the embarkation platform.

14:21 PM

It was now just over three hours since the incident on Westminster Bridge. Police officers were interviewing everyone who had been in the vicinity. The boyfriend Len Harris saw that the record button on the camera had been depressed, he stopped it while his girlfriend Ginny was being treated at the First Aid Centre incorporated inside the Old County Hall building, while waiting for an ambulance. Due to the atrocious weather, many hospitals were inundated with accidents, so the wait was agonising.

He replayed the recording, if only out of curiosity, to see what Ginny had seen worthy of filming. Len Harris sucked in a deep breath as he saw on the camcorder screen that Ginny had zoomed quite close in on the man's body, taking far too long an interest on the spot below his navel.

The man was well aroused and fairly well endowed too. Len immediately felt inadequate and really cheesed off, that Ginny felt it necessary to look at the man at all, let alone at his erection.

He was about to delete the file. He wondered how Ginny had managed to zoom and focus – to keep the image tight and clear was uncanny, given she hadn't properly used the device before.

Len winced as he replayed the sickening landing several times. Then he took out his mobile again and dialled nine-nine-nine.

DS Roma Clarkson was quickly informed of *any* unusual death occurring in and around the Metropolitan London area, and suburbs.

She was about to inform DCI Lomax but recalled that he'd asked her to take charge until he contacted her again. She studied the file that had landed on her desk in the Incident Room less than twenty minutes earlier. Inside the yellow envelope was the folder with the case notes, and the CD-ROM with the camcorder recording file that had been copied onto it.

Opening the CD-ROM/DVD tray on her PC, she took the disk and inserted it, then pressed the close button. Immediately, the file came up in a dialogue box within the Windows® Media Player system-program, she left-clicked with her mouse to accept it.

As soon as it was downloaded, she clicked the play icon.

'Jesus,' remarked DC Crosse, as both he and DC Greggs watched over DS Roma's shoulders at the 17" flat screen monitor, as it played the unfolding scene from earlier that day.

'Do you think this has any bearing on our case?' asked DC Greggs, speaking to Roma, his tone clearly devoid of sympathy for the victim.

'Why? Don't you?' She asked back.

'I-I'm not certain, but from what I've seen on that film, it could just be some young guy, who's had his fill of life, and he's decided to end it. Simple,' DC Greggs said.

'Why go to all that trouble of removing his clothes? Why stand out in such a public display and say or shout something before he runs and dives off the bridge?' asked DC Crosse. 'I mean look, he dumps all of his clothes on the pavement. Okay there's hardly anyone paying him any heed due to the shitty weather, but why still do that in hailstones? It just seems bizarre behaviour to me. Totally out of keeping with most suicidal tendencies.'

'Well DC Crosse, that's exactly how I see it,'DS Clarkson said, tapping her pen against her right cheek. Her eyes narrowed and a V-shaped crease appeared in her skin just above the bridge of her nose. Roma was in deep thought, albeit not entirely to do with the case.

'So,' began DC Greggs, pausing for effect. 'What's our next step?'

'Shouldn't we inform DCI Lomax of this latest connection?' asked DC Crosse.

DS Roma Clarkson shook her head. 'No. Look, DCI Lomax's father is seriously ill, I think he needs to be with him at the hospital. Don't tell him I told you.'

Leaving her alone in the office she shared with Lomax, DC Crosse returned to his desk to continue his work. DC Greggs left the briefing-come-incident room, telling Crosse he had to go to the staff toilets. Instead, Greggs left the building entirely and walked along the street, until he reached a small cafe where he used the public phone inside. He was on the phone for just under five minutes, then he returned to the nick.

***

Monday 7th January 9:56 am.

Shortly before the incident on Westminster Bridge took place, Lomax had come to. His head felt as if it was on fire. Even though his head was restricted he could see that he was in a sort of laboratory, banks of benches with strange looking equipment, machines – some of which he recognised as similar ones to those in the secret laboratory in Amanda's apartment – Lomax could also distinguish pungent odours, some he thought he recognised, some he couldn't place.

With his hands tightly bound behind his back, his ankles and knees still restricted of movement, and the tape still covering his mouth, Lomax was aware of a few things: firstly, he was possibly allergic to the adhesive on the back of the tape; his skin and especially his lips were feeling increasingly sore and dry.

Secondly, that the journey in the elevator took several minutes, meaning that wherever he'd been taken, the destination was very high up. Whatever he'd been injected with had taken longer to render him fully unconscious than whoever had stuck the syringe into him had anticipated.

The five people surrounding him, as he lay propped at an angle on a motorised medical stretcher, wore balaclavas with only a narrow opening for the eyes, and two small holes for breathing. He was moved from the laboratory along a corridor and across a small foyer to a set of doors to another elevator. The motorised stretcher was manoeuvred into the car and the doors closed, then he felt the unmistakable slight lurch as it began to rise, yet again.

Lomax was able to determine that one of them most certainly was female. He briefly wondered why he hadn't been blindfolded as well, but then since these people, whoever they were, and whomever they worked for, had contained their identities completely it was pointless to cover his eyes. Added to this, he had absolutely no actual idea where he was.

The elevator shuddered to a halt in such a way that Lomax felt there was something vaguely familiar about it. He was wheeled out into a darkened space. He heard the rubber wheels *skishing* through a fairly thick carpet material.

He recalled how his leather-soled boots made a similar sound, such as they did on varying surfaces. He was wheeled to another set of elevators. A button was depressed.

Pet-ting.

The electronic and mechanical opening of the doors also seemed familiar, but still Lomax wasn't quite certain. After a short ride he was wheeled out, again through a darkened area, and yet Lomax could see huge windows with lights from the outside from the other nearby buildings clearly visible.

He now realised where he was. The gaffer tape covering his mouth was swiftly and callously ripped free, causing Lomax to wince and curse under his breath.

His bladder *accidentally* released some urine. It was probably an involuntary response to the fact that he'd been brought back to the very building where Amanda Waterman had died. He felt the warm trickle of the liquid as it seeped through his underpants and went down his leg.

He squirmed, trying to adjust the position of his penis, whilst concentrating on controlling his bladder. He knew it couldn't be full. However, he was absolutely glad he was wearing dark trousers.

The stretcher was one where the 'bed's' angle could be adjusted and Lomax was propped up in front of an expensive dark red leather armchair, facing a large expansive desk, virtually clear of anything relating to whoever's office this may be.

The office lighting was dimmed. Then a bright light came on and was aimed directly into Lomax's face. He squinted.

Footfalls clicked on the highly polished wood flooring, and the low squeak of an office chair alerted Lomax that someone new had entered the room and sat down. More than likely behind the desk, and even more likely somebody with a very high-ranking position within Vortexa Pharmaceuticals.

The voice was deep. Exuding utter calm but tinged with an edge of malevolent malice. 'Mr Lomax. Philip… you don't mind me being informal, do you? No? Good. It seems that you have given me a significant predicament. I'm really not sure quite what to do with you.'

'What is it you'd like me to do? Look, shithead, whoever the fuck you are, although I have a fairly clear idea who you could be... I'm a copper. A Detective Chief Inspector. I'm paid to investigate crimes, whatever they may be, but murder or suspicious deaths are my forte. You can threaten me. Kill me even, but you'll have tens of hundreds more coppers on your arse,' Lomax spat vehemently, his voice firm and controlled.

He felt a sudden jab in his side from one of the thugs. Possibly the muscular woman. It felt like a fist punching him fast and hard just above the right kidney. He grunted and wheezed.

'That wasn't polite Detective *Chief* Inspector Lomax, was it now?' The tone was definitely sardonic.

'I apologise,' Lomax said as convincingly as he could, although he didn't mean it.

'Good. I accept your apology. Tiger, apologise to the nice policeman for hitting him,' the stranger's voice commanded.

A deep rasping voice cut close to Lomax's right ear. 'I'm sorry, mate.'

'No problem,' Lomax replied.

'So,' began the VIP's voice, 'what exactly have you discovered about Amanda's untimely demise, Mr Lomax?'

'Very little to be truthful. The autopsy results aren't completed as far as I'm aware. I haven't received any reports from the Coroner's Office yet, but then I've been dealing with my ailing father's health. But you already know about that, don't you?' Lomax said.

'So, you know nothing about any results? That's good, I'm pleased about that. Would you be so kind as to tell me precisely where her body was taken? That question unfortunately Mr Lomax is due to my people losing track of the vehicle transporting her to whatever mortuary here in London that she'd been earmarked for. Damned congestion, it's abominable,' the stranger's voice said.

'I don't have that information as yet. I'm still waiting for the preliminary forensic report as we speak. Most of the mortuaries are backed up here in London, due to the high number of elderly that have passed away over Christmas, it's a sad time as I hope you can understand, so it's plausible to assume she may have been taken outside the city. What about the police van which blew up? Did you happen to have anything to do with that?' Lomax asked, his voice relaxed and non-accusatory.

'You're very astute, DCI Lomax. It's no wonder you have reached this far up the career ladder, at such a young age. Very well then. I shall tell you this much, I need you to keep this case under the radar... if you continue to investigate it, I will act on my earlier threat concerning your family. I take it you did alert your commanding officer of your situation?' The voice asked.

'Look,' Lomax began saying, thinking of how he was going to explain things in a way that even this dumb-arse might actually comprehend, 'I really don't have the authority just to stop investigating a case, just because you say so. Even if I took myself off the case as a result of your threats to my family, they'd assign another team, and nothing I could say or do would prevent them from going ahead. I'd have thought, you being an educated and intelligent sort, would have realised that.' He hoped the sarcasm in the words he'd chosen wouldn't result in another, harder jab to his body.

He didn't see the hand, but he felt the strike as a vicious slap stung him on his right cheek. He presumed it was delivered by the masculine-looking bint.

'That wasn't necessary, Lomax, however you brought that upon yourself for being lippy,' said the voice. 'I do understand and accept your opinion though. It does make sense. Okay Mac, you may proceed. While you're being prepared, Philip, I'll concede that it would be impractical for me to try and prevent the investigation. Too many alternatives to contend with. Nevertheless, as much as I feel the need to dispose of you right now, that in itself would also cause me a great deal of issues, so I shall let you live. Take him back down to street level then keep him there in the van until about eight o'clock this evening, then dump him somewhere, your choice.'

Lomax felt his left jacket sleeve being pushed up, followed by his shirt sleeve-cuff button being undone and that sleeve pushed up as well. Something was tied around his bicep and pulled tight, the inside of his elbow was patted and a vein appeared, a small cotton wad was soaked in medical alcohol and wiped across the target area, then a syringe appeared from nowhere. Lomax caught a glimpse of something opaque and pale green in the cylinder. Whoever was brandishing the syringe depressed the plunger and a small amount squirted into the air.

At least they're doing it right this time. Lomax thought to himself. But he still felt jittery, wondering what it was they intended to inject him with now. He felt the prick as the needle broke through the flesh's integrity and went into the vein. As soon as the plunger was depressed, Lomax's muscles contracted. Whatever it was it was freezing cold. It felt as though his entire blood supply was being frozen solid inside.

When the substance reached his brain, Lomax felt very relaxed. It reacted very swiftly, and he began giggling like a little boy. The effects of the substance also relaxed his muscles so that what urine his bladder did still hold suddenly rushed free. The unmistakable odour of his urine became obvious.

'Ooops. He's pissed himself,' said the questionable female.

***

Three of the *henchmen* took Lomax back to the ground floor, still secured to the stretcher. He was unsecured and laid in the same van which brought him to this location. The van was driven back into the West End.

Lomax continued to giggle as he lay in the rear of the van, then when it stopped the side door opened, and he was hauled unceremoniously out and dumped into St. James's Square just off Pall Mall. The van roared off once more, and in his confused hysterical state, Lomax just caught a slight blurred image of the registration plate.

He lay for almost fifteen minutes on his back, gasping for air as he hyperventilated. His heart was racing, well more than one hundred and ninety per minute; he could feel the thumping organ bouncing against his chest wall. He closed his eyes tightly until he saw flashing moving lights running in front of his eyelids.

Rolling over onto his knees, he splayed his hands out, palms down straight into a puddle which smelled absolutely rank. He cursed, and he suddenly felt nauseous. His stomach somersaulted and he vomited, heaving what little food he'd consumed earlier in the day back up along with acidic bile. He rose to his feet and staggered semi-blindly around St James's Square and then right into Duke of York Street heading north. Soon he was in Jermyn Street where he turned left and crossed the road, almost getting himself run over by a van, whose driver hammered his horn. Members of the public seeing him advancing towards them swiftly averted their gaze and their direction, turning up their noses as they caught a whiff of the disgusting smell emanating from him.

Even Lomax himself winced and gagged when he sensed the odour, and he felt embarrassed. He walked along towards St. James's Street, whereby he collided with a small glass-topped table outside Franco's, an Italian restaurant, knocking one of the two customers' drinks over, spilling it into her lap. Her beau stood up immediately and grabbing Lomax by his coat lapels shoved him backwards away from the two of them and other customers. Lomax stumbled away and eventually disappeared around the corner. In his befuddled state, he had no idea where the fuck he was going. Moving along Piccadilly Road, into and through the bright square with its neon lights and screens, with Eros and The Grand Hotel on his right, the Trocadero on his left, several buses, cars and cabs drove past, blaring their horns, some nearly running him over.

His head swam, as he opened his eyes to the bright lights and the neon's blazing out from the theatres, cafes and bars, it brought him to a semblance of normalcy. He stood up and cussed as he saw that his overcoat and the front of his trousers were dirty and wet in patches. He could also feel the tenderness from where the acidity of his urine had affected his thighs. This made him feel self-conscious and embarrassed.

He began moving towards the brightly lit area. Looking at his watch, he saw that the face glass was cracked and the hands of the Sekonda had stopped at 21:08. It had probably been broken during the scuffle of throwing him out of the van. He wondered how long he'd been wandering aimlessly. He cursed once again, then remembered his mobiles.

Strange that they'd given both of them back to him.

As Lomax regained his composure, and his senses began to improve, if not his appearance, he tried to understand what was really going on here.

He dug a phone out of his inside jacket pocket. It was switched off. He couldn't recall turning it off himself, but then considering his recent situation, and the fact that he'd been rendered incapacitated, perhaps they had turned off it when they searched him…or perhaps they'd placed trackers in both and cloned the sim cards. *'Shit!'*

Now he'd have to get another new one or two, more bloody expense. *'I wonder if I can put an expense claim in to CS Warwick?'* He shook his head, knowing what the answer would actually be.

He reached the junction, squinting as the bright lights of the buildings assaulted his eyes. Passing pedestrians looked at him suspiciously, taking wide berths to avoid making eye-contact. He stumbled out into the road and moved awkwardly.

Across the street a huge throng of people stood around in groups, talking, laughing, and some eating from foil containers containing Chinese or Thai takeaway food, from the many establishments in the area. Lomax stopped on the pavement facing the shops and switched on his LG mobile. He waited for it to boot-up.

After the main screen appeared, he shuddered. A thought suddenly occurred to him, and he removed the back cover, took out the battery and looked inside, but apart from the SIM card, he couldn't see any differences.

Being ever cautious though, especially in these days of Big Brother surveillance, and the fact that he believed that whoever had abducted him may have planted some type of device upon his person, he removed the battery, just in case, then he removed the SIM card and discarded the main body of the phone, lobbing it into a nearby bin. The 'unofficial' phone he realised had been misplaced by whoever had abducted him.

'Stupid bastard,' he said aloud to himself, drawing looks of suspicion from the passing public. He looked up and saw two uniformed police officers walking towards him; both had serious and suspicious frowns upon their faces. 'Thank God. There goes the old saying…' he said out loud.

'What old saying would that be, sir?' asked the male copper having overheard Lomax and stopping close to him. A tadge too close, as he could smell the strong odour of urine. A tall man in his thirties, the flat-cap hat above his green eyes with a yellow waterproofed cover, looked incongruously large.

'That there's never a copper when you need one,' Lomax said.

'Excuse me, sir,' began the second officer, a slightly shorter female officer, a blond-haired fringe just visible under her soft rounded hat, the checker pattern just above the brim, with the Metropolitan badge in the centre front. Her brown eyes above her narrow and medium sized nose gave Lomax the impression she was the nicer of the two. 'Have you been drinking?'

'No. Look…' Lomax reached into his inside coat pocket to retrieve his wallet with his CID warrant card, but both officers reacted far too swiftly, and grabbed him, forcing him to the pavement. Almost immediately a crowd gathered, gawking and pointing, laughing. Many made sarcastic comments not only towards Lomax, but some harangued the officers, telling them to stop being heavy-handed.

One man who hadn't said anything near the front had a pen and notebook and began scribbling. Tall and slim, he had short, cropped hair and a neatly trimmed goatee beard and moustache. He also sported a beige-checked Burberry flat cap. He'd just exited The Comedy Store theatre across the street, taking a short break during comparing a stand-up show and came across this unfolding drama. 'This should be good for one of my novels,' he thought to himself smiling, as the uniforms yanked the stranger upright now, securely cuffed and bent over a street railing as one of the officers radioed for a van. The observer continued making notes as he watched the scene unfold.

**

DS Roma Clarkson hadn't been able to concentrate. Her mind wandered back to that night she'd spent with Philip Lomax, that wonderful lovemaking session they'd both enjoyed.

Thankfully she was alone in the office. Everyone else had gone off duty. The clues were drying up, no fresh leads had been found, and the forensic tests were still ongoing. The officers were directing their efforts with the ongoing cases which needed follow-ups.

Home Office pathologist, Sally Hickton, was still finalising her post-mortem report on Amanda Waterman, which was taking longer than she'd anticipated.

Roma decided to get herself a coffee. Passing the radio room on the second floor, she overheard a radio message. 'We have some joker here, claiming to be a CID officer who'd just been kidnapped.'

'My name is DCI Philip Lomax, Earl's Court CID, you fucking berk...' came the recognisable voice DS Clarkson clearly caught in the background.

She barged into the room and grabbed the microphone, 'Officer, this is DS Roma Clarkson, Earl's Court CID, does the man you're holding have a scar on the left side of his back?'

The male officer pushed the coat to one side and lifted Lomax's shirt. Sure enough, the scar was there. 'Er... yes, he does.'

'Good. Then in that case I suggest you let him go, that's DCI Lomax. Where are you situated?' Roma demanded.

'Piccadilly Circus, outside The Trocadero, almost opposite Oxendon Street,' said the female officer.

'Stay there,' came back the command from a very angry Roma Clarkson.

Twenty minutes later, with car sirens wailing, lights flashing, and an unmarked car sped towards the area then screeched to a halt. DS Clarkson jumped out, flashing her warrant. By then Lomax had been relieved of the cuffs, and he'd taken his own warrant card out to prove his ID.

To say the two uniformed officers looked decidedly sheepish would be an understatement.

'Perhaps next time you'll try listening rather than acting on impulse,' DS Roma Clarkson said angrily at the two uniformed police officers.

'Thanks for coming to my rescue. I didn't relish being put in a cell,' Lomax said, a knowing grin on his face. 'And by the way, officers, I was reaching for my warrant card when you forced me to the ground.'

'Where the hell have you been?' Roma asked, the timbre in the tone showing much concern in the question.

'I'd been on my way back home from the hospital. My fath…' the words stuck in his throat.

Roma placed her right hand on his left arm.

'My father died. Shit. I need to… get home.'

'I'll drive you. You're in no fit state.'

Roma drove like a woman possessed. Even with the blues and twos alerting the other road users that she was coming through, Clarkson weaved the Vectra through the late night traffic, narrowly missing some oncoming and same direction vehicles with scarce millimetres to spare.

Motorists would shout, scream, shake their fists and swear at her, but neither she nor Lomax heard them, or even cared.

Even with such a distance to be covered, somewhere between six and eight miles across London, DS Clarkson did it in substantially less than twenty minutes. Lomax went to jump out before the car had stopped near his front garden gate, but the seat belt caught and restrained him. Cursing, he quickly unclipped it and ran to the door.

Roma alighted from the car and followed her superior into his home. After making them both a cup of tea, they sat down in the kitchen at the small table and Lomax told Roma what had happened. He felt that if whoever it was that had had him abducted was listening in at that very moment, via listening devices from within his home, or from somewhere outside, he didn't really care at that particular moment. He kept his personal feelings towards Roma out of the conversation, showing her the battery and SIM card from his phone. She nodded to show she recalled the note he'd written previously.

Lomax got up and went to his bathroom, to shower, and to change into some fresh clothing. He returned downstairs, and threw the dirtied clothes into the washing machine, and set it to wash. He wrote on a notepad.

Let's go somewhere else. Any ideas?

Roma took the pen and pad and wrote her response.

Back to my sister's?

Lomax simply nodded.

Roma listened as Lomax explained what had happened at the hospital with his father, once they arrived at her sister's place. Ensuring to the best of their ability that they hadn't been followed. Roma had inserted a compilation CD into the player and set it on random/shuffle. It wasn't until *"The Living Years"* by Mike & The Mechanics began to play before Lomax began to feel awkward.

His stomach began to tumble, and his heart fluttered, then his eyes welled up. When Roma saw Lomax bury his face into his hands and sob she stood up, moved to the sink. Looking out into the darkness of the garden, feeling her heart pounding in her chest she looked back at him and waited until his emotions had been cried out. As much as Lomax always believed it *more* masculine, rather than a weakness to allow his emotions to have their release – albeit preferably not in public – he still felt it lessened him as man, and so he tried not to allow them to come to the fore. But this was a time when his emotional state was so intense, and raw.

Lomax took a deep breath before he began to speak again.

'He was still breathing, but it was so shallow as to be almost unnoticeable. I tentatively reached out and took hold of Dad's right hand, intertwining his fingers with mine. I was shocked at just how skinny my father looked lying there in that bed, those sterile white sheets covering him.

'"Dad… I'm here. I'm sorry I took so long to get back to you. I just want to… want…" I began saying, as I looked at my father's face. The man lying in the bed didn't really look anything like the man I had loved, admired and respected. The eyelids seemed to open slightly, though the eyes themselves seemed as if the light had been diffused by the diseases raging within.

'"Dad… this isn't easy for me. I know that I haven't been around much lately for you, and I'm sorry for having a go at you today, I mean, yesterday."' Lomax flinched, took a deep breath after he recounted more or less what he'd said to his father. 'I'm certain I felt his fingers tighten around mine. I told him that I-I-I'm ashamed to say I should have done something officially about Gerald sooner. It was his fault my father became so ill so quickly, as much as it is mine. I told my father that I just wanted him to know I loved him, and always have. Dad, and Mum… they cared so much for all of us.' He thought about what he needed to say next, but he recalled how he felt his father's hand relax and go limp, or at least the memory which caused his fingers to tingle, goose bumps rose.

He recalled how he'd looked at his father's face and chest, which rose and fell a few times then became still. He recalled the final rasping breath being exhaled.

'No,' Lomax said, the word coming out barely audible. Tears flowed freely and he began sobbing again, his head falling forwards onto the kitchen table top.

After sitting quietly in the living room with a cup of strong black coffee, DCI Lomax then told Roma that he felt guilty having signed an NRO form – No Resuscitation Order – when he came in with his father, and even now he still felt as though he'd been dressed like the grim reaper, brandishing the huge scythe, standing at the bottom of his father's hospital bed.

Waiting.

'His organs were packing up, one-by-one. The doctor had to put him on Morphine to ease the pain he was suffering, he told me after joining me in the corridor.'

"Doctor Kilprine took blood samples to run tests, but it was obvious that your father was not likely to last much longer. We believe he was waiting for you to come here before… he passed over."

Roma desperately wanted to go to him from the armchair and offer her condolences, give him her support. But something convinced her to be patient, let *him* approach her, if and when he needed to. He opened his eyes again and looked into Roma's eyes a pained expression formed on his features, sad, forlorn, melancholy, self-accusatory, as though he blamed himself entirely for what had happened.

Roma couldn't read Lomax's thoughts implicitly and decided to move over from the armchair. She sat next to Lomax, reaching out; she grasped both of his hands into her own and she spoke softly, comfortingly. Telling Lomax that he shouldn't blame himself at all, for any reason. Out of all of the three surviving children, Philip Lomax was the only one, as far as Roma could ascertain, that took the time to ensure that James Lomax in his twilight years was well looked after, and she also told Lomax, '…from what I've witnessed, Phil, you were the only one that truly cared about your father and loved him. I'm certain he always knew that.'

Hearing Roma say this was what caused Lomax to crack again, he began to sob, tears escaping freely, his chest heaving as Roma wrapped her arms around his shoulders and pulled his face into her chest.

Twelve

Monday 14th January.07.21 AM.

It had now been a week since DCI Lomax had suffered two harrowing experiences in his life. Yet what currently bugged him at the moment as he sat in the Briefing Room of the Incident Office area on the fourth floor of Earl's Court CID, was having to stare blankly at the whiteboard, with only a few extra different colour penned comments in two lists.

The first related to Amanda Waterman:

Age:42 years.

Occupation: Executive Overseas Marketing Manager for Vortexa Pharmaceuticals Ltd.

Criminal History:N/A

Preliminary Cause of Death:Deceleration trauma from height.

Vincent Robardi:

Age:32 years.

Occupation:Bar Waiter at Rossini's Italia Club, Trafalgar Sq.

Criminal History: Breach of The Peace and Assault 1998, Brighton, Sussex.

Cause of Death: Attempted suicide by drowning in The River Thames, after deliberately throwing himself off Westminster Bridge. Resulted in hard surface impact, broken neck and severed femoral artery and associated injuries on steel cover of passing barge.

Lomax sighed loudly. He closed his eyes.
He wished he knew the answers.

'Weren't the trace forensic material recovered from Vortexa Pharmaceuticals, Miss Waterman's covert laboratory and the Thames barge incidents results due to be handed in by now, sir?' asked DC Crosse, seated at a desk thumbing through some case notes.

Lomax opened his eyes once more and turned to look at his underling before he spoke. 'From what I understand, the tests are taking longer due to a backlog.'

'Can't we get a warrant to search the Vortexa building thoroughly, in case we've missed anything? I have the distinct feeling there's something screwy going on there. Especially if as you said, that's where you were taken against your will, sir,' DC Crosse said.

'Unfortunately,' DS Roma began saying as she entered the room, 'whoever was responsible for Miss Waterman's death at that location, if that happens to be the same individual that accosted *The Boss*', they've succeeded in locking down any legal matters relating to our obtaining access.'

'Roma's right,' Lomax added. 'I've argued with the Top Brass, but they've said, "…our hands are quite literally tied." It seems that their lawyers have quite literally pulled the rugs from under our feet.'

'This is bollocks,' DC Crosse said.

For three more hours they argued whether or not to try something… something ever so slightly risky. Then Lomax asked the team to go over all of the case notes and information they had to date, then as long as they'd been thorough, everyone could finish at five o'clock.

***

21.49 pm.

The huge office had been thoroughly vacuumed, wiped, polished, and disinfected the moment Lomax had been removed the previous week. No surface was left untouched; even though the captive had not been able to handle anything there was still a possibility that a small amount of DNA evidence may have been left.

The imposing figure drank from the snifter of whiskey, cradling the large piece of glassware at the base of the bowl above the short stem in his meaty large left hand. His thick dark eyebrows on the slightly pronounced brow were like canopies of dense foliage above the one intense eye, which exuded a most intense sense of foreboding from the man, towards anyone unlucky enough to find themselves at his displeasure and gaze. Such as the young woman being held before him at this moment.

She couldn't see his face. The bright lamp made her eyes sting, but she was unable to close her eyelids, as they'd been forced to remain open with short strips of medical tape.

'As I'm certain you're well aware,' the voice had the same air of contempt for those he felt were way beneath him, and it caused the twenty-six-year-old to shudder. 'I'm not one to suffer fools gladly, and nor do I appreciate my staff making calls to the police.'

'I didn't. Why would I?' the young woman said, her voice faltering into a sobbing wail. She breathed a deep breath to try to calm herself, 'I love working here. You've made a mistake. I haven't done anything I shouldn't.'

That was far from what the person seated behind the very same large oak topped desk, and the bright lamp, wished to be told. He stood up abruptly from the high-backed executive office chair, sending it rolling far behind him across the carpet and banging into the huge plate glass window with a hard thud.

Marching round the expansive desk, he decided he didn't care if she saw him. It wouldn't matter, not in the long run.

She was naked, restrained on an adjustable stretcher by straps to her wrists, thighs and ankles. An extremely attractive young woman with a blond bob-cut hairstyle which accentuated her natural beauty. Hazel eyes, red-rimmed from the soreness around her eyelids and bloodshot from continuous crying still shone with a degree of vulnerability, particularly now.

Her thighs were parted enough to expose her intimate area; her slender legs led the man's eyes to the well-trimmed thatch of pubic hair. Her legs were also slightly bruised, as were her upper arms from being gripped by vice-like hands. Her stomach was almost perfectly flat. She had pert but small pointy breasts. Nipples erect due to the chill she felt from the fear of what she was going to endure at the hands of this man.

He stepped into her line of sight, blocking the brightness of the lamp, but it took a while for her eyesight to recover. When she was able to see, albeit blurred, she noted that he'd undone his trousers and dropped his red boxer shorts, his shirt came undone next, and not only did she see his erect and circumcised penis, but that he was athletically perfect and in great shape for his age. The only thing that caused her to balk was the sight of his disfigured face.

He advanced, moving himself against her, sliding himself within her body, briefly finding slight resistance as he bore his manhood inside of her, grinding against her body, and picking up his pace. He caressed her breasts.

She cried out, 'Don't… please stop, don't do this to me.'

He grunted, ignoring her pleas. He continued thrusting while she cried, trying to block out this abuse; she would have tried to buck and resist, but being of a slight build, and him being much bigger and heavier, she knew it would have been pointless.

He took a few more moments before his release. He ejaculated; gave a final grunt, his face contorted. She felt him. Felt the warmth of his seed, something she'd not experienced before. Wanted to... but not like this. Not with this bastard of a man, but with Nathan. When they were married... on honeymoon in the Seychelles.

This was rape. Pure and simple. Unjustified.

He pulled his flaccid organ out, a satisfied grin on his face. The sudden sound of a loud crack reverberated within the office, making both of them jump. This resulted in a trickle of his semen to seep from between Gillian Radcliffe's legs.

He pulled up his boxers and trousers, walking towards the sound. He saw a huge crack in the glass. It began to creep its way up and down from the point of impact, where the back of his chair had struck the glass pane, spidering outwards towards the edges where the sheet glass was fixed to the framework.

Pressing a button on the intercom unit on the desk, he bellowed a command.

Moments later two burly men entered.

'Release her but guard the door,' the man said as he looked back at the cracking glass, which continued to split. 'Fuck it.'

The straps were relaxed, but not one of the men thought to keep a hold of the young woman. As she lay unrestrained she thought about what had just happened to her. She wondered if Nathan would ever forgive her for allowing this to happen; would he even still love her? She thought about this for only a few moments before she saw her one opportunity to resolve this awful situation; then, as her bare feet touched the carpeted section of the large office, she slipped between the men and charged towards the man who'd brutally raped her. She knew she could barge into him, hopefully sending him and herself through that window...

He caught a glimpse of the young woman's reflection in the glass as she made a dash towards him and he side-stepped at the last moment. Gillian Radcliffe struck the glass which instantly gave way with a thunderous ear-shattering *'kkrakk'*. Razor-sharp splinters of differing sizes lacerated her flesh across her body as she broke through the weakened ten-millimetre-thick glass.

Huge rents opened in her face, shoulders, chest, hips, thighs and feet as the splinters effortlessly sliced her skin deep to the bone. She found herself surprised, in shock, in acute agony and floating in mid-air for brief seconds as her body tumbled forwards, then gravity took hold, turning and rolling she plummeted to the ground, with other larger shards of glass raining down after her.

She struck the two-metre-high boundary wall that surrounded the southern wall of the building and provided an anti-flooding barrier to the building at West India Dock South. She impacted the surface on her right side and bounced over into the water where she floated briefly before she moved away with the tide.

The raining glass shattered on the concrete and broke into much smaller pieces.

It was fortuitous for the CEO that since Amanda Waterman's tragic *'accident'* late the previous year, he'd had the presence of mind, after her body had been removed, to close off the area to the public, by using the excuse that essential repairs and improvements were planned; tall wooden boards were erected to seal the section from public access. The only part that was open, strangely enough, was the exact spot where Gillian Radcliffe's body fell onto the boundary wall and *'bounced'* over into the water.

The man peered down past the framework, holding onto the face of the glass next to the now missing panel. A bitter wind passing through the gaping maw caused him to shudder and retreat to another smaller office on that floor, where a young man stood.

'Sir. I don't mean to sound impertinent, but two deaths from the same building within a couple of weeks, isn't that going to attract unwanted attention?' asked the slimmer man, David Carter, who'd entered moments after the two guards had accompanied their employer into the ante-office.

'David. My dear boy. You worry too much. I have everything under control.' Looking at his two high level operatives, Liam Garratt and Del Kingsley, he gave them a command. 'Get down there, clean up the glass. Find the body or make certain it's no longer possible to be connected with us. And David, call the maintenance dept., get them in to replace the window, I'm not freezing my bollocks here much longer. Oh, and make sure they use the specialised glass I requested last time. If they try screwing me over once more, I'll have their heads.'

David Carter seemed uncertain. He stood stiffly in his expensive Walter Hilfiger silver/grey three-piece suit, staring down at his Languin-Zoltar tan suede loafers. His white silk shirt with red piping around the collar and cuffs, and red tie with gold tie-pin shaped as an Egyptian ankh symbol.

David Carter a thirty-year-old post graduate in business economics from Cambridge University. He had been recruited as a result of his unorthodox business acumen. He had worked for his current employer for just over six years, and he had a nervous yet vicious streak of his own, which was being nurtured by the CEO of London's Vortexa Pharmaceutical Division.

'David, I want you to go back to the labs and prepare to immediately transfer the data logs of our *Special Project* back to Berlin, with back-up copies to our US, Australia and New Zealand divisions,' the CEO said as he approached the younger man, slipping his thick muscular arm around the younger man's shoulder.

He spoke in a low voice as he led Carter back to the door. Then he went back and looking down out of the rent where the large glass panel had been, with the cold breeze of a wintry evening entering the building and enveloping his body, he smiled.

***

Four floors of the Vortexa Pharmaceutical building housed the legitimate laboratories which comprised of the experimentation development and production facilities. Then there were the two floors that contained the *special* laboratories, and it was these which were centralised deliberately in the middle of the legitimate production and research laboratories and kept well away from the prying eyes of the police, as they held some extremely secretive aspects. The officers that had conducted the initial crime scene surrounding Amanda Waterman's death, and the subsequent tour of the offices and laboratories, were only shown the legitimate side of the business. The tour had been deliberately designed so as to disorientate those attending, to make them think that they'd actually seen all of the laboratories, when in fact they had been shown two laboratories twice but entering from different directions. Different staff had also been drafted in from other departments, told to follow routine procedures including the donning of white lab coats or all-in-one suits and associated PPE.

Set over the six floors in the upper section of the building, just below the executive office level, two of the floors were legitimately dedicated to humanitarian research and development of medicine. The central two levels contained the *specialist* laboratories. The smaller one for production of hybrid organisms, the other and largest one, had sinister and nefarious purposes.

Vortexa's CEO had been on an extensive expedition in the South American countries of Peru, Chile, and Venezuela, Ecuador, and Bolivia as well as the western edge of the Brazilian rainforests. Taking with him some specialist scientists that sought to collect as many of the most potent plants and creatures that have the means to defend themselves.

They collected the poisonous blue and yellow tree frogs, which exude a poisonous secretion through their skin, as well as the red one. They captured poisonous snakes and regularly de-venomed them during their stay until they had accumulated enough samples.

With the sufficient supply acquired, they shipped the 'cargo' back in specially designed cartons, made to appear as though they were transporting contagious and diseased human organs for study, and therefore could not be opened and scrutinised.

For the past three years, specialist chemists and bio-geneticists worked hand-in-hand developing a number of different toxins. But there was one type of synthesised combination that the CEO was particularly interested in.

He had specifically placed a team of eight scientists to work solely on his 'project' which he had code-named 'Overlord'. They worked, slept and lived on the one floor that only they had access to apart from the CEO himself. Not one of those eight people were able to leave the building under any circumstances either. When their twelve-hour shifts were over, they went to an area contained within that floor, which served as their living/sleeping/rest quarters. The police were being kept at extreme arm's length regarding obtaining permission to make a second detailed search of the entire building. The CEO's lawyers were certainly earning their money, keeping the CID and in particular DCI Lomax and his team at bay through placing legal barriers in their path.

The tests conducted in the early stages had mixed results. The number of people going missing had increased way above the national averages for those periods when it was almost accepted that a certain number of people would disappear, usually between mid-October and late February. The fact that many of those that went missing, they would more often than not only be reported missing many weeks if not months later. This of course proved to be very awkward for DCI Lomax, his team and the investigation as a whole.

Men and women from the street, often unemployed and usually homeless, aged between seventeen and thirty-six were generally targeted, usually enticed by the promise of a financial reward, although Amanda Waterman was the exception to the rule when she died. Verity Bracknell and Dean Morgan were also exceptions, as Vortexa's CEO was keen to see if 'ordinary' people could be drawn into his tests, albeit his method of acquiring Verity and Dean was far more deviously deployed.

Vortexa's other legitimate corporate divisions, headed by lower importance but still high management employees, were also completely unaware of the vastly illegal processes and activities. They reported to their own high-level executives, who then supposedly reported to the CEO. Lomax's attempts to secure the opportunity to question every member of Vortexa's personnel was thwarted directly by the company's lawyers.

To say Lomax was becoming increasingly angry concerning the lack of progress was extremely accurate.

***

Tuesday 15th January.

DCI Lomax lay in the bed, his eyes wide open. He wore his new watch – the old one had broken during the kidnapping – bought for him by Roma; he looked at the luminous dial. It read at being just after seven ten am.

He felt the soft arm move slightly across his stomach. Looking down he ran one of his hands through the thick dark hair of the woman, whose face lay resting on his chest, rising and falling with his breathing. Roma murmured softly, her skin aglow from the sexually charged few hours they'd spent making love at her sister Helena's home while she was away in the Maldives.

They'd both agreed it was best, as they also felt their own homes may be compromised. That's not to say, that if they've been followed recently without being aware of it, that this place was now under surveillance as well, but it was a risk they were willing to take.

Lomax felt relaxed, contented and he knew that without fail he was definitely falling for his colleague in such a way it could easily cause problems at work if it became public knowledge.

But he *didn't* care. It had indeed been a while since he'd been closely involved with a woman. He hadn't intentionally gone all out to seduce DS Roma Clarkson, but over the last couple of years working together, (and working particularly well, developing an excellent rapport with her), he'd noticed that on the odd occasion she'd been covertly flirting with him. He knew, as did she, the ramifications of a work-related relationship.

The last couple of weeks had been shitty. Mega shitty. Yet being with Roma had given his conscience some respite, and his confidence one huge boost. He found himself being drawn deeper into developing true loving feelings for his thirty-three-year-old colleague, whose body had been well maintained, and she only *appeared* to look in her twenties.

He was reminded of a woman whom he'd previously been extremely fond of. And had seriously been prepared to commit his life to several years before.

Hannah-Faye Houghton was twenty-five years old when she and Lomax had been together. He was also twenty-five, back in 1991, and Lomax was a lowly beat copper pounding the streets of London.

He and Hannah-Faye had not long been involved.

Just over seven months since he'd saved her from dying in a near fatal traffic accident on New Oxford Street, at the junction with Bloomsbury St.

A stolen red Routemaster 66 London Transport bus rammed into the driver's side, killing Hannah-Faye's favourite cousin Jamie, who was only just eighteen at the time, and had been driving the Mini. The car erupted into flames almost immediately, enveloping the small vehicle. Lomax knew that due to the speed and weight of the bus, there was little or nothing he could have done for the driver. He got to the passenger side door, and after a tense few minutes, wrenched the door open, unclipped the safety belt, pulled her free, moving her far enough away before the car and the bus blew up, showering the street with shrapnel.

Innocent bystanders were showered with white hot pieces of metal and plastic. Lomax had covered Hannah-Faye with his body. It was a scene of utter chaos and carnage.

It was discovered that the thief was a lone Iraqi terrorist transporting a bomb towards the main shopping area of Oxford Street and preparing to detonate it during the busiest time of day on a Saturday, in the summer. Jamie was turning into Bloomsbury St., from New Oxford Street when the bus driver panicked and swerved, losing control, and crashing into the small car that was seriously damaged, causing the fire to spread quickly.

Lomax was hailed a hero, and Hannah-Faye began dating him. But as the fickle hand of fate was tempted to screw things up for

Lomax, as it usually did, Hannah-Faye died in late 2000, by ovarian cancer which was a specifically aggressive strain and particularly difficult to treat, let alone diagnose, until it was too far advanced. Lomax was distraught, as he'd recently been accepted into the CID as a rookie DC, and he was getting ready to propose marriage.

The mobile on the bedside table began to vibrate and warble. He answered it, though the conversation was very brief and to the point. He said goodbye and ended the call.

'Who was it?' asked Roma, sleepily, as she looked up into Lomax's deeply captivating eyes.

'DC Crosse. It seems I've, sorry… *we've* got ourselves a *'floater'*,' Lomax said, a serious expression on his weary face.

Roma nuzzled his stomach, kissing his slight paunch and running her fingers through the thick mass of chest hair as she worked her mouth further down towards his rousing organ.

'Stop that,' Lomax said, a hearty guffaw exploding from his lips, 'we've got to get dressed and get to the SOC.' However, they made love again in the shower, then cleansed themselves and each other, hoping to clear any 'evidence' from being detected by their colleagues. It was just after eight-fifteen when they left. Dressed smart and comfortable.

Roma drove the silver pool Vectra, which she'd retained overnight having finished late, with Lomax not far ahead in his Maestro, hoping to give the impression they'd intended to meet at the scene. Lomax hoped that neither he nor Roma had given away too many indications for anyone to suspect that they were involved.

They parked up within metres of each other and barely nine minutes apart.

DS Clarkson climbed out of her pool car and walked the twenty-seven metres towards the steps cordoned off with the blue and white tape with the legend - *POLICE LINE DO NOT CROSS* - printed along its length. She saw Lomax squatting beside a pale, bloated corpse, with another person who she instantly recognised as Dr Sally Hickton. Roma flashed her warrant card at the uniformed female officer guarding the steps and who happened to be the very same one who had nearly arrested her superior officer recently. It was obvious the WPC recognised DCI Lomax when he approached her, and now she had to bow deference to DS Clarkson. Roma made her way down the steps gingerly, as they were covered in a light film of green moss and patches of seaweed.

Roma made her way across the mud and shingle mudflat, wearing her own pale blue wellingtons with a daisy flower pattern. As she arrived on the scene, just a few feet back from where DCI Lomax crouched, she saw the dark marks which randomly spotted the wrinkled flesh, which were obviously bites from the marine life in the Thames, taking the opportunity to feast upon a fresh food supply.

Several rib bones protruded from the right side of the upper torso. It was also possible to see severe abrasions on the entire length on that side of the body.

'Sir?' Roma said, keeping about ten feet back on the fine pebble and sand/muddied shoreline. Wearing her matching dark blue velvet skirt and jacket suit, the skirt's hem finishing slightly above her knees. DS Clarkson gave the appearance that she was on her way to a social family event, rather than coming to view a corpse, apart from the wellington boots.

'Be with you in a moment, Detective Sergeant,' Lomax replied, trying to sound just officious enough without upsetting her.

Dr Sally Hickton knelt on the special plastic boards placed atop the soft quaggy mire near the water, a distance from the slightly more stable area, where DS Clarkson stood. She wore her obligatory all-in-one paper forensic suit, with a pair of white wellington boots smeared with the slimy foul-smelling green mud and was making observational comments into a portable diction machine. Wearing latex gloves, with a small ice-cooler sized box containing her tools and equipment beside her, Dr Sally Hickton worked meticulously as she examined the corpse.

'The body was washed onto the mud-flats, on the northern bank close to Victoria Embankment, and discovered at oh-six-forty-seven by a middle-aged female jogger, on her daily run, approximately three hundred metres west of Temple Pier,' Sally Hickton said, her voice devoid of emotive inflection. 'Approximate age, twenty-one to twenty-five years. Blond hair natural. Eyes hazel. Severe bruising to upper and lower arms and the same to legs especially the inner upper thighs, within the genital region. Evidence of multiple glass incisions, maybe from a fall from height through an industrial strength window? I have removed small glass pieces from the flesh of the upper arms, and fleshy sections of the hips and thighs, and placed them in sterilised evidence phials, prior to autopsy. Potential evidence of sexual intercourse present although likely to be compromised by contamination by river water. Approximate time of death, somewhere within the last twelve to eighteen hours.'

Lomax jerked involuntarily. 'You just said possible glass incision, maybe from a fall from height and through industrial strength glass?'

Sally nodded. 'Why do you ask... oh,' she remembered. 'The Vortexa building in Docklands. The window with the slight defect?'

'Yup. I don't suppose you recall what floor that was on, do you?' Lomax asked.

'Forty-eighth, I think. The executive offices floor. That tower has fifty floors in total, the top two incorporating the maintenance for elevators, heating, climate control and the uppermost housing a covered heli-pad,' Hickton said.

'Smart-arse. How do you know that?' Lomax asked.

'I'm interested in modern architecture,' came the simple reply.

DC Crosse stood a few feet away, as did DC Greggs. 'How does the pathologist know she's a natural blond?' DC Greggs asked.

DC Crosse sighed. 'Don't you know nuttin'? By looking at her pubic hair of course. The pubis area of both male and females is very sensitive to the high-profile branded hair dyes, and usually reacts, often painfully, if they're used in areas they're not intended for. Therefore, most people don't dye their pubes, leaving them in their natural colour, or shaving them.'

DC Greggs shrugged his shoulders. 'Oh... I see, yes, of course.'

DC Crosse grinned knowingly, 'of course, had she been a black woman, we'd never be too sure now, would we?'

DC Greggs sighed again. 'Arsehole.'

DC Crosse laughed, patting his colleague on the back.

'I'll meet you back at the mortuary, Sally,' Lomax said. 'Continue with the PM as normal, and if you could get your report to me ASAP, I'd very much appreciate it.'

'I'll do my utmost,' Dr Hickton announced, not even looking back as Lomax rose and walked back over the tread-boards put over the mud to reach and make retrieval of the body easier.

'Any idea who she is?' Roma asked as they walked back up the stone steps to where the cars were parked on the main road.

'No, I asked Sally that as soon as I arrived. There were no items that could give us a definitive clue as to her identity. She may well have floated for some distance. Completely naked, no personal effects. No rings, bracelets. No tattoos or body piercings. No apparent operation scars. Nothing,' Lomax said, adding, 'It's likely that she could well be completely disassociated with our case altogether.'

'I don't suppose it would be worth trying the MPD?' She asked.

'Give it a go,' he replied, 'you never know what may turn up.'

DS Clarkson went to the Vectra and called the Incident Room Secretary. 'Check the Missing Person's Database for the past four weeks, see if anyone's reported a twenty-one- to twenty-five-year-old female, IC-one, blond hair, no distinguishing marks known at present, but that doesn't mean she may not have any. Liaise with the pathologist for updates on any body tattoos, piercing, and birthmarks. This is essential. Please keep me informed of any progress, good or bad, thank you.'

Lomax's mobile rang, and he answered it. 'Lomax here.'

'Chief Superintendent Warwick. Lomax, I need to see you urgently. Be in my office within the next twenty minutes, if you wouldn't mind,' came the curt response.

The call was ended before Lomax could respond. He momentarily considered calling back and stalling this intrusion into his investigation, but his curiosity was piqued. Although Chief Superintendent Warwick's tone didn't sound too officious, it wasn't friendly either.

'Detective Sergeant Clarkson,' Lomax began, speaking clear and loudly so the others could hear, 'I have to go to headquarters, as I have been summoned by God's Underling.'

'Do you want me to accompany you?' DS Clarkson asked, moving up to her boss, and speaking quietly.

'No thank you,' Lomax replied, also keeping his voice low. 'I'm expecting to get my bollocks shredded yet again, and I don't think you'd appreciate bearing witness to that,' he said, a slight grin appearing on his face, as he remembered how they'd spent the previous night, as well as barely an hour earlier.

As he drove away, he smiled to himself. His emotive state was on a massive high.

At least it was, until he walked into Chief Superintendent Warwick's outer office at twelve-fifty-five and was greeted by Brigitte Ellis. Her expression was, as normal, unreadable.

'Hello, Detective Inspector Lomax. I'll let Chief Superintendent Warwick know you've arrived,' Brigitte Ellis said, seeing him enter her domain from the hallway door, as she filed some folders in one of the many filing cabinets that lined the west wall.

As Brigitte knocked and entered the inner sanctum that was Chief Superintendent Warwick's kingdom, Lomax smiled. Brigitte obviously forgot that he'd been promoted, or she simply wasn't aware.

'Send him in,' bellowed the loud voice of Chief Superintendent Warwick, overly emphasised for Lomax's benefit. This probably wasn't going to be as straightforward as he'd originally thought.

Brigitte stepped back through and held the door open for Lomax. Her new expression said it all.

This *was* going to be bad. *Bad indeed.*

'Sit,' the deep resounding voice of Warwick commanded, gesturing towards the only vacant seat in the room, on a mediocre sofa in tan cloth set against the side wall. Lomax stepped over and plonked himself hesitantly on the sofa.

For some unknown reason, his hands felt clammy. Hoping not to be noticed, he loosened the top button of his new shirt, and the red tie he wore, bought for him by DS Clarkson.

In the room were two strangers, seated in the more comfortable chairs. A man and a woman.

Warwick stood up, went to the window and looked out across Holland Park, which he could just glimpse above the roofs of the school and the Post Office ahead of him. Some citizens were walking their dogs, even in this cold weather.

Turning to his left he looked at Lomax, who chanced to look his way. 'Detective Chief Inspector Lomax, I'd like to introduce you to two Interpol officers, Inspector Claude D'Ebeauville and Sergeant Marianne Clourette.'

Lomax stood up and stepped towards the newcomers. They both stood up and shook hands with Lomax.

Inspector D'Ebeauville was tall, standing just short of six feet. He had a puffy face, but he was still handsome. Dark brown eyes, bright and alert. A slender nose and beaming mouth. Olive skinned. His jet-black hair was slicked back and parted in the centre. He wore fashionable rectangular spectacles.

By contrast, Sergeant Marianne Clourette was stunningly beautiful. Shorter by a full foot in height than her superior. An hour-glass figure. Chestnut hair framed her face in a casual style then at the rear cascaded a long way down at the back and formed a slightly curved shape in-line with the piping line of her jacket across her lower back just above her buttocks, which were encased in the almost skin-tight trousers of the dark red cotton suit she wore. The white blouse was open to the collar of the jacket and stopped upper-chest and showed an ample amount of décolletage. A small pendant hung around her neck on a gold chain.

Marianne's face was slender, a chiselled chin which jutted significantly forward much like Sophie Ellis-Bextor, whom Marianne reminded Lomax off immensely. She had similarly big oval eyes, a pointy small nose and a large-lipped mouth. She wore a deep red lip gloss, and her general make-up was stunning. She certainly was a looker. Lomax swiftly averted his gaze from the female guest and swiftly looked at his boss.

'Bonjour monsieur Lomax,' she said in French, though seeing the puzzled look, she then spoke in flawless English, 'do you speak French?'

Lomax watched her lips, mesmerised by her mouth, then he chastised himself inwardly. 'No, I'm sorry. Nothing at all.'

'Never mind, perhaps one day you'll learn,' she said.

'Please excuse my colleague, Mr Lomax... Marianne has this terrible affliction towards English men,' Inspector D'Ebeauville said. His own accent clear, receiving a playful tap on his arm from Marianne.

Chief Superintendent Warwick sighed impatiently. 'Philip. I've agreed with Interpol for these two officers to join your team as observers at first. They may be brought into the case, as they have acquired some information from installations in Europe, connected to Vortexa, and which may have implications concerning your investigations.'

'Sir, I don't mean to sound impertinent, and I apologise to you both, but why? Why this early into the investigation?' Lomax asked.

'Philip... from what I've observed so far regarding your handling of this case, especially since your father's recent passing away, there have been very similar deaths in northern European countries, such as Holland, France, Belgium and Germany which defy explanation.

Apparently, the information I have been made aware of may well be directly connected with your investigation, but then again it may not.

'This is why these two Interpol officers will remain as observers only, but also to explain the information they have kindly imparted to me, and until further information leads me to conclude that we shall definitely be joining forces. Of course, they have already agreed that this information is to be made available to you and your team.' Warwick's determination with his decision was obvious.

Lomax drove his car the short journey across London with his passengers back to Dunne House. Lomax led the way back through the six-storey building to the Investigation Room on the fourth floor, where the current case was being worked. DS Clarkson, DC Crosse and DC Greggs who had returned from the crime scene about forty-five minutes earlier, were collating what information they'd acquired onto the computer system, and what little there was being penned on the whiteboard, which painfully showed that they had very little to go on. Even though quite a significant number of events – drastic and painfully fatal events for the victims – had occurred in a considerably short time. So, with the assistance of a force technical specialist, all the information gathered so far was being entered into HOLMES, the Home Office Large Major Enquiry System, which cross referenced every minute detail of the investigation, including all of the results from the post-mortems, and correlated them into something that, in time, would break the back of this case. If not, perhaps give the officers something tangible to tie into whatever suspicions or leads they had.

Lomax introduced the Interpol officers to the senior members of the team, and then the other officers and civilian assistants.

'Since Amanda Waterman's death, on the thirtieth of December last year, there have been a further two unexplained deaths, which cannot be classified as natural causes,' Lomax began saying, as a lead-in to explaining the mainstay of the case, which was clouding his waking hours. For the next fifty minutes or so, he ran the two Interpol officers through most of what he and his team had witnessed, discovered, and what evidence had been retrieved from the scenes.

DS Clarkson sat at her desk, in the small office she shared with Lomax. The door was open, and she could see him speaking to the two Interpol officers. The moment Roma clapped eyes on the French woman, the green pangs of envy – closely followed by the red haze of jealousy – sparked into life.

She knew it was foolish, childish even, yet she immediately felt that she could be in danger of losing her place in Lomax's life, *his private life.*

She thought about eavesdropping. Lomax unexpectedly glanced back into his office, and just caught her looking pensively his way.

He looked away again.

Lomax asked Crosse and Greggs to show the Interpol guests around the CID suite, and then to take them to the nearest hotel, where they'd been allocated a room for the duration of their stay.

After dealing with a mountain of paperwork, taking numerous telephone calls, and making several more to his various sources, Lomax decided to stop for the day. He was feeling both tired and elated at the same time, but he had also felt a slight tinge of concern. He glanced at the clock on the wall above the main door.

19:59 PM.

'You shit,' Roma said, when Lomax turned up at her first floor flat in Lansdowne Walk, Notting Hill later that evening. Lomax had decided to ask the tech team to go over both his own house as well as DS Clarkson's own place, for any covert listening devices or secreted video equipment. The outcome was that the tech people found nothing whatsoever.

DS Clarkson had left the Incident Room at five-forty, in a decidedly frosty mood, long before Lomax. Since the two Interpol officers had arrived at the station, she'd had no direct contact or conversation with Lomax for the better part of the day since he returned from seeing CS Warwick.

'I saw you ogling her tits as you briefed those Interpol officers,' she said.

Lomax could that tell she was upset. Very upset. He felt terrible.

Christ. They'd not been involved five minutes and already things were turning really shitty... again.

'I suppose you'd like to come in?' Roma asked. She stepped back pulling the door wider so he could step through. He hesitated briefly. She slammed the door shut after he passed by her, keeping his front facing her; behind him he had a carrier bag containing flowers, wine and chocolates. He waited for her go by and then followed her to her living room.

Roma was wearing a short towelling bathrobe in a pale shade of lavender. It stopped about mid-thigh, and the tie-belt wasn't pulled taut. The top was low cut, showing a large expanse of oiled cleavage, as was the rest of her skin. Roma regularly lotioned her body to try to keep herself younger and she was succeeding. It smelled of coconuts, reminding Lomax of his favourite confectionery, second to Mars Bars: Bounty.

She took the glass of white wine she'd been drinking before he'd arrived and took a sip, eyeing him over the rim, trying to read his expression.

He was looking pensive. Wondering whether it was such a good idea to come here at all. But then he'd recalled last night, and how much he – and, he hoped Roma – had enjoyed the closeness. The intimacy.

'Look,' he began, his voice sounding feeble, slightly panicky, after setting the bag down on the nearby armchair. 'I'm sorry if you believe I was flirting with that French Interpol officer. I was only trying to be polite, and besides...' he tried to think of the correct words to explain.

'Besides what?' Roma asked, her tone cutting, suspicious, painfully bitter.

'She's married,' he said. 'I thought I'd already told you, I never mess with married women, and in any case...'

Roma raised her eyebrows, her eyes widening in expectation of some surprisingly amazing piece of information. She felt her heart rate speed up, her breathing laboured and she also felt suddenly dizzy.

'Inspector Claude D'Ebeauville is Marianne's husband,' he said, matter-of-factly.

'How do you know?' Roma asked.

'I saw her wedding band, they were kissing passionately when they were waiting to be taken to their hotel. DC Crosse caught them and told me.'

'She's a tad too flirtatious though, isn't she? I mean the way she dresses in public, like that? Besides, I clocked the way she was looking at you,' Roma said, trying not to sound too relieved or too scathingly bitchy at the same time. Before Lomax could answer the question, she placed the wine glass on the coffee table, and ran to him, throwing her arms around his neck, jumping up wrapping her legs around his waist, almost knocking him off balance, and planting her lips firmly against his.

Their tongues slipped over each other's, exploring the warmth and wetness of each other's mouths.

Lomax immediately caught the strong odour of the scent she wore, Lace by Yardley. It was one he particularly favoured, and one he bought for Hannah-Faye for their first week's anniversary.

He felt Roma's hands move, stroking his neck, following the line of his cheekbones to his chin. Minutes later, the bathrobe was flung off to one side. Lomax was soon naked too, Roma had swiftly undressed him, while at the same time she teased his flesh, running her hands over his body, and kissing his legs, his knees, and his thighs. She played with him, even though he needed little encouragement to become fully aroused.

He responded equally. Even though she'd bathed, or showered, she still gave off that hint of female muskiness; that heightened sexual odour, released by the hormones, triggered when aroused.

By the time they'd finished some time later, they were both bathed in a sheen of perspiration. Their hair was matted and 'stringy', then when they made as to separate their bodies from one another after the final kiss, their flesh having adhered to one another, he peeled himself away stickily with a resounding *'squelch'*.

Lomax was the first to start laughing loudly, swiftly followed by Roma giggling like a schoolgirl.

'That's rude,' Roma said, then adding, 'and disgusting.'

'Well… it wasn't me,' Lomax claimed, bursting into laughter once again.

'I'm sorry for accusing you earlier,' Roma said, kissing his shoulder lightly. 'I'm just so afraid of being hurt like I was before. You've told me about Hannah-Faye, and I realise that you still have feelings and strong, deep memories about her. You've been so honest and up-front about your past, right from the beginning. Although I've held back from telling you about my past experiences…'.

'Tell me whenever you're ready,' Lomax said simply. His tone comforted Roma.

Thirteen

Wednesday 16th January 08:28 AM.

Vortexa's CEO glanced down once more at the file set before him less than twenty minutes earlier. He'd studied them meticulously; it would be fair to say that he was definitely far from pleased by the results of the experiments.

'How many test subjects are we left with at present?' he asked the person seated to his left at the twenty-foot-long conference table in the briefing room on the forty-seventh floor. One level down from his expansive office suite.

'Nine, in total,' Sandranna Jorgensen the Swedish female replied. Originally hailing from Stockholm's Institute of Infectious Disease Kontrol, she was the atypical platinum blonde, slim Swedish female. Her flesh was almost like porcelain; a creamy white with no blemishes whatsoever, no moles, no freckles, and not one single scar.

A health nut, who preferred to live on vegan-style foods, and natural yoghurts which she always prepared herself from freshly purchased ingredients on a daily basis. Sandranna was a no-nonsense person. Thirty-seven years old, she completed a doctorate when only nineteen at Stockholm University for Biological Studies and Viral Complexities in Hormones and Hypnotic Causalities.

Jorgensen was discovered by the CEO when he discovered she was being investigated by the FBI when she visited America in 1996, aged twenty-five, and was implicated in several unexplained deaths of young students at a college in Alabama. She'd been caught conducting several experiments with various hallucinatory fungi, and copious mixtures of class A drugs.

Realising how she would benefit his endeavours, he acquired the services of a few 'experts' that succeeded in intercepting the convoy taking her from the courthouse to the penitentiary. With a masterful degree of brilliance, the 'experts' disposed of the accompanying police vehicles, and after rendering the guards incapacitated, Sandranna was freed and taken overseas by private sailing yacht out of San Diego and US waters.

Sandranna was one of five top scientists the CEO employed to develop his personal endeavours, and she was in fact the second-in-command, behind Austrian chemist Helmut Grüber-Stahlmann. A world-renowned past Nobel Prize Winner in 1997 and recognised for his work in developing cancerous cell inhibitors using some of the compounds from the most toxic substances found in plants and amphibian and sea creatures, through some unexpected and remarkable experiments.

Experiments which were conducted on human test subjects (mostly life imprisonment members from some of the world's prisons – who had been offered a degree of reduction of, or commutation of their sentences as a prelude in getting them to sign the appropriate official paperwork.) However, most of them died from complications and serious reactions to the test sample doses.

'Out of those nine,' Grüber-Stahlmann began saying, 'five are totally unacceptable to work with. Sandranna feels that their history of heavy drug dependence would react in a negative fashion to your compound. The abuse their bodies has taken from the illegal drugs would cause the compound to totally fry their insides, resulting in total organ failure. I was certain that your choice to bring in people off the streets, or abducting them from drug-rehab clinics, would pose problems.'

At sixty-four years of age, Grüber-Stahlmann still sported a full head of thick wavy jet-black hair. His chiselled Germanic/Austrian features had made him an extremely handsome man, and his intense green eyes usually captivated the attention of any woman who met him. In his latter ten years he was a bit of a womaniser and had sustained a fair number of facial disfigurements from the boyfriends or husbands of the women he became involved with, which caused him to hide away. That is of course until Vortexa's mysterious CEO learned of him, enticed him to move to London.

As with the other scientists and subordinate workers taken on to develop the project, Grüber-Stahlmann lived in lavish furnished quarters in a section of the main floor containing the secret labs and was directed never to leave the building under any circumstance. Even in the event of a fire, or any other major catastrophe. This came after three low-key employees concerned with developing the materials and substances were severely punished for attempting to slip out to go into the city and have some fun. It was a painful lesson, not only for the unfortunates, but also those who obeyed the rules. The CEO proved himself to be a fearful employer.

Overseen by Helmut Grüber-Stahlmann and Sandranna Jorgensen, the shift-pattern workers constantly synthesised the raw products and inserted them into specially designed devices, which could be used by assassins all around the world.

Sandranna cut in. 'However... we have set up a test with the latest batch of your project, and with two of the more favourable prisoners we have available.'

The lab was segregated into eight separate sections covering the entire forty-fourth floor of the towering building. The exterior walls had similar thick sheet glass panels as that covering the majority of the building, but behind the glass were solid four-foot-thick reinforced concrete walls. In a glass walled room, off to one side of the lab, a section of the floor opened as a sloping surface rose from below. A smart young man, aged approximately twenty-eight, dressed in a dark blue cotton bathrobe, lay seemingly asleep. His thick dark brown hair was cut to a short but neat style. He was decidedly handsome for a man who'd been abducted two days earlier, on his way home from his job at an accountancy office near Trafalgar Square.

CCTV cameras linked directly to the office a few floors up, showed the man beginning to wake up. A small earpiece was fitted in the man's right ear, where as he was regaining consciousness, he began to hear a pre-recorded command.

When the woman enters, you will greet her with a handshake and a smile. Then you will kiss her passionately; she will resist, you shall throw her onto the bed removing her garments, and you will force her into having sex. Afterwards, you shall take the knife from under the mattress without her seeing you do it, you will then cut her throat.'

The door opened, and a beautiful young woman entered. She too had been pre-programmed by a sedative/hypnotic drug-induced suggestion. She wore a pink see-through negligee showing just a small pair of panties and matching bra.

He approached her, grabbing her hand and kissed her, she reciprocated. Then he began to slip his tongue into her mouth while ripping her nightwear from her body. She was twenty-seven years old. She started resisting but he was stronger. Carrying her onto the bed he forced her into submission. After he had finished, he rolled her onto her back, her legs splayed wide, bruises forming from the aggressive attack. He took the large hunting knife from its hidden place and drove the point into the hollow in the girl's throat.

The flesh yielded effortlessly, as soon as the razor-sharp point overcame the brief resistance and was driven past the musculature within the neck. As he drew the serrated blade across, from side to side, major blood vessels were severed and the crimson liquid gushed freely. Her eyes widened, and as her blood poured back into her throat she gurgled and her body flinched briefly for a few seconds, then went limp. Blood seeped from the nasal passages and her mouth, down the side of her face and onto the white bed sheet, the material soaking up the coppery fluid.

The male test subject stared blankly for several moments before his eyes glazed over. He turned his head from side to side, a puzzled and frightened expression forming on his features – a look of remorse? Then he promptly removed the knife from the woman's throat, turning it round he plunged the point of the blade into his own chest, directly into his own heart. He slumped on top of the woman.

'Damn,' the CEO bellowed from his office.

'That's the *heart* of the problem,' Grüber-Stahlmann began saying, 'for some unknown reason, the compound when introduced directly into the pituitary, isn't being absorbed proficiently enough to take overall control of the subject's subconscious. It also appears to cause immediate suicidal tendencies.'

'I think though that your expectations of using this method of undermining enemies' morality through sexually contrived means will never succeed in any case,' Jorgensen said.

'And why is that?' asked the CEO, his tone showing his mood was still to be lifted.

'Because the sexual drive of individuals is something that is far too complex, that's why, sir. The sexually emotive state of humans is far different than that of animals. The animal kingdom isn't driven by thoughts of love and affection as we humans are. Animals mate purely for instinctive reasoning, to procreate and to keep the bloodline going, even though many species do pair up for life in general.

'The human brain has developed over tens of thousands of years into a living organ, far greater than any computer we could build to do all the tasks in life.' She took a breath and a sip of water before continuing. 'Think about it, if the human race hadn't developed the way it has with intelligence, we wouldn't be sitting here now in this tower. There'd be no transportation, cars, planes or ships, no computers, no internet, no TV, radio or even space travel. Humans have,' she paused to collect her thoughts and to give a valid explanation, '…in all essence become an overwhelming plague on this planet. We kill in the name of religion, because of our faiths and beliefs. Humans take land from others without remorse, without concern for the others' welfare. They steal other men's wives or girlfriends, husbands or boyfriends dependent of gender, just because they're jealous of what another has. So, they take indiscriminately, regardless of how it makes the other person feel; they have no morality. They value beauty, or handsomeness above intellect. I also believe that conceit and narcissism play an integral controlling role in the overall psyche of the human mind.'

'So, basically what you're actually trying to tell me, Sandranna, is that because of the human mind's structure, total brainwashing is impossible? In other words, hypnotists like Paul McKenna are frauds?' The CEO asked.

'In short, yes. I've never held any belief in hypnotism. The conscience element of the human mind is far too intricate. No matter what someone does to force the mind to do, after trying to put the person into a trance, the mind will always fight against any adverse commands which it believes is contrary to its individuality. Fictional novels and films are simply playing with an idea that cannot be proven to succeed,' Sandranna said.

'And just what is *your view*, Helmut?'

'I'm afraid I agree with Sandranna. Her extensive tests on the subjects acquired have proven without a shadow of doubt that your project will always remain flawed, as the human brain is far too complex to control one hundred percent, or without something going amiss. I'd have thought that the recent example of the man on the bridge was evidence enough.'

'I need the two of you to continue working on that. I need results and I need them to prove my theory, I need you to concentrate on making this product a success, otherwise should this entire project fail it is something which *the two of you* cannot afford to let happen.' The CEO left the conference room, with a dark cloud hanging over him. What portion of his face they were afforded to see, left nothing to the imagination.

Sandranna and Grüber-Stahlmann both knew exactly what the CEO implied with that statement.

The CEO sat down on the sofa in his private suite next to his large open-plan office, with a large snifter glass of Rémy Martin whiskey being swirled around. He'd had his idea for this hypnotic 'product' for several years, and he'd intended that it would be placed on the international 'black market', using a specifically mega-encrypted web site targeting known terrorist organisations.

The CEO of Vortexa was operating his own system of distribution of deadly bio-virus weapons, which in all honesty, the remaining directors in the offices and development laboratories in Berlin (Germany), Hamilton (New Zealand), Montgomery, Alabama (United States of America), and Rotterdam, (Holland), knew nothing about.

***

District Line, westbound tunnel
South Kensington heading to Earl's Court tube station.

The high-pitched screech of metal upon metal reverberated through the tunnel, but the unfortunate driver of the tube train didn't stand a chance. Three bodies were dropped from a section of the tunnel roof one after the other just as the train passed an electronically wired sensor. The speed of the train was sufficient to send each one spiralling forwards, from the impact out of the dark maw, directly into the brightly lit area of track where the packed platform would witness the carnage.

Limbs were torn from the bodies as they were struck, and the bloodied pieces of flesh and bone either bounced off the tiled walls where posters covered as much advertising space available, or rolled along the tracks, causing electrical sparks to arc out. Other pieces and streaks of blood and other bodily liquids and matter sprayed out across the newly installed Perspex exterior Platform Anti-Suicide/Accident Barriers. (PASABs).

Several people passed out immediately. One person died of a heart attack caused by the shock and several vomited; the majority backed away and began stampeding towards the exits, causing a wave of hysteria.

Tony Grant, a London Underground supervisor was on duty at the time monitoring the passengers during rush hour, tried to restore calm, but his calls were unheard above the screams and shouts. He grabbed his radio walkie-talkie and quickly ordered the westbound District Line between South Kensington and Earl's Court to be shut down, so that no further trains followed and ploughed into the rear of the train that was now stationary, and would no doubt remain so for some time.

As the stream of fleeing travellers bounded up and out of the station, British Transport Police officers Paul Ross, Chel Parrish and Bob Davies were fighting their way through the mass of screaming and shouting men and women, some dragging their screaming and crying children or carrying them. An elderly man, partially blind and using a white stick to guide him, was knocked to the ground then trampled by several people during the mad escape.

If PC Paul Ross, a huge example of mankind at well over six feet, and broad to match, hadn't barged through the exodus and yanked the man out of harm's way, the gentleman would have easily perished. Emergency paramedics arrived on the scene, along with the fire service and street police officers, and the elderly man was taken to safety and cared for.

Once the fleeing crowd had thinned out to a few bewildered stragglers, Tony Grant was joined on the platform by the three BTP officers. The tube train had stopped well short of its normal spot, but the driver, Vicki Connors, was still screaming in her cab, the damaged windscreen covered in blood and entrails.

Finally passing out from shock, Vicki was soon released from her cab by several fellow workers from the Emergency Event Rescue Team, once the override switch was operated to open the platform barrier doors.

'Can someone move this train forward please?' asked Tony Grant.

'Not yet,' came the voice of British Transport Police Superintendent Ian Howarth. Dressed in his official uniform, with the peaked cap adorned with the customary yellow bands around the peak, and the silver pips on his shoulders, he was an imposing man of fifty-one years. Tall and slim, with greying hair at the temples, his green eyes shone with determination and fairness.

He strode purposefully over to Tony Grant, a five foot three short, stocky man of forty years, with a shock of curly dark hair from his Italian roots, along with his Mediterranean tan which being natural never faded. Tony usually had a permanent smile, being of a pleasant disposition, but his face currently sported a very serious expression, mixed with concern.

'The train needs to remain where it is until the forensic people have been and concluded their work,' Superintendent Howarth said.

'There might be people still alive under the tra...' Grant tried to say.

'Unlikely,' Superintendent Howarth responded. 'Ten minutes ago we received an anonymous tip-off that one person would die, along with two corpses which were to be engaged in a barbaric show of contempt towards British justice and our government.'

Tony felt his stomach twitch. 'You mean to tell me someone deliberately placed three people inside the tunnel, and that two of them were already dead? The other one was to be deliberately killed by being struck by a train? Good God.' He felt awful, and ran away to the wall as his stomach, influenced by his mind trying to absorb the information, caused him to vomit, and he stood hunched over by one of the waste bins he'd managed to reach and throw up into.

Three SOCO teams arrived within twenty minutes of being deployed; comprising of fourteen members in total, each one wearing all-in-one white lightweight waxed paper suits, blue plastic overshoes, latex gloves and obligatory masks and goggles, carrying their individual kit-boxes containing the necessary tools of their trade.

After a short briefing with Superintendent Howarth, the Lead Forensic Officer, for this shift, Sergeant Darren Tipplely, instructed the team members to their designated tasks.

This was going to be a very difficult job indeed, and not just for the SOCO members. Tony Grant, feeling better after having some bottled water handed to him by the female BTP-uniformed officer Chel Parrish, called the main HQ Dispatch Office Manager, via his radio-transceiver and ordered public announcements and displays to close this section of the underground to the public, effective immediately.

'Look, don't you think I *know* how much this is going to disrupt the services? We have three dead people scattered over the tracks, and several others on the platform. Besides which, how do you expect the police forensics people to do their fucking job?' Tony Grant hung up the walkie-talkie on his belt, and switched it off, wondering whether he'd still have a job the next day.

Shit.

He shuddered, then when he turned he was looking into the faces of Superintendent Howarth and BTP officer Paul Ross.

***

12:17 PM.

Sitting in his office, DCI Phil Lomax was leaning backward in his chair, his hands behind his head, legs stretched out, and eyes closed. On his desk, the computer monitor was showing his report, on page fourteen. He was struggling to word the current paragraph which dealt with his abduction by the unknown kidnapper and his injuries sustained by the assailants.

Although he made clear his conviction that he was abducted by somebody of very high status, associated with Vortexa Pharmaceuticals Ltd, if not the resident CEO of the London site in Canary Wharf himself, and assisted by his employees, he had little or no evidence to back up his theory.

Crosse came to the partially open doorway. 'Sir, we've just had a report of a serious incident down at our local tube station. It happened just after eight-thirty this morning.' He pushed the door open more.

Lomax slowly opened his eyes and turned his head to his door. He then glanced at the large clock on the office wall, a decisive frown immediately appearing on his forehead. 'And you're suggesting this is connected to our investigation? When did we get updated on the incident?'

'Yes sir, and just under two hours ago,' Crosse backed away.

Shit. It would happen today of all days.

The day of his father's funeral, which was to happen in just over two hours' time. 'Crosse, look, do me a favour, take Greggs with you and get over to Earl's Court tube, speak to whoever's in charge of the situation, ask Dr Hickton to make sure she PM's the bodies as soon as she can, and make certain the SOCOs get photographs as the scene stands. Take DC Pete Greaves, he's our resident David Bailey. I have to get ready for my...' his voice faltered slightly.

Crosse nodded in understanding. 'Sir, you get away and get yourself ready. We'll take charge of this for the time being. Judging by the way it looks and sounds, it could definitely be connected to your abduction, and most if not all of the strange deaths too. By the way, the report of the incident came in from a Superintendent Ian Howarth of the British Transport Police.'

Rising slowly, Lomax walked to the door which Crosse opened wider and stepped aside to allow his boss to move past. Lomax nodded and smiled briefly, patting his subordinate on his shoulder as a way of thanking him.

Fourteen

Lomax sat on the first row of the mahogany pews at St. Mary's Church, Kensington, for the main service. The heavens had opened, as predicted. The fine drizzle that had been forecast gave way to a deluge of what seemed like biblical proportions. The overcast sky gave the impression of impending doom preparing to befall the entire city. Lomax imagined the rain changing to a maelstrom of fire and brimstone, crashing without remorse upon every single member of the congregation, who claimed not to have sinned.

He'd be one of the first, he was certain.

Then as a few of James Lomax's closest friends and acquaintances gave brief eulogies, Philip Lomax had to struggle to hold his head up high with pride, as his father's mates made passionate speeches. Stinging tears rolled freely down the DCI's cheeks.

His elder sister Hillary, who sat beside him, had insisted that he keep his feelings in check. She didn't want to be embarrassed with others seeing her brother crying. Not while she was this close.

It was the same at each of the funerals of his mother and younger siblings, Ruth and Byron. Hillary had kept a close eye on the younger Philip Lomax for their mother's, Byron's and for his sister Ruth's internments and then at age twenty-two for a cousin's funeral. Lomax had always hated his sister in all honesty, for her hard and ruthlessly bitter attitude to emotional expression. It really wasn't surprising that she didn't want any children.

She loved herself far too much to extend any love for any others.

Especially as she had done her utmost to control the family home, after their mother had died. Lomax recalled often the instances of Hillary dictating to her father how to live his life, and how after putting up with her intolerable behaviour for ten years, James Lomax had had enough and told her, 'Just fuck off you control-freak. I've had enough. God knows how you ever found a man to put up with you. Go get married, I ain't paying for it, make that poor bastard loser's life a fucking misery. Stupid fucker probably doesn't realise what he's letting himself in for.'

Inwardly Philip Lomax grinned. That was one of his favourite memories, and one that he always kept to himself. He felt slightly nervous at this moment, what with her sitting right next to him. He always had this fear that Hillary was capable of reading his mind, and that she would strike him down dead with one of her vicious glares.

However, he had survived more often than not, so he felt safe in the belief that she indeed had no such power. Lomax wondered if Hillary would get up and say a few words, but when the vicar looked at her, she shook her head almost imperceptibly, her hard eyes declaring clearly to the vicar that she had nothing at all to say. In truth Philip Lomax wasn't really surprised and he always believed that his sister held a deep burgeoning grudge for the way his father spoke to her when he kicked her out.

It showed in the cheap and very small wreath of flowers she'd purchased, and the short terse message on the card she'd had printed, *'Bye Dad, see you much later. Hillary.'*

In contrast, Phil's was much, much larger, and bore the more personal message, written by hand, *'Dad, you were my rock. You may have been proud of me, I just wish I could have been there and done much more for you, the right things, in your time of need. Love you always. RIP. Philip xxx.'*

Hillary stood at the graveside, and as soon as the vicar had finished the final part of the internment prayer verse, with the constant depressing rain continuing to fall, she turned and walked off. Lomax never saw it, but she had the definite smile of someone who had an alternate motive.

Lomax stood alone at the bottom end of the grave, staring down at the coffin lid with its brass plate bearing his father's full name, date of birth, and date of his death. Slightly covered with some wet dirt thrown in by the mourners. He'd shaken the hand of the vicar, and accepted his condolences, as he had with everyone who had been kind enough to speak to him. His overcoat was drenched, his shoes almost filled to overflowing from the slimy mud walking across the almost grassless cemetery grounds. He didn't have an umbrella, or a hat, so his brown hair was slick to his scalp, and raindrops slid down the back of his coat, making him feel even more depressed.

As he looked into the six-feet-deep maw, at the coffin containing his father's body, Lomax wondered what the rest of his life held for him. He recalled a recent comment James Lomax made to him, back at his father's house, concerning Philip having children. The thought immediately made him consider quite where his current relationship with Roma might well take him. Might it lead to him getting married, *and* having children?

Part of him hoped so, and the *other* part made him feel ever so slightly unnerved. He also wished that she was there with him, right then, holding hands, sharing the moment. He shook his head, and cleared his mind, bringing himself back to reality – out of his Walter Mitty dream world.

There wasn't going to be a wake. Lomax couldn't really see the point, as there were only he and Hillary left as far as the immediate family were concerned. On this matter Hillary agreed, she felt the cost would be an unnecessary 'extravagance'.

This was something that Lomax found very strange. Then it hit him. The realisation. Her husband wasn't there at the funeral, but then if he also came to think about it, he'd never actually met the man… at all. He hadn't even seen any wedding photographs, so he didn't know what Hillary's husband looked like. Hillary had never bothered to invite Phil to her wedding or her house in all the time she'd been married to her husband. Christ… what was his name?

Lomax usually had a pretty good memory for names. For some strange reason, his brother-in-law's name evaded him. Maybe if he'd met him, even once, he would have remembered it.

Even during the drive back to Earl's Court CID Lomax tried to remember, but he doubted he ever actually knew the name. He used a trick; he'd run through the alphabet thinking of names, but after the eighth run-through he still couldn't get it.

Entering the office area that housed his team, Lomax faced his three top subordinates as he pushed through the two swing doors. They each sat at desks in the middle of the floor and arranged so that a triangle of space was created around one of the upright RSJ supports, where the cabling to and from the computers and phone lines congealed on the floor, like a bad case of regurgitated spaghetti.

Lomax stood next to the desk occupied by DC Crosse. 'So, what's the story? What happened at the underground?' He asked no-one in particular.

'You're not going to believe it,' DS Roma Clarkson said. She explained the situation in which she and the two DCs had been given a statement by the British Transport Police Superintendent, Ian Howarth, and the three uniformed officers, as well as the London Underground supervisor, Tony Grant, and the female train driver, Vicki Connors, once she had recovered from the shock.

Lomax listened intently. Moving his eyes from each officer in turn as they explained what they'd been told and were about to finalise their reports. 'Okay, write it up as your preliminary reports. Tag all photo evidence recorded by DC Greaves and make an extra copy of everything you've written regarding this incident, then attach it to everything we've got on Vortexa Pharmaceuticals/Amanda Waterman and the other two deaths.'

'We're still not clear on whether those other two *are* indeed connected though… are we?' asked DC Greggs.

'No, not officially,' Lomax admitted. 'But I am expecting Dr Hickton's report to confirm my own suspicions on that matter. I'm going home for a while.'

***

Lomax arrived home forty-three minutes after leaving the station. Popping into his local market to get some fresh supplies of food, toiletries and essential household items. He didn't plan to go back into work that day. Not after his father's funeral, but he needed to find out what had happened at Earl's Court tube station.

As he unlocked the front door to his house, a pile of mail was pushed aside. One of the top envelopes was unstamped, and seemed to bear the handwriting of Hillary, his sister.

He bent down and picked up the collection placing it on the hallway table but keeping the one from his sister in his hand. He went into the kitchen placing the bags on the small table there, and then dropped the one envelope on the kitchen work surface. He unpacked the bags and set the kettle to boil, got a mug ready.

While he waited for the kettle he put his shopping away, his eyes straying towards the letter. Once his drink was brewed and ready, he sat at the cleared table then took a sip of his drink and using a knife to cut the top of the envelope he pulled out the single-page, hand-written letter.

He read quickly the first time.

Then reading much slower, he felt his anger rising. He felt so appalled at the audacity of his older sister, asking this *'favour'* on the very day of their father's funeral. Talk about bad taste. But then when did Hillary ever have good timing for her abrupt and selfish nature?

He heard his home telephone start to ring, and he decided to ignore it for now. It was probably someone offering their condolences, so he'd let the call go straight to the answering machine. He still felt emotional, and knew that whoever it was, their message would only set him off again.

He read the note once more.

The letter read:

Dear Philip,

Now that father is gone, we need to discuss the sale of his house. I apologise if this comes across as insensitive, so soon afterwards, but I would appreciate it if we might come to an understanding, by way of getting the property onto the market.

I've decided to leave the country and go to Egypt. Please call me soon.

Hillary

Scrunching the letter up into a ball, he lobbed it towards the open-topped bin in the corner. It struck the wall above the rim then bounced down into the waste receptacle.

'Fuck it, she can damned well wait,' he said. Then his hearing caught Clarkson's voice from outside.

Lomax opened the door and moved aside to allow his colleague entry.

'I parked a couple of streets away and used the alleyways… just in case,' Roma said, her expression serious. 'Are you feeling okay?' she asked him.

'I'm all right. It's just everything seems to be fucked up lately,' Lomax said. 'The brick through my father's window. Me being kidnapped by that bastard who I believe is behind these crazy deaths, and then my father… losing my father. Now Hillary wants to get her hands on any inheritance there might be on the house. Jesus.'

Roma moved towards him.

She wrapped her arms around Lomax's neck and shoulders, planting her mouth to his, kissing him firmly, passionately. Breaking off she said, 'You need to relax more, let me help you,' her tone was seductive, and it had the desired effect.

Lomax lay on the bed, still naked and with the sheen of perspiration gleaming over his body. His hair matted. An expression of contentment on his face, although he did feel a little guilty for allowing himself to engage in some rampant love making, today of all days. All the same, he did feel better for it as well.

The sound of water cascading in the shower was audible from his room. His appetite for sex had increased a hundred-fold since becoming involved with Roma, it was as though she'd re-lit his fire, making him want to go in there with her, make love to Roma yet again, but he was exhausted enough as it was. Physically *and* mentally.

She reappeared wearing a bathrobe, her hair covered by a towel. Her face and body flushed with a glow from the shower she'd just had, but more so from the extensive bout of energy she and Lomax had expended.

She sat on the bed, and twisted her body to look at him, resting her left hand on his hairy thigh. His organ twitched as she stroked his leg. Lomax smiled.

'Down boy,' she commanded, and it quickly became flaccid once more. Lomax looked disheartened. 'Do you think… that our being involved, will compromise the investigation?' she asked.

Lomax coughed, clearing his throat and smiled that endearing smile of his. 'No. No, I wouldn't think so. Why?'

'Because…' Roma paused, trying to think of the best way to tell him. 'Because I've fallen in love with you Phil. Deeply in love. I've never felt this urgency about a man before. I care about you so much, it hurts when we're apart, even though we work together.'

Lomax moved his left hand onto hers, still resting on his leg. He pulled her towards him, the robe opened and they kissed. 'I love you too,' he said.

They made love again, albeit Lomax took his time, conserving what little energy he had left, yet at the same time making the experience that much more pleasurable for the both of them.

***

The hidden cameras and microphones picked up everything. It was all recorded digitally on the instruments and equipment contained within the van parked in the next street.

'If this doesn't destroy him, nothing will,' said the man operating the equipment, wearing a headset.

'It isn't my intent to *destroy* the man. Just imbalance his future credibility within the Metropolitan Police Force. Besides, I don't actually wish to kill him, just yet, unless he makes it necessary,' replied the voice on the other end of the digital connection. The tone was as clear as day.

'When do you intend to play your hand?' a third distant voice intervened. A female voice with a hint of harshness to it.

'Not for a while yet. This is my trump card, which I shall use as and when he's close. At the moment he doesn't have enough evidence. I, however, have important things to do.' Abruptly, the connection died.

Fifteen

Thursday 17th January 07:40 AM.

Earl's Court Police Station: Major Incident Room. "Operation Freefall"

Lomax entered the room carrying a large tray of plastic cups filled with coffee from the vending machine on the floor below, along with a couple of packets of biscuits. He set the tray down on a desk. 'Here you go lads and lasses, help yourselves.'

DC Crosse selected one of the cups and almost dropped it, the burning liquid inside so damned hot Crosse felt as though it would melt the plastic container.

Apart from Crosse, who'd been working since half-past six that morning, the room had a few people already in attendance for the briefing, including uniformed officers. Two were civilians, one male and one female. Craig Nethwell, a twenty-nine-year-old statistician and corporate crime specialist, and Felicity Bower, a forty-six-year-old legal secretary, whose job it was to ensure there would be no issues in how the case affected legal matters with potential prosecutions later on. Both drafted in from other departments to assist with the day-to-day filing and cross referencing of all data accrued by the officers investigating the current case.

Lomax had requested this case be given a higher profile, as he believed things were becoming far more urgent. He'd had a very difficult time persuading Chief Superintendent Charles Warwick the previous evening, but eventually he'd succeeded.

'Philip, look…' Warwick had told him in his office, 'I understand that you have a personal interest in this case.

Your association or relationship with the first victim, Miss Waterman, has obviously clouded your judgement, however, I'm allowing you the benefit of my doubt that you will conduct yourself professionally in this matter,' Chief Superintendent Warwick had told him.

'Thank you, sir,' Lomax had said, as he sat in the comfortable chair facing his superior.

'Cut the "sir" crap, Philip. It's late and I'm wanting to get away, I have an important dinner party I'm *supposed* to be attending tonight,' Warwick said, a slight grin showing across his ragged features. 'You keeping me behind at work isn't going to put me in favour with my wife.'

'I'm sorry, Charles. Tell Diane to blame me then if you get a right tongue-lashing.'

'Don't worry, I shall.'

Lomax rose from the chair. Warwick stood up as well, extending his hand which Lomax took and they shook. 'Thank you, Charles. I really do appreciate this.'

'Just don't make me look a fucking idiot Philip, for showing confidence in your judgement. If this case goes tits up, it won't just be your career going down the shitter,' Warwick said, keeping his tone as serious as possible.

Lomax smiled as Roma entered the Investigation Suite. She nodded to him, a faint smile appearing on her face as well. She sat in one of the chairs facing the whiteboard, which had copies of some of the photographs taken by DC Pete Greaves, who was still there, having only just finished sticking the photos up with pieces of tape.

'Okay then,' began Lomax, after he'd mentally checked everyone was in attendance. Then the two Interpol officers he'd already met unexpectedly arrived, with a third member of their team. Lomax had forgotten about them to be truthful, as they hadn't been in contact for a few days; he hadn't been able to spend a great deal of time with them anyway, and he'd assumed they'd returned to Paris. Lomax nodded and motioned for them to take seats. 'As of today, this case has been designated with the code-name 'Freefall', which seems uncannily appropriate as our first few victims each died as a result of sustaining serious injuries caused by falling from great height.'

'Shouldn't that be serious *fatal* injuries, sir?' asked Greggs, who smiled sarcastically as he slouched in his chair.

Lomax gave Greggs a sour scowl. 'Ignore that prick's comment. I apologise to our guest officers from Interpol, Inspector Claude D'Ebeauville and Sergeant Marianne Clourette, I'm afraid I haven't been introduced to your fellow officer.'

The newcomer stood up again, and proffered his right hand, which Lomax accepted and they shook. 'Constable Bernhard Kleist, mein Herr,' he said in a clearly discernible German accent.

'Jesus. The Krauts are invading again,' Greggs said.

'Yes, we are… and ziss time ve're going to win,' Kleist said, mocking the British police officer. Greggs flushed. A murmur of muted laughter erupted from several members of the assembled officers and civilian staff, accompanied by disparaging remarks towards Greggs.

One of the uniformed officers in a seat a little way behind Greggs said audibly, 'What a jerk,' culminating in another bout of raised laughter. Greggs turned round in his seat but he couldn't tell who'd spoken, as he didn't know every uniformed officer explicitly. As the faces changed to a serious expression he glared at all of them, hoping that the one who'd spoken would give himself away, but he was unsuccessful. He turned back to face Lomax.

Lomax decided right as of this moment, he liked the German Interpol agent. He motioned for the man to sit back down before he went on. 'Now that we're all properly acquainted, I'll give you the lowdown on the progress, or rather the lack of it, so far. Since my brief abduction, there have been no reports of anyone going missing. Apart from the MPD listing of missing persons over the past few months, the database has not been updated with anything that matches the criteria concerned with our casework.' He glanced at his notepad, and continued, 'It is my own opinion, that whoever is behind these people's deaths, is possibly using members of the public finding those who simply wouldn't be missed by family, friends or acquaintances, who have eluded the usual radar, as guinea-pigs in some very nasty experiments he is conducting.'

'Excuse me,' asked Sergeant Clourette, as she raised a hand. Lomax nodded. 'I recall you mentioning that you were trying to get a search warrant to gain access to every floor of the building in Canary Wharf, London. What is the status of progress in that matter?'

Lomax looked directly into her face, then immediately switched to Clarkson's before looking at the room in general. 'Unfortunately, the as yet unidentified CEO of Vortexa Pharmaceuticals' lawyers are still playing hard to get and are stalling us at every turn.'

'Perhaps we could always try a different tactic?' asked Crosse.

'What do you mean?' asked Lomax.

'We could always sneak in?' Crosse answered. A knowing smile appearing on his face.

'You mean, make an illegal entry and search of the CEO's office suite? You have to be joking. Do you not realise how much shit *I'd* get into if we did that?' Lomax said.

'You might,' began Marianne Clourette, the female Interpol officer. 'But myself and Bernhard, could get in… unofficially as far as this investigation is concerned, of course.'

Both Lomax and Roma Clarkson were stunned by the audacious claim; the look of utter shock which appeared on both their faces was almost comical. Then Lomax smiled; the dimples which appeared in his cheeks and gave his facial features an appealing quality seemed to lighten the mood, but only ever so slightly.

'Okay, so what's your take on this?' Lomax asked.

Along with inspector D'Ebeauville, Marianne and Bernhard explained their idea, each member of the Interpol team explaining what they'd come up with. The meeting closed with Lomax assigning the uniforms to go out and canvass the neighbours of Amanda Waterman once again, and also the witnesses to the man who'd jumped from Westminster Bridge.

***

Sixteen

He picked up the receiver of his office phone before the first ring had subsided. 'Yes? DCI Lomax speaking.'

The call lasted no more than thirty seconds.

'Who was that?' Asked Roma.

'It seems we have a friend, who shall remain nameless for the time being,' Lomax said, then added 'It also seems that another piece of the puzzle has reared its head. Roma, you're with me. Everyone else continue with your work, dig deep and see what you can get for me.' Taking a light grip of Roma's left elbow he guided her towards the door.

It wasn't until they'd reached the car park and climbed into the older pool Vectra, with Roma behind the wheel that Lomax spoke once more. 'Your place or mine?' he asked, winking.

'Are you serious?' she asked, her expression incredulous.

Lomax burst out laughing, then after a few moments, he said, 'Sorry… even though I'm feeling frisky, we have to get to University College Hospital, which is where the deceased and the injured have been taken.'

'Aaww… I was up for a bit of fun too. But… but I suppose duty does have to come first. May I ask, why University College?' Roma questioned, as she kept her eyes on the road, concentrating on her driving.

Lomax brought her up to speed with what he'd been briefly told by Chief Superintendent Warwick during the briefest of calls.

'Goodness. Really?' Roma exclaimed.

'By order of the Prime Minister, there's been a media blackout. Even though the 'incidents' were in plain public view and involved several members of the general public being killed or injured, their vehicles being written off, anyone even remotely involved has been rounded up, and sworn to secrecy,' Lomax said, his tone not actually conveying much.

The media blackout was put in force so that not one of the global television news channels or radio stations would be allowed to cause hysteria by alluding that there were a number of maniacs running around London, randomly shooting up anyone from within 4x4s.

'So… University College Hospital it is,' Roma said, '…due to its low profile no doubt. I never realised that it had an operational mortuary. I thought all deaths, natural or suspicious were sent to Home Office-approved mortuaries in Central London?' Roma asked.

'True. Normally they would,' Lomax said. 'But these incidents definitely have an unusual connection with Vortexa Pharmaceuticals. The male passenger from the red Mitsubishi Warrior came to while receiving medical treatment at the scene and gave enough information to give us an idea where he and the female driver, as well as those in the black vehicle, came from. But apparently the hospital doctors thought he was simply delirious,' Lomax said, knowing that by giving Roma the information in snippet-form, he could keep her talking and her interest piqued.

She drove on, taking Wimpole Street from Wigmore Street, then left on Devonshire Street straight into the rear of University College Hospital. Roma parked the Vectra in one of several spaces usually reserved for the occasional visits by the Home Office pathologist.

After alighting from the car, Lomax led the way through the maintenance dept., and through the maze of pale-yellow corridors, with the unmistakable tang of strong disinfectant that always pervaded the air. Their shoes continually squeaked on the worn linoleum which had seen better days, then they made their way down some stairs and into the depths of the building. They turned a corner where a large elevator was connected to all ward floors, for the removal of any unfortunate person that died regardless of the medical care being provided.

Ahead were two light green coloured doors, with square wire mesh windows at head and chest height. Lomax shoved one door open holding it for DS Clarkson to pass by, and her right hand came up to lightly stroke his face as she walked through into a short passageway. Lomax overtook her and turning right he pushed through a pair of swing doors, again holding one aside for her. She smiled and stopped, once again placing the palm of her right hand on his chest; moving closer Roma was about to plant a kiss on his mouth when a recognisable voice from beyond called out, echoing from even further within the bowels of the building.

'Phil, come on, I don't have all day,' Sally Hickton said.

'Typical,' Roma said grinning, her eyes showing that she was sexually aroused, and those alluring dimples in her cheeks appeared, which made Lomax feel the same.

Moving into the main mortuary examination room, Lomax and Roma were confronted by three bodies lying on adjoining dissection tables. Each were covered by an opaque plastic sheet. Their clothes already removed and bagged, each right big toe had a buff-coloured toe-tag with 'Identity Unknown' written by hand. There were several trolleys scattered around the room, each with a corpse covered by a thin opaque plastic sheet.

Men, women and children of differing ages, were present on the trolleys, and Sally Hickton's face showed exactly how she felt, being placed under this much pressure.

Both Lomax and Roma gasped upon noting how many people had lost their lives in such a short time. Although this was indeed a serious event and counted upon the random yet deliberate actions of the drivers of two large and dangerous vehicles, one seemingly intent on submitting injury or death to those in the other. This wasn't in reality considered as serious as those acts of deliberate terrorism, which occurred in July 2005.

Presiding over the examinations of all of these victims of the carnage, Sally Hickton looked far from pleased at being dragged across London to an unfamiliar mortuary, and needing to bring her personal tools.

'Hi, Sally,' Lomax said, cheerily.

Hickton's expression conveyed without any doubt whatsoever her dismay at being ordered to conduct the autopsies. 'I might have known you were directly involved,' Hickton said gruffly, sweeping her fingers through her thick light brown hair.

'Hey,' Lomax countered, his tone convincingly hurt, 'it wasn't my idea to bring the bodies here. That was down to the Chief Commissioner, Stonehouse. He made the decision, taking into consideration the recent events, besides which, and I haven't told you this, there's a possible leak within the investigation that's getting back to the person causing all these deaths.'

'I do hope that you're not suggesting that I'm giving unauthorised information out to any...' Hickton began saying.

Lomax held up a hand. 'No, of course not Sally. You're the second-to-last person I'd *ever* accuse of doing something like that.'

'Good. Besides which, this situation only makes my work that much more difficult. I suppose that you're already aware that every one of these victims has been held in cold storage since the incident?' she asked.

'No... I wasn't aware of that until earlier. I had a short discussion with Chief Super Warwick who's only now made me aware of the incident in the first place, also that there are two people I need to speak to who survived the carnage, and who might have vital information.'

***

Marianne Clourette and Bernhard Kleist walked towards the entrance of the Vortexa Pharmaceuticals building in London's Canary Wharf complex. They both looked up at the impressive redevelopment, and specifically at the glasswork of the windows with their gold sheen gleaming from the bright sunlight peeking through the clouds and striking it.

Standing there for a few moments admiring the architectural vista, they then moved towards the main doors. Even with all the recent events, and more specifically the number of deaths related to the building, there was a hive of activity on the concourse inside and outside the building.

Businessmen and women, most brandishing expensive briefcases, moved singularly, in groups or couples, usually in deep conversation; whether business related or not, who could tell?

Earlier that morning, inspector Claude D'Ebeauville had called Vortexa, posing as a pharmaceutical businessman and having spoken to their Marketing and Public Relations department heads, had finally secured permission for two of his 'employees' to visit and be given a guided tour of the building, and an insight into its success.

His call had been, he hoped, as convincing as it possibly could. Yet he had an uncomfortable sensation in the pit of his stomach which made him feel cautious, especially as his beautiful wife was, to some extent, placing herself in danger. That said, he knew that he could trust Bernhard Kleist to look out for Marianne; not that she was incapable of looking after herself.

Marianne was an accomplished martial arts instructor. Judo, karate and kick-boxing being her favoured sports. She also had excellent markswoman-ship in weapons use. She had played a major part with the UN in keeping the peace in war-torn Iraq during the Saddam Hussein trial and had been caught up in several attacks by insurgents, killing many with single shots.

She felt no remorse towards those she'd killed. Mostly because she felt and accepted in her mind that they were aggressively intent on killing her and her fellow officers, as well as innocent Iraqi civilians. Marianne had excelled herself as a UN peacekeeper, and when she decided to transfer to Interpol, they jumped at the chance to have her on their side.

Marianne had been with Interpol for just over two years, at the age of twenty-nine, being a good twenty years younger than her husband. She preferred older men; she found them more reliable in many ways. She was instantly drawn to him; his attractiveness was intensive, and she liked his boyish charm, as well as his bright intelligent eyes.

As soon as the Interpol officers entered the main foyer, they were met by Ceri - *(pronounced Cherie)* - Fallontyne, from the publicity department. Ceri, was a twenty-three-year-old with sparkling green oval eyes, long bright red hair which framed her thin porcelain face, a small nose which was very pointy, and accompanying tight mouth. She wore no make-up, and her flesh was pasty on a very slim figure, emphasised by the pencil skirt and jacket in matching mid blue, the black shoes and slender legs which seemed to have no real shape to them.

To some men she would be attractive, but to others, she was too thin... too... Kate Moss, or Victoria Beckham.

'Mademoiselle Clourette? Herr Kleist? My name is Ceri Fallontyne, I've been asked to give you the standard public tour. However, we usually only give tours on Tuesday and Thursday mornings, but we've had a few… structural problems recently, so we've had to cancel the regular tours. Your CEO was adamant you should have the chance to tour as you're leaving in two days for South Africa?'

Bernhard Kleist was about to query the question, but Marianne spoke quickly, calmly, 'Yes, that is correct. Cape Town, there's a facility there that we've been informed is developing some fantastic new anti-cancer drugs, and also radical non-invasive chemotherapy routines.'

Although she was up to speed on her own employer company's mainstream production of legitimate pharmaceutical products, Ceri wasn't fully aware of other *foreign* companies' lines. 'I see, very well… would you both please follow me?'

The tour lasted just over two hours and was indeed very thorough.

Only not *too* thorough. There was of course a particular section of the building that was by no means accessible, under any circumstances. It was totally off limits to the general public of course, however, even respected dignitaries, Her Majesty the Queen for example, should she have requested a comprehensive tour, would have been denied.

The two visitors were led to the upper executive floor, after the tour guide's bleeper went off as she neared the end of her talk. She checked the message that flashed up on the small screen, and then she told the two visitors that they had been invited to speak with the CEO of the company personally.

Marianne and Bernhard exchanged quizzical glances at each other, conveying their surprise without alerting any suspicion towards their companion.

Watching the visitors throughout the two-hour tour, Vortexa's CEO admired the audacity of the authorities, but he also felt a strong degree of anxious anger. Were they getting close? Who were these two people from Interpol? Why were they here? He knew their true identities from the moment they entered the foyer; now he became concerned that they were indeed connected to the British police investigation.

He had his suspicions that DCI Lomax was most definitely the major thorn in his side. He was also exceedingly peeved off that the warning he'd given to Lomax not too long ago had fallen on deaf ears.

He might need to apply some more pressure upon DCI Lomax. He knew about Lomax's father dying. He himself was indirectly implicated with Gerald's death, which only left Hillary, Lomax's elder sister. He had no inclination of becoming physically involved with that ugly bitch. Besides, she was too old, *far* too old for his preferences.

Perhaps, however, he could use these visitors to his advantage. There was always the possibility that the latest development in his control product might succeed this time. He'd had some positive results coming through from the lab.

So what that two of his prisoners had, somehow, managed to escape? It was ironic that his security officers had died, yet their uniforms had no insignia that would directly link them to the company, or more importantly, to him directly. Yet there was the issue of the black 4x4, which *was* a company vehicle and was licensed to Vortexa. He'd have to find a valid reason to explain how and why one of the company vehicles was involved, and how and why three heavily armed persons were firing weapons from it and causing mayhem on the streets of London. That is, should he find himself investigated by someone with a much higher profile than that damned DCI Lomax.

For now, though, he had other more important things on his mind.

The main door of the elevator to the floor he occupied opened, and the guide motioned with a sweep of a hand for the two visitors to continue along the corridor without her and walk straight ahead. Ceri barely nodded before she left to return to her duties.

Marianne and Bernhard walked without speaking or making eye contact with each other, which might alert the man they were about to meet of their concerns. The door to the main office opened automatically, and with only the slightest of noticeable hesitation, Marianne entered first.

Both she and Bernhard moved with purpose towards the huge desk, behind which stood the imposing figure of the man facing them. He seemed much younger than they expected. His smile, albeit lacking any sense of decency or trustworthiness, made her feel decidedly uncomfortable. Marianne felt a distinct shiver course through her as she studied Vortexa's CEO, she found his returning stare unnerving to say the least.

Gesturing with a hand for his visitors to be seated, the CEO sat down and took a few moments to carefully observe his guests as they took their seats. He knew that by not speaking, or offering his hand in welcome, these two Interpol officers would indubitably begin to feel uneasy. This was exactly what he had intended.

'May I offer you both something to drink? Tea, coffee? Or something stronger?' he asked. 'By the way, my name is David Carter. I have the honour of being the CEO of Vortexa Pharmaceuticals.'

The true CEO was in another room, communicating with David Carter via an earpiece, directing him in what to say, and being able to hear everything.

'Er, yes, thank you, coffee for me if you don't mind,' Marianne said.

'Same for me,' Bernhard agreed.

Without speaking, the visible CEO pressed a button on the surface of his desk, then he leaned back in his expensive executive leather chair and, forming a pyramid with his fingers, he began making small talk concerning his visitors' tour of the facility. Directed by the actual man, Carter performed with some aplomb.

'I was wondering,' Bernhard asked, 'just what you produced in those off-limit laboratories, we were *not* allowed to see.'

'Ah-ha,' the CEO murmured, a sly smile appearing on his face. An Asian man wearing a white collarless tunic and blue trousers entered the office carrying a crystal glass tray with similar cups, steaming with coffee which smelled of an expensive Colombian brand. He waited until the servant had handed the visitors their cups and exited once more, then after having sniffed the aroma of the enticing beverage and taking healthy sips of the liquid from his personal engraved glass cup, he spoke. 'I see that your inquisitiveness might just get the better of you. You know the saying regarding the cat?'

Marianne raised her eyebrows. 'Excuse me?' she said.

'Curiosity. It tends to lead people into situations, or dangers, that they wouldn't usually expect,' came the cryptic response.

As the two visitors cradled their cups of coffee, the CEO seemed to be getting a little anxious, almost fretful that these two wouldn't actually drink their coffees. 'Please, I'd hate for your drinks to get cold. This brand always tastes best when consumed hot,' he said, hoping that he wasn't coming across as too forceful.

Almost immediately after taking their own first sips of the aromatic beverage, both Marianne and Bernhard felt strange. The drug they had unknowingly ingested worked almost instantaneously upon their auto-nervous system, rendering their muscles useless, their motor neurones were immediately blocked by inhibitors which interrupted the flow of signals from the brain to the muscle groups that were commanded by voluntary actions. Mostly walking or using arms and hands. Speaking.

Involuntary groups such as the heart and lungs continued to operate normally, if not slightly reduced. However, it was how the drug controlled the mind that gave this product its greatest potential, and the greatest satisfaction to Vortexa's real CEO. He watched via a large flat screen TV from the other room, a gleeful smile forming.

Both of the Interpol officers lost their abilities to grip the cups voluntarily and watched them slip to the floor, spilling the remaining liquid over the officers' clothing and the carpet. As their bodies became listless, their muscles relaxed swiftly so that they slumped in the chairs almost to the point of falling off the seats, if it wasn't for the two henchmen standing nearby, who had entered through a secret doorway hidden behind the panelling along one wall of the huge office. They moved forward swiftly to quickly haul the Interpol officers back upright, then began using cable ties to their arms and rope around the captives' chests to secure them.

Even though both of them were unable to resist the bodily effects of the drug, their minds were able to distinguish what was actually going on around them; although they couldn't speak, they could still see, hear and comprehend.

The real CEO entered his office and stepped into their line of sight. His expression severe, maniacal, and yet at the same time almost serene. He leaned in towards the two officers, and keeping his voice low, he spoke. 'You will both now act for me. The British police investigating my London operation are becoming a tiresome bore. I need you both to lead DCI Lomax off on a different tangent.'

For almost an hour, the CEO lectured the two Interpol officers as their minds were subjected to the mind-control drug, and they absorbed their new orders.

Before he sent them on their way, he took liberties with Marianne by leading her into his private bedroom and satisfying his perverted preferences for more than three hours.

Seventeen

Later the same day.

Dean Morgan was sitting up in the hospital bed; his wounds were non-life-threatening, but still serious enough to be painful. He looked at the faces of the two police officers who sat either side of his bed. DS Roma Clarkson on his right and DCI Lomax on his left. Dean found that answering the barrage of questions and turning his head one way and then the other was causing him some discomfort.

'Look… could you two sit next to one another? Answering your bloody questions is making me feel queasy, and I hate tennis,' Dean said angrily.

Roma stood up and moved her chair around the bed and sat on her superior's left, keeping a good three feet apart.

'So… are you going to tell us exactly what happened or not?' Lomax asked, his tone obviously stressed. He scowled intently at the patient in the bed.

'I will if you tell me how Verity is,' Dean demanded.

Roma stood up once more and left the private room in which Dean had been placed for his own security. Verity was in another private room a little way down the corridor on the fourth floor of the private hospital. Both Dean and Verity were checked over and treated for their injuries at University College Hospital, and then transferred to a private hospital facility.

Roma went to speak to the male nurse on duty. A few minutes later she returned to Dean's room and re-took her seat. 'Verity's comfortable at the moment, but she is still sedated, as her injuries were a bit more serious than yours. Obviously due to the bullet wounds needing extensive surgery. DCI Lomax and I have only you to rely on to give us the information we need regarding the *incident*,' Roma said, her voice carrying the necessary timbre of authority that was required to convey their irritation at Dean's stall tactics.

She held the scowling stare long enough to cause Dean to relent. 'Okay… okay… I'll tell you everything.' He began by explaining that both he and Verity had been at the same club in Soho, *Clandestine*, on the same night. That he'd been chatted up by a stunningly attractive brunette, and that Verity had been chatted up and bought a drink by a very handsome man.

'Drugged,' Lomax stated, 'probably a hybrid mixture of Rohypnol and GBH, or something similar. Perhaps a new variation.'

Roma nodded. 'I'll ask if the blood tests can shed any light on that enquiry.'

Dean then explained that Verity and he had also both been stripped naked. He explained also that Verity had been subjected to a violent attack in her cell, and almost forced to receive a hypodermic syringe filled with some unknown substance, whilst at the same time being sexually molested by two of the guards, while a female was about to administer the drug, or whatever it was into her bloodstream.

Dean refrained from giving any details about him and Verity making love and skipped that part of their dilemma; he then gave a very crucial and detailed description of how they managed to find their way out.

'Verity found that a key on the bunch of cell door keys belonged to that dark red 4x4, which we managed to drive away in. It wasn't until we got out of the underground garage that we realised we were in the Canary Wharf financial district.'

Lomax's eyes widened in surprise, and a knowing smile spread across his face. 'Can you describe what the building looked like as you drove out from beneath it?' he asked. He could feel his spirits being lifted as he hoped that Dean would describe a particular building he'd already visited twice, the second time not of his own volition.

Roma, although seated a couple of feet away, could feel his excitement buzzing through the air towards her.

'It was tall, but then most of the buildings are there, I suppose,' Dean began. 'It had somewhere around the upper forties in floors. Glass covered most of the exterior, and there were at least two corner lifts that I could see. There was at least one freight elevator. The glass shimmered golden in the sun, and if I remember, the name of the company was emblazoned across the middle section of the wall facing the riverside, V-O-R-T...'

'Vortexa Pharmaceuticals,' Lomax shouted out, a little too loudly, causing Roma and Dean to flinch. Dean grimaced as a fresh wave of pain shot through his entire body. Although his injuries were in truth very minor in comparison to Verity's, his fractured ribs, a sprained ankle and a collapsed lung, badly sprained wrists (from using the Glock.45 weapon) and being thrown about violently in the truck as Verity fought to stay out of danger from their pursuers, caused him a great deal of discomfort.

Mind you, he felt safer than ever now. 'So, what's all this about then?' Dean asked, as the pain finally subsided.

'I'm sorry,' Roma began saying. 'I'm afraid you're not privy to that information, suffice it to say that your part in this investigation is paramount, and everything you can tell us would be considered extremely important in closing this case.'

Dean concluded this meeting by telling the two CID officers everything else that had happened leading up to when the two 4x4s finally collided and the black one ended up on its roof after a spectacular crash.

'So? What's on your mind?' Roma asked Lomax as they left the hospital.

'I *could* tell you, but you'd probably slap me for certain,' Lomax replied, grinning salaciously.

Roma gave him a mock matronly scowl, then grinned as well. 'As was said before, your place or mine?'

'Let's get back to base first,' Lomax said, looking at his watch and noting that it was way past eight in the evening. 'I'd like to check on progress… stick my head in the door and see who's still working the case. You go home and I'll meet you there, yes?'

'Are you still suspicious about your office having been 'bugged' and your own place after what you said about those devices at your father's house?' Roma asked, then mentally chastising herself for mentioning Lomax's father.

Lomax nodded, 'Yes, in fact I'd be surprised if the majority of the people working on this case weren't under surveillance, going by the degree of 'bugging' I've already been subjected to. Perhaps you should go home, grab some essentials and we could maybe meet separately at your sister's again? Or we could always find a decent hotel?'

Roma smiled and said, 'This case is certainly proving to be a tough nut to crack.'

Lomax nodded as he stared out of the windscreen, then said, 'Even with all of the complexities we're being presented with, I believe that with everything that's occurred so far it is simply *the tip of the iceberg.*' He remained silent for the remainder of the journey. Roma dropped Lomax back at Earl's Court nick, then drove off to her own place.

She opened her eyes, but the scene which befell them was very blurry. Marianne Clourette blinked several times; eventually her sight cleared and as the scene came into focus she gasped loudly when she saw her reflection in a large mirror. She saw that she was strapped to an aluminium table and inclined about sixty degrees from the horizontal plane. She also noted with much disdain that she was totally naked, her beautiful body exposed for all to see and admire.

She hoped that that was all it would be exposed for. She could tell that she was in some type of laboratory, a sparsely equipped one, yet a laboratory nonetheless. As she craned her now relaxed neck from right to left around the room, she saw benches fixed to the back walls, with gaps for the doors, and for storage cupboards.

Atop some of the benches were the usual paraphernalia associated with chemistry: complicated series of tubes connecting to large glass bottles with glass tubing and tap/valves with electronic sensors to open or close the valves as necessary. The obligatory Bunsen burners with orange rubber tubing feeding the gas from taps, seated under various supports with the pyramid-shaped flasks containing strangely coloured and clear fluids, which were being heated to set temperatures, and then as she watched, when the desired temperature was reached, a valve was opened and a clear fluid was drawn through the glass pipe via a vacuum effect towards another receptacle, during which another valve opened and a colourless gas was released, causing the clear liquid to change to a dark purple colour.

Marianne had no idea what was causing this chemical reaction, but what she was certain of was that the contents of those containers and the end product once formulated were surely destined to be injected into her and Bernhard. Bernhard. She looked around again but she was definitely alone, her colleague wasn't there.

A hiss alerted her, and as she turned her head back round she saw a door begin to open in between two sections of workbench and people entered, three of them in laboratory coats. One was a female, a striking blond, tall and slim.

The other two were the man that she'd first met in the executive office with Bernhard when the tour guide left them, and another stranger. Marianne recalled that neither she nor Bernhard had been formally introduced to him, so she had no idea of his name, or whether he was directly connected with what had been going on.

The unknown man approached Marianne, running his appraising gaze all over her body. She felt not only humiliated but extremely violated, being subjected to such a degrading situation. 'You have a very nice figure,' the man said, smiling as he continued eyeing her from head to toe.

'Don't even think of trying to have sex with me,' Marianne said forcefully, and her voice in the lab startled her as much as it did the man in charge. The striking blond in the white lab coat grinned but changed to a serious expression when the man glared at her. 'You're too late to have prevented me from enjoying myself in that regard young lady, besides I had intended to use you to work on my behalf in another capacity, but I changed my mind to a degree.'

As the realisation that this stranger had violated her without her being aware of it, Marianne shuddered then angrily spat out at him.

'Administer the drug,' the man said. Then as the blond woman nodded and gave instructions to her two colleagues, the man stepped closer to Marianne, holding a hand up to the blond scientist woman to temporarily hold off on the intended proceedings. 'You know it was a very clever ruse by your husband Claude D'Ebeauville to obtain permission for a tour, but you see madame D'Ebeauville, I am fully aware of your status within Interpol, and more importantly, I am fully aware of what you intended to do with whatever information you hoped to acquire.

'Allow me to assure you,' he went on, 'that no-one in the British police service, in particular that infernal Detective Chief Inspector Lomax, will succeed in solving what I intend to do, and it's highly doubtful that he will live very much longer. Or any of his team for that matter. And… in fact, now I have decided that you shall be instrumental in ensuring that DCI Lomax and everyone on this investigation, will soon be removed.' The man nodded, and the two other lab-coated employees advanced and after inflating the cuff of the blood pressure device, they then took a firm grip of Marianne's knees, holding them still while the woman with the syringe advanced.

After swabbing Marianne's left elbow crook with medical alcohol, the woman slapped the spot, satisfied when a large vein appeared; she pierced the flesh and inserted the needle deep, she drew back the plunger so that some of Marianne's blood was drawn back into the glass tube and mixed with the contents, then the blond woman, who never spoke once during the entire procedure, depressed the plunger, forcing the mixture into Marianne's circulatory system.

She then withdrew the needle and one of the other two slapped a swab of cotton wool over the puncture site and then placed a large square plaster over the top.

It took mere seconds for the substance to rush through Marianne's circulatory system and begin taking effect. At first, she felt a warming sensation flowing through her body as the unknown substance began its job, which wouldn't really be fulfilled until it reached the brain and affected the desired sections that dealt with the conscious mind.

The drug had been re-tested on the remaining abducted prisoners, after several adaptations and changes to the various compounds of which it was made. It was the two of the third set of prisoners that presented the ultimate success of the drug, and it was this key aspect that afforded the CEO's hope of using Marianne to undermine Lomax and perhaps even remove him entirely from this planet.

Unfortunately, what the Swedish scientist hadn't taken into account was whether the substance would cause an allergic reaction, as Marianne unexpectedly began convulsing when the drug reached her brain. Grand mal seizures suddenly erupted within Marianne's brain, as blood vessels bulged and some erupted from the unexpected pressure; she responded by freeing her legs from the grip of the two assistant technicians and both her feet from the restraints holding her down.

With her legs freed, they thrashed about randomly and as the two employees went to retake their grip and hold them back down, the heel of Marianne's right foot connected forcibly in the face of the man under his nose and drove it inwards and upwards, breaking the sphenoid bone and driving the pieces straight into his brain. The shards of bone severed the frontal lobes and several major blood vessels. The man's eyes rolled back up into his head showing only the whites, and after a short bout of a reflexive spasm he fell to the floor, blood pouring from his nose and mouth where he'd bitten a large portion of his tongue off.

Marianne's other leg struck out at around the same time, catching the other employee's chest with such force that the sternum and the ribs either side of were detached. Two of the man's ribs were driven directly into his left lung and straight through the aorta, the largest and main blood vessel coming from the heart. Three ribs exited the chest wall like small spears creating an escape route for the blood being pumped by the still beating heart, allowing it to gush freely under pressure and soak through the laboratory employee's garments. He too slumped to the floor, a crimson pool spreading across the linoleum floor from his chest and frothy foamy blood from his mouth.

The CEO watched open mouthed as the two fallen workers lay on the floor, still twitching, gurgling sounds emanating from both. David Carter's face swiftly paled, then he turned and ran to a nearby waste bin, where he vomited profusely, the retching and heaving noisy within the small lab.

The CEO's attention was drawn away from Marianne, as was Sandranna Jorgensen's, the Swedish scientist, looking at the prone form of both men, lying still. Helmut Grüber-Stahlmann, observing the scene, cautiously moved as far away from the carnage, fearing that the female test subject might attack him also.

Marianne's wrists now became loosened from the straps, as a result of the strength she now possessed. Even though she was still suffering grand mal seizures caused by the substance having such a diverse and extraordinary effect upon her, she grabbed a scalpel from a nearby tray while jumping off the examination table. She crossed the small space between her and the man, lunging wildly at the CEO, catching him on his left forearm about midway.

The razor-sharp blade cut effortlessly through his jacket and expensive silk long-sleeved shirt, cutting through into the muscular flesh of the man's forearm, severing blood vessels and into muscle and nerves. Blood seeped freely, staining his expensive clothes, and he reacted swiftly, with such anger, bringing his right balled fist around in a swift and deliberate arc smashing directly into Marianne's face, breaking her jaw, loosening several teeth and breaking the lower orbit bone of her right cheek.

She was sent spinning by the blow towards Sandranna who looked on in muted shock and was unable to react in time as Marianne still clutching the scalpel in her right hand, collided with the Swede and plunged the scalpel blade deep into the woman's neck, severing the carotid artery, and as she continued falling to the side, the blade cut the flesh aside sufficiently to allow the jet of blood to escape and create a fountain of red liquid to spray out.

Helmut Grüber-Stahlmann looking to his right saw a door, and edged himself towards it, and checking where the CEO was looking the Austrian-German scientist opened the door and slipped out of sight.

Marianne gave a sigh as her brain was unable to fight the effects of the drug, and it immediately began shutting down all involuntary systems, breathing, heart and muscular abilities. She collapsed on the floor heavily face first, her forehead striking the hard surface with a sickening crunch, then almost immediately she lay still.

The bulk of Sandranna Jorgensen's blood supply was practically exhausted within two minutes, then as her heart emptied of its contents it collapsed inwards and she slumped to the floor a few feet from Marianne's limp and still body.

The CEO was gripping his arm trying to stem the flow of his blood whilst at the same time moving to a wall intercom system. He raised his injured left arm whilst keeping pressure on the wound with his right hand, and using his middle finger with a lot of effort he pressed the security button and waited. 'Yes sir?' Came the response from one of the higher-ranking security staff.

'Get a medical team down here immediately. I've been seriously injured...' he then slumped to the floor, his back to the wall as tears began to flow and he began to shiver as he went into shock.

Eighteen

Friday 18th January 06.15 AM.

The shrill of the mobile phone's incoming call woke Lomax and Roma from their deep slumber. Lomax sleepily answered the phone picking it up off the floor by the side of the bed. 'Hello?'

'DCI Lomax?' asked Crosse, the surprise evident in his voice.

'*Shit,*' thought Lomax to himself as he remembered that he had just answered DS Clarkson's mobile instead of his own. 'Yes, Crosse. What is it?'

'Well sir… seeing as you're there with DS Clarkson, we've found a body, but you're not going to like knowing who it belongs to,' Crosse said.

'You've identified the body already?' Lomax enquired.

'Yes sir. It… I mean the body is that of the female Interpol officer. Sergeant Marianne Clourette. She looks like she's been through a grind mill,' Crosse said.

'What about Constable Kleist?' Lomax asked.

'There is no news concerning him at all so far, sir. Inspector D'Ebeauville has been trying to contact him via his cell phone, but without success. He's very distraught about his wife as I'm sure you can imagine, sir,' Crosse answered nervously.

'Very well, Crosse. Thank you for informing me. We'll be in as soon as possible.' Without waiting for a reply, or a chance for Crosse to try and squeeze any further information as to why he answered Roma's phone at that time in the morning, Lomax ended the call.

He rolled over onto his back in the double bed and immediately noticed his phone was on the other bedside table. During the night he and Roma had swapped sides during their lovemaking. *'Shit,'* he said to himself once more, as he gazed down at the still sleeping form of his colleague and lover. Roma was lying on her front, the cotton sheet half-covering her rump and one straight leg, her other leg bent at the knee and her shapely thigh exposed and tantalisingly so close, Lomax wanted to caress it. Instead, he traced his fingers from just above the gap between her buttocks at the small of her back and ran them gently up towards her face. Roma stirred as the tickling sensation awoke her.

She rolled over to face him while opening her eyes and smiled.

'Chris just called. I'm afraid I answered your bloody phone. I'm not sure, but at this time in the morning, I'll hazard a guess that that clever dick's just put two and two together,' Lomax said, a mocking concerned frown appearing on his face. Roma burst out laughing, and Lomax was unable to stop himself from joining in, regardless of the news he now had to tell her.

'So… apart from calculating that he's gotten the square root of the hypotenuse angle of an obtuse square, what did Crosse have to tell us?' she asked, feigning concern.

'Sergeant Marianne Clourette's body has been found in Highgate cemetery, lying near the grave of Karl Marx,' Lomax said, raising his eyebrows at Roma's reply concerning Crosse's mathematical expertise.

Roma said. 'If the CEO found out that she and Kleist were investigating on our behalf, and not acting as bona fide overseas visitors, surely that means there has to be a leak within the investigation. But we don't know who it could be.'

'I'd put a pound to a penny there is a definite link,' Lomax said. 'That bastard whoever he is, is killing innocent people left, right and centre. It started with Amanda's murder. Since then, there have been too many other people losing their lives as a direct or indirect result of what that madman is up to. Now, this morning Marianne's body turns up in Highgate cemetery.'

'What about Kleist?' Roma asked.

'Nothing. His body hasn't been found as yet, but that doesn't mean he's still alive,' Lomax said, wondering what he'd be able to say in sympathy to inspector D'Ebeauville when he saw him.

Roma gently caressed Lomax's left arm as he faced her on the bed. 'I'm just glad he let you go after he abducted you,' she told him.

'So am I,' Lomax agreed. 'That still makes me wonder just what that bastard's agenda really is. He threatened me, my family. I'm just glad,' he paused as he tried to think of the right way to express himself, then continued, 'I'm glad my father died when he did. I know I wouldn't have been able to live with myself if he'd been subjected to unspeakable violence at the hands of that bastard.'

'What about your sister, Hillary?' Roma asked, as she climbed out of the bed and made her way to the bathroom.

'To be honest… I'm not really sure,' Lomax replied. 'I cannot really see him trying to frighten me by threatening to kill her, or harm her in some way. If his abilities to gain confidential information is of any consequence, he'll know that she and I are not on the best of terms. But then again, who can say what's going on in his mind, what with all the recent destruction and deaths he's caused,' Lomax called out as he heard the water in the shower begin flowing.

He knew it would be pointless trying to hold a conversation from the bedroom, so he slipped into the bathroom and joined her in the shower. As they exited the shower, he continued to explain his ideas as they dried themselves down. 'I just wish I had an inkling of what's next.'

Crosse and Greggs were seated at their desks when Lomax and Clarkson entered the incident room at just after eight-twenty-five.

'So, would either of you two care to elaborate on just what state Sergeant Clourette's body was in when she was found?' Lomax asked bluntly.

Crosse stood up and handed Lomax a set of A4-size papers, including standard sized colour photographs taken of the body in situ, which he swiftly flicked through, reading the report word for word. 'We placed the enlarged photographs on the board,' he added.

Roma moved over and began examining the photos, moving left to right scanning the twelve enlarged 10x8 images arranged in four columns of three on the clear section of the whiteboard. As she looked at them, she found her pulse rate begin to quicken, and she covered her mouth with her right hand as the horrific images showed just what trauma Sergeant Clourette had been forced to endure.

Lomax finished reading the preliminary SOCO and post-mortem reports as well.

Greggs spoke up, as Lomax moved over to join Roma at the board. 'It seems that Sergeant Clourette had been subjected to an as yet unidentified substance injected into her bloodstream via her left elbow. Toxicology results are yet to be determined and seeing that our suspect is potentially the as yet still unidentified CEO of Vortexa Pharmaceuticals, who has unlimited access to any number of different drugs and potentially illegal compounds etc., etc., this is surely going to make the job of pinning down what the drug of choice was that much harder.'

Crosse went to answer the phone on his desk. After a brief discussion with the person on the other end of the line, he replaced the receiver and joined the others at the board. 'That was the toxicology lab technician. Unfortunately, they cannot pinpoint the substance down to any known drugs, such as Rohypnol, cocaine, heroin, LSD, amphetamines or even a cocktail of any or all of them. From what they told me, this is proving extremely difficult to categorise as the gas spectrometer and all the other machines appear not to have been programmed with any of the compounds being used to create this specific substance.'

Lomax heard his phone ringing in his office and left the others to answer it.

His phone was still ringing; he picked up the receiver. 'Hello? DCI Lomax.'

'I have Deputy Chief Commissioner Conway on the line for you Detective Chief Inspector, please hold while I connect you,' came the abrupt reply from DCC Conway's PA.

Lomax had no idea he was in the firing line to receive a person-to-person call from Felicity Conway. If anything, it was likely not to be good news at all. 'Yes, Deputy Chief Commissioner Conway, what can I do for you?' Lomax asked tentatively when the connection was put through.

'Detective Chief Inspector, you're aware of the recent incident concerning the death of an Interpol officer I presume?' Conway asked.

'Yes, ma'am I am. I was informed by one of my DCs, and I have just been reviewing the reports and the photographs,' Lomax said.

'Can you tell me why she had been seconded onto this case, and what part of the investigation she played, which has now cost her... her life?' DCC Conway asked.

Lomax could hear the anger in her tone, but he knew immediately that his next response would definitely not go down well at all either. 'I'm afraid I wasn't made aware of Sergeant Clourette's involvement into the Waterman case ma'am, other than as an observer. I'd suggest that you take this issue up with Chief Superintendent Warwick, and Sergeant Clourette's husband, Interpol inspector Claude D'Ebeauville. Now if you'll excuse me ma'am, I have some policing to be getting on with.' Without waiting to hear the reply, Lomax replaced the receiver and exited his office, to continue working with his colleagues in the incident room. One thing was clear in his mind however, that everything he and his team were doing, was being closely scrutinised: *too closely for comfort.*

***

DCC Felicity Conway had been using the speakerphone, and she smiled when the click signalled that Lomax had closed the connection. She looked into the faces of Chief Commissioner Sir William Stonehouse who sat off to the right of her desk on the red leather sofa, and another man. Detective Superintendent Miles Hancroft.

Both men were in civilian clothing.

'It would appear,' began Detective Superintendent Hancroft, rising from the sofa, 'that my earlier concerns regarding DCI Lomax's involvement on this case were warranted after all. It's clear to me that the first victim, Miss Waterman, was merely the catalyst and since DCI Lomax began his investigation, he has compounded his credibility by having an affair with his Detective Sergeant, Roma Clarkson, thus potentially creating an even greater risk of public humiliation for the Police Service if their assignation were to be discovered and made public.'

'That is something we simply cannot allow to happen.' Chief Commissioner Stonehouse said bluntly, adding, 'however, what makes this situation that much more awkward for us, is that if we were to suspend Lomax his entire team would more than likely quit, and delete their progress on the computer system, forcing us to start afresh. That in itself is something we also cannot afford. I propose that we allow him to continue working the case, and perhaps, if we're indeed fortunate, this situation will be resolved satisfactorily. Then, once the furore of the media has died down, we can discuss what would be the best thing to do about him and his team at Dunne House.'

Both Hancroft and Conway could indeed see the logic in CC Stonehouse's argument. Removing Lomax wouldn't really serve any benefit at this moment. If anything, it would potentially increase suspicions.

DCC Conway stood up from her desk and walked around to the front and leaning her rump against the edge, she looked at her immediate superior and the officer from the Internal Investigations department, 'Perhaps when this is all over, we could charge Lomax with dereliction of duty, or conduct unbecoming, fraternising with his subordinate in a sexual relationship? Surely that's grounds for dismissal?'She asked.

Chief Commissioner Stonehouse smiled at Conway, and she immediately felt uneasy.

A sudden pang of guilty conscience?

'I've had Detective Superintendent Hancroft deploy a team of officers keeping Lomax and his entire team under close watch since he was brought back from his vacation by Chief Superintendent Warwick to investigate Miss Waterman's death,' Stonehouse stated matter-of-factly. He then added, 'It is my decision that he be allowed to continue this case to its ultimate conclusion, regardless of the ramifications that brings. It is of course unfortunate that certain individuals connected with Vortexa Pharmaceuticals have been instrumental in causing excessive damage and loss of life in such a short time. However, unless we allow Lomax and his team to continue, we won't be in a position to clear ourselves with the publicity debacle.'

DCC Conway nodded her head. 'I agree, the flak we've been getting recently from the media is proving extremely difficult to control, and as the incidents continue to occur it's going to get that much harder. But I'm certain we can and will weather the storm. I'll speak to my PA and ask him to begin preparing a press release. He's extremely excellent at spinning the truth.'

Stonehouse's eyes widened and his brow became filled with deep furrows. 'If he's that good, how come he wasn't snapped up by the prime minister?'

'He was at first... but he found that he just couldn't spin the bullshit that the PM and the rest of the government ministers wanted him to,' DCC Conway replied. 'Our bullshit is by far much easier to deliver to the media. Although to be honest, I doubt the public are as stupid as we'd like to believe they are.'

***

During the rest of the day, DCI Lomax and his team continued to try and piece together what information they had, working it into different possibilities, and discarding if it appeared too outlandish.

At just after six pm, after an exhausting and demoralising day without culminating in any further progress, or being able to piece together what evidence they had acquired via the collective members of their incident room staff in a cohesive way that made any more sense than they had already concluded, Lomax decided to take Roma, DC Crosse and DC Greggs out for a meal and a few beers.

Lomax chose a more select establishment, and one unlikely to place them in any danger: The Moon Under the Water, a Wetherspoon's in Leicester Square, where all four enjoyed a meal and a few drinks, discussing the case in low voices for an hour, before relaxing and discussing other things. At nine-forty-five, both DC Crosse and DC Greggs left the pub. They went in different directions.

Having turned left after exiting the pub, DC Greggs turned left into Irving Street, right onto Charing Cross Road, passing the Portrait Gallery, crossed the road to Duncannon St, and made his way to Charing Cross railway station. There he made a call using a public phone.

Lomax and Roma left the pub soon afterwards and went to the Odeon cinema, a couple of doors along from the pub and took in a late-night screening of a movie, some kind of romantic comedy. Then they went back to Roma's sister Helena's home for the night, and both hoped they wouldn't be disturbed at all.

***

11:51 PM. Private Hospital, somewhere within Greater London.

Dean Morgan was asleep, albeit fitfully. The sedative medication was wearing off, as was the morphine he'd been given almost two hours ago. As he began to wake up, he thought he heard strange noises coming from somewhere along the corridor, a shuffling, and scuffling series of sounds which he thought were unnatural.

He sat up and swung himself painfully around, his legs now dangling over the side of the bed. He rubbed his eyes and listened. Silence; nothing.

Lowering his feet to the floor, he cursed 'Shit,' as the cold linoleum sent a shock through his body. He found the hospital slippers, put them on and grabbed the dressing gown from the hook on the door of the room. Slowly and carefully, he pressed down the lever and opened the door to his room which he was surprised to discover wasn't locked.

He cautiously peered into the dimmed corridor and noted that the uniformed police officers stationed outside his and Verity's rooms were gone. As he looked more carefully, he noticed lying in the doorway of one of the other rooms a police radio, which had obviously been dislodged from the officer's uniform.

But by whom? And why? Then as he carefully exited his room and began moving along the corridor towards Verity's room, the realisation dawned upon him, and it struck him like an icicle being thrust into his heart.

He shuddered.

That bastard from Vortexa, whoever he was, had discovered where he and Verity were, and either planned to kidnap them and take them back to punish them, continue with the experiments, or simply just kill them.

Dean wondered why the hospital staff weren't around, and as he approached the nurse's station he discovered why, as he saw the piled unconscious forms of the two uniformed police officers as well as the three hospital on-duty staff, each with a dart penetrating their chest, arm or neck.

At least they weren't killing innocent professionals indiscriminately, Dean thought to himself. He wondered why they hadn't gone to his room as well, but he knew that he had to find out urgently if Verity was still okay. He moved as swiftly as he could along the corridor, trying not to make any noise, but the soles of the slippers squeaked on the linoleum.

Why was it that even in private hospitals they had awful noisy linoleum instead of carpeted flooring? Dean cursed and removed the slippers. The cold of the lino made him shudder once more, and he did his best to ignore the chill running up from his feet. As he crept even closer and reached the door, which was ajar, he could hear two whispered male voices coming from what had to be Verity's room.

'She's definitely heavily sedated,' said one of the men.

'That's fine,' said the other. 'Makes it easier to dispose of her, then we can go find the young man, and deal with him.'

'So, how should we kill her? Smother her face with a pillow?' asked the first man, whose voice sounded uncertain. Dean felt that he must be new to this line of work and was possibly being mentored by the more confident individual.

'Nope,' said the male with the deeper voice. 'I have something here supplied by our employer, which I can simply inject into that drip. He'd prefer for this woman to appear as if she simply died from a stroke as a result of her injuries.'

'What about the younger man? How are we going to dispose of him?' asked the other man, more stress and nervousness becoming obvious.

The older and more experienced man was becoming annoyed with the constant questions being thrown at him by his younger charge, and this showed how much the younger man was inappropriately suited for this type of work, and even to be a security officer, in the nefarious side of their employer's business. The older, more experienced *assassin* approached the bed, holding the syringe ready to inject the luminous green substance contained therein into the small rubber stopper in the Y-shaped connecter attached to the dextrose-saline drip bag tubing hanging from the stand beside the bed.

Dean looked at the backs of the two men as they assessed and began to implement their plan. They appeared to be wearing similar uniforms as those in the 4x4 that had chased him and Verity from Canary Wharf.

Although he still felt weak, and his injuries were beginning to jolt back into the discomfort zone, Dean could feel his muscles begin to stiffen, but he knew he wasn't about to stand by and let these two murder Verity in cold blood. Not like this.

He saw the hands rise: one to steady the tube's injection site, and the other to pierce the stopper and depress the plunger, forcing the contents into the drip-feed line. It would take anywhere up to three minutes for the substance to find its way into Verity's bloodstream, and possibly the same amount of time for it to take effect, possibly less, before effectively closing down her brain's control of her body's involuntary functions.

Dean backed away from the door and took a deep breath. He knew if he didn't act now it'd be too late. He didn't have time to call DCI Lomax. Taking one last slow deep breath, he eased himself to the gap and peered in once more. What he saw chilled his blood when he saw that the syringe needle had now been inserted into the tubing, and the larger, older of the two men was slowly depressing the plunger.

Dean froze. He'd been ready, albeit ill-prepared, to attack these two men. He watched for a few seconds and saw the substance begin to mix with the clear dextrose-saline solution already in the transparent tubing.

He had to act.

Now.

As his rage built to a frenzy, Dean barged the door open so that it crashed against its stop. The younger assassin, startled by the unexpected sound and the rushing figure towards him, had no chance to avoid being struck by the fire extinguisher Dean was brandishing like a club. Dean swung the extinguisher with all his might, and the bottom connected heavily across the face of the younger intruder.

The sound of bone being crushed and the squelch of flesh being split seemed loud in the silence of the room, even under the hood the younger man wore. His hands rushed to his face as the pain engulfed him and he fell to his knees on the floor. Dean swung the extinguisher again and struck a second time across the back of the man's head, sending him to the floor, unconscious.

The back of his head opened and blood began seeping freely from the cracked skull and torn flesh, finding its way through the black woollen hood to pool on the linoleum flooring of the room. Dean scrabbled, sucking in a deep breath as his cracked ribs protested, over to the out-of-contention assassin and took something from his still form.

Dean then readied himself before he rushed towards the much larger and far more formidable opponent, who was focussed on completing his task regardless of his associate's fate. He turned to face his intended next victim. Dean glanced towards the bag suspended from the stand, and he could see the green coloured substance moving through the dextrose solution in the clear tubing downwards, closer towards Felicity's arm.

If the intruder had thought about it, he could have adjusted the flow to ensure Verity's death came that much sooner, but thankfully he hadn't. The larger man took a couple of steps towards Dean, his face glaring, his near perfect teeth gleaming in contrast to the camouflage face paint he wore to try and disguise his facial features.

The man stepped agile-like over the prone form of his barely still breathing accomplice but didn't notice the pool of urine laying on the linoleum flooring, and because he was wearing leather soled shoes he immediately lost his balance as his right shoe slid away from under him. His arms began to flail wildly as the bulkier man fought to regain his composure, so Dean used this opportunity to strike.

Bending over, Dean rushed into the larger man head first, directly into the man's stomach. It felt as though he'd just head-butted a brick wall. Dean bounced backwards and had managed to assist the man to regain his balance instead of compounding it. This resulted in Dean receiving a massive blow to the right side of his head from the man's left fist which sent Dean flying, being lifted off his feet by the force of the strike and sent several feet across the room. Dazed, and with his vision blurred, Dean looked over at the bed and saw the green substance was still a distance from entering into Verity's arm, but it wouldn't be much longer.

The larger man used his right foot to hook underneath his unconscious colleague's stomach and shoved him away forcefully to crash against a wall, his head being slammed ferociously against the edge of a cupboard, accompanied by a sickening and bone-crunching sound. A low grunt escaped from the other man's lips as he partially regained consciousness, but only briefly, and then immediately died from a broken neck.

Although the sound of the drip was pretty much indistinguishable amongst the other sounds occurring in the room, such as the heart monitor, Dean was sure he could hear each drop loudly as it escaped the dextrose-saline bag and fell into the collective valve before travelling along the tubing, forcing the unknown substance closer to Verity's bloodstream.

The huge man laughed, then spoke condescendingly. 'I like the way you believe you can outsmart me and overpower me, my foolish little friend.'

'I'm *not* your friend,' Dean hissed back. He rose to his haunches after the briefest of glances around the room, and then once again at the tube leading from the valve towards Verity's arm. The green substance was passing though the collective valve and now only about seven inches away from the cannula, getting closer to entering Verity's body.

The larger man glanced over and grinned. 'Hhmmm… not long now,' he said. Then he distinguished a familiar click, as that of a specific type of mechanism being operated.

When he turned to look back at Dean his expression changed dramatically, when he found himself looking at the silenced barrel-end of his now dead colleague's weapon. A Glock.45 machine-pistol, the same type of weapon that Dean had used a few days ago during the car chase.

Dean's hand was shaking, so he gripped the weapon with both hands, and it became steadier. The stranger took a step closer to Dean, testing the younger man's spirit, testing to see if he still had the courage to fire.

He soon found out.

Dean squeezed the trigger. The weapon bucked wildly at first as the rounds spat out on the rapid-fire setting, and several impacted with the walls of the room, sending huge chunks of plaster flying around, along with small clouds of plaster dust. Dean re-aimed the weapon just as the larger man made a diving action with a huge, bladed combat knife – *his weapon of choice* – raised in one hand and ready to be plunged into Dean's chest. As the larger man closed in to land on top of Dean, he pulled the trigger once more, twenty rounds escaped the end of the silenced barrel, speeding through the air at more than 3,000 feet per second, and obliterated the attacker's head and upper body. The powerful force of the rounds mashed into the face, reducing it into a colander of holes, smaller ones in the front obliterating the man's features, and tearing much larger rents out of the back of the man's skull as the pressure created within from the rounds forced the cranial sutures to part and send the macerated brain matter, severed main arteries, to spatter blood, bone and flesh across a wide area.

Dropping the weapon on the floor as the unknown assailant's almost headless corpse slumped lifelessly between Dean's legs, blood pooling quickly from the gaping maw, Dean got up and rushed to Verity's bedside. The strange green substance was almost at the point of entering the cannula, and reluctantly, Dean knew he only had one choice. He ripped the sticking plaster-tape holding the cannula in place away, and as quickly and carefully as he could, he withdrew the medical item and dropped it into a metal kidney dish set on top of the bedside cabinet.

The green substance began to drip from the end of the cannula, as blood seeped from the puncture wound in Verity's wrist.

Verity unexpectedly came to as Dean was applying pressure to the entry site.

'Dean? What are you doing?' she asked him. Her voice was crackly, dry, so Dean passed a beaker of water to her lips, and she accepted the liquid, taking short sips.

He shifted his position slightly and nodded over to the far wall. Verity glanced and balked when she saw the final positions and conditions of the two men. The younger and smaller of the twos head was pushed backwards at an acute angle, but it was the state of the larger and older, more experienced male's head that caused Verity's stomach to do several somersaults. She covered her mouth and moaned.

'Will you be okay for a few moments? Keep pressure on here, I need to find a nurse, and call DCI Lomax,' Dean said.

'Who? Who's DCI Lomax?' Verity asked.

'He's the police detective investigating the case, in which we were, sorry, are involved in. I'll explain later. I need to find someone to see to you. I won't be long,'

Dean said, then after ensuring that Verity was applying sufficient pressure, he leaned in close and gave her a gentle kiss on her left cheek. He then took a spare bed sheet from a nearby table, and after unfolding it he threw it across the two bodies. The blood and released body fluids seeping on the floor soon became soaked into the material.

Dean stood up after making sure the bodies were covered, and went to the still open door, which due to the force he'd asserted when entering had come adrift from the bottom hinge. As he exited, it was only then that the three nursing staff and the two uniformed police officers began to come to from the effects of the tranquilliser darts. Dean wondered why they hadn't been killed, but for now he wasn't really too concerned.

He glanced up at the clock on the wall above and behind the nurse's station desk. It showed that the time was now eighteen minutes to one in the morning. He ignored the police officers and tended to the nurse that was virtually fully conscious. After helping her to her feet, he explained about Verity.

One of the police officers came to and started to rise, albeit unsteadily, but with Dean's assistance he was aided to a nearby chair. 'How do you feel?' Dean asked, although he was fairly certain he knew what the response would be.

'Fucking awful,' the officer replied.

'Does your radio still work?' Dean asked.

'I think so, why do you ask?' the officer replied. Then without warning he retched a few times and then vomited onto the floor, narrowly missing Dean's bare feet.

'I need you to get in contact with DCI Lomax immediately. Tell him to get here as fast as he can and bring some extra officers as well,' Dean said, then he returned to Verity's room, after helping the others to come back to their senses.

**

DCI Lomax got the call at just after two-ten in the morning. He immediately called DC Crosse and DC Greggs, as well as Chief Superintendent Charles Warwick, who it must be said was far from pleased at being woken up at that time in the morning.

As for Roma Clarkson, she found out at almost the very same time as Lomax, listening to her superior as he explained the situation to Chief Superintendent Warwick, as calmly and concisely as he could, barring the expletive-filled interruptions from their superior. Lomax managed to eventually calm down Chief Superintendent Warwick's concerns by promising that he would do everything he could to ensure that this situation didn't reach the media, and therefore cause further complications with those higher up in the Metropolitan Police hierarchy.

After hastily getting dressed, Lomax and Roma drove at high speed to the privately run hospital, with Roma behind the wheel. The scene was one of utter destruction in the private room that Verity had been occupying, although by the time Lomax and his team arrived she had been moved to another room. The two uniformed officers were questioned by Lomax and Clarkson, while the three nurses were interviewed by Crosse and Greggs.

Dean and Verity were interviewed by Lomax and Roma in private after the SOCO technicians were called for to take forensic evidence from the hallway, nurses, police officers, the room, and from Dean and Verity, prior to the two corpses being removed from the crime scene.

'I have a very strong feeling the top brass aren't going to be very happy, when they hear about this,' Roma said to Lomax as they climbed back into the Vectra in the car park of the hospital. The coroner's vehicle had already arrived and removed the two dead men, to take them to Dr. Sally Hickton, who was already waiting patiently for them at University College Hospital's mortuary. She was far from best pleased at being told she had to drop her current caseload and go immediately to UCH.

'Where to?' Roma asked, as Lomax glanced at the older police vehicle pool Vectra's integrated dashboard clock, which showed the time as coming up to four-twenty-five in the morning. She'd changed vehicles the previous afternoon again, at Lomax's suggestion, in the hope that if whoever had been planting bugging devices on the pool cars being used by Roma would leave the older vehicles alone, but he couldn't be certain he was right. Roma had used her own initiative by travelling to Bromley police station to visit a friend and colleague there, sabotaging the vehicle and requesting her friend's commanding officer there, Inspector Trevor Ellson, if she could borrow one of their spare pool vehicles, which he graciously obliged as a professional courtesy. Mainly however, it was because he was attracted to Roma, and hoped that she would accept his offer of a meal and a drink; yet to his dismay, and once she'd acquired the replacement vehicle keys, she blew him off.

Roma told Lomax who laughed, despite the recent events, and told Roma he wasn't at all surprised, seeing as Inspector Ellson was a notorious lech, a womaniser who had already been divorced three times in the last eight years.

'Seeing as we have a *clean* car, why don't we slope off back to my sister's?' Roma suggested. 'Catch up on the *sleep* we were recently deprived of? Oh and, perhaps we could turn our damned phones off this time?'

'Okay,' Lomax agreed. Roma drove, while he called DC Crosse and told him that he and Roma were following a potential lead and would be travelling outside of the Greater London area for a few hours. He also told DC Crosse that they wouldn't be back in until late morning.

To be frank, at that exact moment in time, he couldn't really give a damn if anyone from his team did *suspect* that he and Roma were *involved* intimately. Regardless of whether it was in breach of protocol or not.

Nineteen

Saturday 19th 10.29 AM.

Raymond Deakins felt a tingling sensation creeping up his lower legs; beginning in his toes, moving to his ankles and lower part of his legs, over his knees and then when it hit his lower abdomen, that's when it began to get painful; *very painful.*

He felt as if his insides were being squeezed in a vice. His intestines, spleen, kidneys, liver. Then the pain continued up to his lungs and his heart. They felt as though they were all on fire; burning from inside, as though he were spontaneously combusting, and he could sense, feel it as it was happening to him as every millisecond passed by. Every sensation heightened by an acute sensitivity, caused by whatever had been injected into him via the hypodermic syringe, which now lay empty in the medical tray at the side of the bed.

Raymond Deakins' eyes were being forced to remain open by eye clamps which looked like uncomfortable medical instruments taken from a museum of torture. The semi-circular bars rested against the eyeball top and bottom; the eyelids forced back by spring-loaded hooks. He looked startled, his nostrils flaring as his breathing was increasing in short but rapid bursts, he began to sound as if he was going into hyperventilation shock.

Suddenly he felt calmer, his breathing became slower, easier and the pulse monitor attached to his right index finger detected and showed on the ECG machine nearby that his heart-rate was returning to a near normal rate of between sixty-eight and seventy-two beats per minute.

Due to the CEO's chief female neuro-biochemist Sandranna Jorgensen being killed during an earlier procedure being conducted upon the female Interpol officer, who unexpectedly had suffered a severe allergic reaction to the various compounds that made up the sub tropic-neuro-inhibitor compound, it was lucky that Helmut Grüber-Stahlmann had been keeping a close eye on Sandranna's work, even to the point of spying on her whenever she refused to share much of her discoveries.

Now that she was dead, he could persevere with her work, study it closely and make whatever amendments and recalculations for the formulae to correct the mistakes she'd obviously made and overlooked. Grüber-Stahlmann felt that much more superior to that of his now deceased colleague, even though he'd recognised that his employer, the CEO, had been smitten by the Swede, favoured her over the elder man for obvious reasons, even though she regularly shunned his amorous attentions.

Grüber-Stahlmann approached the examination table. Deakins' arms and legs were secured in a much more superior fashion than the Interpol officers were, having seen the video footage of what had occurred before, and observed how the *'test subject'* had reacted badly to the test sample resulting in the CEO suffering from a particularly nasty wound to his left forearm, which was now stitched and covered by a pressure sleeve.

Grüber-Stahlmann had assured the CEO that he had discovered the errors made by Jorgensen, and had adjusted the ratios appropriately for the different compounds, then after testing his adaptation on the lab animals, specifically the chimps and one of the gorillas held in captivity in a secure area, he found it humorously ironic that he was about to culminate his efforts by testing on a human; a human animal rights activist of all people.

The CEO had decided to watch the effects this time from a safe distance, namely his office via a closed-circuit

TV system. He had no intention of being wounded a second time, or worse. Joining him were six other people, three of whom had travelled over from the now defunct Dutch facility. The German woman Patricia Kohl, the Dutchman Kurt Anderlich, the Texan Max Burroughs along with Liam Garratt, a British thug in the CEO's employ, acting as a trouble-shooter and enforcer, and his two associates, Del Kingsley and Peter Tyler.

Grüber-Stahlmann had already inserted a cannula tube and like with the Interpol officer this had a rubber stopper, in which Grüber-Stahlmann carefully inserted the needle of the syringe until it had fully penetrated the stopper and he depressed the plunger, forcing the contents down into the clear plastic tubing.

The substance that had been injected was swiftly making its way towards Deakins' brain. He began to feel light-headed, yet at the same time his eyes felt as though they were on fire and burning from behind the orbits. He screamed, but nothing escaped from between his lips, his vocal cords had been paralysed; the screaming voice must have been inside his head.

'How long before we see a positive result?' asked the disembodied voice of the CEO, coming from the speaker set into the panel on the wall.

Grüber-Stahlmann smiled, and turned to look at the speaker, which also had a built-in camera lens. There were other lenses set at various points in the small lab, all directed at the table where Raymond Deakins lay.

'The drug should have taken full effect within the next twenty minutes. I am certain that you'll have full, unrestricted control over his mind, and he will be utterly unable to resist your commands,' Grüber-Stahlmann stated, confidently.

***

At the same time that Raymond Deakins was being experimented upon, Roma tried her phone once more. She'd been trying to call Raymond Deakins' father, her uncle, Neville, but he'd refused or simply failed to respond to any of the messages she'd left for him. This riled Roma no end, and now as she stood outside Neville Deakins' house in the leafy suburb of Leatherhead in Surrey, she could feel her rage was on the increase. Seven times she'd pressed the doorbell, in the last fifteen minutes. And still… no answer.

'C'mon. Let's go,' Lomax said. 'This is a waste of time. He's either not in, or if he is he's still very angry with you… I mean…us.' Lomax turned to leave and had only taken five steps away from the house when he overheard Roma swear very loudly. He turned to look at her and saw a curtain twitch in the downstairs front bay window. 'Roma… come on, let's get back to the station,' he said loudly but trying to sound annoyed at the same time.

Reluctantly, as she turned away from the door, her face like thunder, Roma started to walk towards Lomax. Reaching the gate, and out of earshot he spoke again. 'Someone's home. I saw a curtain twitch.'

'Did you see a face or a hand?' Roma asked.

'No. Just a movement of a curtain. Why?' he asked.

'They have a cat, that's all. All the knocking and ringing the bell might have disturbed it,' Roma replied.

'Damn,' Lomax said angrily.

'Why are you annoyed?' Roma enquired as they climbed back into the third older pool car. As she inserted the key into the ignition of the dark blue Audi A4, she turned to look at Lomax. He wasn't looking best pleased.

'I just thought he was avoiding us, that's all,' Lomax said.

'Where to, then?' Roma asked.

'I need to speak to Sally Hickton,' Lomax said succinctly.

Roma nodded, started the engine and selecting first gear she released the handbrake and pulled away, heading for Sally's usual place of work. It would take them at least two hours to get back into the city and reach UCH, where Dr Sally Hickton was swamped with corpses; the backlog was proving to be taking its toll on her nerves and her sense of humour. Her stress level was at breaking point, and when Lomax and Roma arrived Sally wasn't in the best of moods. Mostly as she'd been requested to return to her own mortuary at St. Thomas's Hospital for an urgent autopsy case her boss demanded she conduct.

'So you're telling me,' began Lomax as he sat in Sally Hickton's office at the main coroner's office suite attached to St. Thomas's Hospital, after she'd told him about her findings concerning the Interpol Officer's death, 'that the strange substance is still unidentified?'

'Yes, that's exactly what I'm saying,' Sally retorted testily. 'Due to the fact that every one of the compounds used in the substance retrieved from her body have been carefully prepared, and from what I can ascertain, they belong to out-of-the-ordinary plants and creatures from far off lands or seas. I'm not a specialist in these substances, however, purely from an amateur interest, I'd be inclined to think they were derived from plants and amphibians and sea creatures' venoms and have been specifically reverse-engineered. I've sent samples to some colleagues at various labs here in the UK. I'm hoping to receive some confirmation as soon as is possible,' Sally said, hardly pausing to breathe, due to her state of tiredness and anxiety.

Lomax huffed loudly. He was becoming more and more agitated by this case. Being driven by Roma right across London to where Sally preferred to be based, even though her work as a Home Office pathologist meant that she could (and was on far too many occasions) called to perform examinations of deceased in situ at suspicious scenes of crime. Once in attendance Sally would be required to confirm whether the person was in fact dead, then, if possible, give an approximate time of death and then follow up with post-mortem examinations. 'When you get the results,' Lomax said, his voice low and showing just how tired and dejected with this case he really was, 'please call me immediately, no matter how late,' he asked.

Sally told him she would.

Lomax felt certain that when he'd attained the rank of DCI and had been assigned this office, he'd arranged the tables, filing cabinets, shelving units and even the few framed pictures on the wall, and would have definitely noticed anything out of the ordinary.

He closed his eyes for a few moments and then opened them again and stared at the spot again, then moved around the room, searching for anything different. After a fastidious examination of his office, he looked at the phone on his desk. He wondered if they'd somehow managed to remove the camera and replace it with a 'bugging' device in his phone. Although he immediately discarded that notion, seeing as he rarely really used his landline for exterior calls, he found himself feeling much more uncomfortable. He returned to his chair behind his desk and reached for the phone, repositioning it just off to his right near the corner of his desk. He took the handset off the cradle and began to punch out Roma's official landline number at her private residence. Then he looked at the clock.

It was almost half-past one in the morning. Although he wondered if she was awake at this hour, perhaps even wondering about what she was up to. With the handset still in his hand, he moved it closer to his ear as the dialling tone changed to a continuous tone. He listened for a few moments, then pressed the button to reassert the dialling purr. Then he heard it.

Something he'd feared hearing, but from his knowledge of covert surveillance and listening devices in the past, and even with the most sophisticated electronic devices being developed today, interference with the phone's internal wiring and speakers was inevitable. He replaced the handset and wondered who it might actually be keeping him under a very close watch. His thoughts immediately went to the unknown person that had him abducted not that long ago, and had continued to threaten him, concerning the evidence collected from Amanda Waterman's secret home lab at her apartment.

With his father now no longer at risk and his brother Gerald dead, the only person left from a family perspective was his sister Hillary, and as difficult and perhaps even heartless as it was to admit it, he really couldn't care less if she was to be killed as a result of this investigation. Needless to say, he refused to deliver the evidence as forewarned to do so at the directed place and time.

The only other person that might be at risk was Roma. If the people behind this investigation knew of their intimate relationship, then why hadn't she been taken hostage already? He took a deep breath and sighed. He hoped he was worrying for nothing, but he knew he'd have to keep his wits about him.

Because he'd closed the door to his office, and only had the light from a small desk lamp shining down onto the top of his blotter pad with a low wattage bulb providing the illumination, Lomax felt strangely at ease, and leaning back in his chair he swiftly fell asleep in the silence.

04:20 am.

A loud bang brought him awake from his slumber, startled as he was normally a light sleeper. Lomax only detected the shuffling sounds after several minutes, coupled with the faint but unmistakable deep breathing sounds coming from beyond his office door. He looked at the clock and cursed under his breath and assumed that the loud bang was someone coming in early from the investigation team to begin work.

Rising from behind his desk, his heart beating fast from the unexpected alert, Lomax went to his door and with his hand around the lever ready to push down. He saw through the frosted glass pane a shadowed figure walk by, illuminated by the few lights still left on in the larger suite.

Lomax faltered slightly at the door, as the hairstyle of the figure was nothing like anyone on the team that he recognised immediately. Lomax could make out that the hair was spiked up, and it was also the height and body-shape that made him hesitate before he dared to push the door lever down and release the catch. From his side of the door, Lomax could hear movement. Drawers being opened and closed.

The seven drab, scratched and dented grey metal filing cabinets had their drawers opened, and slammed shut after papers were withdrawn and unceremoniously dropped onto the floor. Lomax's hearing was pretty acute at the best of times, and even through the thin walls of the partitioned office, and the standard door to his office, he could easily make out the footfalls on the thin corrugated industrial brown carpeting, as the intruder (as this could *never* be one of his team members behaving in this manner – at least he hoped not) moved about. He knew that most of his team wouldn't begin to arrive until just after six in the morning, in the main part of the station where the brunt of uniformed policing occurred, at this time of the morning. With the main workforce out on patrolling set routes in London, there were only three officers on duty, and one was the desk sergeant. Lomax couldn't rely on any of the three to rush to his assistance, even if he did press the panic alarm.

When the investigation suite went unnaturally quiet, he retrieved something from a small two-drawer pedestal cabinet under his desk, unlocking the lower drawer; he winced as the hinges gave out a quiet but noticeable squeak. Lomax carefully opened his office door. He pulled the office door open slowly and peered around the leading edge into the vast space of the incident room, trying to make out shapes in the dullness. The low-level illumination given off by the lamps was negligible and it made it that much more difficult to make out the furniture.

Cautiously he stepped out into the larger space and remembered that the main lighting switches were on the far side near the main double doors that lead up from the lower floors. He moved out and kept looking about quickly, changing his line of sight after a few seconds, and as he moved deeper into the space, he unfortunately caught his right thigh on the edge of DC Crosse's work-desk very hard, and the ceramic cup which held his pens etc. near that corner was knocked over by the severe jolt, spilling its contents with an annoying loudness to which Lomax muttered under his breath, giving himself a severe admonishment.

He heard a movement off to his right, and as he rubbed the spot on his leg where he was certain a lovely bruise would form, he stepped around the desk front and slowly moved to where he thought the sound emanated from.

He saw a metal waste bin roll on the floor, having come from around a corner of one of the filing cabinets and fully into view, some of the screwed-up balls of paper from inside spilling onto the floor.

Then it happened. Lomax was caught totally off guard as the arm unexpectedly wrapped itself around his neck in a choking hold. He could feel the coldness of the flesh of the wiry and seemingly hairless arm pressing in against his own skin, and he reached up with his free left hand, trying to get his fingers in between his throat and the arm. He dug his fingernails into the flesh of the person choking him, pressing as much strength through his fingers, hoping that whoever was attacking him would release his grip.

Lomax could feel himself losing consciousness as he was being starved of air. He could also feel something being pressed into his back, then he felt the agonising jolt of electricity being passed into him once the arm was unexpectedly removed from around his neck. He was immediately disorientated, gasping for air, and then he felt a new agony from the effects of a stun-gun or Taser device. Lomax's body convulsed and he fell heavily to the carpeted floor, twitching.

He'd fallen unconscious, but he was unsure for quite how long. Minutes? Hours? Where was he? He opened his eyes and realised that he was still in the office area, but he'd been lifted into one of the office chairs and tied to it by rope the intruder had obviously brought with him. Bound around his chest to the backrest, wrists to the arm rests and his feet tucked under the seat and tied to the rear two wheeled feet sections.

As he regained his senses, he felt the pain shoot through him from where he'd been tasered. The searing pain caused his eyes to water profusely, so he blinked to clear his vision. Then the unexpected intruder made his presence known. Lomax stared open-mouthed as Raymond Deakins' face was illuminated by a light that was switched on. 'You,' Lomax shouted out, although his voice had been affected by the pressure exerted by Deakins' arm around his neck, and it came out more as a croak.

'Yes… it's me, Lomax. And as you can plainly see, the reports of my death were… shall we say greatly exaggerated,' Deakins said, an almost feral sneer appearing across his face.

As Lomax studied Deakins, he noted with disdain that Deakins had Lomax's handgun stuffed down the waistband of his jeans. The Browning 9mm pistol, Lomax's personal choice of handgun, and one he'd fought hard and determinedly to retain his use of even though the Police Service were favouring the new lightweight Heckler & Koch .50mm round weapons.

Lomax had to laugh, though. It wasn't loaded at present, it had an empty magazine in it; well, empty that is of 'live' rounds – Lomax preferred to use blanks, they were noisy enough and usually had the desired effect. In fact, he'd never ever shot at anyone he'd been chasing, regardless of whether they'd had real bullets in their weapons and had ungraciously fired at him with the intent to kill him. He did have magazines with live rounds in a secure metal box in his office, but he usually kept the gun 'loaded' with the blank rounds.

He wondered if Deakins could tell if the gun wasn't actually loaded with live rounds. He doubted that Deakins had much if any real experience with firearms, unless it was the wrong end of the barrel being shoved in his face, and his being threatened to pay up what he owed for the drugs he'd been getting on tick.

The only weapon types Deakins was known for were knives and machetes.

'Are we feeling better?' Deakins' sarcastic tone enquired, while he gently caressed the handgrip of the handgun as it rested within the waistband of his jeans.

'Fuck you,' Lomax replied, regaining his voice slightly and spitting the words towards the younger man, who stood before him grinning like the proverbial Cheshire Cat.

'That's not nice, is it?' Deakins said, then he stepped closer and with a swiftness even Lomax couldn't have expected, Deakins punched Lomax on the right side of his jaw, causing the DCI to swivel as far as the ropes tying his feet to the supports on the chair would allow, while they dug into his flesh through his trousers, compounding their effect, by burning through friction.

The head blow hurt like hell. His skin stung and Lomax thought that it had loosened one of his back teeth. Lomax had bitten deeply into one side of his tongue, and he spat blood out onto the carpet narrowly missing Deakins' left foot. 'What are you doing here? And if you wouldn't mind, dare to tell me where you've been hiding?' Lomax asked, running his sore tongue around the back of his mouth, but feeling nothing that resembled a loosened tooth.

Deakins took a few steps away, still staring at Lomax. He sat in a chair facing the detective and after clearing his throat, he spoke calmly. 'I'm here... because you were warned to release the evidence concerning this case you're obviously still working on, and because you have refused to do so, I was sent here to recover said evidence, or if upon failing to acquire it myself, to force you to hand it over. Whether or not you lived or died was left up to me. As to where I've been hiding... that I cannot say, as I have no idea.'

'I'd already ascertained that you'd been kidnapped. For what reason and by whom I am still investigating. Although judging by the fact that you've been sent here to recover *the evidence* relating to Vortexa Pharmaceuticals, the only conclusion I've come to at this moment is that the person that sent you here to retrieve the 'evidence' pertaining to the current case, has to be the very same person that previously had me abducted and threatened me and my family,' Lomax said bluntly.

She'd entered via the rear door of the station building, using her personal coded entry pin. Bypassing the uniformed section, Roma climbed the stairs that led up to the CID offices. Wearing a pair of soft-soled shoes, her steps on the concrete stairs made hardly any sound. At that time in the morning, just after half five, it was still far too early for the main team to be in attendance; they rarely arrived before seven-thirty, unless specifically requested to do so.

Roma had found it difficult to sleep, mostly due to the fact she was alone. She'd been wondering about Lomax, was about to call him, but decided he didn't need any additional emotional pressure on him at present. So Roma had decided to come in and go through her case notes, and check the evidence again, see if there was anything they'd all missed.

When she reached their office floor, she heard voices. She recognised both, but she held back before barging in. The right-hand door was moving slightly, caused by a draught coming down from above in the stairwell.

Roma left the doors and climbed up to the next floor where she found an open window, the vertical security bars bent apart to allow someone to climb through, using a hydraulic car jack, and who had obviously come in via the roof, a nylon climbing rope flicking about outside as it was caught by the wind. When she peered outside the open window, she noticed a holdall clipped to the rope hanging just below the window sill. She carefully hauled the bag in through the window and silently set it down on the floor. Opening it, she found several knives and swords.

Because she was unarmed, she grabbed three of the larger knives and took the stairs back down to the CID area. Reaching the doors once more, she edged closer and listened.

'You know… it's ironic that you broke into my flat with the intent to arrest me, and that it was that bitch of a cousin of mine that actually did the deed. If only I could see her now, this minute…' Deakins said.

'What? What would you do to her if she was here, right this minute?' Lomax asked.

Deakins grinned salaciously, licking his lips. 'We're cousins, right? I mean she's damned attractive, even if she is a few years older than me, and an officer of the filth, but then again… she's definitely a hottie. Blood related or not.'

'It's not advisable for first cousins to be intimately involved, any more than it is for brothers and sisters you know,' Lomax said. He hadn't been looking directly at Deakins as he spoke, he had in fact been staring beyond his abductor, to the double doors where Lomax had noticed Roma stealthily enter.

'Ah-ha. I know where you're going Lomax, you two are invol–' Deakins had been so enraptured by his sudden realisation of Lomax and Roma's relationship his distraction was enough to allow Roma to creep up behind Deakins and using the more dangerous looking knife she dug the tip of the blade into his lower back sufficiently enough to make him jump. Deakins turned his head and saw his cousin.

'Carefully remove the gun from your waist and drop it to the floor,' Lomax said firmly.

'Or what?' Deakins asked, still smirking. 'She might have surprised me and got the drop on me. But…' Deakins said defiantly as another person made his presence known from a darkened area of the office.

Bernhard Kleist gun was pressed against Roma's head. Lomax's eyes opened wide in utter shock, combined with anger. Kleist spoke. 'DS Clarkson, I'd suggest that you drop that knife, otherwise you'll force me to shoot you, and I'd prefer not to. My employer is eager to meet you while you're still alive,' he cocked the weapon. The sound echoed loudly in the otherwise silent room.

Sighing loudly, Roma relaxed and drew the knife away from Deakins' back, dropping it to the floor. Deakins in turn turned sharply and slapped Roma hard across the face, sending her backwards, where she stumbled and fell to the floor onto her rump. She raised a hand to caress her cheek which stung, the skin reddening from the strike.

'Deakins… you bastard,' Kleist snapped. 'You were told not to harm either of these two. Our employer wishes for another audience with them. Lomax in particular, especially as you correctly said, he refused to comply with the previous request to deliver the evidence.'

'It won't do you any good anyway,' Roma said from her position on the floor. 'Getting rid of whatever evidence associates your employer with the recent deaths, and the accidents caused by the two escapees being chased by his security employees, we've made copies which have been locked away by our Commander. Even we cannot access them, so in reality, your employer is well and truly fucked.'

'That is indeed unfortunate, if that is the case,' Kleist said.

'So, I take it you were the one that set up Marianne Clourette?'Lomax asked, addressing Kleist directly.

Kleist coughed. A sign of guilt. But he didn't say anything at first, then after he'd thought for a few moments in the silence, he did speak. 'My benefactor had in fact orchestrated my inclusion onto Inspector

D'Ebeauville's Interpol team using his European contacts, who successfully enabled me to be placed at the Interpol inspector's disposal.

'I'm not surprised really, as I felt that for you and Marianne to be granted a tour, especially after the recent incidents, was surprisingly unusual,' Lomax said, a smile appearing on his face. 'Okay guys, you can come in now,' he said, nice and loud.

Unexpectedly for Deakins and for Kleist, they were immediately surrounded by over twenty heavily armed police officers.

Deakins dived for Lomax's gun and was shot in the lower left leg by one of the STG officers before he was able to grab, lift, aim and fire it. He shouted loudly in agony and clutched at his wound, as several officers from the STG squad moved in to slap handcuffs on him.

Kleist was forced to relinquish his weapon which he did, realising that there were several semi-automatic weapons trained upon him; he too was cuffed forcibly, and held firmly by three officers.

Roma grabbed the knife from the floor and went over to Lomax where she cut through the ropes, freeing her superior. 'Great plan. Although I'm surprised it actually worked,' Roma said as Lomax stood up and stretched.

'Me too,' Lomax admitted. 'I just wasn't too sure how long to wait before I called in the infantry.'

Kleist looked worried. He turned to Lomax. 'How did you know that I was the one who caused Marianne to die?' he asked.

'I didn't, not really, but you definitely gave me reason to be suspicious. Inspector D'Ebeauville was also concerned when you agreed to go along with Marianne for the visit to Vortexa, especially when it had been hurriedly organised.

'I find it incredible that your employer, whoever he is, was so gullible to allow this visit, unless he had certain prior intelligence which alerted him to Marianne's true official status as an Interpol officer investigating the company. And then there was the fact that there was little news of what had actually happened to you. No body, and no ransom demands for your release.' Lomax allowed himself a little smile. 'Okay, take these two to the cells, we'll interview them later.'

'What about this one's injury?' asked one of the STG officers.

'I'll get a duty doctor to assess him. If I decide he can be taken to hospital for treatment, I'll need a few of you guys to accompany him, if that's okay?' Lomax asked.

The senior officer nodded, and then left following his colleagues, as they man-handled their charges down the stairs to the cells.

***

Chief Superintendent Warwick's office
08:43 am

DCI Lomax and DS Roma Clarkson sat serious faced before their superior. Chief Superintendent Warwick had been appraised of the situation by Det. Superintendent Miles Hancroft, by way of an urgent phone call, and who it seemed had sources everywhere, and these sources were focussed directly upon Lomax and his team.

'Your handling of this case appears to be falling apart, Lomax,' Chief Superintendent Warwick said, the concern in his voice clearly evident. 'Philip, you're a damned fine detective. But this case… it seems as if this is racing away from you. From what I understand, you have very little specific proof against this as yet unidentified adversary. You've told me that you believe that this person is directly behind the bizarre deaths which have occurred since Miss Waterman's. The two men that were killed during the aborted murder attempt on the two young, escaped prisoners at the hospital. You've suspected that you and your entire team have been under unscrupulous surveillance by some unknown party, potentially connected to the perpetrator behind all these deaths.'

'Sir,' began Roma, carefully choosing her words, 'since this case began, we've had obstacles placed before us, which in my mind are definitely connected, but also by someone even closer.'

Chief Superintendent Warwick's face changed immediately, and he stood up glaring directly at Clarkson. 'Are you accusing me of organising a covert surveillance on one of my own officers, Detective Sergeant?'

Roma shook her head firmly. 'No sir, not you, not at all. But Phil, I mean DCI Lomax confided in me and told me that you'd warned him about a Detective Superintendent Miles Hancroft from the Internal Investigations department. So, I did some digging around of my own. I haven't told DCI Lomax this yet, as I was still collating intel, but it seems that we have bigger problems from within the service itself, and more urgently, from far higher-ranking officers than yourself, sir.'

Both Chief Superintendent Warwick and DCI Lomax looked startled at Roma's revelation. 'Who, exactly?' Chief Superintendent Warwick asked.

'This isn't easy for me to say, sir, yet the evidence I have acquired,' Roma pulled photographs along with voice recordings made by Hancroft to Chief Commissioner Stonehouse and his deputy Conway. She handed out copies to Lomax and Warwick and using a CD player, played the first of several conversations.

'Good God,' Chief Superintendent Warwick blurted out far too loudly, so that his PA/secretary Brigitte Ellis stepped into his office, a concerned expression on her face. He waved her back out and tried to smile, but it was forced.

'I'm sorry sir,' Roma concluded, keeping her voice as calm as she could.

'Well… that explains a hell of a lot,' Lomax said, a cheeky grin appearing across his face. 'At least we now have a clear indication of who else we're up against. If it wasn't bad enough having to deal with that wanker in charge of Vortexa, having his goons try and abduct me again for God knows what purpose.' He started to think carefully. 'Any ideas on how we deal with this new development, sir?' Lomax asked, the cheeky grin now firmly fixed on his handsome face.

Charles Warwick began to chuckle, and he felt more relaxed. More than he had since this sorry case first forced him to contact DCI Lomax while he was on a much-needed break. 'To be honest Phil, no, not really. But I'll see what I can do to put a stop to this.'

Twenty

11:48 AM.

In interview room #4, Raymond Deakins sat behind a battered and scarred white Formica-topped table. Next to him was his 'brief', a solicitor who'd acted on Deakins' behalf on many previous occasions, Frank Whitcombe, a thirty-nine-year-old from a long-established London law firm.

On the other side of the table sat DCI Lomax and DC Crosse. Lomax made the customary explanation of the interview recording procedures to Deakins and his solicitor, and unwrapped the two new recordable compact discs, inserting them into the machine. He pressed the record button. 'The time is one-forty-seven pm. My name is Detective Chief Inspector Philip Lomax, I am accompanied by Detective Constable Christopher Crosse. This is the interview with Mr Raymond Deakins, who is accompanied by his solicitor,' Lomax held out his hand towards Frank Whitcombe for him to speak and introduce himself. He did so in his practised and professional manner.

Lomax hadn't met this particular solicitor before, and he was indeed a very striking man. Dressed in a medium blue suit which he wore with aplomb, coupled with highly-polished black leather shoes to show that he was someone who knew his job. Whitcombe was of average build, handsome features, medium brown hair and brown eyes, high cheekbones and a chiselled chin with a healthy complexion yet tanned from spending a fair amount of time on vacation abroad. He stood at five feet nine inches and had an experienced tone of voice.

Lomax began the interview. 'Raymond Deakins. On the second of January myself and three other police officers arrived at your bedsit at thirty-four Bayliss Road, Lambeth, SE11 in order to detain you for questioning in relation to break-ins connected with Vortexa Pharmaceuticals' laboratories and other animal testing centres. Also, to enquire exactly what your relationship/involvement was with Miss Amanda Waterman, an employee of Vortexa. After a brief and discourteous fracas with myself, you were arrested and placed inside a police vehicle for transport for interview.

'Unfortunately, we, that is the police, were fooled into believing that you were the victim of a deliberate attempt by an as yet unidentified person, or persons, to kill you and thwart our intentions to question you on the matters we were interested in. Can you explain what actually happened and where you were subsequently taken to, and what these people did to you?' Lomax asked.

Frank Whitcombe looked directly into Lomax's face, he spoke firmly, 'My client retains his right to silence and will not answer that or any questions whatsoever regarding your investigation, of which I am assured he has had no involvement whatsoever.'

'So,' DC Crosse began saying, 'in your professional opinion, you're saying that apart from the obvious fact that Deakins—'

'Mr Raymond Deakins, if you wouldn't mind showing some professional courtesy, Detective Constable Crosse,' Whitcombe said, keeping his tone firm and forceful, also for the benefit of the recording. Though Deakins found it very hard to suppress a sarcastic smirk as well as a chuckle.

DC Crosse resumed speaking. 'So, with *Mister* Deakins about to be detained on the earlier declared date as specified by DCI Lomax at the beginning of this interview, and since he was, as it turned out, abducted by said unidentified person or persons, you *Mr Raymond Deakins* are refusing to explain exactly what happened to you, and you refuse to name those responsible for forcing you to stage an attempted kidnapping of DCI Lomax?'

Deakins leaned in to whisper to his solicitor. He leaned in to listen.

Whitcombe leaned back to face the two police officers. Deakins felt a sudden adrenalin rush speed through his system. His pupils became diluted, expanding to almost cover the coloured irises.

The drugs that were still flowing through his system were reacting with his natural adrenalin. That was the concern facing him, as the drugs effecting his mind were continuing to have an unexpected effect upon him, one that he was losing the battle to control.

***

Interview Room #1.

DS Roma Clarkson and DC Neil Greggs had already gone through the same procedural process prior to beginning the interview. In this room, they were trying to get Bernhard Kleist to answer questions relating to Marianne Clourette, his Interpol colleague's death, and his direct involvement with those determined to thwart DCI Lomax's case.

Kleist's male Dutch solicitor, who also acted in Vortexa's Overseas Legal Department and having been brought in by Kleist's unknown employer, was being as difficult as Deakins'. Wilhelm Ubrecht was tall, slim, and good-looking with piercing blue/grey eyes under a shock of platinum blond hair. His mouth was wide with normal lips, a large almost Roman-shaped nose and a narrow chin with dimpled cheeks whether he smiled or not.

Usually not. Ubrecht was not known for his sense of humour.

Speaking in perfect English, almost without a trace of any Dutch accent, Ubrecht spoke firmly. 'My client prefers not to speak under any circumstances. You have no jurisdiction over my client, you also had no right whatsoever to arrest him. Under EU rules, you are not even allowed to arrest Herr Kleist, as he has diplomatic immunity, as agreed via Interpol policies.'

DS Clarkson's anger rose furiously, but she counted to ten before she spoke, her eyes hidden behind her long-lashed eyelids. 'However, you seem to be missing the point. I have here…' DS Clarkson began saying, as she opened a red-coloured A4 folder and pulled out a series of stapled sheets of A4 documents. 'Official documents sent to us by Inspector D'Ebeauville directly once he'd returned to Interpol HQ in France, taking his dead wife back with him, and which confirms that your so-called Interpol Agent Bernhard Kleist has no record whatsoever with Interpol, and therefore he does not fall under *any* diplomatic immunity against arrest.'

Each of the sheets was emblazoned with Interpol's crest in the top right corner. There were two sets, one of which she passed across the table to the Dutch solicitor, who leafed through the paperwork, reading quickly but assuredly, taking in the information. After he had finished, he lay the sheets down on the table, carefully adjusting its position so that it was virtually straight. Ubrecht then turned to look at his client and leaned in to speak quietly into his ear for several moments.

As he did so, Kleist's face drained of colour almost at once. After a few moments of discussion and some time to think, Kleist, through Ubrecht, requested some time to speak to his solicitor in private.

'Interview with ex-Interpol agent – or should that be *fake* Interpol agent Bernhard Kleist and his solicitor

Wilhelm Ubrecht suspended at...' she checked her watch against the wall clock's time, pausing deliberately, at 'fourteen-twenty-one.' Clarkson and Greggs exited the room, standing directly outside with a uniformed officer nearby; they didn't say anything at all, they just looked really pissed off.

In interview room #4, Deakins had steadfastly refused to answer any questions. He sat grinning, daring Lomax to launch himself at Deakins and start a fight, right there, right then.

'My client wishes to confer with me in private. To discuss his options,' Deakins' solicitor, Mr Whitcombe said.

DCI Lomax reluctantly nodded and suspended the recording for the interview in the same official and practised manner as Roma did in the room down the corridor. He then left the room along with Crosse.

The room was soundproofed, and contrary to common belief the British Police *DO NOT* covertly watch or listen in on private conversations between arrested suspects and their lawyers. Even though it is commonly believed that the arrested suspects usually admit to committing the particular type of crime they've been placed in custody for, or parts of the crime or crimes, any information acquired would be deemed inadmissible in a court of law... much to the chagrin of the officers conducting the interviews.

Crosse went to the canteen to get a coffee and something to eat. Lomax went to use the nearest toilets. A uniformed police officer stood outside the room.

Frank Whitcombe was quietly thinking about the options he had to try and facilitate the release of his client, when Deakins suddenly stood up and wrapped his hands around Whitcombe's throat. Using his thumbs at the sides, Deakins squeezed hard at a certain point on the left side and almost straight away Whitcombe passed out. Deakins began using his fists to strike Whitcombe's unprotected face; his limp form fell out of the chair onto the floor after several strikes and landing on his back his right foot kicked out and struck the wooden chair which clattered loudly against the wall of the room.

It was common for an arrested suspect and their brief to disagree when speaking in confidence and Lomax and Crosse, having returned just at that moment, hearing the sounds from the interview room through the partially opened door rushed inside.

The sight that greeted them was extremely disturbing. Frank Whitcombe was unconscious again having been struck by Deakins hard in his face Blood oozed from a split on his top lip.

It took a few moments for both Lomax and Crosse to react, but then Deakins glanced over as he continued to strike at Whitcombe's bloodied face.

Lomax stormed over and, grabbing a handful of Deakins' greasy hair, he snatched the younger man away from the solicitor and threw him hard against the wall, then he drove his right knee directly into Deakins' groin.

Crosse ordered the uniformed officer, who'd been staring at the badly beaten legal representative, to go and get a first aid kit and the paramedics. After a short beat, the officer tore his eyes from the scene and ran.

Crosse removed his jacket and was about to cover the man out of respect. His body was shivering, going into shock; however, Crosse realised if he had he may compromise any DNA evidence from Deakins. He did however check his vitals, pulse, breathing and airway.

'Wassamadder?' Deakins cried out as Lomax pulled his knee back, and then drove it in harder this time. Deakins folded up, grimacing in acute pain. Lomax stepped away then as Deakins spat at Lomax, the phlegm spittle sliding down the DCI's face, Lomax pulled his left hand back holding Deakins' hair, then Lomax swung in with his balled right fist directly into Deakins' face, smashing his nose, loosening a few top teeth, and fracturing the man's left upper jaw.

Blood oozed from the suspect's mouth. Lomax could feel and see where Deakins' teeth had connected with the skin over his knuckles, leaving deep depressions. He released his grip of Deakins' hair and the man dropped to the floor groaning.

Roma had come rushing along the corridor at the sounds of shouting through the open interview room doorway. DC Greggs looked in and was astonished to see Deakins lying unconscious in a heap on the floor, the male solicitor lying a couple of feet away, also badly beaten. Lomax drew back his foot ready to kick him in the head, but Crosse grabbed Lomax's arm and yanked him backwards.

After throwing Deakins back into a cell, after having him checked over by an on-call doctor, the paramedics arrived to check over Frank Whitcombe and transport him to hospital.

'Jesus. What the fuck happened in here?' DC Greggs asked.

DC Crosse answered. 'Deakins just brutally hit his solicitor.'

'What? In there? For Christ's sake. Chief Superintendent Warwick's going to have all our balls for breakfast over this,' DC Greggs said, the concern obvious in his tone.

'Hey. He wanted to confer with him due to the line of questioning, so we had to leave the fucking room. Police procedures. Warwick will understand that. He'll also understand that with Deakins' recent involvement with the prime suspect, aka the CEO of Vortexa, he'll be well aware that Deakins was probably likely under the influence of the drugs he's been subjected to. Don't go blaming DCI Lomax or me, you prick.' DC Crosse felt as though he wanted to go over to his fellow CID officer and punch his lights out, but a look from DS Clarkson soon removed that desire.

Roma took Lomax by the elbow and led him along the corridor. Once there, she spoke quietly. 'Greggs is right in a way, but then so is Crosse. Due to this substance being so damned difficult to isolate in blood tests, and Sally's inability to test it thoroughly and see just what it does to people, neither you nor Crosse could have predicted how Deakins was going to react,' she said.

'I agree, Greggs is right... I think even Warwick's going have a hell of a job keeping this away from Chief Commissioner Stonehouse, Deputy Commissioner Conway and even that Internal Investigations officer, Hancroft,' Lomax said, his voice low and showing to Roma that he felt like this was going to be a case that would definitely get the better of him.

Lomax was still feeling vulnerable since he was abducted and threatened by the unknown CEO.

He felt that this was going to be the major case that he failed to solve. Yet at the same time, he knew that he couldn't allow that to happen. For one thing, he owed it to Amanda Waterman, and secondly, he owed it to his father and to Roma and the rest of his team and to Chief Superintendent Warwick.

Mentally chastising himself, Lomax excused himself from Roma and went to speak to Chief Superintendent Warwick unannounced at his office. Roma watched him leave with a heavy heart, seeing her superior carrying such a burden. Then she left the station; there was someone she desperately needed to speak to.

'He'll see you now, Detective Chief Inspector Lomax,' Bridgette Ellis said. She opened the door to Chief Superintendent Charles Warwick's office and Lomax entered. His heart almost stopped when he noticed the dour expression on his superior's face.

'I've already been made aware of what happened, Philip,' Chief Superintendent Warwick said, his voice filled with concern.

'May I ask by whom, sir?' Lomax asked. Dreading in all honesty who it might just actually be, and at the same time he had an uncomfortable feeling in the pit in his stomach he already knew.

'Detective Superintendent…' Chief Superintendent Warwick began, before Lomax finished it for him.

'Miles bloody Hancroft,' Lomax sighed audibly. 'It's not that difficult to believe, is it? Now, considering that he couldn't have been anywhere particularly close, as in right inside the interview room, and to be able to notify you of precisely what went on within what?' Lomax looked at the clock on the wall off to Warwick's right and his left, then he continued, 'The last twenty-two minutes, with exact details unless… unless somewhere inside our interview rooms, my office, the investigations suite, and potentially even in this very room as we're speaking, sir, there could be hidden cameras and microphones.'

This realisation hadn't actually occurred to Chief Superintendent Warwick, and he shuddered visibly. 'Shall we continue this discussion somewhere else, Philip?'

Lomax agreed. 'I think that would be advisable, sir.'

More than two hours later, after a long round robin trek around Central London using a hire car which Roma Clarkson had acquired using cash given to her by Chief Superintendent Warwick himself, she drove the two men who sat in the rear of the maroon-coloured Audi A6 as they discussed the less than satisfactory results of the interviews with Deakins and Kleist. The main focus however was on what had happened in the short time

Deakins had been allowed to have a private consultation with his solicitor.

'This is very bad, Philip. This event is going to have such a serious impact, not only on whether we can afford to continue investigating this case in the first place, but the ultimate backlash from the media, should they ever get wind of this,' Chief Superintendent Warwick said.

Roma had been listening in the front, with her other ear on the BBC News channel on the car radio as she drove, and swiftly pulled the car over sharply to the kerb when she caught something. 'Sir... Philip, listen.' She turned up the radio.

The three of them sat listening for three full minutes as the radio news presenter spoke.

'...*Raymond Deakins has died whilst being transported by ambulance to an undisclosed hospital. Mr Deakins is also reported to have been viciously attacked by a senior police detective from Earl's Court Police Station. A solicitor acting on behalf of Mr Deakins has been reportedly beaten by a senior ranking police officer investigating the case involving Mr Deakins.*'

'Good God,' Chief Superintendent Warwick said. 'How the fuck did the media get a hold of this obvious load of bullshit?' he asked no-one in particular.

'It's like Phil's been saying, sir. Somehow our offices have been infiltrated by someone with an axe to grind, and I now firmly believe that DCI Lomax is being set up. Possibly by that CEO from Vortexa, and the more I think about it, the more I'm convinced that that CEO has definitely got certain high-ranking police officers in his back pocket.'

'You're speaking of course about Stonehouse, Conway and Hancroft?' CS Warwick said.

Roma nodded, adding 'Of course, I would never surmise that you were implicated in *any* way, sir.'

'I for one, am very glad to hear that, Detective Sergeant.' Warwick paused, stroking his chin, looking decidedly perplexed. As Roma glanced to her right something caught her eye in the driver's side mirror. Before she could warn Warwick and Lomax in the back, an American SUV pulled up in front of the car and another directly behind, boxing them in. The side doors opened as well as the passenger sides and several meticulously suited men and women alighted and surrounded the car facing outwards.

An officious man approached the rear passenger door where Chief Superintendent Warwick sat and opened it; he bent down to peer inside, and in his left hand was his warrant card opened to show his photo and identity.

'Chief Superintendent Charles Warwick. Detective Chief Inspector Philip Lomax and Detective Sergeant Roma Clarkson, would you all please get out of your vehicle and accompany me and my team,' the man said, his voice low, controlled and authoritative in its American accent.

Chief Superintendent Warwick looked at the man with utter disbelief. He climbed out of the car slowly. 'What in God's name is this about? Who are you people?' he asked.

Lomax and Roma both opened their doors and got out. They looked as perplexed as their superior. All three were herded into the minivan that had also pulled up quickly nearby. All three vehicles had the obligatory blacked out windows, which were probably bullet-proofed as well. Once all three police officers were secured in their seats, the man who had approached got in and sat facing them. The sliding door was pulled shut and locked.

The minibus was then sandwiched between the SUVs as they moved away.

'What's going on, for Christ's sake?' Chief Superintendent Warwick demanded, glaring directly at the man facing them.

'If I may? DCI Lomax?' the American said, addressing Lomax. 'You may not be surprised to know that your earlier concerns about being placed under covert surveillance were completely correct. However, where you were in fact wrong was that it wasn't the CEO, who we have recently discovered is none other than one Gerrard Banksworth-Tilburne, an Anglo-American who was born in Richmond, Virginia a few months after you were Mr Lomax, here in the UK. His parents split up in nineteen-seventy-nine, when you were eight, and his mother, a British woman by the name of Patricia Banksworth brought her son Gerrard back to the UK. She enrolled him at...'

Lomax butted in, 'Parrott St. Primary School in Acton in nineteen-seventy-three, when I was about seven going on eight years old. Yes, I remember Gerrard Banksworth, although I think his mother dropped the Tilburne name once the divorce was finalised.'

'That is correct Mr Lomax, however, he seems to have reinstated the Tilburne and dropped the Banksworth,' the man said. 'Just how well did you know him while at school? I only ask to get your opinion of him, as a character reference from his school years if you like.'

Lomax thought for a few moments. 'Basically, he was a bully... right from the offset. He swiftly built up a small gang of nine other children, who he *commanded* through fear, boys and girls. In fact, he had a habit of chasing Amanda mainly when he and I were at the comprehensive level of education. She constantly told him to get lost, that she wasn't interested. I think he had this idea that he could get her one day.

'I had several run-ins with him over Amanda, as he believed I'd stolen her from him, so he and I regularly came to blows,' Lomax said.

'Hmmm... That's very interesting,' the man said.

'Just who the hell are you, where are you taking us and why?' Chief Superintendent Warwick asked, still angry.

'I'm sorry,' the man said. 'My name is Agent Kevin Donaldson, Federal Bureau of Investigation, London Division. The others with me are field agents, some seconded from Northern European countries, Germany, Holland and France. We've been investigating Vortexa Pharmaceuticals Worldwide for the past three years, and when they set up in Canary Wharf, things suddenly went very quiet in their other laboratories.'

The journey to the destination didn't take very long. The minivan stopped and after several doors were opened and slammed shut on the other two SUVs, the sliding door of the minivan was pulled open. Agent Donaldson alighted first and beckoned his three guests out.

Lomax, Roma and Warwick undid their seatbelts and climbed out, to find themselves standing in a brightly lit underground parking garage.

'Where are we?' Roma asked. Her voice echoed eerily in the subterranean void, bouncing off the concrete walls.

Donaldson spoke quietly. 'FBI London HQ,' he said simply.

'And where might that be exactly?' Chief Superintendent Warwick asked.

'I'm afraid I cannot tell you that, at least not just yet. Perhaps after we've had a talk. Please, follow me,' Donaldson said, leading the three police officers to an elevator. The doors opened almost immediately, and the FBI agent entered first. After Lomax, Chief Superintendent Warwick and Roma entered, three of the field agents also got into the elevator, all of them keeping their expressions neutral and impassive. The doors closed and using a special card Donaldson inserted into a slot above a keypad, he then pressed an unmarked button above the numbered ones.

The ride upwards was smooth and virtually silent. It took about three minutes to reach the floor required. When the elevator car stopped, the doors opened and the three police officers found themselves looking into a penthouse suite-sized office area. Tables set around and in the centre of the room had flat screen computer monitors connected to a mainframe system somewhere else within the building. There were windows, but they were covered by wood boarding and in front of them were large multiple screens at a comfortable eye-line.

They were all in operation, showing various scenes across London from both street level and from above. Various screens on the desks were filled with streams of data with operatives carefully scrutinising them.

Donaldson led his three guests through the operations centre to his office at the far end. He gestured for them to take the three chairs set in front of the medium-sized wood desk, with its smoked glass top set before the large window which overlooked the Tower of London.

'So... we're in this part of London,' Lomax said.

Donaldson smirked then pressed a button on a control panel on his desk and the image suddenly switched to one of Central Park in New York from above.

'That's very clever,' Roma said, with a hint of sarcasm. 'You obviously don't want us to know *where* we are, do you?'

'Please, be seated. Would you care for something to drink? Coffee? Tea?' Donaldson asked, ignoring Roma's attempt at humour.

'Yes please,' Warwick replied.

'Okay... as long as it's not poisoned,' Lomax said.

'I'm with DCI Lomax,' Roma added. Then she regretted using those words, then Lomax glanced at her slyly and winked.

As they waited for the beverages to arrive, Donaldson began to explain. 'The reason why the FBI have been brought in is because the President has been informed of a potentially damaging political threat, in which a rogue CIA team have joined up with Tilburne and are planning a worldwide attack on the financial stronghold of the entire planet's banking system. It's basically an extortion attempt to blackmail every single country, which has the finances, the means and the will to give up their entire monetary assets.'

'Jesus,' Warwick said. 'Are they serious? Would you mind telling me just how they intend to do this?'

'The recent events whereby certain individuals have been killed after being subjected to being given an as yet unknown substance, we believe these are simply the guinea pigs, test subjects to refine the properties of the purposely designed drug. Thankfully insofar they still haven't perfected it,' Donaldson said, a brief satisfied smile appearing on his face.

'I wouldn't have thought so,' Charles Warwick said angrily. 'Do you know the death count so far? At least twenty-four fatalities, and that includes two police officers, several innocent pedestrians across London, men, women and children alike. As well as at least one hundred and seventy-nine seriously injured casualties. As a direct result of this madman's plans, far too many innocent people have died or been injured. What *I'd* like to know is how long you've known about this, what you've been doing, and also what you intend to do to help us get that bastard?'

Donaldson paused briefly. 'Look, I'm really very sorry about the deaths, and the injuries sustained by the people concerned, however, no matter what we might have tried to do by intervening too soon, collateral damage is unfortunately inevitable; what I hope you'll appreciate is that I have two covert operatives still undercover within Vortexa's employees.'

'Still have?' Lomax enquired, his forehead developing concerned furrows. He suddenly had an uncomfortable ache in his stomach, as though he already knew what Donaldson was about to say. So, he spoke instead. 'You're speaking of Amanda Waterman; she *was* your prime operative, your spy? I suppose she was also as you Yanks often say *expendable*?'

Donaldson spoke. 'It is regrettable that Amanda died the way she did. I have to admit though, her reports faltered shortly before she was lost. I can only ascertain that perhaps she was scared that Tilburne may have become suspicious.'

The coffees came along with some sandwiches and fruit.

'So, just how exactly did Amanda become embroiled in all this?' Lomax asked.

Donaldson paused. He coughed then began to explain. 'Amanda had discovered the nefarious intentions of Tilburne's covert black-market intentions, and more importantly what he actually intended to use the other special drug for, and she was appalled by it. She got in contact with the FBI when she discovered that her employer was in league with who she thought was the official CIA, so she knew she couldn't go directly to them.'

'She always was highly intelligent, and cautious,' Lomax said. 'That's why she and I never got together,' he smiled.

'So… as it turned out we asked her to remain employed at Vortexa, and to get as much information as she could from the mainframe in London. That's why she had that secret laboratory of her own, due to the fact that she also had a degree in micro-biological chemistry. We helped her equip the lab and we even paid for the apartment lease. She felt that if she could obtain samples of the substance, she could inform us when, or if, she ever cracked how it was all put together.'

'And it got her killed. Murdered,' Roma said, the sympathy evident in her voice. She glanced at Lomax. He glanced back. Their eyes met, briefly.

'Yes. I truly am very sorry about that,' Donaldson said, taking a sip of his coffee. 'However, I have to justify the fact that without the intelligence Amanda – Miss Waterman – had acquired for us, we wouldn't have been able to begin our own in-depth investigation. I can only promise you Mr Lomax, she will not have died in vain.'

'Thank you,' Lomax said. 'I appreciate that. What about this rogue CIA element? Have you discovered anything about them that we may need to know about?' he asked.

'Actually yes, we have,' Donaldson said. He pressed a button on his desk and the huge screen behind him changed, the image of Central Park replaced by six photographs. One was the current image of Gerrard Tilburne, much older than how Lomax remembered him, a lot flabbier in the gut, and a fearsome expression on his face. Donaldson used the cursor to pick out Gerrard's face. 'This was taken a few years ago, shortly before his father died in the States under some very suspicious circumstances I might add. Tilburne Snr was found in his mansion in Beverley Hills with his throat cut at around the same time Gerrard was known to be in the area. Unfortunately, the ensuing court case to prove that even though Gerrard wasn't in the mansion at the time, and that he was responsible for his father's death, was thrown out of the Supreme Court.' Donaldson's face showed the utter contempt and resolute failure regarding that case. 'We became aware that the police detective who had investigated his father's murder was so certain Gerrard had paid someone, a hit man if you like, to kill his father while he was in town but where he had numerous high-profile alibis as to his whereabouts at the time, so that the case was dismissed due to a severe lack of substantial evidence. After Gerrard Tilburne was acquitted, the police officer eventually committed suicide. He was only twenty-nine years old.'

'That's awful,' Roma said.

'That's not the half of it,' Donaldson continued. 'The police officer was married with two young children at the time of building the case against Gerrard Tilburne. His wife and children were thrown into the background as the police detective built his case against him. Unfortunately... much of the video and stills photography imagery taken of Gerrard went missing, as did other important items. Det. Lt. Vincent Vicenzo was sure that someone within the department had been bought off to destroy or remove evidence. Then when the judge threw the case against Gerrard out, Vicenzo threatened that he would do all he could to get Gerrard, but Gerrard struck first. Vicenzo's wife and children were found horribly mutilated. His wife Louisa had been raped by several men then set alight with gasoline. The two children, a boy and girl aged nine and seven years, had their throats cut and they too were set alight.'

Roma felt ill. Her face became ashen and she found it difficult to swallow, her lips and tongue felt dry, she thought she was going to be sick. She filled a glass of water from a jug and took short sips.

Donaldson swiftly concluded this part of his story. 'As I said, Vicenzo couldn't be expected to continue in the force, so he was let go shortly after his family's funeral, which was when he committed suicide.'

Lomax nodded; his expression serious, sympathetic. As was Chief Superintendent Warwick's.

A tear slid down Roma's cheeks. Lomax noticed and fished around in his pocket for some tissues which he handed to her.

Donaldson coughed quietly. 'How bad was your relationship with Gerrard exactly?' he asked Lomax.

'Oh, the usual stuff,' Lomax said, preferring not to recollect in too much detail. 'We simply didn't see eye to eye on many things. Apart from the fact that he didn't like the way Amanda preferred my company to his for one thing, and because I would regularly stand up to him and his gang of thugs, either as a collective lot or individually. Gerrard had a habit of bullying younger kids at school and out of school hours, usually at weekends.

'I'd step in and pull him up about it, then we'd end up fighting. Often his gang would join in outnumbering me, but,' he grinned knowingly with some satisfaction, 'I'd manage somehow to get the better of them. By that, I mean that I didn't exactly fight by Queensberry rules.'

Donaldson smiled. 'Okay, thanks. These other faces belong to the suspects involved in the rogue CIA unit. Unfortunately, we haven't been able to identify any of them conclusively, and I'm hoping that we do very soon, but that could be easier said than done as we have no idea where they happen to be at the moment.'

Lomax studied the images from his chair, then he stood up and stepped closer to the screen, but the images became fuzzier, blurrier. 'Can you make these images clearer?' he asked the FBI Unit Director.

Donaldson nodded and using a mouse pad built into the desktop he made the image clearer and more centralised on the main screen, overlapping the others. 'Is that better?' he asked once he'd finished.

Lomax stepped backwards then forwards once more. He looked at the bottom right face in the background, and Donaldson brought that one up and reduced it as well, then placed it next to the first one. He then pressed another button which changed the profiles of both images. Straight on to the camera, a left-side shot then a right-side, then they began alternating so it appeared that the person was moving.

Lomax took his time studying the two faces. He reached into his pocket and pulled out the new unregistered mobile phone Roma had bought for him, but Donaldson spoke. 'I'd rather you didn't use that here. Who do you need to call?'

'Sally Hickton, a very friendly and helpful Home Office pathologist friend of mine,' Lomax answered.

'Here,' Donaldson said, pushing a landline phone set towards him. 'Would you mind putting it on speakerphone?' he asked.

Lomax nodded. He dialled the number he knew off by heart. After several rings he was about to replace the handset when Sally answered. 'Hello? Sally Hickton here, how can I help?'

Lomax flicked it to speakerphone. 'Hi Sally, Phil Lomax here.'

'Oh, hi Phil. What is it you want this time?' Sally asked.

'I need some info. The two stiffs from the attempted hit on Dean Morgan and Verity Bracknell at the private hospital on the thirteenth of February. Do either of them have any tattoos on their necks?' Lomax asked.

'Hang on one sec while I get my notes.' The sound of Sally's handset being set down on the table was heard. After about thirty seconds she returned. 'Yes, one of them, the larger of the two, had a coloured dragonfly tattoo with large teeth in its head and a dragon's tail with a forked end on the right side of his neck. The smaller younger man had a scar running down the right-side cheek from the outside corner of his eye down diagonally to stop just past his upper lip near his fulcrum. The younger man also had his right earlobe missing, probably a birth defect, but I cannot be certain, it may have been an injury that was badly repaired. Why do you ask, Phil?' Sally asked, her interest piqued.

'Just something I'm working on at the moment. I just needed to know. I'll let you know if it was important. Thanks, Sally. Bye for now,' Lomax said, then cut the connection. He turned to the images once more, scrutinised them closely for a few more moments then nodded. 'Well… these two we can scrub off our wanted list.' He tapped the two images in turn. 'I'm inclined to believe that these two boys were supposed to be the top assassins for this rogue CIA team. But what I cannot figure out is why they were sent to kill the two escapee prisoners, or how they discovered their whereabouts in the first place.'

Lomax looked at her. He nodded slowly, pondering.

After another forty minutes Lomax, Roma and Chief Superintendent Warwick were driven back to where their hire car had been left.

Twenty-One

Monday January 21st. 14.07 PM.

DCC Felicity Conway was en route for a meeting. A very urgent and important meeting she was requested to attend, along with her superior Chief Commissioner Sir William Stonehouse. Detective Superintendent Miles Hancroft had arranged the meeting in the main hall of the Natural History Museum. She was due to be there at half past two in the afternoon.

Dressed in civilian clothes, she wore a black trouser suit with a light blue blouse, and black ankle boots. Due to the brisk weather, she also wore a thick beige woollen overcoat and a red silk scarf covering her head. She had a large suede handbag slung over one shoulder. Travelling by public transport as advised to do so, she mingled with the throng of passengers on the London Underground, which made her feel both vulnerable and very uneasy.

She had a high-profile job and was often seen on television, usually alongside her immediate boss, admonishing the criminals of London for their activities. She hoped that she wouldn't be recognised by anyone she may have helped put in prison in the past. Thankfully, with the new anti-suicide barriers being put up across the London Underground system she felt a little safer, but that wouldn't prevent her from being seriously injured if someone did recognise her and either shot her or knifed her, even in full view of the public.

Being alone was the worst thing. Hancroft had insisted they arrive separately and by different forms of transport. Stonehouse was en route via a black cab. He too was in civilian attire. Jeans, trainers, a woollen white sweater over a cotton pale green shirt and a brown leather bomber jacket with white wool fleece collar. He also wore a ski hat. This was for his own safety, similar to the reason for Felicity Conway.

Conway arrived first, exiting the passageway from South Kensington tube station, and feeling increasingly unnerved when she was observed for several moments by a busker set on a spot along the tunnel just before the exit into the grounds of the National History Museum. With him was a scraggy mongrel which looked as if it was at death's door.

She craned her head slightly to her right and looked carefully, to see if he had risen and began to follow her. But no... He was still sitting, legs crossed in front of him as he strummed the guitar and made a feeble attempt at singing a James Blunt song.

Sighing under her breath, Conway stepped into the grounds of the museum and made her way towards the main entrance steps and then in through the door. She was accosted by the security staff who insisted on looking through her handbag which she happily allowed them to do. She had nothing to hide; she wasn't a terrorist and she almost had the urge to show the female security officer her police warrant card.

However, she'd been instructed not to by Hancroft.

Why was he calling the shots? How come he seemed to be ordering the two most powerful, high-ranking police officers in the UK's capital city of London? Insisting that they followed the demands of a subordinate officer from the Internal Investigations Division?

Conway had begun to feel increasingly uncomfortable taking orders from Hancroft, and yet she was already in far too deep to escape the ramifications, if all hell broke loose, and her involvement became public knowledge there would be an almighty outcry. The media frenzy would crucify not only the government's handling of this, but the police service would suffer irreparable damage; or at least it would take a damned miracle to put things right again. Therefore, her hands were tied. She and Sir William Stonehouse were caught in a huge trap. A trap baited with an extraordinarily huge amount of money at stake. Even these two high-ranking police officers were unaware of who their benefactor was or what he looked like, as they had never met him face-to-face; yet they had both already received some financial reward for their assistance so far.

But, *if* they were to be discovered having played a major part in such a diabolical scheme such as this, then they'd more than likely face the rest of their lives in prison.

The call from Hancroft had sounded urgent, so urgent both Conway and Stonehouse had dropped all plans, all meetings and appointments were immediately rescheduled. Conway began moving towards the main display, where the huge skeleton (or rather the *fake* model of the dinosaur) welcomed the visitors to the museum. The museum was relatively busy, although not particularly packed with visitors during this time of year, there was a decent throng of passing members of the public.

She walked slowly past the exhibit, barely bothering to give it a glance. Her focus was centred on the door to the right of the stairs. As she approached the stairs, she caught sight of Hancroft standing just off to one side, near one of the archways leading to another exhibition hall.

Stonehouse had by this time stepped through the main entrance doors of the museum. After going through the same security procedure as every member of the general public, he was ushered through and he marched purposefully ahead, past the same dinosaur exhibit which he too neglected to take any notice of. He took his place next to Conway, on her left. Ahead of them, Hancroft, who had seen Stonehouse arrive moved to the door and, producing a key, he unlocked the door that led along a hallway towards an auditorium which seated approximately one hundred and fifty people at a time. He ushered Stonehouse and Conway through the door then he closed and relocked it.

He then moved ahead of the two higher ranking officers and led them to the education facility, where lectures were regularly conducted by prominent and distinguished academics. The renowned naturalist Sir David Attenborough had often presented lectures there.

Hancroft guided the two officers to seats at the very front of the auditorium, and he remained standing. He then tapped his foot three times on the wooden parquet floor before him.

Lights came on illuminating the small stage area, providing light to reveal an expensive black leather chair set direct centre of the stage; it had its back to what would be the audience. Conway mused to herself whether this was a dramatic version of Mastermind. She grinned inwardly to herself. Her smile swiftly faded however when the chair swivelled round to reveal a larger-than-life individual sitting in it. His expression was dour beneath the mask which covered most of his face, and yet severe almost so incredibly menacing enough, to chill the blood to ice.

It was the fact that the mask covered one eye, and the majority of the stranger's face that made the two high-ranking police officers shiver where they sat.

'Mr Tilburne, may I present to you Sir William Stonehouse, Chief Commissioner of the Metropolitan London Police Service, and his subordinate, the Deputy

Chief Commissioner, Felicity Conway,' Hancroft said, then he sat down.

Tilburne stood up and stepped forward from the chair, his expression never changing for an instant. He glanced from one to the other, only allowing his gaze to settle for mere seconds on the two faces, of these so-called high-profile persons, and who it was he believed had the powers to deal with that interfering Detective Chief Inspector Philip Lomax and his team.

'I am in essence extremely displeased that your efforts to chastise and put in his place that infernal busybody detective Lomax have failed miserably. As the old clichéd saying goes, "if you want a job done properly, do it yourself." And this does indeed seem a case in point. I asked Hancroft to request of the two of you a simple task on my behalf. Unfortunately, even with your capabilities and powers you have at your disposal, yes, disposal, I like that word... you have not in any way achieved my wishes.'

Stonehouse stood up. His face ashen, now after such a long time, being in the presence of his benefactor, the person who had paid nearly fifteen million pounds into an account at a Swiss bank in Zurich. Ten million into another account for Conway. Stonehouse faltered for a few moments to collect his thoughts and to bolster his confidence. 'To be truthful sir, if I were, along with DCC Conway's assistance, discovered having done something untoward and more importantly illegal, such as killing DCI Lomax or any of his team, including Chief Superintendent Warwick, and whoever took on that investigation thereafter... there would *have* to be an investigation, and the fingers of suspicion would most certainly fall upon us. That would potentially then follow on to lead whoever was placed in charge of that case, to your doorstep.'

'I see,' the benefactor said. 'And you found there to be no significant method in which you might utilise the skills of the many criminals Lomax has successfully put away behind bars in the past? Surely you would have the necessary records to hand that you could have a quiet word in the ear of someone Lomax has put away for life? Someone perhaps who bears a long-time grudge against him and would jump at the opportunity to see him dead?' the man said, his voice filled with utter contempt.

Conway stood up. 'Excuse me, sir, but I'm afraid that even trying something like that would indubitably find its way back to us. Hancroft there, who I'm certain you're more than aware of, might have had a better chance of pulling off such a dangerous scheme, being in the background of policing, his department usually dealing with corrupt coppers or those that bend the rules of police procedure, might have been a better candidate.' She sat back down, keeping her expression neutral.

'Hhmmm,' the formidable man said.

Hancroft suddenly looked alarmed. As though he was now concerned the ball was being firmly thrown into his side of the court. 'I do hope you're not considering expecting me to take charge of this problem now?' Hancroft said.

Tilburne sat down and made a pyramid with his fingers in front of his face. His expression was serious but soon changed, a devious smile spreading swiftly across his features. 'Never mind. I have decided on another tack. However, this doesn't mean that I have dispensed with your continued use to me. You will both still play an important role, and to that end I shall leave it to Hancroft to explain to you in due course what tasks I require of you. That will be all.' He turned and exited via a door at the back of the stage. Within minutes he was in his limousine and being driven swiftly back to his office.

Twenty-Two

Franco's Italian Restaurant, Jermyn Street, Mayfair.
18.22 PM

Lomax sat in the main waiting area, nervously twiddling his fingers with a small glass of lager set between his hands on the table. Beside his right leg was a fancy looking bag containing a couple of expensive gifts, a red rose and a box of chocolates as well as a bottle of wine.

He was dressed smartly but conservatively, and having shaved the five-day stubble from his face he'd showered and splashed on some aftershave, something he rarely did at any time. Usually he'd spray some cheap deodorant or anti-perspirant before he went to work, and even though he had done so, straight after leaving work at just after five-thirty and having gone home to get ready for this *"special date"*, his fingers tingled with expectation, wondering how Roma would arrive and what she'd be wearing.

He noticed the maître d', other waiters and the female receptionist all looking at him intently with accusatory expressions. He was about to call one of them over and demand what their problem was, but he decided against it lest it cloud his already anxious demeanour.

The door opened and in waltzed Roma, wearing – even in February, on a chilly evening – a light thin black leather jacket over a knee-length red dress with gold sparkly details, with a décolletage that almost left very little to the imagination. As Roma's bosom was ample and firm, they filled the upper section of the U-shaped dress, and her cleavage was beautifully accentuated. She wore knee-length matching red leather boots. With just an adequate amount of make-up, and her hair washed and set in her favourite loose style, her eyes shone and her pale-pink lipstick she'd applied to her lips, she pouted deliberately as she swanned in and met Lomax's admiring gaze.

Both of them felt a little guilty taking pleasure by going out for a meal, especially after the recent deaths and injuries connected to the case they were working on. However, given that today was a Monday, and after the unusual events on Saturday with their unexpected meeting with Donaldson of the FBI, it was a necessary and deserved indulgence. They'd agreed to go out for a meal, which seemed like a worthy opportunity to have a brief respite from the pressure of their jobs.

The head waiter returned to take their orders for the meal. As the meals arrived and the champagne flowed, during their light-hearted discussions on matters not related to the ongoing case Lomax presented Roma with the card, flowers, chocolates and the special gifts, in the boxes from a well-known Hatton Garden jewellers.

Roma gasped as she opened the boxes to reveal a necklace and matching earrings and bracelet. She caught her breath as he took the necklace and hung it around her neck, clipping the clasp into place.

Other diners watched in anticipation, expecting the man to drop to one knee and make a public display by proposing to the attractive woman he was dining with – but that *didn't* happen.

***

19.00 PM

In Bedfordshire at Chief Commissioner Sir William Stonehouse's private residence, the man sat stony-faced on the sofa facing the expensively large flat screen which was showing a 24hr news channel. After arriving home after the impromptu meeting at the Natural History Museum he had tried to relax, but he couldn't. He was on edge – partly due to meeting his covert financial benefactor, who it appeared didn't usually enjoy face-to-face meetings with those he employed – in particular, those supposedly in powerful positions within the law.

He looked at his hands; they were visibly shaking, partly from fear, but mostly from anger. His face and brain felt like they were on fire, yet the rest of his body felt as though it was encased in ice. The cigarette between his index and middle finger of his right hand was burned down to the filter, but he hadn't taken a single drag from it. His phone rang, and he reached over with his left hand and picked up the receiver. 'Yes?'

'Hancroft here, sir. Just making sure you arrived home safely, that's all.'

'Yes, I did, but why would you be concerned that I had...' he stopped speaking and looked around the room. He hadn't noticed it when he'd arrived but set on top of the slim DVD player on the TV stand was a black box. Stonehouse frowned, 'What is the meaning of this, Hancroft?'

'Nothing really, sir. Mr Tilburne asked me to simply convey his gratitude for your assistance that was all.'

'My assistance? I don't really think I played much of a role, to have been of any significant assistance,' Stonehouse admitted.

'No sir... and neither does he.' A red light had begun to flicker at the back of the device, meaning that it had been covertly activated, slowly at first but picking up speed. There was no sound, no 'clicking' or any audible warning.

'Goodbye, sir... It was an honour to work with you,' Hancroft said, a hint of sarcasm in his voice. The line went dead. Then it happened just as Stonehouse jumped up from the sofa, dropping the cigarette from his fingers as he turned to run for the hallway and the front door. He reached the doorway of the lounge as the detonation took place. The Semtex/liquid chemical explosion was intense. Stonehouse and the room he'd been in were totally obliterated/vaporised into nothing but tiny floating particles of what had been human tissue, bricks and mortar, wood furnishings, architrave and electronic components.

Everything that had constituted a human being, and a large portion of the house no longer existed. The huge fireball of orange/yellow and red erupted upwards for three hundred or so feet. A large dark cloud formed above as the colours dissipated and the miniscule particles that had formed floated on the breeze to be carried away.

19.16 PM

DCC Felicity Conway had returned to her office at the Metropolitan Police central offices in Central London, not far from Downing Street. She had arrived just after a quarter to seven, and she too was still shaking. She, like Stonehouse, was reeling from the truth that they'd both been played as fools by the unknown person who had tricked them into doing as he wished. Although quite just what they had been involved with concerning DCI Lomax and his team on this specific case was still amiss from her full understanding, as she hadn't actually played a significant role as far as she was concerned.

Allowing themselves to be manipulated like marionettes by Hancroft. An underling, a subordinate police officer from another department, who both Conway and Stonehouse had allowed to orchestrate an element of power over them, to control them as deemed necessary by the stranger, who had paid them so much money to do his bidding. To keep Lomax out of his way and specifically to ensure that Lomax or any of his team were thwarted in their efforts to discover exactly what was going on.

She booted up her laptop, and after accessing her covert bank account in Switzerland she tried to check her balance. It showed zero. Zilch. Nothing. Stonehouse hadn't even considered checking his own Swiss account; perhaps if he had, he might have been forewarned.

She picked up her phone and dialled the Swiss bank number. When the connection was made, she asked to speak to the person in charge of her account. When she was put through she suddenly didn't know quite what to say, how to put her concerns into words. She coughed then spoke. 'Er, hello... my name is Felicity Conway, I'm having problems accessing my account with your bank via my computer here in the UK. It shows that a transfer hasn't been made, would you please clarify for me?' she asked.

'I'm afraid no transfer has been made in that name,' came the curt reply from a woman with a Swiss/French accent but speaking in fluent English.

'Are you certain?' Felicity asked. She immediately felt as though everything was falling apart. The woman on the other end of the line confirmed then closed the connection abruptly.

***

17.22 PM

Conway's secretary entered the office without knocking. His face was ashen, pallid and his eyes wide in stunned shock and horror. 'Deputy Conway... Felicity? Sir William Stonehouse... he's dead.'

The phone on Conway's desk rang. She picked up the receiver. 'Hello?'

'Miles Hancroft here, Deputy Chief Commissioner Conway. Just a courtesy call, to say thank you for everything you have done for us.' The line went dead before she had the chance to answer, not that it would have made the slightest difference...

Then an instant later, her office and a major part of the building overlooking Whitehall Road, just a few hundred metres towards Trafalgar Square from Downing Street, was enveloped in a fireball explosion. The package secreted in the drawer of her desk detonated after an electronic signal received via her phone and triggering the device set off the Semtex/liquid chemical bomb.

With a similar conclusion to the one that obliterated Sir William Stonehouse's being and destroyed his private home in Bedfordshire, the explosive device ripped through the office. The bomb-proofed windows facing the street contained the blast well, but the subsequent age of the building's walls, weakened by weathering and age, buckled and the concrete/brickwork blew outwards into the street, showering the pedestrians below with masonry. Conway and her secretary were, like Stonehouse, vaporised into tiny unrecognisable particles. The resulting concussion blast blew the bomb-proof windows out into the street along with the plume of dust that was once the furniture and fittings of her office, as well as Conway and her male secretary/PA's vaporised remains, sucked through the gaping maw by the sudden change of pressure. Alarms began to scream as small fires erupted in the adjoining offices not completely gutted or destroyed by the explosion.

People rushed to assist those in the street, the police were called from neighbouring stations and buildings, ambulances and the Fire and Rescue Service were called and soon the street was awash with people; several innocent pedestrians became victims of the blast, a few were killed outright by the falling masonry, and many more were injured.

The news swiftly filtered back to Dunne House, whereby DCI Lomax and DS Roma Clarkson along with Detective Chief Superintendent Warwick were very quickly informed of this totally unexpected development. Even the FBI Agent Donaldson became aware of this development almost at the same time as Lomax, who inadvertently answered his phone when he recognised the caller ID, while he and Roma were still at the restaurant.

Back in his office at Dunne House forty minutes later, cutting the intimate meal short, Lomax sat behind his desk, leaning forward with his hands flat on the top of the blotter, his expression serious, thoughtful and concerned, even though he was staring at the wall opposite him. Roma sat on a chair on the end of Lomax's desk, her left hand resting gently on top of his, her fingers caressing his. She wanted to speak, to say something, but she just didn't know how to choose the right words or whether they would make things any better.

'Phil? What're you thinking?' she asked at last.

He turned his face to look at her. 'To be honest, I think this caps it all. Stonehouse and Conway were definitely involved in a big way. I'd even go as far as to suggest they were in the pay of Tilburne for some time. No doubt Tilburne has covered his tracks, his involvement with these two, but that still leaves Hancroft. We now know for certain that he had close links with Stonehouse and Conway. More than likely, he was the *'middle-man'*, their contact and the one that told them what they had to do to thwart our investigation.'

'I'd say they obviously outlived their usefulness to Tilburne. Either that, or they seriously pissed him off due to their failure to put you in your place,' Roma said allowing a trace of a smile to begin forming, forcing those seductive dimples to appear in her cheeks.

Lomax stood up. 'Come with me,' he said, a knowing smile growing across his handsome face.

Just over an hour later they lay together naked and covered in a sheen of perspiration, the beads of moisture rolling down across their flesh and onto the sheets on Lomax's bed. Exhausted, they lay panting on their backs, both their chests rising and falling. Roma's right thigh lay across Lomax's left, the skin slick and yet also sticky. Lomax's left arm under Roma's neck, his hand still snaked around her shoulder and resting lightly atop her full left breast, the bud of her nipple still erect and pressing into his palm as he cupped the mound lightly.

Roma murmured, closing her eyes as Lomax's right hand lightly caressed the inside of her right thigh. Slight shivers flowing through her body as her lover's tender touch kept her senses aflame.

***

Tuesday 22nd 06.10 AM

After they'd showered and dressed, they sat in Lomax's living room drinking coffee. The TV was on the BBC channel, the focus on the terrifying events of the previous day.

Then the doorbell rang several times in quick succession. Roma put down her coffee and went to answer the door. She was immediately barged out of the way as DC Greggs thundered into the house. Roma's head struck the wall behind her, and she was momentarily dazed.

She didn't notice what Greggs held in his right hand.

Storming into the living room, Greggs held the Glock.45 up level at waist height, directed straight into Lomax's stomach. Lomax grinned as Greggs, his face serious and his skin pulled tight against his bones, stared at the DCI. 'I had a funny feeling it might be you, Greggs,' Lomax said, his tone sarcastic. 'By the way, good morning, nice of you to drop by.'

'Yeah? Okay you smart-arsed fucker, see if you feel as smug with a 45 slug buried in your skull,' Greggs said, trying to sound confident and tough.

'You're not really suited for this henchman type of work, are you?' Lomax said smirking still. 'How long have you been working— sorry, taking bribes from a high-level criminal?' Lomax asked, keeping his eyes fixed on Greggs' trigger finger, seeing it twitch slightly, pulling the trigger backwards a couple of millimetres, and hoping the gun didn't have too much of a hair-trigger mechanism. 'I suppose Miles Hancroft was in charge of what role you played in all of this?'

The last thing Lomax needed or wanted was another scar on his stomach. Or worse still to be killed in a situation like this, more importantly at the hand of a fellow – if dirty – police detective constable.

Greggs looked puzzled. 'How did you find out?' he asked.

Lomax smiled again. 'Well, you've just confirmed my suspicions that someone in my team was batting for the other side as well,' Lomax said, adding, 'and I don't mean by being a raving homosexual, although I wouldn't be surprised if you were one,' Lomax said grinning, then he said something that caused Greggs to react wildly. 'You should have made sure that you'd disabled DS Clarkson completely when you barged through my front door.'

Roma, having shaken off the dizziness of being shoved unceremoniously out of the way when Greggs had forced his way into Lomax's home in Shepherd's Bush, made her way unsteadily back past the front room door and into the kitchen from the hallway. She could hear everything that was being said between the two men. Roma retrieved something from her handbag and entered the living room from the kitchen archway brandishing the object.

Greggs spun around to look behind him; his gun hand twitched, and his index finger pulled the trigger of the Glock.45 sending a bullet straight into the wall between the kitchen and the lounge/diner. The loud retort in the room was deafening, but Greggs opened his eyes wide in shock as he saw DS Clarkson had by this time brought the canister of CS gas up to face level and she pressed the button, sending a vaporous mist directly into Greggs' unprotected face.

He dropped the weapon as he covered his face, but the potent CS gas affected his ability to see and breathe. He fell to the floor heavily on his knees, gasping and retching.

Roma immediately felt queasy, and she turned and ran to the kitchen and threw up in the waste bin. Lomax opened the windows, while keeping away from the area where Roma had sprayed the incapacitating gas.

Lomax called in DC Crosse, requesting two uniformed officers as well, confident that he was as straight as anything and could still be trusted not to have been seconded, as Greggs had certainly been, into working for the opposition. Crosse arrived within twenty-three minutes, alone as requested.

Lomax let him in and showed Crosse where Greggs' lay moaning, his face wet from the tears cascading from his eyes and the mucus dripping from his nostrils. A knowing grin spreading across his face, Crosse said 'I never did trust that prick. There was just something about him that didn't sit right by me. Too smarmy and overly confident for one thing. Plus, he was far too negative concerning Roma's authority over him. I guess he just didn't appreciate being overshadowed by a woman, especially one that looks younger and prettier than him.'

Lomax chuckled. He patted Crosse on the back. 'Take Greggs and that weapon back to the nick, see if you can cross-reference the serial numbers with any missing or stolen guns. I want to know how Greggs obtained that weapon. After he's been seen and treated for the CS gas, put him in a cell, leave the door open and have two uniforms watching over him at all times. Make Chief Superintendent Warwick aware personally, tell him yourself, and don't phone him. I'll be back soon. Also, try and see if you can find out with FBI Agent Donaldson's assistance where that DS Miles Hancroft is likely to be this afternoon. I need to find him and have a few words with that bastard. I think he's responsible for killing Stonehouse and Conway on behalf of Tilburne.'

'Are you going after Hancroft and Tilburne, sir?' Crosse asked.

'Yes, I am. Why do you ask?' Lomax said.

'Because I want in. Greggs might have been on the take, and he was an arsehole, but all-in-all he wasn't really all bad. I think he got swayed by the money. That's all,' Crosse said.

Lomax grinned. 'Okay then, Chris. Get that information I asked for. Here's Donaldson's number.' Lomax handed Crosse a card given to him by Donaldson. 'I'm taking Roma to hospital to get her checked out first. Then we'll pop into the office, double-check on whatever information you've acquired for me, after a quick detour to speak to Chief Superintendent Warwick about getting the assistance of security supervisor Dee Wilding. I think she'll be the key to getting inside the Vortexa building at Canary Wharf.

Besides, I have a very old score to settle with Tilburne, now that I know he was the one that had me kidnapped a while ago.'

'By the way,' Crosse began saying. 'The identity of the second young woman has been made, using info from the MPB database. Gillian Radcliffe, aged forty-two. She was...'

Lomax's face showed more surprise than he intended it to. 'Don't bother... I knew her as well. Now I think I understand just what Tilburne's beef is with me. He's killing off all of the girls from school I ever knew and had befriended, in particular those that had rebuked his advances, and had sought my protection. The more girls he tried to shag at school, the more I would do my best to stop him. God knows how many more he's holding prisoner. Chris, another favour, will you?'

Crosse nodded, a serious expression on his face.

'Phone up these schools and colleges. Cross-reference my attendance with Tilburne's by using my police file records, here's my authorisation,' Lomax handed Crosse a short hand-written note with his signature, then continued. 'There should be some records of Tilburne's bullying. Make a note of all the girl's names he'd been accused of assaulting at school or college, then check and see if those names crop up on the Missing Persons Database, would you?'

'You thinking Tilburne has a secondary agenda primarily set against you personally? That he's kidnapped all of the young girls you protected at school, and now he's trying to get back at you by abducting them?'

Lomax nodded. 'I also think that this is the primary reason why he's developing certain drugs, both for the black market for foreign sales as potential military threats, but also those as a form of a hypnotic control drug which he's planning to sell to perverted fuckers that find it near damned impossible to get a girlfriend in the normal manner. By the way, also check and see if Tilburne ever got engaged or married. If not, this could be the underlying reason why he so intent in getting his revenge against me.'

Crosse nodded. 'I'm just surprised he didn't just get a gun and shoot you himself, all those years ago.' Then he left Lomax's house. Lomax grinned and said more to himself, 'Thanks a bunch, Crosse.'

***

To say that Gerrard Tilburne was angry, *very angry,* would be an *extreme* understatement. His face was florid, the veins and arteries on the sides of his neck stood out like ropes and he thundered around his office throwing items across the vast expanse, smashing anything that was fragile, expensive or simply whatever he could grab at any specific moment. Along with his child-like tantrum, during which he was sweating profusely, the majority of his diatribe being targeted at both Lomax and at the man standing rock still in Tilburne's office.

'You are by far the most incompetent assistant I have *ever* employed,' Tilburne raged as he stomped from one side of his office to the other. He stopped admonishing David Carter and stared out of the huge window.

Tilburne was finding it ironic that even after all these years since he'd left school and had built up his successful career as an exceedingly aggressive businessman, that the only way he'd been able to have much of a sex life was by using Rohypnol, the date-rape drug, and Viagra; it was due to his subsequent failures at consummating his relationships after all the hard work of even persuading them to go out with him in the first place that he decided to develop a specific and powerful sedative/hypnotic drug which would give him ultimate control over any woman he desired.

The unmistakable thought process of a despicable village idiot.

Once he had calmed down a little, Tilburne returned to his desk and sat heavily in the leather executive chair, surveying the damage during his childish strop. Hancroft sat quietly throughout the tantrum musing to himself and wondering how he had allowed himself to agree to work for such a deviant prick.

Miles Hancroft had been particularly sneaky himself. Unbeknownst to Tilburne, Hancroft had been spying on the man, his 'unofficial' employer, and had recorded several occasions whereby Tilburne had failed miserably to seduce and have sex with a considerable number of women in his private suite a few metres away from the very office he now sat in.

Tilburne had even attempted to lose himself in the company of prostitutes and hookers. Tilburne had thought that those women on the game would have made it that much easier for him, as they had lesser inhibitions about 'sleeping' with their clients.

But no... He was in all honesty completely useless. This made him angrier, and as such the violence within him raged deeper.

After several minutes of just sitting across the desk staring at Hancroft, Tilburne spoke. 'I want Lomax brought in again, forcibly if necessary,' Tilburne said, a menacing timbre to his voice.

'Why exactly?' Hancroft asked.

'Why?' Tilburne repeated, 'That is not of your concern.'

'I only ask because if you had intended to kill him, why didn't you do it when you had him brought here last time. Surely it would have been simpler to have done it then. Plus, you could have had the added enjoyment of torturing him personally,' Hancroft said.

Silence. At least for a few moments.

'Yes… perhaps with hindsight that would have been far more satisfactory, and it would have removed Lomax from being such a thorn in my side. But nevertheless, now would seem like the perfect opportunity to deal with this problematic irritation once and for all. That is why I would like you to lure him here, on the pretence that I wish to have a formal meeting with him, perhaps even an 'official' interview regarding the recent events.'

Hancroft nodded and after another twenty minutes of discussion, he left. The time was now nine-forty-five at night. He decided he would contact Lomax the following morning. Hancroft went to his apartment in Kensington and Chelsea, in a four storey Georgian building in Cromwell Road, a few hundred yards from the Natural History Museum, on the opposite side of the road.

Twenty-Three

Wednesday 23rd. 07.00

Lomax awoke to find the space next to him in the double bed empty, apart from an envelope, a pale blue envelope with his name on it. Then he heard the *clink-clink* of cups being prepared downstairs, and the smell of coffee being prepared in the percolator, along with what also smelled like a full English breakfast.

Lomax licked his lips, swung his legs over the side of the bed and sat up. He slipped into the bathroom where he realised Roma had already showered as the mirror was steamed up and the shower stall still streaked with water. He had a quick shower and shaved, then after putting on the clean and pressed set of clothes Roma had laid out for him, he joined her in the kitchen holding the envelope in his hand, which he waved at her once she'd turned to face him.

He sat on a kitchen chair, admiring Roma's shapely form, opened the envelope and pulled out a note, which simply read:

Darling, as coppers we're the best. I of course am more superior to you, being a woman, but I love you so very much. Thank you for being there when I need you.

Roma, xxx

Lomax laughed, and as Roma went to move past him he grabbed her around her waist and pulled her onto his lap on the chair which creaked suspiciously under the combined weight. He kissed her fully on her lips and she responded running her fingers through Lomax's hair.

Roma stood up. 'Eat your breakfast. Think you're going to need it today. I've got a funny feeling in my bones.'

'Sorry,' Lomax said grinning, and adding quickly, 'I'll keep my hands where you can see them in future.'

Roma cut in, a mock expression of sadness and horror in her face, 'Although that surprise meal in Franco's was lovely, I was thinking you might have had something more elaborate planned for me?'

Lomax looked blankly at her, as though he wasn't quite sure what she was referring to. Her expression changed in an instant and she stormed over to the cooker, dished out the food and dropped the plate in front of Lomax then stormed off out of the kitchen.

Lomax wasn't too certain whether she was messing around, or whether she was seriously upset. He knew that he had to eat the food, otherwise she'd be even more pissed off with him. He'd virtually finished eating the piled high plate of food when Roma returned to the kitchen, clutching her holdall with her belongings.

Lomax stood up, his mouth open wide in muted guilty concern, his eyes wide. Roma saw his guilt and burst out laughing, then dropping the 'empty' holdall to the floor she rushed into him, wrapping herself around him. They kissed passionately for a few moments; Roma could taste the breakfast on his tongue. When they released themselves from the embrace, Lomax said, 'I don't know what I have to do to understand women in general.'

'We're a strange species, which is true. What you really need to do, especially where I'm concerned Phil, is try to imagine what I'm thinking, what I really want from you.'

'I'm sorry,' Lomax said after peeling his lips from hers. 'I'm not sure I'll ever succeed in that, but I'll make it up to you as soon as this case is over. I'll treat you to a night or two in a country hotel somewhere,' he said.

'Only *a night or two?*' Roma replied, smirking again.

DUNNE HOUSE

The mood on this Wednesday morning in the Investigation Suite was dire to say the least. The loss of two high-ranking police officers in such a barbaric display of contempt was prodigious and heart-breaking, even if it turned out they were indeed dirty. Added to which another two police officers, one in Lomax's own team and one from the so-called Internal Investigations Divisions, were also on the take. Lomax knew he could confide in just three people: Roma, DC Crosse and CS Warwick.

Yet the rest of the team remained assiduous in their tasks, each man and woman, whether full-time or civilian, pursuing the day-to-day enquiries, following up on leads and calling those agencies who might be inclined to be of assistance.

The phone rang on Lomax's desk

'DCI Lomax?' asked the voice on the other end of the phone. Lomax recognised the voice immediately.

'Yes. Hancroft,' Lomax said. 'I was going to call you when I got to the office. I need to speak to you on a very urgent matter. I'm busy until about one o'clock this afternoon. Would you meet me at the Sherlock Holmes pub near Charing Cross train station at about one-twenty-five?'

'Yes, that would be fine. I would have preferred an earlier meeting but seeing as you're obviously very busy dealing with your current case, I do understand. By the way,' Hancroft began saying, 'I take it you've heard about Chief Commissioner Sir William Stonehouse and Deputy Commissioner Felicity Conway? Terrible news, isn't it?' The line went dead.

Lomax stared at the receiver for a few seconds then placed it back in its cradle on his office desk. He grinned. He thought about how asinine Hancroft really was.

Roma and DC Crosse, both sitting on chairs facing Lomax, had puzzled expressions, even though they both clearly heard the conversation as Lomax had switched the external speaker on and turned it away from him so his two colleagues could hear the conversation.

DC Crosse gave a knowing smile. 'Hancroft just let on far more than I believe he meant to with that remark.'

'What do you mean?' Roma asked, her thin carefully plucked brown eyebrows forming two arches above her inquisitive eyes.

'Well… it wasn't specifically in his choice of words, rather the *way* he said them. *'I take it you've heard about Chief Commissioner Sir William Stonehouse and Deputy Commissioner Felicity Conway? Terrible news, isn't it?'* If you ask me, he had prior knowledge of the event long before it became *public*.'

Lomax nodded his head in agreement. 'I think you're right there, Chris.'

'So? What do we do next?' Roma asked.

Lomax looked at the clock. It showed the time as just after nine-fifty-five. 'Well, I don't know about you two, but I'm going down to Gino's Cafe. I'm starving,' Lomax said.

'After that full English I cooked for you this morn…' Roma said, then felt herself reddening as DC Crosse glanced up at her with a grin so wide his teeth flashed brightly.

'Come on… my treat,' Crosse said. 'I'm feeling peckish as well, and I had a full English this morning.'

By five past ten, all three were seated in Gino's cafe, a few minutes' walk from Earl's Court nick, and close to the post office in Kensington High Street. Lomax sat at a table by the wall near the middle of the cafe, with Roma directly opposite him.Crosse sat next to Roma next to the narrow aisle and facing the counter. Gino stood next to Crosse, facing all three patrons. He was Greek from Athens, unusually tall at five feet ten inches, courtesy of his father's side of the family. His mother was Italian, hence why he'd been given the name. He had slicked back black hair tied in a ponytail at the back under a white baseball style cook's hat with webbing on the top.

Above the peak was an emblem proudly showing a caricature of Gino carrying a tray of steaming food, with an exaggerated smile on his face. Crosse ordered for all three after they'd made up their minds what they fancied to eat. Gino returned with their coffees and orange juices then returned to the kitchen where he personally prepared the meals.

'Hmm... At least it's nice and warm in here,' Roma said.

'They forecast bitter cold winds tonight after eleven,' Crosse said. 'I plan to be between the sheets of my bed, snuggled up against a warm body. How about you two?'

'Thanks for the offer,' Lomax said adding, 'but I don't go in for threesomes.' All three burst out laughing, although Roma felt a little embarrassed as she caught a glimpse of Crosse winking at her.

Gino brought the meals and set them down. All three began to eat, relishing the hot, savoury and spicy food.

After they'd eaten and washed down the food with an additional coffee, Crosse paid for the meals, and outside they spoke briefly as the biting January wind cut down Kensington High Street towards Earl's Court Road, then Crosse returned to the station Incident Room Office Suite to do some last-minute checks.

'Do you fancy a quick...' Lomax began saying.

'What? Now?' Roma answered, feigning disgust.

Lomax grinned. 'No… not that, although I would never refuse, what I was going to say was how about we delay meeting up with Hancroft and spend an hour or two walking around the Natural History Museum up the road?'

'Why not? It's been a while since I've been in there,' she replied, hooking her right arm through Lomax's left elbow, they then crossed the street and made their way towards the NHM.

***

He watched them from a distance, mostly since they'd first exited the police station, and all three walked in the bitter cold along to Gino's, sat down, ordered their meals and drinks, ate, drank and talked.

Hancroft held a parabolic microphone aimed at the window of Gino's Cafe where Lomax, Clarkson and Crosse sat. He picked up every word as clear as a bell through the headphones. Then after they left and parted company with Crosse, who returned to the office, he turned off the microphone and as discreetly as possible alighted from the rear of the red coloured old 1967 Bedford van, which in its pristine condition should have been in a museum of its own; he followed the two senior police officers as they strolled casually along the pavement.

Back at Dunne House, DC Crosse was checking up on something which had been bugging him for quite some time. He sat at his desk in the Incident Room. He casually glanced over at his ex-colleague, Neil Greggs' desk, which was still festooned with old paperwork, three used and partially drunk coffee cups, crisp and sweet wrappers, and the assorted pens, paper clips and notes stuck to the bottom edge of his flat screen computer monitor.

Tutting to himself, Crosse wheeled himself over to sit before Greggs' desk, shoving the other chair aside. He preferred his own chair. Crosse then began sifting through the detritus accumulated on the desk with a pencil, flicking items aside, often over the edge of the desk into the nearly empty metal waste bin. Crosse then pulled his hanky from his trouser pocket and used it to pull open the drawers on the desk, but there was very little in there of interest.

Crosse switched on Greggs' computer terminal and waited for the screen to show the welcome message but was surprised when it showed upon waking up that Greggs had forgotten to officially log off; the computer was still connected to his home PC via a public internet VPN that allowed customers to access their home network or office files from various locations wherever they happened to be.

Crosse stared at the screen for a few moments, then he jumped when a hand landed on his right shoulder from behind him. Startled, he snapped his head around to his right to see Chief Superintendent Warwick standing there. 'Sir.Jesus… you made me jump.'

Chief Superintendent Warwick chortled. 'Sorry, DC Crosse… I never intended to startle you. What're you doing at Greggs' desk?' He pulled Greggs' chair back and plonked himself down on it.

'Well sir, I've had my suspicions about Greggs since shortly after this particular case kicked off. He began acting very cagey about things, mostly where he was going after he finished work, whereas before he'd be quite open about his plans. I wondered whether he'd found himself a new lady friend and wished to keep her identity secret until they'd established their relationship.

'So, one night last week I followed him, as discreetly as I could. I know it wasn't good protocol to do so sir, but there was something that was nibbling at my gut instincts. Anyway, as I said… I followed him to a pub in Leicester Square, The Moon Under the Water, if I remember correctly. It was pretty well-packed in there. I managed to find a spot in a corner, and having ordered myself a drink, I watched him. Then who do you think I discovered he was meeting up with?' Crosse asked rhetorically.

Chief Superintendent Warwick's expression became serious, as he felt he knew this wasn't going to be good news.

Crosse continued. 'Detective Superintendent Miles Hancroft.'

'Good grief,' Chief Superintendent Warwick exclaimed.

'Yes, that's what I thought. Hancroft had been in the toilets at the back of the bar, then he joined Greggs and they sat and chatted for a good forty minutes or so. The bar thinned out a bit in that time, when they both stood up from the table they were at and about to leave, I thought that they would have surely noticed me as they passed me by less than four feet away. But thankfully a large group of patrons had just entered and both Greggs and Hancroft were forced to turn their backs to me and squeeze their way out through the throng of people,' Crosse said.

'Have you any idea why those two had planned to meet up?' CS Warwick asked.

'No sir, but then I wondered why Greggs had never even mentioned it to me in passing. If it was simply two colleagues meeting up for an after-work drink, then that's fine as far as I'm concerned. But then they both went to…' Crosse paused for a second. 'Sir… they both went into a gay bar in Soho. I didn't clock the name at the time, but I'm sure I'd be able to find it. Anyway, I hightailed it back home after that.'

'Okay. Have you told DCI Lomax any of this yet?' Warwick asked.

'No sir. Should I tell him?' Crosse asked.

'No, at least not yet, I don't think it's relevant. What exactly are you doing at Greggs' workstation?' Warwick said.

'I think I need to check these e-mails, sir. If you can see,' Crosse used a pencil to tap on the screen at the sender's email address, 'these seem to originate from an outside source, which is outside the official police Internet Communications Directorate Compliances rule. As you know sir, any unofficial communications between officers and the general public… or worse a criminal for whatever reason, is considered a breach of protocol, and could lead to dismissal if it were found that any officer was acting as a go-between for criminals, by sending sensitive case information to their lawyers or whoever.

'But for some reason, Greggs' PC here seems to have glitched and turned off the security mode for these messages he'd accessed from his private PC at home. Either that or the dumb fuck simply forgot. The important fact is sir, these messages all seem to come from Hancroft, and if I can get one of the tech guys in here, as I'm bloody useless with this stuff, I'm sure he'd be able to tell us where exactly these messages originated. Hancroft's office, home or somewhere else.'

'Very well then, Detective Constable Crosse. Go ahead, request for a tech guy as you put it to come in and see if he can help. If this pans out and you're spot on the money, I'll see that you're promoted to Detective Sergeant,' Warwick said, smiling. He got up from the chair and patted Crosse on the man's shoulder.

Crosse looked up at his superior, and cracking a gap-toothed grin he said, '*Only* Detective Sergeant, sir? I'd have thought *Detective Inspector…* at least.'

'You'd better watch it Crosse, you might live to regret that,' Warwick said, laughing as he left the Incident Room.

Crosse returned his attention to the monitor for a few moments, then picking up the phone receiver on Greggs' desk he dialled the Tech Division which dealt with solving any problems officers had with the computer system.

Just over one hour later, Crosse had the necessary information, and it shocked him to the core of his bones and turned his blood to ice. He tried to call CS Warwick, but he was unavailable. He then tried Lomax and Roma, but their mobile phones were switched off. There was one crafty trick he knew he could try however, but Crosse needed to be certain.

He phoned CS Warwick and requested that he accompany Crosse in an Interview Room to question Greggs.

CS Warwick addressed Greggs with a stern expression. 'As your former superior commander, I have to say that I am greatly disappointed with your conduct in this case, Greggs. To that end DC Crosse has a few important questions he'd like to ask of you. I would add that in my personal opinion, it would be to your advantage to answer him truthfully.'

'Is this an official interview?' Greggs asked.

'For the moment, no it isn't, which is why it's not being recorded,' Warwick said.

'Isn't that a breach of police procedurals?' Greggs said, more a statement than a formal question.

'Perhaps it is, but then again, depending on your answers it might not be,' Warwick replied, allowing a sarcastic sneer to appear across his face on purpose. Its intention was to unnerve Greggs, and it succeeded. Every question Crosse put to Gregg received an answer, although the two detectives would have to decide how honest Greggs was actually being.

Even when it appeared that Greggs had clammed up, potentially through the sudden realisation that he might come to harm from Tilburne's people, which he obviously feared more than having to face going to prison. He rationalised swiftly that spilling the beans might just save his life.

Crosse knew now how CS Warwick had attained his rank, and he also had a renewed respect for his new commanding officer of the S.M.E.T division.

Twenty-Four

Hancroft looked at his watch. It showed the time as almost a quarter to three. He was angry as he followed Lomax and Clarkson around the National History Museum. He'd intended to go to the pub near Charing Cross as arranged, then wait and see when and if Lomax would turn up, but having overheard Lomax tell DS Roma Clarkson by using the parabolic microphone that he'd keep him waiting for goodness knows how long, it annoyed him greatly.Before he entered the building, Hancroft phoned Tilburne and appraised him of the current situation.

Hancroft kept his distance as he trailed the two detectives while they meandered around the huge building, turning away sharply whenever the two officers suddenly changed direction, and pretending that he was engrossed in something on a display.

They were now in the midst of the dinosaur section, walking along the metal catwalk suspended from the ceiling, and supported from below by the angled tubular legs and above by similar supports. Either side of the catwalk were exhibits of the various skulls and limbs suspended on industrial-strength steel cable. Set onto the handrail of the catwalk at the appropriate locations were small rectangular descriptions of the dinosaurs these skulls and other bones belonged to.

Lomax and Roma made small talk as they meandered along, seemingly unaware that they were being followed. Although it was a request that patrons switched off their mobile phones during their visit to the Natural History Museum, Hancroft had neglected to do so, but he had inserted his Bluetooth earpiece and set his phone to vibrate in his pocket.

It vibrated, and he swiftly touched the unit on his ear and spoke barely above a whisper. 'Yes?' He listened for several moments then responded, a gratuitous smile swiftly replacing his earlier angry temperament. 'That can be arranged, yes. In the Lecture Auditorium, very well, in forty minutes. It shall be done.' The line went dead and Hancroft noticed that Lomax and DS Clarkson had disappeared from view.

He rushed along the catwalk, barging past the tourists and visitors and getting some unmistakably unsavoury remarks in the process.

Hancroft caught up with his two 'marks' where the life-sized automated replica of a Tyrannosaurus Rex juvenile stood, moving its head up and down and side to side, opening its mouth and a pre-recorded growling sound emanating from nearby. Lomax and Clarkson were holding hands and standing even closer to one another, something Hancroft hadn't really noticed properly earlier, and this pleased him.

He checked his watch again and waited until they'd left the T. Rex exhibit area. He saw a phone on a wall near the exit to this section, but there was a security guard standing close to it. Slightly put out, Hancroft fished his police ID out and showed it to the guard, a young woman of Afro-British appearance, with long black straight hair below shoulder length framing a very pretty face. Hancroft approached her smiling as warmly as he could.

'Excuse me miss,' Hancroft said in a warm friendly tone, 'I believe two of my colleagues are somewhere in the museum, and I wondered if you could make an announcement using that phone, to ask them to meet me in the Lecture Department Auditorium on the ground floor of the museum. It's very urgent police business.'

Because he'd only very briefly shown his warrant card to the young female guard, he hoped she wouldn't have been too observant. Luckily for him, she hadn't. After giving her his name and rank as Chief Superintendent Warwick of Southwest 5 Division, he requested that she put out a public address announcement for Detective Chief Inspector Philip Lomax, *and* Detective Sergeant Roma Clarkson to meet him in the Museum Lecture Auditorium, as soon as possible. Hancroft also asked the guard to arrange for the door to be unlocked in readiness, and to ensure they wouldn't be disturbed.

Hancroft then ran back the way he came against the flow of tourists, receiving additional irritated abuse from those he shoved out of the way.

Hancroft arrived well before Lomax and Roma, and he asked the museum staff person to relock the door after he'd entered, and only reopen it when DCI Lomax and DS Clarkson arrived. The man said that he would, even though he found this situation extremely unorthodox.

'But then… who am I to argue?'

Hancroft ignored the man and went through the doorway, pulling the door closed behind him and waiting to hear the lock mechanism being engaged once again. He then ran along the corridor and opened the doors to the auditorium. He knew the 'house-lights' were controlled from the small lighting area just off the right-hand side of the small stage, and where the emergency fire exit doors were, where his unofficial employer had unofficially entered and exited the other day to address Stonehouse and Conway.

Hancroft heard a knock and went to the doors; using the spare set of keys he had acquired. He disarmed the alarm and then the lock on the door and opened it. Gerrard Tilburne stood there dressed in an immaculate three-piece Armani suit in shining medium grey, a pale blue silk shirt, and matching tie, dark grey socks and black brogue shoes. His slightly greying dark hair was slicked back, and his steely blue/grey eye looked even more menacing than it ever did before. He wore the mask to cover the majority of his disfigured face. Tilburne entered and took the seat as before. But Hancroft was unprepared to see three other men arrive, two of them carrying a coroner's black body-bag.

One of the men Hancroft had seen a few times before in an ante-office next to Tilburne's office high up at the Vortexa building. He recalled the man's name as being Liam Garratt. Someone Hancroft had had the unpleasant benefit of dealing with a long time ago, when he was a young rookie police officer.

Garratt made it clear he recognised Hancroft by snorting at him as he passed him, and with his two fellow tough-guys they entered and placed the two *unoccupied* body-bags out of sight on the other side of the stage, where they all stood quietly, patiently.

Lomax and Roma arrived at the door after the public address system requested them to make their way there. They were met by the museum staff member, who after asking for their identities unlocked the door and ushered them through.

Lomax asked the man why they'd been asked to meet Chief Superintendent Warwick here, but he told them that he had no idea. 'The officer gave me the impression it was urgent. But he did say he'd tried to contact you via your mobile phones.'

Lomax and Roma began walking along the corridor, then quite unexpectedly, Lomax's mobile began to vibrate in his pocket. He was certain he'd turned it off. He stopped walking. Fishing it out he looked at the screen and saw the envelope flashing, alerting him he had a message. He pressed the button to open it and read. Twice. The message was a warning from DC Crosse:

Hancroft is at your location: NHM... He's definitely a traitor. He's been in league with Greggs who was definitely the mole from our team. BTW, both Greggs and Hancroft were potentially 'lovers'. Beware you might be walking into a trap. Will be there shortly to back you up.

Lomax showed the message to Roma. She gasped covering her mouth then whispered, 'What now? That man just locked us in here.'

'We go on in,' Lomax replied.

They arrived at the auditorium doorway and Lomax opened it, expecting the one hundred and fifty seat auditorium to be in total darkness. It was lit up, and there was a chair on the stage; it had its back facing where the audience would sit. Lomax guided Roma towards the front row of seats.

A voice echoed around the room, amplified by the microphone fixed to the chair through the sound system. 'We meet again Philip, and this time you've brought a friend to join us. A very pretty friend as well.' The chair swivelled around and for the first time Roma saw the unmasked face of the man in person, instead of the dated images she'd seen what DC Crosse had dug up from the research Lomax had requested from school photographs, and the images FBI Agent Donaldson had shown them. This was the face of a monster. She caught her breath and felt immediately ill, her stomach flipped.

Horrendously disfigured from having acid thrown at him more than ten years previously, the flesh around the eyes and covering the nose, cheeks and mouth appeared as though it had melted and re-solidified. The plastic surgery had failed to repair the damage caused when a young woman Tilburne had accosted several times, demanding that she sleep with him, had resorted to her own drastic action to make her response very clear to him.

His disfigurement was not only the main reason why he'd developed his misogynistic attitude towards women in general, but it had caused him to be a recluse from mainstream public attention and put his endeavours into creating such a deviant drug which he believed other men struggling to succeed with women would happily pay for to achieve their goals.

Tilburne had inherited five billion dollars from his father's estate in the United States, after it was decided by the US Supreme Court that he played no part whatsoever in his father's death, so he used the money to buy the building in London, refurbish and equip it with state of the art technology, employ the necessary people to create the legitimate drugs, and be in direct competition with the other mainstream pharmaceutical companies around the world.

He also employed other unscrupulous employees with chemistry and microbiological expertise to develop the black-market drugs and chemical weapons for modern warfare. More importantly those he needed to develop the drug he so desperately wanted for his personal use, and those men he knew struggled with the opposite sex.

Tilburne's right eye was cloudy, and constantly weeping with a milky liquid that caused a permanent stain down his cheek, after a cataract operation to correct the damage inflicted by the acid attack failed. His left eye was still okay, but the disfigurement was so stomach churning that even Lomax found it difficult to look at Tilburne for too long.

Tilburne replaced the mask he held in his right hand to cover his face, leaving just his left eye and chin exposed where the injury was minimal. He spoke again. 'Philip, you may be wondering why I allowed you to go free after I spoke to you in my office?'

'The thought did cross my mind, Gerrard,' Lomax said, as Roma moved away to take an aisle seat and keep her focus away from what she'd just seen. 'In fact, using DC Greggs to act as your mole was both an act of genius, but at the same time flawed, especially as Hancroft there is no longer a serving police officer.'

'It took you long enough to discover it,' Hancroft said, a cynical laugh escaping from his lips.

'It's a shame Greggs didn't fuck things up sooner, otherwise we would have discovered just who you were indeed working for. But that doesn't really matter, as it's perfectly clear that you've crossed the tracks. In more ways than one,' Lomax said, the bitterness of his tone cutting deep into Hancroft's confidence.

Hancroft made as though to step forward as if he intended to attack Lomax.

'Stop,' Tilburne ordered him, and Hancroft hesitated then stepped back again. Tilburne smiled, although under the mask it wasn't easy to notice. 'So, Philip… you've finally discovered the prime link between those two that enabled me to utilise their other, more official skills,' he chuckled.

'You could say that,' Lomax answered, adding, 'although they succeeded in hiding their relationship for so long it would have been only a matter of time before they *screwed up* – if you'll pardon the expression – and we would have discovered their secret. Don't get me wrong Gerrard, I'm not a homophobe, I have no issues with gay rights, and homosexuals or lesbians don't worry me at all. But the upper echelons of the Police Service might have taken a dim view, due to the implications that these two officers may succumb to blackmail by criminals in order to secure their obedient servitude, to someone with a black heart such as yours.'

Tilburne laughed loudly and slapped his thighs.

Lomax's mobile phone vibrated once more. He retrieved it from his pocket and saw he had another message, only this one was from Sally Hickton. 'Do you mind if I read this message, it's from my sister?' Lomax lied.

Tilburne merely waved his hand.

Lomax pressed the button to retrieve the message. It read:

Phil, I've just received some disturbing results from samples of your father's blood, taken before he died. The results show that an as yet undetermined poison had been introduced only a matter of hours before he died and may have been why he deteriorated so quickly. Will try to discover the poison's identity.

Sally

Lomax's blood froze. He shivered involuntarily, dropping the phone on the floor. The rage within Lomax began to rise and he felt compelled to rush towards Tilburne, who sat grinning smugly back at his audience of two.

Roma moved over and picked up the phone, and she read the message. It froze her blood. It made her feel awful and saddened as she knew full well what the message inferred, and she also knew exactly what Lomax had already concluded.

'Good news, I trust?' Tilburne asked, the glaring sarcastic smile not wavering for one second.

Lomax exploded in anger. 'You knew damned well that the pathology result on my father's blood results would show that he'd been deliberately poisoned. I can only guess someone you employed went into the hospital and contaminated his IV solution. I ought to just go for you, right here, right now, and throttle the fucking life out of you.'

'I wouldn't do that if I were you, Lomax,' came the voice of Liam Garratt, as he made his presence known.

Lomax balked as the huge frame of Liam Garratt moved fully into view. Lomax and Roma had both had dealings with this man in the recent past, arresting him in connection with drug-related crimes, and multiple threats of violence against ordinary citizens who'd borne witness to criminal activity, and had been due to be called as witnesses in major court cases. They were frightened off once Garratt made his appearances.

'Garratt,' Lomax said. 'I might have known you'd be mixed in this somehow. You've been off the radar for a while now, I had no idea where you'd gone. I had hoped you'd curled up and died somewhere.'

'That's enough!' Tilburne shouted. 'Take them to my office, I cannot risk our being interrupted here. Deal with these two, after you've rendered them incapacitated.' Tilburne said sarcastically.

Out of sight of Lomax and Roma, the two other thugs had slipped out and along a side corridor from the stage, each carrying a tranquiliser pistol. They shot Lomax and Roma in their backs. The darts injected the two police officers with a fast-acting knock-out drug.

***

It took less than forty minutes for Tilburne's henchmen led by Liam Garratt to transport Lomax and Roma's unconscious bodies in the back of the transit van from the Natural History Museum back to the Vortexa Building at Canary Wharf.

Strapped to trolley/stretchers they were removed from the van and taken via the freight elevator normally used for transferring incoming materials and outgoing products in the central core of the building, to the forty-eighth floor, where Lomax had been a couple of weeks earlier, and then transferred to the executive office of Tilburne, where he waited with bated breath to explain just what he had in store for his nemesis and the female detective.

Once placed into position, the stretchers were tilted so that both occupiers were slanted to enable Tilburne to converse with them more easily. He nodded to Garratt who, retrieving another two syringes, injected their contents into Lomax and Roma. It took several minutes for the tranquiliser to be counter-acted and for Lomax and Roma to begin recovering.

Both felt as though their heads were about to explode, the pounding thud which seemed to them as if their brains had solidified, threatening to smash their way out. When they finally opened their eyes they swiftly shut them, as the bright illumination was like having white hot needles poked directly into the pupils.

'Oh dear… is it a little too bright in here for you? Hold on one moment,' Garratt said, and he nodded to Tilburne who using a dimmer switch on his desk, reduced the lighting level.

Lomax slowly opened his eyes, and the pain didn't return. Roma did so as well.

'Aahhh. That's much better, I trust?' Tilburne said.

Both Lomax and Roma tried to rise but found that they'd been securely tied with cable-ties to the stretchers. They could move their hands at the wrists, and their heads could rise slightly and turn enough to look to the sides.

Lomax looked back directly at Tilburne whose face still exhibited that self-righteous, smarmy smile. 'Fucking tosser,' Lomax snarled through gritted teeth and pursed lips.

Tilburne laughed. 'Such language, and in front of your beloved too.'

'Okay… so what exactly do you have planned for me?' Lomax asked.

'Oh? Not *just* you Philip, but you and your very delicious lady friend there. Although I'm fully aware that you and she have been involved in a quite steamy relationship for a while now, I'm not bothered too much about having to sample second-hand goods,' Tilburne said, his tongue snaking out from between the scarred and almost non-existent lips, leaving a slick wetness to them.

Roma shuddered at the very thought of having that grotesqueness of a man even considering doing anything to her sexually. But what concerned her the most was that if she was forced to succumb to Tilburne's forced sexual gratification, how would Lomax feel afterwards? Especially if they were both to survive this ordeal?

'I'd rather die than experience you touching me in any way whatsoever,' Roma declared defiantly. She spat the words towards Tilburne, who merely winked at her with his one good eye.

'Garratt, turn Lomax's stretcher around so he can see what I'm actually about to do to his girlfriend. Or should I say, who I'm about to allow to have some fun with her after me,' Tilburne said.

Lomax had an immediate thought, something he'd wondered about and he felt now might be the best time to enquire. He hoped it might distract the man from his intentions. 'Gerrard, excuse me for asking, but what happened to your parents, and more importantly, how did you come to afford to create Vortexa in the first place?'

Garratt moved over and did as he was asked. He pulled Lomax's stretcher back then turned it so that he had a better view of Roma. Lomax was now on Roma's left side, and only a few inches from her feet to his left. Garratt returned to the sofa where he too had a reasonable view of the proceedings.

Tilburne pondered the question and smiled knowingly. 'I see what you're doing Philip, and you're very clever. All the same, you're sadly mistaken if you think it will stop me. However, in order to placate your curiosity, my father left my mother and me in nineteen eighty-five, a couple of years after leaving school, from which I am certain you recall our regular altercations.

'It wasn't until the late nineties when I had a chance to visit him in the States, and discovered that he'd made his fortunes in pharmaceuticals, although he was still a bastard to me. He never sent a dime to my mother for us to have an easy life. I tried to convince him to make it worth my while to leave him alone and not pester him for financial gain, but he bluntly refused and ordered his security to throw me out. A couple of months later he was murdered, after I had secured the services of his own lawyer to change the details of his will to favour me and my mother, who died before she had the chance to enjoy the benefits of his wealth.'

'So… you're telling me that you had your father murdered?'

'Not directly. I was arrested and initially charged with his murder. The police investigated, yet there was no substantial evidence to place me at the scene, and besides I had cast iron alibis. Then, the US Supreme Court decided the case was flawed and I inherited a portion of my father's estate. Five billion dollars to be precise.'

Tilburne moved towards Roma's stretcher, and as she was wearing a skirt and flesh-coloured stockings he ran his right hand up from above the top of her right mid-calf-length boot up over her upper calf around to her knee, then he caressed her lower thigh moving his hand up further. Then his hand disappeared under the skirt squeezing her thigh, then he hooked his fingers over the stocking top and yanked, the seamed band was freed from the fastener clips.

He continued moving his hand over her skin, and Roma tried her best to squeeze her thighs closed to prevent him going any further. Tilburne's expression changed, and with his left hand he viciously slapped Roma across the face; her head snapped sideways from the force of the blow, and across her cheek a red mark immediately appeared, stinging sufficiently to cause her to cry out.

Garratt grinned and chuckled in the background. He was enjoying this.

Lomax's anger rose and he strained against the ties binding him to the stretcher, wishing that if only one would fail, he could possibly get an arm free. He closed his eyes and concentrated.

Tilburne's attention was still focussed upon Roma, moving his hand back up between Roma's legs. He used his strength to ease his fingers in between Roma's clenched thighs, until his fingertips brushed against her panties. Just then Tilburne's PA unexpectedly entered the office. David Carter had not long returned from Berlin where he'd been overseeing the data transfer as Tilburne had instructed him to do days earlier.

Dressed in his dark grey suit, Carter was still engrossed on checking his report as he entered when he collided with the stretcher on which Lomax was secured to, knocking it hard up against the one Roma was secured to.

The cable tie securing Lomax's left wrist to the support rail began to split, he could feel it weakening and as it was now out of sight, Lomax covertly yanked his wrist and it became free. Neither Tilburne nor Garratt appeared to have noticed.

Carter looked up immediately as he'd struck something he knew shouldn't have been in that part of Tilburne's office. He saw both of the stretchers, and that there were two people securely tied to them, one male, one female, and with Tilburne's right hand out of sight beneath the woman's skirt.

Tilburne looked up immediately when the stretcher had been knocked by the one holding Lomax, without Garratt in a position to prevent it, and turned to face Carter, his face decidedly maniacal, his one good eye almost shut with rage, the other staring blindly at nothing. He swiftly withdrew his hand.

'What the fucking hell do you want?' Tilburne roared, as he moved away and stepped towards his desk chair, his angry, scarred face glaring at his underling executive secretary. Carter had never seen his employer's face unmasked in all the time he'd worked for him; this was the very first time he'd seen just how disfigured Tilburne actually was.

Now he was seeing it extremely up close... far too close, for he could now also smell a decidedly fetid odour, as though Tilburne's ragged flesh was decomposing right there and then on the man's face as he watched. Trying not to gag, Carter glanced back at his notes, but Tilburne angrily swiped them out of Carter's hand, sending the sheaths of paper scattering across the office. 'Er, I thought I'd better come to see you straight away, sir. I've done everything you asked of me in Berlin, and I have amalgamated all of the Northern European assets and associated data to your preferred location database.'

Tilburne's anger subsided momentarily. But he was still fuming at Carter's lack of judgement in returning at this hour, unannounced and, more importantly, at this momentous occasion. 'Very well. But you haven't heard the last of this, David. I'd prefer it if you didn't witness anything further, if only for your own sake.'

Lomax wasn't being observed during the conversation by Tilburne, the newcomer Carter or even by Garratt. He decided to act. As he looked at Roma he smiled at her, she smiled back briefly although Lomax could clearly see the concern in her eyes. He raised his now unrestricted left wrist, and moved it to the exterior of Roma's left calf-length boot, where he deftly retrieved the flick-knife he knew she usually secreted there in a sheath, discreetly camouflaged as part of the boot's design, and slipped it out of sight into the palm of his hand, handle first, sliding it under the sleeve of his shirt, the four-inch-long blade cold against his flesh.

He was surprised that none of Tilburne's goons had even considered looking for a weapon on either officer, given how he'd been frisked when he'd been abducted, but for once he was grateful for small mercies.

Lomax kept glancing over to the desk where Tilburne had guided Carter, then Tilburne did something that both Lomax and Roma found much unexpected. 'Liam, would you escort David back to the main elevators, I'm finished with him tonight. Thank you.'

Garratt stood up from the sofa and moved over to the door. David Carter was then guided by Tilburne, with an arm draped around Carter's shoulders, to where Garratt held the door open, then he and Carter disappeared from view. Tilburne returned to Roma's stretcher, barging Lomax's stretcher aside a couple of feet, and poised himself to return his hand where he'd last had it.

Roma braced herself again, but Tilburne had been faking. Instead, he took a firm grip of Roma's blouse at the topmost button and yanked it downwards, ripping the buttons free and exposing the lacy bra beneath.

Roma shrieked.

Lomax slid the flick-knife down from his sleeve as Tilburne's attention was focussed on Roma's upper body. Lomax cut through the cable-tie on his right wrist, he then swiftly cut through the extra-long one around his chest, enabling him to sit up and cut the ones securing his thighs and ankles in quick succession.

Lomax managed to cut himself free before Tilburne noticed, his attention focussed on fondling Roma's body. Lomax was off the stretcher and heading toward Tilburne by the time he caught the movement reflected in one of the mirrors on the wall. Tilburne pulled his hand away as he was about to grasp Roma's right breast in a vicious squeeze; instead, he viciously punched Roma in the face, rendering her out cold. Lomax lunged and prodded the tip of the slim blade directly inside Tilburne's right ear, or what was left of it, the tip pushing in just enough for Tilburne to get the point.

'Back away from her you vile bastard, or I'll ram this blade so far inside your ear...' Lomax said quietly, emphasising that he would have no hesitation in pushing the blade all the way in. Lomax cautiously eased himself backwards, using the slightest pressure of the blade inside the hole, the chill of the steel to entice Tilburne to do the very same.

As they backed away, Tilburne's right leg brushed the stretcher Roma was on turning it slightly.

'You know,' Tilburne began saying, 'I'm sure there is a way that you and I can work something out, Philip.' He tried to speak in a calm, friendly manner, but it was lost on Lomax.

'Why do you even think, Tilburne, that you and I can resolve this in a *friendly* fashion? You've always hated me, and the feeling is mutual. I'd prefer nothing better than to see you rot in prison for the rest of your pathetic life. But to be honest, considering what you've accomplished in the last few weeks, and beginning with the rape and murder of Amanda Waterman, who spurned you at school, I'd sooner just launch you off the roof of this building.'

Garratt returned to the office unseen by Lomax. As Roma began to come to from Tilburne's punch, she saw Garratt had re-entered, albeit through blurry vision; she tried to shout a warning to Lomax but the words stuck in her throat. Lomax had his back to the door where Garratt had entered and had stopped only very briefly, where he removed his footwear, and then he crept towards Lomax as quietly as he could across the polished wood flooring.

As he neared Lomax's turned back, Garratt looked at Roma and pressed his index finger to his lips in a *shushing* mime along with a knowing grin, and with the DCI unable to see the oncoming attacker in the reflection of the huge window due to Tilburne being in the way, Lomax continued to urge the man towards the windows, where he'd planned to make his point understood.

Roma finally managed to scream out a warning, but it was too late. Just as Lomax turned sharply, Garratt brought his clasped hands down together onto the nape of Lomax's neck. The crushing blow forced Lomax to pull the blade away from Tilburne's ear and sent him flying off to the side out of harm's way, although not without inflicting the slightest nick to Tilburne's skin. Lomax lost his grip of the flick-knife which spiralled in mid-air, came down and struck the desk's edge by its handle and bounced onto the floor, skittering away out of sight.

Lomax fell to his knees, his neck aching as though it had been struck by a ton of rock. It was one hell of a blow by Garratt, who had used most of his powerful muscles to get Lomax away from his boss. Garratt pounced onto Lomax, grabbing him around his throat from behind and digging his beefy fingers deep and hard into Lomax's flesh, pulling the DCI back upwards almost back onto his feet whilst almost cutting off the air from getting into his lungs.

Lomax kicked his legs behind him, and after a few misses he managed to kick hard enough to throw the muscular Garratt off balance, his weight being slightly off-kilter due to the way he was leaning over Lomax from behind, while holding the police officer's weight, and exerting the pressure on the larynx and windpipe. Lomax's kick forced Garratt's left foot to slip on the polished wooden floor, as he'd removed his shoes and had crept to attack Lomax in just his socked feet.

This was obviously his downfall, quite literally, as Lomax managed to free himself from Garratt's hold around his neck and throat, then Lomax scrabbled forward and grabbed the flick-knife from where it had landed, after which he got into a crouched position, facing Garratt, rasping for air. Garratt leapt toward Lomax, his features set in a rictus of rage.

Lomax anticipated this desperate move by Garratt and had in fact been counting on it. Garratt expected to land heavily on top of Lomax, hoping his excessive weight would be sufficient enough to cause serious injury, if not death. Lomax rolled away just as Garratt was being pulled downwards by gravity coupled with his weight, and the muscular man landed heavily face first onto the floor, unable to realise that he'd mistimed his attack.

Lomax swiftly dived across Garratt's lower back and plunged the knife's blade deep, crossways into the thick thigh muscle, barely two inches below the upper dermis so that it came out the other side on a horizontal plane. Garratt cursed and twisted his injured leg suddenly. Lomax's grip was steadfast on the handle, and where the blade met the handle it snapped, leaving the blade embedded. Blood seeped slowly from the wound.

Garratt's rage intensified and he thrust himself upwards from the floor, throwing Lomax aside effortlessly. Lomax rolled a couple of times, and as he was about to get up once more Garratt, using just one fist, connected with Lomax's skull at the back of his head and he was sent spinning again to the floor of Tilburne's office. Lomax slid across the wooden floor, but by the time he came to rest he was out cold.

Tilburne grinned. He'd enjoyed this show of defiance by Lomax. He knew from the time at school that Lomax wasn't a man destined to give up easily, that was a certainty. 'Put Lomax back on the stretcher, Liam, then remove them to lab number four. You know what I want you to do... I hope?' Tilburne asked of Garratt.

Garratt simply nodded. He was going to make the most of this opportunity. Inwardly he was seething; he couldn't believe that Lomax had managed to get the better of him with the knife and inflicted a painful injury. Garratt could feel his blood seeping from the wound. 'I'm just going to dress this wound first, if you don't mind?'

'Very well. I shall observe your objectives via the CCTV. I sent the non-essential staff home earlier. Carry on, Liam... I'll enjoy this.'

Roma was about to say something as Garratt placed Lomax back on the stretcher. He felt that he'd slugged Lomax hard enough to keep him incapacitated until he got them both to the lab in question. Garratt looked at her, then without warning or mercy he slugged her on the left side of her face, with just sufficient force to send her into unconsciousness.

For Roma, everything very quickly went black, she barely groaned in pain. Peter Tyler and Del Kingsley, two of Garratt's associates, who had returned with Garratt, remained close by but not daring to interfere.

Chief Superintendent Warwick was feeling peculiarly exhilarated. He'd previously and regularly reprimanded DCI Lomax for his cavalier and often brash, maverick methods of police work, but now, finding himself doing just what his subordinate did most if not all of the time, it was definitely giving him a buzz.

Of course, in situations like this, Warwick should follow strict and official police procedural practices and call in the SCO19 Squad, whose officers were properly trained to use automatic weapons. He knew that if Lomax had had the opportunity, whatever was going on would have been over and done with ages ago, if only Lomax or Roma had been able to use their officially sanctioned handguns, but it occurred to Charles Warwick that DC Crosse's concerns were well justified.

The two men had rucksacks on their backs, both filled with loaded magazines for the police-issue weapons they each carried in shoulder holsters. Warwick also had two of his favourite weapons, which were ex-police issue Browning 9mm pistols, each carrying magazines with thirteen rounds.

Crosse preferred the new Glock.7.62s; they were lighter and less prone to jam when loading a fresh magazine into the handgrip. Crosse also carried an Ithaca 12 bore short-barrelled shotgun. Just in case.

Each man had over twenty spare full magazines, and Crosse also carried more than fifty spare cartridges for the Ithaca.

Warwick followed Crosse towards the freight elevator in the underground garage of the Vortexa Building and waited until the car came back down. They could have taken the stairs, but at Warwick's age, and his state of fitness, it wouldn't have been prudent to do so, climbing more than forty storeys worth of stairwells. Even though the senior police officer regularly attended the gym, Crosse decided that it would have been a disadvantage if they ran sweating, wheezing and gasping out-of-breath into some of Tilburne's goons part way up, and both of them being far on the wrong side of forty years.

Both Warwick and Crosse were surprised that they hadn't run into *any* of Tilburne's personal security staff by now, both men tensing themselves just in case.

Crosse's mobile buzzed in his pocket. He was about to ignore it, but thought better of it. He pulled the device from his pocket and smiled.

'Hello, Dee,' he said, smiling.

'I have you on CCTV in the garaging area by the freight elevator. DCI Lomax asked me to assist you in any way I can. Wesley and George are waiting for you once you get to the first laboratory level, but they won't be able to go any further. I, however, will be able to help. I'll meet you there,' Dee Wilding said, adding 'by the way, Wesley hacked into the building's security system and apart from the central laboratories, he has been able to disable the system to the upper floors. Also, you'll be pleased to know there doesn't appear to be any other members of the CEO's private security.'

'When I spoke to Lomax recently,' Crosse said, 'he thought there may be other prisoners somewhere on-site. The two who escaped couldn't be sure if there were any others, but perhaps George and Wesley could go and look in the sub-garaging levels, and release them before the shit hits the fan?'

'I'll see that they do, plus it'll give them something to do and get them away from here. I'll brief them before they meet up with you,' Dee said.

The elevator slowed as it neared the garage level and made a noisy stop. Both Crosse and Warwick realised that they were standing directly in front of where the doors would open.

Crosse motioned for Warwick to move aside out of harm's way, just in case. They took positions either side of the doorway just as the double door slid open. They then waited, Crosse counting down from five using his fingers and thumb, curling each digit in turn. Then just before the doors automatically began to close again, Crosse chanced to peer around the edge. He sighed when he saw the car was definitely empty. He pressed the button on the panel again, and the doors opened once more.

'Come on,' he said, motioning for Warwick to get into the freight elevator. 'What floor, sir?' Crosse asked.

Warwick grinned, then said, 'Ladies lingerie or top end electricals? Your call, Detective *Sergeant* Crosse.'

Crosse looked at his superior with a mixture of humour and cynicism. Was he being serious about the promotion? At a time like this? Crosse pressed button number forty, the highest level the freight elevator went to, and for the lowest laboratory. Once there, they'd have to transfer to another smaller freight elevator system that served all six of the labs, particularly the ones that were designed and equipped to create Tilburne's product.

The elevator began to rise once more. Both men stood silently watching the buttons change colour beneath the accumulated grime.

Crosse wondered how long it was going to take for this bloody elevator to reach its destination. He turned to Warwick, a thought entering his mind to take some of the tension he was sure they were both experiencing out of the situation. 'Lovely weather for the time of day, isn't it?'

Warwick chortled. 'Well, at least this elevator isn't playing *"The Girl From Panama."* or whatever the name of that song is.'

Crosse guffawed. He knew what song Warwick meant, but even he couldn't remember its exact title.

The elevator stopped suddenly, but when both men looked at the indicator it showed that they were in between floors thirty and thirty-one. 'Shit. The bloody thing's gotten stuck between floors,' Warwick stated.

'No shit, Sherlock,' Crosse said, and he kicked the wall of the elevator just below the panel, then the elevator car growled and jerked a couple of times, then with an ear-splitting shriek it began to climb once more. 'Oh well, if in doubt… give it a fucking good kicking,' Crosse said, a sigh of relief in his voice.

'I'm wondering if having this elevator in such a poor state of repair, making noises like that, is Tilburne's cheapskate form of security alarm,' Warwick announced. 'I just hope we don't have a welcoming committee when we reach our destination,' he added.

'Me neither,' Crosse agreed.

When the elevator finally reached its uppermost point, the small, illuminated floor indicator showed it had stopped at the desired floor, and the doors opened. Both Warwick and Crosse repeated their earlier tactic by keeping as much out of harm's way, just in case there were any armed security personnel, but thankfully and strangely enough… there weren't.

Both men stepped outside the elevator and cautiously scanned the foyer of the lower laboratory for anyone, but it too seemed to be completely devoid of people. There was absolutely no sign of staff, no lab technicians whatsoever.

'Maybe Tilburne's laid everyone off,' Crosse said, keeping his voice low.

'Or they've all gone on holiday… at the same time,' Warwick whispered.

'Or perhaps… they're all dead,' Crosse remarked, and immediately wished he hadn't thought of that possibility. Both men shuddered.

The two men moved slowly, purposefully scanning each way as they moved further into the complex. Because the other elevators which would take them up to the top executive floors and have access to each of the laboratories were on the far side of the laboratory facing them, they now had to find a way of circumnavigating the security system, which was by no stretch of the imagination going to be damned near impossible.

Neither Warwick nor Crosse had obtained an entry-identity-flash card because they hadn't come into contact with anyone likely to have one available for them to acquire. Crosse approached the floor-to-ceiling opaque industrial laboratory glass doors, with acid-etched legend LABORATORY #1 on the right-hand door, then he pushed the large chrome handle. Sure enough it was secure. 'Locked. Just as I suspected,' Crosse said. 'Perhaps I could shoot it?' he said.

'Or maybe I could just smash them with that? We might need to conserve our ammunition,' Warwick suggested, indicating a fire extinguisher attached to a hook on the wall just outside the laboratory. Without waiting for a response from Crosse, Warwick dropped the rucksack he'd been carrying with the spare weapons and ammo, and he crossed the small space and took the extinguisher from the hook, raising it above and behind his head. He was about to launch it at the glass doors when a voice shouted out.

'Oi! What do you think you're doing?' George Murray yelled, while Wesley Jenner grinned.

Warwick dropped the fire extinguisher down to his side, looking slightly sheepish. 'Nothing.'

'Good, 'cos Dee asked me to give you this,' he handed Crosse a pass key and a piece of paper with some codes on it, as well as a short-wave radio. 'These are for the laboratories, but they won't work for every door, it'll be hit and miss which ones you get to, and which codes work for which entry panel. Dee's sorry but she wasn't able to get the information any sooner. Dee will be watching you on CCTV, the radio's pre-set to Channel seven, just press the transmit button on the left of the digital display to speak to her but use the ear-piece.'

'That's okay,' CS Warwick said. 'Thank you for your help. Dee said you'll go and check the sub-basement levels for us?'

'That's where we're going now, then we're high-tailing it away from here, else we'll be out of a fucking job!' George and Wesley got into the freight elevator Crosse and Warwick had used and disappeared from view.

Crosse grinned. 'Yeah. Me too.' Using the card which unlocked the first of the lower-level laboratories, they entered, Warwick having retrieved his rucksack, and they moved cautiously through the expansive area, looking fleetingly at the equipment.

Crosse inserted the earpiece into his left ear as suggested by George. Warwick left Crosse's side and made his way around one of the elongated sections, casually looking at the glass containers with bizarre looking labels, giving algebraic formulae expressions with Latin names as well.

Static fired through the earpiece, startling Crosse before he heard a female voice coming through. 'Hello? Can you hear me?'

Crosse raised the small Motorola unit and pressed the transmit button. 'Hello, I read you.'

'Look, meet me in the security office.' Dee then gave them directions of how to get there from LABORATORY #1 on the fortieth floor.

A few minutes later Dee answered the door. Both men looked straight into her face. Her short brown hair was spiky with several dyed red and blond flashes running through it. She had a pretty, slim face, large brown eyes, a small, pointed nose and full pouting lips above a rounded long chin.

Warwick asked her why she was here at all.

'Covering sick leave. One of my male colleagues, Jake Bunton, called in sick. Leaving only me, George and Wesley to hold down the fort,' Dee said. 'What do you intend to do?'

Crosse looked at his watch. It read six-fifty-three. He knew it was cutting it close if he and CS Warwick were to be effective in rescuing Lomax and Roma. 'CS Warwick and I have to get to our colleagues. Gerrard Tilburne has captured them, and we fear for their safety.'

Dee nodded. 'Is there anything you'd like me to do to help?'

Warwick answered her question. 'It would be too dangerous to involve you any further, Miss Wilding. I would prefer it if you joined George and Wesley and left. But I can tell by your expression that you have no intention of doing so.'

Dee laughed, 'Not bloody likely. You need someone to watch your backs. Don't forget to use the radios and earpieces George supplied. I'll be watching you.'

***

Because of the nature of Dee and her colleagues' access to the majority of the floors, apart from the central two laboratories, their security access flash-cards worked for the most part. Dee had been advised to remain locked in the CCTV control room for the time being. Warwick did, however, suggest 'If you hear anything that doesn't sound healthy, get the hell out of the building.'

While they waited, Dee flicked a switch on a small pad connected to the security office's monitoring system that now gave her unlimited access to the building's entire CCTV system, even in the executive suite and the covert labs. They watched as the two stretchers with the unconscious forms of Lomax and Roma were being wheeled out of the freight elevators and into one of the central two labs.

Dee pointed to one of the labs. 'That's the lab you need to head for… and you should get there before they do, if you leave right now,' she said, adding for good measure, 'it's on floor number forty-one. There's a set of stairs on the northeast corner that links the two central laboratories where with any luck you won't be spotted.'

Just before they exited, Dee said, 'Be careful… those guys look like really nasty pieces of work.'

'They haven't met us yet,' Crosse replied, grinning. It was here that they parted company with the security officer.

With bare minutes to spare, Crosse and Warwick arrived at the lab before Garratt, Kingsley and Tyler. Crosse hid in a small office-come-control room, separated from the lab by a door with a single narrow vertical glass panel. They decided to lay back and wait.

Dee had managed to covertly override some of the controls for the freight elevators, causing them to stagger Garratt's arrival, and making him angry with Tilburne's tight-fisted lack of maintenance.

Warwick had found a small storage room in a corner of the lab, where cleaning equipment and supplies were contained.

He pulled the door to, leaving it ajar in case anyone did return. It was a short time before he heard movement and saw two trolley/stretchers being manoeuvred into this very lab, each one with people he knew lying atop;

Roma was still secured by cable ties and Lomax was currently still out cold from the blow from Liam Garratt.

The two stretchers were positioned close to one another, three feet apart. Garratt gave the other two men orders to re-secure Lomax, telling one them there were spare ties in a cupboard nearby. Garratt left the two men while he went into a small annexe-room to unlock a safe and retrieve the vials of VPT184-505, the code for Tilburne's project, and to prepare two syringes.

Lomax was beginning to come to, as one of the other two men found the spare ties and returned to the foot end of Lomax's stretcher, passing several ties to his associate. Lomax stirred. Tyler, standing at Lomax's chest, grabbed hold of both arms and pressed them onto Lomax's chest, using his position and weight to hold him still.

Kingsley began preparing ties to secure Lomax's feet and upper legs.

Twenty-Five

Warwick came into the lab as stealthily as he could, choosing this moment while the larger man in charge was otherwise engaged in the smaller annexe room.

Creeping right up behind Kingsley, and using his extendable baton, Warwick swiped hard across the shoulders of the smaller of the two men standing with his back to him, who'd been holding Lomax's legs down on the trolley/stretcher. Del Kingsley cried out from the force of Warwick's strike and released Lomax's legs, allowing Lomax to kick upwards; the heel of his right foot connected viciously hard with Kingsley's chin, breaking his jaw and dislodging several teeth, three of which flew out from his open mouth along with a large spurt of blood. Kingsley's eyes rolled upwards and he collapsed onto the floor, barely making any noise.

Although still weakened from the fight with Garratt, Lomax was swiftly realising that this was going to be a tough situation to get out of alive. Both for himself, and more importantly for Roma.

Tyler was still holding Lomax's arms, and as such he couldn't dare let go, otherwise Lomax would be able to fully jump away.

Warwick then ran for Peter Tyler, only slightly smaller than Garratt, but almost as strong. Tyler was holding Lomax's arms and chest as still as he could, but now with his partner in crime rendered out cold, and with Lomax virtually fully conscious, he knew he was going to have a hard time fighting off two police officers.

'Garratt!' Tyler called out.

'Alright, I'm nearly ready,' came the agitated response.

Warwick thrashed at Tyler with the baton rather than using a noisy weapon in the confines of the laboratory, attempting to force the man to release his grip of Lomax's arms, giving Lomax the chance to get up. Tyler leaned back to keep away from Warwick's baton making contact. *'Garratt!'* Tyler called loudly again, 'Get your fat arse in here, you stoopid twat.'

Garratt ignored Tyler as he was busy preparing the second syringe for Roma. He thought both Peter and Del could cope with Lomax.

Warwick knew he had to act quickly so he thrust himself forwards, bringing the baton from behind and above his head, striking Tyler across his face with enough force to cause the man to cry out loudly as the skin on his left cheek split open wide, a long gash of more than three inches at a diagonal slant from the bridge of his nose downwards. Tyler cried out.

Blood splashed out as the wound splayed open exposing the fatty layer and the cheek muscle, and the sudden stinging sensation forced Tyler to release his hold of Lomax's arms and take his weight away. Lomax swiftly sat up and swung his legs over the side of the trolley. He jumped off to the floor, his legs buckling slightly, then he regained his balance and he advanced upon Tyler, who was backing away. 'Garratt!' Tyler tried to shout, but his cheek muscles stung.

Warwick came in from the other side and they cornered Tyler. Lomax brought his right arm back, his fist balled up, and he struck Tyler hard dead centre, crushing his nose into his face. Then he brought his left fist around and connected with Tyler's right temple. The force sent him to the floor, out cold.

Just then Garratt came out from the annexe room, holding a shining metal tray containing the two filled syringes, and was shocked to see Lomax standing next to the second trolley cutting through the cable ties restraining Roma's arms, wrists, thighs and ankles with a scalpel.

Warwick turned his head and saw Garratt reappear as Lomax was trying to wake Roma as best he could, gently shaking her as she was still out cold from Tilburne's strike.

Garratt was aiming the weapon at Warwick's head. Warwick held the baton down at his side; he knew it would be pointless to even attempt to strike at Garratt.

Garratt pulled back the hammer. The click seemed extraordinarily loud in the lab. His hand was steady. Lomax heard the noise. Warwick was staring down the business end of the barrel, and he felt awkwardly useless. 'So? Now what do I do?' Garratt asked. 'I only have enough of VPT184-505 to inject into you, Lomax, and that stupid bitch copper.' He peered to his left and saw that she'd been unsecured but was still unconscious.

'So?' Warwick asked. 'What *are* you going to do, shoot me in cold blood?'

Garratt smirked. 'Only if you're brave enough to try and smack the gun out of my hand,' he said, testing and goading Warwick to try his luck. Garratt slowly moved into a new position so that he had a clear vantage point to keep both police officers in view.

'Why haven't you fired?' Warwick asked.

Garratt grinned menacingly and laughed before he spoke. 'Mr Tilburne wishes me to prolong your experience. He's watching us as I speak.'

Lomax pulled the sleeve of his jacket down to cover his hand and quickly moved to his right, reaching for a large glass chemical jar which was set atop a stand above a lit Bunsen burner on a nearby workbench. The pale-yellow liquid inside was still simmering, and in one swift motion Lomax grabbed the jar and, turning as fast as he could, he flung it towards Garratt. Garratt caught the movement and turned his head slightly, yet kept the gun trained on Warwick. He very gently began squeezing the trigger.

Garratt had to make a split-second choice, shoot Warwick and then the jar, or vice versa? He opted for the jar. It was the mistake both Lomax and Warwick hoped for. Garratt fired once, the bullet escaping the barrel in excess of nine hundred feet per second, and it hit the jar when it was only two feet from him; the boiling liquid fanned outwards along with the shards of the thin glass.

Only a few drops struck Garratt's flesh, yet not enough to cause him any concern, and some splashed over the giant of a man's clothes. The glass shards fell onto the floor with small tinkling sounds.

Warwick waited until Garratt began to swing the gun back in his direction, but he had been preparing the baton, covertly bringing it up behind himself and moving closer in one fluid motion. Lomax could see what Warwick was intending to do, so he remained clear. Warwick timed it perfectly just as Garratt brought the weapon back almost into position and struck forcibly with the baton directly underneath Garratt's wrist. The force was so intense the baton broke Garratt's grip, but only briefly. The chief henchman's hand rose slightly but he held onto the weapon. As he tried to bring it back down again an unfortunate thing happened.

He pulled the trigger. An involuntary spasm caused by the strike on his wrist. The second loud report filled the room and caused the two police officers to jump. But the bullet struck a metal strip along the front edge of a wall mounted cupboard and ricocheted towards the trolley/stretcher where Roma lay sedated. The bullet struck her right leg just above the knee, passing through the flesh on the right side.

Lomax didn't have time to follow the trajectory, so he wasn't aware of where exactly the bullet ended up.

Instead, he used the disorientating effect to rush at Garratt.

While Garratt's attention was preoccupied with Warwick, Lomax rammed his head into Garratt's chest, but it felt as if he'd just run into a concrete wall. Garratt followed up with an uppercut which took Lomax off his feet and sent him flying backwards into the worktop, his back crunching painfully into the hard marble work surface. He fell to the floor groaning, tears seeped from his eyes, and he grimaced in agony.

Garratt aimed the gun at Lomax and squeezed the trigger, but it didn't fire. Garratt tried several times in quick succession, but it had surprisingly jammed, something Glocks rarely did, so he discarded the gun.

Garratt then pulled a razor-sharp machete out from a leather sheath inside his jacket. He approached Lomax, a menacing glare spreading across his face. 'Tilburne wanted me to inject you and that bitch with his new toy, but now I'm not going to. I'm going to kill you all in my own preferred fashion. Shooting you would be too quick, too easy. So instead, I'm going to dice you up.'

Spittle escaped from Garratt's lips as he spat the words out. He slashed wildly at Lomax as he approached, slicing the air, creating short whipping sounds. Lomax slowly got up but he was defenceless, there was nothing else he could use as a weapon to hand. Instead, he removed his jacket, and wrapped it around his left forearm, hoping that it would reduce any potential serious injury.

Garratt rushed at Lomax, swinging the machete wildly. The blade sliced effortlessly through the material, narrowly missing Lomax's carotid artery on the left side on his exposed neck. Lomax ducked and darted off to his right, keeping his wrapped arm out to deflect Garratt's attack. Garratt countered by sweeping his free left hand around on a level plane and yet again connected with Lomax's chest, slamming him backwards and sending the detective over a moveable sample trolley at waist height. Lomax landed heavily on his knees and hands, feeling the jolts resonate through his body.

Lomax arched his back as he stood up once more, feeling his bones grind a little as a shooting pain slammed across the lumbar region of his back. Warwick drew his own gun, the Browning 9mm. He pulled back the hammer as he aimed it towards Garratt. Garratt heard the sound and turned quickly, pulling a thin bladed knife from his belt sheath. In one fluid motion and with uncanny accuracy, he threw the knife at Warwick who had to try and get out of the way. The knife struck Warwick's right forearm, slicing through flesh quite deeply, causing him to drop the gun and have to tend to his own wound. Warwick moved away towards a bench where some paper towelling sheets were.

Garrett then advanced towards Lomax, holding the wild merciless stare in his eyes; a low growl escaped the man's lips.

Tilburne sat at his desk relishing the scenes being played out on the large TV screen, and as he flicked through the various angles he laughed or groaned depending on what happened.

But Tilburne laughed heartily as Lomax moved around the lab, doing his utmost to keep away from Garratt. He also enjoyed it when Garratt injured the senior police officer with the knife.

Lomax was feeling vastly outmatched by the massive form of his opponent, who had both height and weight advantages. He waited until Garrett was readying the weapon to be brought down in another powerful arc on his upper body, particularly his head. Lomax dropped into a crouched position and threw himself at Garrett's shins, putting his full weight to its best potential.

It was Garrett's own forward momentum that aided Lomax's intentional last-ditch attack strategy, as the larger man tumbled clear over Lomax's back. He struck the hard floor of the laboratory and tumbled heavily into the trolley on which Roma still lay, sufficiently enough to knock the wind from his lungs and to lose his grip of the machete which skittered across the floor and became lost amongst the debris from the fight.

Garratt got up and angrily shoved the trolley away from him so hard that it crashed into a central work island, striking the corner with such force it toppled sideways throwing Roma onto the floor, her unconscious body rolling a few feet until her back slumped up against a side cabinet on her right side. Blood began to seep more freely from the wound on her thigh, forming a widening pool on the floor. Warwick, having stemmed his own wound, quickly went to her side to assist her.

As he tended to Roma, she came to. As she opened her eyes she saw Lomax looking slightly dazed and concerned a few feet away. As Roma tried to rise, she cried out in pain from the wound to her leg. She managed to rise into a seated position with her back against a cabinet, with Warwick's assistance.

Lomax looked over to where Roma lay slumped against a cupboard door, Warwick still beside her, alternately checking her pulse and the wound, and occasionally glancing towards Lomax and his adversary.

Warwick moved a few feet, picking up the dropped gun and aimed it in Garratt's general direction keeping him covered as he moved back to Roma's side.

Tilburne, watching from his office, was outraged. He stood up abruptly and paced around his office, slamming his fists in his palms alternately. 'Can no-one do what is expected of them?' he shouted.

Lomax had to think fast. Garratt was no slouch, and he was intelligent as well. He had speed and agility due to his fitness and strength. Lomax, although reasonably fit, wasn't as powerfully built.

Lomax backed away, his eyes wide in mock surprise and concern as Garratt approached with a sneer that gave away the man's confidence that he was about to fulfil a long overdue wish by killing Lomax. Garratt's attention was so fixated upon Lomax he didn't see Warwick aiming the gun. Warwick was well aware that he could have used the weapon much sooner, while Garratt was fighting Lomax. However, there was always the risk that Garratt could possibly have moved Lomax into the line of fire. Warwick fired, confident in the knowledge he'd waited for the opportune moment. The loud retort heralded the round's escape from the Browning's barrel as it struck Garrett on the right side from the back. At such a close range, the powerful handgun's round sailed across the laboratory, ploughed through Garratt's shirt, into flesh, deflected off the clavicle bone and continued out through the shoulder near the joint where the ball and socket meet.

The pain was intense from the start. Garratt had been shot in the past, yet the exertions from the fighting had reduced his ability to fight off the pain.

He lost consciousness, emitting a low growling groan as he slumped forwards. He hit the floor hard, the flesh on the left side of his face rippling as he landed. Lomax helped Roma into a chair, and opening drawers from the cabinets he found some cloth, so he bound the wound on her leg.

After a few moments, allowing Roma to regain her senses and so that Warwick could gather the weapons, Lomax found the cable-ties intended to be used on him, and with a degree of difficulty he managed to tie Garratt where he lay, using the ties to bind the man's ankles, knees, and wrists. Lomax also rifled through Garratt's pockets and found the man's own pass card. Lomax pocketed it. Unaware that DC Crosse had severed the CCTV system and that Tilburne was unable to observe the events, Lomax, Roma and Warwick exited the laboratory and started making their way to the upper floor offices. They moved along as quietly as they could, Lomax aiding Roma as she kept her weight off her right leg.

***

Tilburne, finally sick and tired of watching his men fail miserably to dispatch Lomax and the other police officers, when the CCTV signal suddenly went offline, and the monitor Tilburne was looking at suddenly became snowy. Unbeknown to Tilburne, the reason for this was that DC Crosse, completely unaware of what had been taking place in the laboratory, had exited the laboratory through a connecting door in the storage room he had initially hidden in into another area, and had been exploring that floor. He heard muted gunfire and had intended to go back, but the door he'd used relocked itself and the key card he had on him failed to reopen it. With no possibility of returning to the lab from here, he'd decided to explore the area and had opened a wall-mounted cabinet with wiring labelled with CCTV codes. He'd been in constant communication with Dee Wilding, although she was now no longer in the control room; having heeded the advice of CS Warwick, she had left the building. He hoped that Dee was safely clear. Using a pair of pliers he'd liberated from a storage room, Crosse randomly cut through the cables and wiring into the private CCTV lines, severing the connection.

***

Miles Hancroft had been observing the events in the lab alongside Tilburne, and as Garratt's failure to dispatch Lomax and Warwick was now causing Tilburne additional consternation, he felt nervous.

Tilburne's tone told Hancroft exactly how angry he was. 'Miles, you'll have to go down there and finish what Liam started.'

'Me? You're fucking joking,' Hancroft replied, felling a discomfort in the pit of his stomach.

'If you still expect to get paid you'll do as I say, now get down there and help out.'

'The CCTV system's out, how will you be able to see? You won't be able to warn me if they see me.'

'They don't know you're here, do they? Now, get down there and help Garratt.'

Hancroft left Tilburne's office, moving cautiously and feeling extremely vulnerable. He took his time getting there as he wasn't really sure what he could do, plus he needed to be wary of coming into contact with Lomax, Clarkson and Warwick, as well as Crosse.

Hancroft immediately felt sick when he moved around the prone form of Garratt. Although he looked down with some semblance of gratitude, since he'd almost been throttled by Garratt back at the Natural History Museum when he tried to argue with Tilburne. He wondered just how Lomax had gotten the better of such a physically stronger man. Hancroft saw the wound in the man's back; the blood had soaked through into the shirt's material and formed a small puddle on the tiled floor. Hancroft knelt down and checked Garratt's pulse. It was still there, but only just. The muscular man's breathing appeared stable, and pulling the shirt away from the wound, Hancroft could tell that the blood was coagulating, preventing him from bleeding out.

Hancroft found one of the weapons which CS Warwick and Lomax had missed picking up – it was Garratt's Glock. He then looked around the lab, noticing that Del Kingsley and Peter Tyler were still out of action. He found a scalpel which he used to cut through the cable ties securing the immobile Garratt. Suddenly, Hancroft wondered to himself why he was doing this, but he had to give the larger man a chance to get away once he came to. After looking around the lab and realising Lomax and the other two were not here, he noticed that there was another pool of blood next to a cabinet, and droplets going towards a set of doors leading to the elevator.

Hancroft realised where they were heading: up to Tilburne's office. He exited the lab and saw the doors closing to the elevator, and moving forward he barged through the door nearby which led to the stairwell. Running up the stairs as quickly as he could, Hancroft arrived on the fiftieth floor just as he heard the car was almost there. He stood before the doors brandishing Garratt's Glock, unaware why the man had discarded it. Hancroft's finger never even reached the trigger. The stock of the Ithaca 12 bore shotgun was brought down into the back of Hancroft's head. Hancroft's face briefly registered what had happened before he fell unconscious.

Lomax and Warwick stepped backwards, protecting Roma as the door opened again and Crosse bent over the unconscious form of Hancroft, pulling him off to the side. Using handcuffs to restrain Hancroft's hands behind his inert form, and a set of leg restraints as well, Crosse left the man lying on the floor.

Twenty-Six

'So,' Tilburne said, as Lomax and his colleagues entered the office and approached him. He was dressed in an expensive business suit. As before, the CEO's arrogance was overwhelming. 'I just want you to know, Lomax, that I *shall* be the one left alive and in a position to leave via my private helicopter, waiting for me on the helipad above.'

Lomax snorted as he approached the desk. His eyes glared at Tilburne, seated behind it. The crooked smile visible on the left side of the mouth, no longer hidden by the mask. The one remaining working eye looked directly at each person in turn, lingering at DS Clarkson's figure and the tip of Tilburne's tongue coming into view licking his lips. 'You're one sick fucking bastard Tilburne, you know that?' Lomax said.

'Do you seriously believe that I am prepared to let you arrest me and put me before a court?' Tilburne goaded. 'I'm more than a match for you, Philip. Let us see if you're prepared for a contest of strength, myself against you.'

Tilburne stood up and advanced towards Lomax from behind his desk, pushing the expensive black leather chair out of the way. It rolled across the polished wooden floor area behind the desk, struck the wall and bounced off at an angle.

Lomax quickly realised that he was at a disadvantage here. The earlier set-to with Garratt in the laboratory had seriously caused Lomax some weakness, added to which he was concerned about Roma. 'I'll tell you what, Tilburne. I'll agree to your request providing you have no objection to Chief Superintendent Warwick escorting

Roma out of the building to get to a hospital for treatment?'

Tilburne paused for a few seconds, then nodded his head. 'Very well then, but your fellow officer there has to stay. I want to kill him after you're dead.'

Foolishly, Lomax turned away from facing Tilburne and insisted that Warwick get Roma out of the building after both began protesting.

Even though Crosse was still watching Tilburne, the man moved remarkably swiftly and wrapped both arms around Lomax's neck from behind in a stranglehold, pulling his body hard up against Lomax's back.

Roma's eyes opened wide. Both Warwick and Crosse took steps towards Tilburne, bringing their weapons to bear but knowing they wouldn't be able to use them due to Tilburne having turned, putting Lomax directly in front of himself. Lomax's face stared directly towards Roma, and she could see his face beginning to drain of colour.

'I wish I'd dealt with you sooner when I had the opportunity, Lomax,' Tilburne spat vehemently into Lomax's left ear. When Lomax smelt the fetid odour of halitosis it somehow brought him back from semi-unconsciousness. Tilburne had only been applying enough pressure to weaken Lomax who had been struggling to breathe, however Tilburne's left arm began to ache from the exertion and a sharp pain went through the limb causing him to fully release the stranglehold.

Lomax pulled himself away giving, himself a few feet of distance between them. He turned to face Tilburne. 'You're a dirty fighter, Tilburne, you always have been.'

Tilburne casually moved back beside his desk, his chair close by. He looked at Lomax and the others with an expression of pure malevolence. 'As I told you, Philip, you won't be taking me to face trial by jury.'

'Really?' CS Warwick countered as he and Crosse followed Tilburne with their weapons, both eager to pull the triggers and end this diabolical scene. Unfortunately, regardless of their mutual desire to remove Tilburne permanently, they both knew instinctively that their actions would as likely involve the both of them being sacked. Possibly all four.

Tilburne sneered at Warwick's singular remark. 'Really.' Tilburne looked at Roma and licked his lips. 'I'm disappointed that I never had the opportunity to show you what it would be like to sleep with me, my dear.'

The few minutes since being released from Tilburne's grip was enough for Lomax to recover sufficiently. Yet at the same time, listening to the man's arrogance and his outdated masculine attitude towards women, even by today's standards, caused Lomax's anger to rise once again.

'You still believe that DS Clarkson would have been inclined to have sex with you willingly, Gerrard?' Lomax asked, rhetorically.

'I believe that she may have come around to it eventually. Although I would have needed to apply the drug at first to make her more compliant. After that she would have willingly enjoyed our couplings. I think it best I take my leave of you all now; my helicopter is waiting on the helipad.' Tilburne laughed heartily, hoping his comments would enrage Lomax.

He wasn't disappointed. Tilburne was aware that Warwick and Crosse were still holding their weapons and covering his movements as Tilburne walked towards the door on his right.

Warwick pulled the triggers of the weapon he held. The discharge was deafening within the office, and everyone's ears rang and ached. Neither Lomax nor Tilburne expected anyone to fire just then and were startled by the blast, as were Crosse and Roma. The glass window behind Tilburne shattered from the powerful discharge of the numerous pellets from the Ithaca 12 bore shotgun. The force from the weapon's shells at that short distance was more than sufficient to blow a large hole on one side of the pane.

The biting cold wind at that height, time of year and night-time, gusted in through the huge maw, the blast leaving differing sized shards attached to the sides of the frame. Held dangerously in place, some of them moving slightly from the biting chill wind.

Tilburne shook his head, trying to dispel the ringing in his ears. He growled as he charged towards Lomax once more. Lomax had moved to the side Tilburne was intending to leave the office by and charged forwards as well. Lomax grabbed the nearby executive chair by the armrests, swung it round and using the backrest slammed the seat into Tilburne's legs, the chair's momentum throwing Tilburne off balance and twisting until he ended up seated in the chair. Lomax then shoved the chair at the gaping hole. Tilburne screamed, reaching his hands out to grab at the window frame to his left.

Two castors of the chair struck the lip of the exterior window frame, becoming wedged in the ridge where it span the chair round with three of the remaining castors hanging precariously outside the fiftieth floor of the Vortexa Building. Tilburne's expression of rage swiftly changed to one of overwhelming fear.

Tilburne's hands were grasping onto a large shard of glass with all his strength, but the biting cold wind streaming in from outside was sapping his ability to hold on. He could feel the jagged edge piercing his flesh.

'Please,' he cried. 'Please help me… I don't want to die!' he screamed at the top of his voice. His grip tightened on the glass, but the sharp broken edge sliced further into his palms, making them slick as the blood oozed from the widening gashes.

Crosse tapped Lomax on the arm. 'I'm going to check on Hancroft and start taking him down. I can take Roma as well if you like?'

'Yes, thank you Chris. Roma, go with him, you've been without proper medical treatment for too long,' Lomax said, smiling at Roma. He waited until Roma and Crosse had exited the office before he spoke to Tilburne once more.

'What about all those people your security personnel killed, when Dean and Verity escaped? Then you tried to have them assassinated while they were still in hospital. You've corrupted so many people over the years, but worst of all you blatantly and selfishly caused far too many innocent people to lose their lives.

'My father included, Tilburne. DC Crosse discovered a file on Neil Greggs' home PC clearly stating that you sent Liam Garratt to cold bloodedly murder my ailing father while he was in hospital.' Lomax sucked in a deep breath from the bitter air streaming in through the broken window, ignoring Tilburne's whimpering pleadings.

'Besides which, you instigated my investigation in the case when you cold-bloodedly killed Amanda, and that was after you'd sexually abused her. Brutally raping her after all these years out of pure jealousy,' Lomax said calmly. 'What really pisses me off though, is why Amanda started working for you when she knew exactly who you were and what your selfish intentions were towards her?'

Lomax spotted a golf bag complete with clubs in a corner. He casually strolled over and, after carefully choosing a suitable club, a 5 iron, and a ball, he set the ball onto a tee that he pushed into a gap in the wooden flooring. He took a few practice swings. The shaft and end of the club created a swishing noise as it cut through the air in the office.

'My father loved watching golf on the telly,' Lomax said, deliberately glancing at Tilburne whose face was filled with utter horror, his grip lessening. 'You said earlier, Gerrard that you intended to fly away from here. Well, you'll be pleased to know you'll be flying alright, but it'll be downwards, not upwards.'

Tilburne's face creased up and he glanced towards Warwick. 'Chief Superintendent Warwick, surely you're not going to allow this?' he cried out, his voice almost barely unintelligible against the cold biting wind charging into the office through the glass-less window. It was by pure luck that the wider section of pane Tilburne was gripping was still reasonably secure in the side framework; it was just Tilburne's blood making it almost impossible to stay where he was.

'Do I look concerned?' Warwick said. If the truth could be known, judging by what Warwick had witnessed within the past hour or so, and also the utter contempt that this man had for Lomax as well as ordinary citizens, in his own mind Warwick was sick and tired of people like Tilburne. He felt, at that very moment, that wasting tax-payers money on a lengthy trial, which knowing Tilburne's fancy high-priced lawyers, would cost a fortune, especially if he ever became acquitted due to some underhand tactics. Also, the media circus would make matters far, far worse than that of the potential outcome.

Then almost as though Lomax could tell Tilburne's grip on the glass was about to fail anyway, he pulled the 5 iron back and, swinging it with all of his strength, he struck the ball squarely, powerfully. The ball shot forward and struck the large shard of glass a couple of inches from Tilburne's faltering grip. The force exerted by Lomax's swing of the club striking the golf ball shattered the large piece into smaller pieces so that Tilburne had nothing now to prevent him from falling out completely. The grip he had was finally gone. He and the chair fell backwards into space, hung there for a few meagre moments as if to emphasise the pending inevitability of Tilburne's demise, and they fell from sight.

Tilburne tumbled, his arms and legs spiralling, and he screamed for all he was worth.

From within the office Lomax called out loudly, 'FORE...'

Only Lomax and Warwick moved to the window as the chair and Tilburne's flailing, somersaulting body struck the concrete walkway below. Six hundred feet above, the two CID police officers peered precariously down and could just about make out from the streetlight coverage Tilburne's body sprawled on the brickwork pathway, with his limbs at acute angles.

Lomax stepped back away from the window and replaced the golf club in the bag. He looked at his boss, and Roma in particular. 'Well... it would seem that I just happen to be an iron man... Number five, I would think.'

***

Having left Tilburne's office, Crosse, accompanied by Roma who was limping, briefly returned to the elevator to collect Hancroft, but he was no longer lying on the floor. Crosse assisted Roma back down to ground level, and as they exited the elevator car he called for an ambulance.

Roma was dispatched to the nearest A&E. Nearby, Dee Wilding waited to be spoken to by Lomax and Warwick. As Dee looked around her surroundings, she thought she saw two men skulking near a walkway leading to a nearby River Cruise Marina, where hire speedboats could be rented. Minutes later the roar of a twin-engine watercraft echoed and swiftly disappeared.

***

Friday 25th January. 10.00 AM

Chief Superintendent Charles Warwick contacted the SOCO teams. He also contacted The Prime Minister Dudley Conran, who he often played golf with, and made him aware of the situation. He told him he would file a detailed report, along with the personal reports of all officers involved in this investigation within the next few weeks.

Epilogue

CS Warwick and DC Crosse were left to do their best in dealing with the ramifications of this investigation.

CS Warwick also had to find someone to replace DC Neil Greggs, whose formal sacking took place while Lomax and Roma were off duty. He was remanded to Belmarsh Prison.

***

In an office in Antwerp, Belgium, a phone rang. The caller relayed the events as the recipient listened intently. His neck veins and arteries became taut in rage and the colour drained from his face as the details were revealed. 'Keep me posted on further developments, I'll have work for you very soon.'

After the call had concluded, the man began setting out his revenge against DCI Philip Lomax and his colleagues in London.